RAVEN, RED

LION AND RAVEN SERIES, BOOK 1

CONNIE SUTTLE

Print ISBN: 1-63478-089-2
Print ISBN-13: 978-1-63478-089-6
eBook ISBN: 1-63478-088-4
eBook ISBN-13: 978-1-63478-088-9

Published by: SubtleDemon Publishing, LLC
PO Box 95696, Oklahoma City, OK 73143

Cover by Renee Barratt @ The Cover Counts.
The Lion and Raven art on the back cover of the paperback by Brittany Johnson.

To Walter, Joe, Larry, Lee, Dianne, Sarah, Mark, Denise and Brett.
Thank you.

In Memory of Jimmie Lou Hasley
1941 — 2019
Rest in Peace

ACKNOWLEDGMENTS

As always, this book is the result of collaboration. If it weren't for the support of my editor, my cover artist and my beta readers, it would be less than it is. All mistakes, as usual, are mine and no other's.

About the Author:
Connie Suttle lives in Oklahoma with her husband and a conglomerate of cats. They have finally banded together to make their demands, which has proven disconcerting to all humans involved.

You may find Connie in the following ways:
Facebook: Connie Suttle Author
Twitter: @subtledemon
Website and Blog: subtledemon.com

Blood Destiny Series:

Blood Wager

Blood Passage

Blood Sense

Blood Domination

Blood Royal

Blood Queen

Blood Rebellion

Blood War

Blood Redemption

Blood Reunion

Blood Recall

Blood Alliance

Legend of the Ir'Indicti Series:

Bumble

Shadowed

Target

Vendetta

Destroyer

High Demon Series:

Demon Lost

Demon Revealed

Demon's King

Demon's Quest

Demon's Revenge

Demon's Dream

God Wars Series:

Blood Double

Blood Trouble

Blood Revolution

Blood Love

Blood Finale

Saa Thalarr Series:

Hope and Vengeance

Wyvern and Company

Observe and Protect*

First Ordinance Series:

Finder

Keeper

BlackWing

SpellBreaker

WhiteWing

R-D Series:

Cloud Dust

Cloud Invasion

Cloud Rebel

Latter Day Demons Series:

Hot Demon in the City

A Demon's Work is Never Done

A Demon's Due

Seattle Elementals Series:

Your Money's Worth

Worth Your While

BlackWing Pirates Series

MindSighted

MindMage

MindRogue

MindMaster

Black Rose Sorceress Series

The Rose Mark

Rose and Thorn

Black Rose Queen

Queen of Thorns and Roses

Future Wars Series

Buffer Zone

Black Zone*

Lion and Raven Series

Raven, Red

Exile, Ancient*

Other Titles from SubtleDemon Publishing:

Malefactor

Transgressor

Underhanded*

by Joe Scholes

*Forthcoming

CHAPTER ONE

*S**eptember*
Costa de la Muerte
Northern Spain

Fierce winds screamed across the sand, blowing spray off the Atlantic and drenching anyone foolish enough to tread the beaches during such a storm.

Locals blamed the winds for nightmares and other unnatural occurrences, while oscillating stones in the area rocked and rumbled, giving life to ancient tales.

Had anyone from the nearby village of Mordomo ventured out, perhaps they would recall their encounter with the *et Inpaenitens*, thinking they'd met the *Santa Compaña* instead.

Perhaps not.

This night, these spirits were especially agitated.

It is gone.

Those words passed silently from one to another, as they found themselves able to break formation.

Then our chance to destroy it has come, whispered throughout the company.

First, we must find it. Belhar, eldest, strongest, and the one who'd enthralled his companions, insisted. *No matter where it travels. It holds us only while it is here.*

Might we travel then, to find it?

Only the strongest among us, Belhar admonished. *I will choose who may go, and who must stay. Remember, your duty is to open the gate, should the opportunity arise.*

The winds whipped into a higher-pitched scream as the *et Inpaenitens* resolved to act accordingly and free themselves forever.

Dispersing completely for the first time in centuries, they left no footprints behind for the winds to erase.

May, the Following Year

Deep Ellum

Dallas, Texas

Arianne Leone looked up from her painting when the bell over her art gallery door jangled, announcing a visitor. She'd bent low to paint the red and yellow colors of the Indian Blanket wildflowers found in Palo Duro Canyon.

Paintings of the canyon were some of her best sellers, so she straightened her spine and stepped back to survey her work. The focus of the painting was a well-known rock formation, called the Lighthouse.

"Ari, it's me," Nico Garcia called from the front of the gallery.

"I'm back here," she replied.

"Oh, that's really good," Nico breathed a sigh as he caught sight of her latest work. "I wish my final project was half as good."

"It was great—you'll get an A."

"Thanks for letting me work on it here—that made a lot of difference. Too many distractions at home," he admitted. "College is harder than I thought."

"At least the semester's over—when will your grades be out?"

"Maybe next week," Nico shrugged. He was worried, Ari could tell.

"You'll do fine," she reassured him. "I just know it."

"The raven came back again yesterday," Nico said.

"Because you're feeding him," Ari teased. "Did you ever figure out what the red patch is under his beak?"

"I still can't tell, and I can't really ask him, can I? He does like tamales, though."

"You working the night shift?" Ari asked.

Nico's parents owned Blue Taco, the Mexican restaurant across the street from Ari's gallery. It was a popular restaurant for standard Tex-Mex as well as authentic regional Mexican dishes offered as daily specials.

"Yeah. Gotta go in at six," Nico answered Ari's question. "Thought I'd come early and see you, first."

"Want to use the studio during the summer?"

"Yes." By the breathless tone of his voice and the way his dark eyes lit up, Ari understood Nico's true purpose in paying her a visit.

"You're welcome to use it anytime. I'll get you a key so you can come and go."

"All right," Nico's enthusiasm spread with his grin.

"I may come to the restaurant for dinner tonight—all this talk of tamales is making me hungry."

"We can go together—you know Papa will not let you pay."

"He needs to let me pay," she said. "He has to cover his bills, just like everybody else."

"The restaurant is doing really well," Nico argued. "Besides, you let me paint here."

"I'm still paying for my dinner. I'm just letting a friend paint in my studio—there are no strings attached. I remember art school, and how much it would have helped me to have an artist's space to do my work. Instead, I had two roommates who couldn't stop talking about guys and getting drunk."

"Mama keeps asking me about a girlfriend. I have girl *friends*, but those are two separate words for now."

"I hear that." Ari and Nico bumped fists. "Want a soda or some water?"

"Water. It's hot outside." Nico followed Ari to the small fridge she kept in her workspace. "Something weird happened last night, though. Papa thought it was a burglar outside. The police came, but they didn't find anything."

"They may have been scared off. Don't let your guard down," Ari warned. "People seem to get crazier during the summer heat."

"Gonna paint some more after dinner?"

"I think I'll go home. This is almost finished, and I have a crick in my back from bending down to do the flowers."

"Is it already sold?"

"Yeah. Somebody in Virginia wants it."

"Cha-ching," Nico laughed.

"Hey, that's rent," Ari poked his shoulder. "Do not diss the rent."

Ari found herself flinging her arms around Nico as a deafening explosion sent them flying across her studio. Time slowed as she reflexively covered him as well as she could before their bodies hit the concrete floor.

Across the street, fire and screams erupted; Blue Taco had been reduced to little more than rubble. The bomb that leveled the restaurant had shaken the gallery and blown out its plate glass windows.

Ari came to her senses first, lifting her head—and her weight off Nico. Her back felt as if it were on fire. "Nico?" she whispered desperately. His eyes were closed and his hair was covered in dust and debris that continued to fall around them.

She'd covered the rest of him, so his clothing was relatively clean. "Nico?" Ari stretched out a shaking hand; temporarily deaf, she couldn't hear his breaths or his heartbeat, and she didn't trust her eyes to tell her whether Nico was alive. Touch was the only sense she had left.

There—a pulse. Ari found herself wiping tears away. Reaching for her cell phone in a back pocket, Ari groaned in pain. Her back felt as if a thousand needles were stabbing her relentlessly.

"Nine-one-one, what's your emergency?" the voice on the other end of her call answered.

"Explosion. Injury. Seven-nine-nine Durrance Street in Deep Ellum."

"We have several units on the way to that area. Stay on the phone; someone will arrive soon."

Nico escaped with minor injuries. A paramedic was forced to pick glass and splinters from Ari's back once the dust settled and first responders arrived.

Everyone inside the restaurant perished.

"He's nineteen and his parents just died," Ari hissed at Detective Norm Little, who'd arrived to ask questions. She'd disliked him on sight, and when he asked if Nico were in the country legally, she almost slapped him.

Another detective joined the first; Ari wanted to snarl at him before he opened his mouth. "Norm," Lance Elliott frowned at Detective Little, "I think you're needed outside."

"But," Little began to argue.

"Out. Side." Detective Elliott jerked his head toward the open space that used to be a door into Ari's gallery.

Ari studied Detective Elliott with a critical eye. *Forties, a little bit of gray, no paunch, single or divorced*, she decided. Elliott didn't budge when it looked as if Detective Little wanted to argue again. She watched with satisfaction as Little turned and walked stiffly toward the entrance.

Once Little left the scene, Lance visibly relaxed. "Sorry about that," he apologized to Ari. "I'll take it from here. I don't suppose you have a security camera outside?"

"Yeah. I can send you whatever it captured—before things blew up."

"Can we do that now? How's the kid?" Lance's voice had gone soft when he asked about Nico, causing Ari to lift an eyebrow.

Bad cop, good cop, she thought to herself, before leading Lance to the back, where Nico shivered on Ari's sofa.

Shock, Ari pulled in a weary breath. "Nico, I have a blanket. I'll get it for you." Detective Elliott could wait—Nico was more important.

"The back of your shirt is bloody," Lance Elliott called after her.

"Damn. And I just changed shirts," she cursed.

Lance hated this part of his job. "I'm sorry, Nico," he handed Nico's driver's license back to him. "But we have to find out who did this. Right now, you're the best source of information we've got."

"Nothing is different," Nico stuttered his reply. Ari had draped a blanket over Nico's shoulders, but the kid was still shivering.

"I have a note here that says your father called Plano PD last night," he said, trying to keep his voice even.

"We thought it was a burglar—Mama heard somebody running beside the house, so Papa called the police. They didn't find anything. I'm not sure they looked very hard."

"He told me the same thing earlier—that they had to call the police," Ari spoke up.

"I'll send somebody out to check again." Pulling his phone from a pocket, Lance excused himself and walked toward the gallery door to place a call.

"I'll call Plano PD," Captain Belwether told Lance over the phone. "Can't hurt to check. Now, what's this beef between you and Norm?"

Lance forced himself not to curse. "The kid just lost both parents," he growled a reply. "Norm decided to air his racism and asked if the kid was here legally."

"Of course he did," Belwether sounded grim. "I'll expect you to file a report on the incident when you get back to the station."

"I'm sure Norm already has his complaint written about me overstepping my authority," Lance grumbled.

"I'll talk to him when he gets back. We don't need this blowing up on the news—that we're this cold-hearted."

"Except Norm is exactly that."

"I'll pretend I didn't hear that. He's close to retirement. He and I will have a talk and he'll choose his words more wisely next time."

"Right. I may have camera footage from a security camera across the street. I'll let you know if there's anything useful."

"Body count is at twenty-nine and expected to go higher," Belwether said.

"Damn. Look, I need to go. I don't know how long the kid can hold up, and I still have questions to ask." After ending the call, Lance walked back to the studio behind the gallery. His phone rang again before he reached his destination.

"House in Plano just destroyed," Belwether barked. "Homes on both sides damaged. We have to get the kid someplace safe. Somebody's after the whole family."

"I'll bring him to the station. We can go from there," Lance studied Ari and Nico, who were now huddled together on the sofa. Ari's arms were around Nico, as if she knew something else had gone wrong already.

Ari followed the detective to his car; Nico walked beside her, still wrapped in the blanket she'd given him. At first, Lance intended to take Nico to the police station, but Nico refused to go without Ari, as if she were his only remaining lifeline in a world gone off the rails.

"We'll get through this, Nico," she spoke softly to him as Lance opened the back door of his vehicle. Ari stifled a scream when a raven, bearing a small patch of red feathers at his throat, landed on top of the car with a concerned *kraw!*

"Don't," Nico begged as Lance waved an arm to shoo the bird away. "He's my friend."

"We can't take him with us," Lance began.

"Come. With. Nico," the bird croaked, sending a shiver through Lance. Ari gasped softly but didn't say anything.

"He said my name," Nico turned to Ari, his eyes wide. "He's my friend," he turned back to Lance.

"Right. Get in the car. Bird, if you're coming, get in and don't make a mess." Lance only said what he did for Nico's benefit—no way would that bird get in the car.

Except he did, lifting off the car's roof and flapping to Nico's shoulder.

"Damn," Ari breathed. "Nico, get in the car. We should go."

"Go now," the bird insisted.

"Right," Lance repeated and slid into the driver's seat.

"I've hauled a lot of things in my car, but I don't think I've ever driven a raven across town," Detective Elliott shook his head as he stopped the car at a red light. Ari sat up front with him; Nico and the unnamed raven were in the backseat.

"I've never seen a raven with red feathers under his chin," Ari sighed. "No idea about this one, or why he showed up now. Nico's been feeding him tamales behind the restaurant, but I've never seen a wild bird settle for riding in a car, even if it is with the guy who keeps him in Mexican food."

"I can't figure that out, either, but then nothing about this case makes sense. Why not include a raven who likes tamales and can talk?"

"Most people would freak out," Ari pointed out. "About a talking raven."

"I think I'm past that now." Lance moved the car forward when the light turned green. "I can't wait to see what happens when we take the bird into the station."

"I-umm right heere," the Raven squawked, making both jerk in their seats.

Ari and Nico were led to Lance's office, where Lance offered them drinks and a place to sit. Ari watched as Lance considered his questions carefully.

"Nico, I know this is hard, but can you tell me whether your parents have acted different lately—anything out of the ordinary?" Lance asked.

Nico was seated on Lance's desk chair while the raven clung to its high back, hovering above Nico's right shoulder. The detective leaned casually against the desk to ask his questions, attempting to put Nico at ease while they talked.

"No. Everything was the same," Nico denied. "School ended last Friday, so I was scheduled to work full evening shifts since then. I usually work weekends when I'm in school unless I have a project to finish and need the time."

One of Nico's feet bounced beneath him, making his entire leg shake—a sign of anxiety. He was doing his best to hold it together, when he'd become an orphan in the time it took to blink. Ari understood his fear and confusion.

Too well.

"Have they taken any unusual trips? Been somewhere they wouldn't normally go?"

"They took a trip to Spain last September. Ever since Mama had us take a family DNA test and she found out she had connections to Garcias in Spain, well, she wanted to go. Papa took her."

"What part of Spain?" Lance scribbled on his yellow notepad.

"Well, they went to Madrid, of course. Went to see lots of things. Ended up at Santiago de Compostela, before going back to Madrid and flying home. Mama had pictures on her phone. She sent me some of them."

"Actual connections—as in relatives?" Lance lifted an eyebrow. He was following a trail Ari hadn't yet considered.

"Distant cousins," Nico's shaking leg ramped up a notch. "They didn't meet any of them—Mama only wanted to see where our Spanish ancestors came from."

"You're saying it was just a tourist trip, then?"

"Yes. They had fun. Came back tired and full of stories." Nico choked on his words. Ari jerked her purse open to dig for tissues—she had some, somewhere. Nico drew his sleeve across his face, eliminating the need. The raven croaked softly and began preening Nico's hair.

Nico sniffled and then chuckled at the attention he was getting.

"Was there anything they brought home besides pictures? Did they have an itinerary—anything on a computer?" Lance asked as the raven inspected his work, then preened more hair, giving Nico a nice lift to his bangs.

"If they did, it's on Papa's computer at home. Mama uses her phone. She hates the computer."

"Nico, we can't get to that computer," Lance said.

"Why not?" Nico raised reddened eyes to the detective.

"I didn't want to break the news like this, but your house was destroyed not long ago. Looks like that call to the police last night should have been investigated better. Do you have anything we can use on your phone? By the way, you shouldn't answer it if anyone calls. We think someone may be looking for you, too."

"Here's my phone," Nico pulled it from his pocket. "Why would anybody want to kill us? We didn't do anything."

"That's what we're trying to find out. Is there anything on here that you don't want us to see? I'll have somebody look through those pictures your mother sent."

"No." Nico shrugged helplessly. "I'll give you my password so you won't have to break into it."

"Lance, a word?" Ari's head jerked around as someone appeared in the doorway.

"I'll be right back," Lance said, straightening and walking swiftly from the office.

"Norm's dead." Belwether didn't waste any time giving Lance the bad news. "Went to ask questions at a business across the alley from the restaurant. He was killed inside, along with both store employees.

Their security system was ripped out and stolen. I've got uniforms all over the place, and forensics checking for evidence."

"We need to look at the recordings Ari Leone sent to my phone," Lance growled. "Damn. Norm wasn't a friend by any stretch, but this really pisses me off."

"We've blocked off half the street, and that won't go well with tourists and visitors in Deep Ellum tonight."

"Maybe it's for the best—we don't need a crowd getting killed if these assholes are still around."

"I was hoping they'd died in the restaurant. Unless there are two teams, they hit the house after the restaurant."

"Yeah, or maybe they planted those bombs at the house last night and detonated remotely."

"I think the Plano cops are getting questioned about their visit to the house last night," Belwether grimaced. "If there were any evidence to find, it's probably obliterated by now. Bomb squad is investigating. I asked for cooperation from the Plano PD. They couldn't say yes fast enough. Get Mona on those security recordings ASAP," Belwether added. "I want to know who or what went into that restaurant and killed thirty-four people."

"How high will the death toll climb?" Lance asked, after wincing at the updated number.

"Restaurant had a max capacity of ninety-five, plus staff and owners. I doubt it was full, but it could be close."

"I think I want to have a conversation with the Plano officers who went to Nico's house last night."

"So do I. We can have a sit-down later. How's the kid?"

"Not the best. Still in shock, but that could crack any minute. He doesn't have any family in the States and doesn't want to go anywhere without Ms. Leone."

"Is she willing to stay with him—at least temporarily?"

"That's the feeling I get. There's something else, too."

"What's that?"

"A talking raven, who refuses to leave the kid's side."

"This isn't the time for jokes, Lance."

"I'm not joking. Didn't you notice the bird on the back of my chair when you pulled me away?"

"Wasn't looking for one. Damn, must be slipping," Belwether mumbled.

"Come back with me. See for yourself."

"I think I will."

Belwether followed Lance back to his office. Just as he'd said, the raven perched on the back of Lance's chair while Nico, arms crossed tightly over his chest and head down, studied his shoes.

Work shoes, Lance realized. Black leather athletic shoes, suitable for employment in a restaurant. The rest of Nico's clothing was black, too, with the Blue Taco emblem on the left shoulder of his black polo.

Everything else the kid owned had been blown apart. All he had was his phone and a backpack he'd carried to the gallery before going to work.

"I'll be damned," Belwether whispered, jerking Lance away from his thoughts. Belwether was looking at the bird instead of the kid. "Does he have a name?" Belwether stepped into Lance's office to ask Nico. Lance, wearing a frown, followed him in.

"I don't know." Nico's arms tightened around himself.

"Mac," the raven croaked.

"Your name is Mac?" Belwether sounded incredulous.

"Cor-mac. Flynn. Call. Me. Mac." There was a frown in the raven's croak, since his beak couldn't transform to convey the message.

"Fucking hell," Belwether swore softly.

"I think you should ask your questions later," Ari stood abruptly. "Nico's had enough for the day."

"What. She. Said," the raven agreed.

"We can put Nico in a safe house with guards," Lance suggested.

"He can come home with me, Detective." Lance understood that Ari didn't like Belwether's intrusion nor his words. She was right, though. Nico looked as if he were barely hanging on.

"Take them to her place," Belwether snapped at Lance. "Ms. Leone, don't leave town. I'll have a unit outside for your protection tonight. Tomorrow, Detective Elliott will call and set up another interview."

"Thanks for all the warmth and hospitality," Ari's eyes and voice had gone so cold Lance wanted to shiver. "We'll be fine."

Nico was up and out of the chair fast. Mac flapped to his shoulder and held on. Ari swept out of the office first, followed by Nico.

"What. She. Said," the raven repeated on the way out.

Ari fumed while Lance drove her and Nico to her house in North Dallas. She knew Lance kept looking her way, hoping to find a way to apologize for the Captain's gaffe, but she refused to allow an opening.

Besides, it didn't take a genius—just someone with sensitive hearing—to know Nico was holding back tears while he stroked Mac's feathers in the back seat. The occasional sniff let her know exactly how things were.

"I'll call tomorrow," Lance said as he saw them to Ari's back door. He waited while she unlocked it and turned off the alarm.

"Thank you, Detective," Ari said before shutting the door in his face. She was grateful to be stronger than she looked as Nico fell into her arms and sobbed. Mac hopped to a nearby kitchen counter and spoke soft mumblings only a raven might understand.

CHAPTER TWO

"*M*ac, are you hungry?" Ari, feeling bone-weary, stared at the raven, who now stood on her kitchen table. Nico slept in her extra bedroom after crying himself out. Ari had glanced briefly at the microwave clock—it showed one-seventeen AM.

"Yes," Mac answered.

"I'm really tired; can you eat an omelet or something easy?"

"Yes. Water?" There was a question in his voice.

"I'm so sorry. Let me get you some." Ari stood and went to the sink, where she pulled two glasses from an upper cabinet. "Ice? No ice?"

"Ice."

"Good choice." After getting ice for both glasses from the fridge, she filled them with filtered water and brought them to the table. "If I weren't so worried, I'd be breaking into the Scotch bottle over the fridge," she confessed, setting a glass in front of Mac.

"Thanks." Mac dipped his beak in the glass and lifted his head to swallow.

Ari sipped her water while watching Mac drink, then rose to put an omelet together. One large omelet should do for both of them. In less than twenty minutes, she set a plate covered by a generous omelet on the table.

"How much do you want?" Ari held a knife and an extra plate in her hands.

"Third?" Mac sounded hopeful.

"A third it is," she said, cutting his portion and pushing it onto the extra plate. "If you want more, I can make another."

"This fine." He fluffed his feathers and began picking at the omelet, tearing off chunks to eat. She'd filled it with ham, cheese, tomatoes, peppers and onions, all of which Mac appeared to enjoy.

"Nico may wake up starving," Ari sighed. "I don't know when he ate last."

"He ex-aww-stedd," Mac croaked. "He eat later."

"You uh, have some egg on your beak," Ari tapped the left side of her mouth. "Here." She pushed an extra paper towel in his direction. Mac dutifully cleaned his beak, wiping it back and forth on the makeshift napkin, then went back to eating.

Unfailingly polite, for a bird. Ari watched him finish his omelet. "You need a perch or a nest or something to sleep?"

"Perch fine. Nest fine, too."

"Well, it's either the back of a chair or a blanket, which do you want?"

"Chair." His pale, nictitating membranes covered his eyes briefly. Ari watched in fascination, as it was his way of blinking.

"Then I'll let you pick the chair. I'm going to bed." Ari rose from her seat, lifted the plates from the table and placed them in the dishwasher.

She froze at the swishing sound outside. "Did that sound like running to you?" she whirled to look at Mac.

"I wake Nico," Mac flapped away from the table toward Nico's bedroom.

"Damn," Ari swore as she pulled her shirt over her head and undid her bra, then shucked her pants and shoes.

The swishing noise came again, this time heading straight for the back door.

"Keep Nico safe," she shouted at Mac, before turning. The door burst open, revealing a foul-smelling human with unkempt hair and an unholy light in his eyes. Ari was ready for him and, spitting and snarling, leapt before the invader could recoil or run.

"I thought you'd be doing your job," Ari snapped at the officer who'd arrived to take charge of the body lying on her kitchen floor. "Instead, I had to fight him off with a knife."

The man's throat had certainly been slashed—deep enough that he'd died quickly. His blood was all over the floor and nearby, a large, bloody kitchen knife lay where Ari dropped it.

"This had better be good," Ari heard Detective Elliott's voice outside the door. "I had to get out of bed for this. Ah," was all he said as he strode into the kitchen and nearly stepped in a pool of blood.

"Where the hell was our surveillance team?" Lance demanded of Officer Gray.

"Not here," Gray shook his head. "Haven't located them or the car."

"They were here when I left three hours ago."

"Not here when we arrived. Ms. Leone dialed nine-one-one."

"And that left this asshole free to kick down her door," Lance shook his head. "I'm glad you were able to protect yourself," he glanced at Ari.

"That makes two of us, detective." Ari's tone conveyed her aggravation.

"The kid safe?"

"He's okay, just shook up. He and Mac are in the back bedroom, if you want to see for yourself."

"We'll have to move you now," Lance sighed. "I'm sorry about that, but they managed to find Nico again. You're lucky to be alive. I'll have a word with the kid."

"Yeah." Ari stiffened as Lance brushed past her, being careful not to disturb the blood or the body on the floor.

"Is there a uh, reason for the bra in the sink?" The officer turned his attention elsewhere for a moment.

"I wasn't exactly dressed for company when this asshole broke down my door," Ari said truthfully. "I barely had time to put the rest of my clothes on before you got here."

"Understandable," the cop agreed and wrote notes on his small notebook. "We'll have to bag the knife as evidence," he added. "And I'll have to ask for the clothes you're wearing—for blood spatter and that kind of thing."

"No problem. I don't need any of it back—if you return it, it'll go in the trash."

"I'd do the same thing."

"Does anybody have to be with me while I undress?"

"This looks pretty clear-cut, if you ask me. Go change and bring me what you're wearing."

"All right." Ari turned and walked toward her bedroom. Once there, she disrobed quickly, shimmied into sweats and a T-shirt, then grabbed what she'd removed and carried them back to Officer Gray.

"It was past my bedtime and I wasn't wearing any—well, if you find blood spatter, it'll be on the inside of those clothes," Ari warned Gray as she handed the clothing to him. "Just to let you know."

"I'll make a note of it." He scribbled more notes on his pad. "If we have more questions, Detective Elliott will let you know. You can leave the kitchen, now, and talk to him and Nico while he decides where to take you from here. We'll get the body off the floor and out of the way. I think we have everything we need."

"Thank you." Ari turned and walked to the back of the house; she could hear Nico's voice as the detective asked questions.

"I only heard Ari yell for Mac to keep me safe," Nico said as Ari walked into the room. "I was asleep until Mac flew in and started squawking."

"So neither of you saw the guy?" Lance asked, causing Ari to frown.

"We. Did. Not," Mac insisted.

"I need this to come from Nico. I don't know how to put a raven as a witness in an official report."

"I didn't see anything. All I heard was Ari yelling for Mac to keep me safe, a loud noise that sounded like a missile hitting the back door, a lot of racket, and then Ari yelling that the man was dead."

"And that's why my back door is hanging on one hinge," Ari said, crossing arms defensively over her chest. "One other thing—that man smelled terrible. Like he'd been rolling in roadkill before breaking into my house."

"We'll get an ID on him," Lance said. "We'll see if he matches anybody in the area or going past your business yesterday."

"You think he was staking out the restaurant?" Nico quavered.

"We don't know anything, yet," Lance told him. "But we have to check every angle of this, you understand. Now, I have to get you someplace safe while we investigate this mess."

"Where will that be?" Ari asked.

"I have a cousin who owns a ranch west of Fort Worth," Lance replied. "I can check in with him—you'd be safe enough there, I'm pretty sure."

"For how long? I can't shut down my business forever, Detective."

"It may only be for a day or two—until we get a handle on all this," Lance attempted to soothe Ari's growing anger. "I'll have somebody check on it several times a day, if that will make things better."

"Good. I need information, and I'll have to replace the broken glass in the front of the gallery."

"It may be better to leave it boarded shut for now. They have your name, Ms. Leone. It's too dangerous to let anyone know where you are or where you'll be, including the insurance company and the glass company."

"Detective?" Officer Gray called out from the hallway.

"Come on in," Ari shook her head as Gray stalked into the bedroom before he was given permission.

"Sorry," Gray apologized. "But we got an ID on the perp. It's weird, too. He's from Corpus Christi. The report says he died three days ago."

"Well, that can't be true, now can it?" Lance drawled. "How long has he been in the Dallas area?"

"We don't know. There aren't any records of him traveling here. In fact, Corpus PD says his body disappeared after he died of a heart attack."

"Then they're wrong. Get back on this—somebody made a mistake," Lance growled.

"I'll have everything double and triple-checked," Gray walked out of the room.

"How soon are we leaving?" Nico asked, reaching for his shoes and socks, which were under the bed.

"I sent text messages to my cousin," Lance said. "When I get a reply, I'll know for sure."

His phone rang seconds later. "Lance, here," he answered.

Ari listened shamelessly to the conversation. "We got the go-ahead," a female voice said on the other end. "He says they'll be ready whenever you get here."

"Nico may want something to eat," Ari interjected.

Lance jerked around to frown at Ari before relaying that information to the woman.

"That's fine," she replied. "You can either go to a fast-food place or they can fix something when he arrives."

"Thanks, Mona. I owe you," Lance said and ended the call.

"Pack a bag," Lance barked at Ari, angry that she'd heard both sides of the conversation. "I'll make sure somebody gets extra clothes for Nico, and whatever it is the bird needs."

"Bird. Is. Fine," Mac declared.

On any other day, the light of a new sunrise spreading westward would have been beautiful to watch as they drove west of Fort Worth on I-20. Ari, hunched in the front passenger's seat and feeling miserable after the night's events, could only stare, unseeing, through the windshield toward the west.

Normally, she'd want to pull over to get pictures and a better look at the spring-green prairie grasses and wildflowers off the I-20 roadside that Lance's vehicle rushed past. Bluebonnets, the Texas state flower, sent swaths of blue throughout the green, and was worthy of a postcard or a painting.

Not today. She'd killed a man who may have already been dead. It left a bitter taste in her mouth, even after brushing her teeth twice and using mouthwash both times.

How could a dead man break down my door? Ari shuddered. It made no sense. The police got it wrong.

Because dead men don't kick down doors with superhuman strength. Ari shuddered again.

"We'll be at my cousin's place in ten," Lance promised after witnessing Ari's distress.

"You o-kay?" Mac croaked from the back seat.

"I'm okay, Mac. For now," Ari hugged herself. "I just feel a little nauseated, that's all."

Lance took an exit, then drove southward along a well-paved farm road. Ari forced herself to stop thinking of the one she'd killed; someone was willing to offer them sanctuary, and she needed to be alert and on her best behavior.

"Is this a cattle ranch?" Nico perked up in the back seat as Lance turned off the road and drove over a cattle guard, the vehicle's tires bouncing across the metal grid designed to keep cows from leaving the property.

"Sure is," Lance told him. "The ranch has been in the family for more than a hundred years. It's huge, and the biggest provider of organic beef in Texas."

"What?" Ari turned swiftly in Lance's direction. "Tell me you're not talking about the Jordan Ranch."

"You know about that?" Lance beamed.

"Turn around. Now. Take me anywhere but here," Ari hissed.

"But we're here." Lance pulled to a stop on a massive, circle drive outside a palatial, three-level mansion.

"No. I'm leaving if I have to walk," Ari wasn't having it.

"Is there a problem? You know my cousin?"

"His family. They did the unforgivable. I'll take my chances at home." Ari was so angry she almost spat at Lance. "Did you give them my name when you said you were bringing us here?"

"I didn't—they only know about Nico, his bird and a companion."

"Call them. Tell them Arianne Leone is here and she wants back what they took from her." Ari's breathing had gone ragged and fast, her arms clamped around herself as she vibrated with fury.

"Wait, here's my cousin. I'll ah, talk to him," Lance opened his car door and stepped out.

"What's wrong?" Nico asked.

"Nico, it's not something I can explain," Ari whispered.

"She says to tell you her name, and that she wants what you took from her back," Lance shaded his eyes as he studied his cousin, Val Jordan.

"What's her name?" Val asked.

"Arianne Leone."

"Fuck," Val cursed and turned his head away for a moment. "You're in the middle of it, now," Val turned back to Lance. "We offered to pay restitution—it's how we ah, handle disputes among us. Her mother refused payment. Called it blood money. I guess that's actually true, in their case."

"You're talking wrongful death?"

"Yeah."

"Fucking hell," Lance swore.

"We're still willing to keep them safe, but now you know why she's upset. Look, I'll get Mom out here—maybe she can talk sense to Arianne."

"I'm guessing this happened during Uncle Brett's lifetime?"

"Yeah. Twenty-six years ago, or thereabouts. It was a big to-do, and the Grand Master was called in."

"I'm not sure I want to know anything else. If Aunt Janie is willing to talk to Ari, I'd appreciate it."

"I'll go get her. She's been worried about that girl ever since, well," Val shrugged. "I'll go get her," he repeated before loping toward the front door. Lance turned back to the car. Leaning down so he could see Ari through the open driver's side door, he said, "Look, Ari, Aunt Janie is coming out to talk to you. Uncle Brett died eleven years ago, and Val says Janie still worries about you."

"Right." Ari shifted in her seat, turning her back on Lance. "I'm guessing you're half, and that makes you outcast," she accused.

"Not in this family; we recognize our own, no matter what."

"Hmmph."

"What's going on?" Nico asked from the back seat. "Can Mac and I get out? We'd like to look around."

"Sure," Lance blinked at Nico in the dim light of the car's interior. "Just don't wander far, okay."

"We won't." Nico opened the door and slid out of the car. Mac flapped after him, landing on his shoulder.

"Look, Detective, nothing you can say or do will ever make me come to terms with any of this," Ari flung over her shoulder.

"Arianne?" Aunt Janie now stood beside Lance and leaned down to get a better look at Ari. "Lance says you're in danger, and that you were attacked last night. At least let us protect you until they find the ones responsible for this mess. We're the best defense anyone can have in a situation like this."

"I have no quarrel with you," Ari still had her back turned to Lance and Janie.

"I made sure you and your mother were fed and taken care of during the trial. I'm sorry there wasn't anything we could do about the shooter. He was told to stay away on the full moon. He wanted the job over with, so he disobeyed. You remember that, don't you?"

"All just empty words," Ari sniffled. "The fucker is still alive, too."

"I told Brett not to hire a human. He didn't listen. I've never been so sorry in my life that he refused to take my advice. Please, come into the house. I know you haven't slept, and I hear you had to protect that boy against a monster last night."

"I guess it's too late to convince Detective Elliott that I used a knife, huh?"

Lance watched as Ari tried to hide the wiping away of tears.

"He's going to swear that's exactly what happened," Janie said gently. "You did what you had to, to protect yourself and the boy. If you'll come with me, I'll fix breakfast for all of you. I have guest rooms ready for you, too, if you want to sleep after breakfast."

"I want to go home," Ari's head dropped against the window.

"I know. Right now, that's not possible. Come with me, and we'll help as much as we can. I know nothing will ever replace what you lost, but can we call a truce until this gets sorted?"

"Ari, this is the best option, really," Lance said quietly. "You don't have to say anything to anybody or do anything you don't want to while you're here. I need to get to work—I've got messages from Mona about Nico's phone, and more information on the man who died last night."

"Fine." Ari flung open the car door and stepped out awkwardly, as if she no longer knew what to do with her own arms and legs.

"She wants to shift," Janie whispered softly to Lance. "And she can't, because of the boy."

"Yeah. Let's go get her." Ari had walked aimlessly toward the edge of the driveway, where she'd stopped beside a mass of flowering lilies. Still hugging herself, Lance wondered if she were crying again.

"I'll get her," Janie put a hand on his arm. "You go to work. Keep us informed, all right? If she needs to get out of state fast because of what happened last night, we'll see to it."

"I don't think it'll come to that, but I'll let you know. Thanks, Aunt Janie. I really appreciate this." He leaned in to kiss her cheek before climbing into the car.

Ari stiffened when Janie Jordan placed a careful hand on her shoulder. "Come inside, now. This sun is blistering already," Janie coaxed.

Without a word, Ari followed Janie into the house. Nico and Mac caught up and walked in with them.

Janie led them toward the kitchen, where the scent of food tickled Ari's nostrils. "You must be starving," she turned toward Nico.

"I kinda am," he confessed. "Are those biscuits?" His eyes grew round at the sight of a large pan of the fluffy, homemade bread.

"We have sausage gravy to go with them, if you want," Janie smiled. "Sit down at the island, I'll bring plates. Does the bird need a plate, too?"

"Bird. Needs a. Plate," Mac declared, making Nico snicker.

"It's good to see you smile," Ari said, sounding weary. "Food smells delicious, Janie. Nico, Janie Jordan, here, is one of the best cooks I've ever met. Janie, this is Nicolas Garcia and that," she pointed toward Mac, "is Cormac Flynn, but he goes by Mac."

"Not sure I've ever met a bird who spoke my language before," Janie nodded to Mac. "Good to meet you, Nico. Now, I have sausage and bacon, scrambled eggs and biscuits and gravy. Who wants what?" Janie bustled around the kitchen, setting out plates and flatware, before placing a platter of meat and a bowl of sausage gravy on the island.

"Saw-sage and gray-vee, pleaze," Mac said.

"And he has manners, too," Janie smiled. "Would you like your sausage patty crumbled?"

"Pleaze."

Nico and Ari watched in fascination as Janie crumbled the sausage on Mac's plate, then poured gravy over it.

"Thank. You," Mac said before scooping up food with his beak.

Nico asked for some of everything, with orange juice. Mac got water with his food; Ari had eggs, bacon, a biscuit and coffee.

"I've never seen a raven with any red feathers," Janie said as she sipped a cup of coffee.

"It's. A curse," Mac croaked.

"Good one, Mac," Nico said. "High five?"

Mac lifted the wing nearest Nico, who tapped it gently.

"Unbelievable," Ari mumbled and finished her coffee.

~

"Here's everything we got from the kid's phone," Mona handed Lance a thumb drive and a file. "Touristy stuff from Spain, emails from his mother, pictures of his parents at restaurants; nothing that would be flagged as out of the ordinary."

"What about the security recordings from the gallery across the street from Blue Taco?"

"We're still going through those but so far, our dead man hasn't been in them."

"He may have been the house bomber," Lance theorized.

"Or one of them," Mona agreed. "If he wasn't alone last night, I'm sure Ms. Leone scared the others away."

"Did you talk to Aunt Janie?"

"I did."

"And?"

Mona leaned in as close as she could. "Mountain lion," she whispered.

"That would explain some things, all right."

"I can give you more later, but for now, I have to keep going through security footage." Mona nodded at her cousin and turned to go.

"Lunch?" he called out after her.

"Sure thing. One-thirty?"

"I'll meet you in the parking garage. Let me know if you find anything elsc on those recordings."

Mona waved a hand in agreement and disappeared around a corner. Lance turned; Belwether expected a meeting on where Nico was and how he was being protected. Lance had to be quick on his feet to refuse police surveillance on the property. He also had to find out if the patrol car and the two on duty last night had been found.

"Belwether wants to see you, and do you want to contribute to the collection for Norm's daughter? She's still in college, you know," Lance's sometimes partner, Kyle Anthony, stopped him in the hallway to ask.

"Bethany and her mother haven't had much to do with Norm for the past five years, but sure, I'll pitch in." Lance pulled out his wallet and handed Kyle forty dollars. What he didn't say was that there weren't many who did have anything to do with Norm if they could help it.

Still, nobody deserved to die like that. With a nod to Kyle, Lance continued his journey toward Belwether's office. He was pretty sure Norm's name would crop up in the conversation somewhere, since Lance was the last one to work with him.

"Come in and take a load off," Belwether motioned Lance into his office. "Shut the door, too. Want coffee?"

"I'll take coffee—not much sleep last night," Lance admitted.

"Well, we got a double check on the dead perp. They insist that's a dead man from Corpus. Fingerprints match, images match. Somebody's trying to screw with us."

"They *are* screwing with us. There's no trying involved," Lance said, taking a paper cup filled with coffee from Belwether's pot, then sitting on a guest chair.

"The kid and the woman are at the Jordan Ranch?"

"As of early this morning. My aunt is taking care of them right now. Val has every hand of his watching for anybody or anything out of the ordinary."

"If they need backup," Belwether began.

"We'll keep you informed," Lance replied. "No worries. They're as safe there as they can be anywhere. Mona's gone through the kid's phone—says there's nothing there out of the ordinary, either here or during his parents' trip to Spain last year. She's still going over the security stuff from Ari's gallery. What are we going to do with the dead guy?"

"I've asked forensics to bump him up their list and take a look. They ought to be able to tell whether the guy was killed last night or died four days ago."

"You'd think so," Lance agreed, hoping his voice didn't betray a hint of sarcasm.

"The kid needs a lawyer—he has his parents' business dealings, insurance and that sort of thing to handle, and probably has no idea what to do. The people who died there may be covered by a business policy, but we need somebody working on that soon."

"Val has a good lawyer on his payroll," Lance offered. "I'll see if he's available or can recommend somebody. There are no other relatives in the country, according to Mona."

"What about Mexico?"

"She's still working on that."

"Tell her to keep me in the loop."

"Sure thing." Lance stood, preparing to leave Belwether's office.

"We've got the kid's car—what's left of it—in impound. It was parked behind the restaurant, next to his parents' vehicle. They're going through it to make sure there's nothing incriminating, or if anything was planted in it by somebody else."

"Should I keep that from Nico?"

"No; it's something to talk to the lawyer about, too. You can feel him out about it if you want."

"This isn't the type of kid who'd murder his folks, you know."

"I figure that's true, but we can't assume anything."

"I'll keep you informed." Lance walked out, tossing his empty coffee cup in Belwether's wastebasket on the way. Something was way off on all of this; he seldom disagreed with Belwether but somehow, the Captain was going down the wrong track on this one—Lance felt it in his bones.

Time for a visit to the Medical Examiner's office; he wanted another look at the man Ari killed.

"What's all the fuss about?" Lance approached one of several officers standing guard outside the Medical Examiner's office.

"There's something going on inside—don't have much information, Detective," the officer replied after Lance showed his badge. "Most of the building has been evacuated. Could be hazardous materials or something."

Lance's phone rang—it was Mona calling. "I have to take this," he waved his thanks to the officer and stepped away.

"Mona? What's up?"

"You're not going to believe this," she began. "Belwether got a call from the ME—says that the cadaver from Ari Leone's house started twitching, and when it got off the gurney on its own, everybody started running. Right now, it's locked inside one of the exam rooms, knocking stuff around."

"What the hell?" Lance couldn't believe what he was hearing. "I just got to the ME's office, and there are uniforms everywhere. One just told me most of the building has been evacuated. The guy's head was nearly severed. No way he can still be alive."

"What if he isn't?" Mona asked. "Those people in Corpus still insist he's a dead man."

"It's just not possible. This is reality, Mona. Zombies don't exist."

"There has to be some explanation for it. It's happening, whether we believe it or not."

"Look, I'll meet you for lunch as planned. I think I'll go back to Blue Taco. We must be missing something in all this."

"I'm still going through that security video. Let me know if anything new turns up at the scene."

Parking his car two blocks away, Lance walked toward the remains of Blue Taco. That portion of the street was still blocked off, and several surrounding businesses were closed until the street reopened.

He stopped outside Ari's gallery first—the windows were boarded up and a closed sign hung on the door. Nico wasn't the only one who needed to speak with an insurance adjuster.

Without any idea how long she and Nico would need to stay at the ranch, he wondered if Ari would like to take her art supplies and canvas to work on while the gallery was closed.

Resolving to send her a text, he turned to gaze at the ruin that was

Blue Taco. His phone rang while he studied the mess, still surrounded by crime scene tape.

"Detective Elliott," he answered the call.

"This is Officer Gray," the caller identified himself. "Now, I don't know if you've heard, but there's been an incident in Austin, very similar to the one at Ms. Leone's house. In this case, the door was kicked in, and the ah, perp took six shots from a forty-four magnum in his head and torso. Still managed to do some damage to the homeowner before he went down. Another case of a man reported dead in San Antonio, who shows up in Austin to commit a crime three days later."

"Where are both now?" Lance asked, swiftly walking toward his car.

"Homeowner was treated and released from the hospital. Perp is at the ME's office in Austin. Why?"

"Call Captain Belwether in Central. Tell him I asked you to describe the events in Austin. He may have other news for you, or for the Austin PD. Thanks for the heads up, by the way. Call me back if you get more information; I'd like to talk to the homeowner if that's possible."

Lance ended the call and jogged the last half-block to his car.

CHAPTER THREE

*A*ri felt as if someone were pounding inside her skull with a blacksmith's hammer when she woke during the afternoon. Events from the day before came rushing back as she sat up and glanced at the bedside clock.

Three-forty-three PM was displayed; she felt mentally drained and sluggish while the headache continued to throb. Dropping her legs over the side of the bed, she fought the desire to lie down again.

Instead, she rose and stumbled toward the bathroom to wash her face. Fog blanketed her thoughts—*what is wrong with me?*

"Ari?" A knock sounded on the bedroom door. "Ari, let me in," Nico tapped again.

"Nico? It's unlocked," she spoke, struggling to release the words— as if speech were deserting her.

Nico arrived just as she sank to the floor, still fighting confusion, unceasing pain and sudden, debilitating nausea.

"Ari," Nico dropped to his knees. "Hold this. Ari, you have to hold this." He placed something in her hand that felt warm from his touch.

"Huh?" It took a great deal of effort to turn toward him, as if doing so had only occurred to her after several seconds passed.

"I was having a dream, Ari," Nico whispered as she blinked at him, still attempting to bring his face into focus. "I dreamed that you were really sick, and you needed to hold my shell."

"Huh?" Ari repeated, but this time, her vision was clearer, and the headache had faded to a manageable level. "What shell?" Looking down at her hand, she found a black scallop shell cradled in her palm.

"You had a dream?" The fog in her brain was dwindling—enough that she could begin to think rationally.

"I dreamed that—the man from last night made you sick, and you needed to hold my shell."

"Nico, I've never seen you with this shell before." Ari studied it, moving it around in her hand.

"Mama called it a pilgrim's shell. They sell them in Santiago de Compostela. She brought it back to me from Spain."

"It feels—warm. Good. I can't really describe it," she admitted. "I don't have a headache anymore." Her voice betrayed her surprise at that fact. "I felt awful when I woke up—like I was really sick and I couldn't think. I think you saved me, Nico," she said, giving him a hug.

He stood and gave her a hand to help her stand. "Wow, I thought I'd have that headache for days," she said, handing the shell to Nico. She wasn't sure it was the shell that did the trick, but Nico's presence had certainly helped.

"Let's go to the kitchen and get something to drink—you look hollow, Ari."

Ari followed him out of the bedroom; he pocketed the shell on the way, as if it were something precious.

It is precious to him, she realized. It came from his mother, and it had felt so warm while she held it—turning her left hand palm up, she drew in a breath.

The imprint of the shell was now on her palm. *Had she gripped it that tightly?*

"Where's Mac?" she asked, dropping her hand and rubbing the palm against her jeans.

"Sleeping on top of my shower door," Nico turned to her and grinned. "He's like a feather ball, all tucked up like that."

They made a turn, walked across a massive family room, then

shuffled into the kitchen. Janie was there, talking to someone on the phone. "They're right here—Ari looks fine," Janie told the caller on the other end. "Do you want to talk to her?" Janie waited while the other person spoke.

"All right—I'll tell her you'll be here for dinner, then." Janie ended the call, stuffed the phone into a jeans pocket and studied Nico and Ari. "Lance just wanted to know if you were feeling okay," she said. "Looks like somebody else in Austin wasn't so lucky when his house was broken into. He's in the hospital, now, and the doctors are going crazy trying to figure out what's wrong with him."

Nico gripped Ari's hand tightly. She understood that he didn't want to talk about what had happened to her only minutes earlier.

"That's too bad—why are they comparing my break-in to one in Austin?"

"The one who broke in—well, he didn't go down easy. Lance hinted at some other problems, but he didn't explain any of it. Somehow, he thinks it's connected, and he wouldn't say that without strong evidence."

"So I can talk to him tonight?"

"He'll be here around seven for dinner, and he's bringing Mona with him. She's the one who's been studying your security camera footage, so there may be some things to look at more closely."

"What's for dinner?" Nico asked, letting Ari's hand go.

"Pork roast with green beans and glazed carrots, and blackberry cobbler for dessert."

"That sounds great. Can Ari and I have something to drink?"

"Absolutely. Would you like water, milk, soda or juice?"

"I'll take water and juice, if that's all right," Ari said.

"I'll have the same." Nico pulled out a chair at the island. Ari sat next to him when Janie motioned for her to sit rather than help with the drinks. They ended up having sliced pears with their drinks, too.

"I guess I was hungrier than I realized," Ari bit into another pear slice. It tasted good—like the best pear she'd ever eaten.

"You've been through a lot," Janie said while rolling out crust for the cobbler.

Mac fluttered in, landing on Nico's shoulder. "Pear?" he croaked.

"Want some?" Ari held out a slice of pear.

Mac hopped onto the island and took the pear slice from Ari. Holding down one end of it with a foot to keep it from sliding away, he set about biting off chunks of the fruit and devouring them. Ari slid another slice his way after he finished the first and offered a glass of water and a napkin.

"Good pear," Mac said after finishing both pieces. "Thank. You."

"He's very polite. For a raven," Nico teased.

"Did. *You* say. Thank. You?" Mac eyed Nico.

"Thank you," Nico told Janie, who laughed as Mac continued to eye Nico suspiciously.

"It's two hours until dinner," Janie said. "There are books, games and a television in the game room. Ari knows where it is if you're interested."

"I wish we could paint together," Nico turned his gaze on Ari. "I think that would block some of this stuff out."

"I'll see if we can't do that. I hope they'll let us go home soon." Ari bumped her shoulder against Nico's. "Besides, I need to finish that commission."

"Val's asked the family lawyer to come to dinner—to talk with Nico about insurance and stuff," Janie busied herself at the stove. "For the house, the restaurant, cars—that kind of thing."

"I have copies of Papa's policies," Nico ducked his head. "Papa always sent me the important stuff—it's on my cell phone. Which I no longer have," he concluded.

"Mona may bring it back to you tonight," Janie said. "I got that idea when I talked to Lance that she was finished looking through it."

"Still not a good idea to be calling anybody," Ari warned.

"Yeah. I'm almost afraid to get it back, but it does have the insurance policy information on it."

"Burke will see to it that everything gets done," Janie said. "Go on —watch television or read until dinner's ready."

Mac hopped on Nico's shoulder; Nico followed Ari out of the kitchen. "Stairs or elevator?" Ari asked.

"There's an elevator?" Nico blinked.

"They have everything." Ari's voice had turned resentful.

"I think you ought to tell me about that," Nico said.

"Not now." Ari hunched her shoulders. "Come on, the elevator's this way."

Ari sat at a window in the third-floor game room while Nico watched sit-com reruns on television. Mac kept him company, sitting on the back of a nearby chair. The bird surprised her, too, flying into the bathroom to take care of business, and flushing before coming back out.

She suspected he was a shifter, but why had he kept the bird shape all this time? Surely, he understood she was the same, and now, being at the Jordan ranch, they were surrounded by werewolves. Only a few ranch residents were human, and those humans would be trusted beyond any doubt.

Except for the one Brett Jordan had hired all those years ago, when his calves were getting attacked by a predator.

Her father had died on a full moon, and the predator continued to prey on the calves until it was found and destroyed. Humans didn't have the nose for what had been attacking and eating Brett Jordan's cattle. Brett was looking for someone who was an expert with a gun, because he and his wolves hadn't been able to get close to the rogue animal feeding off his herd.

A bobcat—a larger-than-normal, non-shifting bobcat—was the real culprit, but Mitchell Franks only saw a big cat when he went out on the night of the full moon. Mitchell killed James Leone from downwind and many yards away.

Fuck you, Mitchell Franks, Ari thought in the man's direction.

Killing her father hadn't been the only thing the man had done, but she couldn't think on *that* without feeling nauseous.

"Ari? Nico?" Lance, accompanied by a woman, stepped off the

elevator and into the game room. "Janie says dinner's almost ready, if you want to wash up."

"I should change clothes," Ari mumbled, looking down at the shirt and jeans she'd slept in earlier. Rising from her chair, she made her way toward the elevator.

"We haven't met," the woman held out her hand to Ari as she approached. "I'm Mona Sparks, Lance and Val's cousin. I work in the forensics department for Dallas PD."

Ari took Mona's hand out of habit, nodding to the woman as politely as she could. "I need to change," Ari excused herself. "I'll see you at dinner."

"We should talk afterward," Lance said as Ari stepped onto the elevator and hit the button for the first floor.

"That's fine." Ari watched Lance and Mona until the door closed and the elevator moved downward. She'd agitated herself, thinking about Mitchell Franks and the fact that he was alive and probably still bragging about how he'd killed a huge mountain lion from a very safe distance.

Fuck you, Mitchell Franks, Ari repeated.

It was mostly small talk over dinner; Ari figured the more serious conversations would occur afterward. She recognized Burke Jordan, Brett Jordan's younger brother, who'd been at the trial, although he hadn't argued his brother's case. Someone else had done that; someone with no connections to the family, at the Grand Master's insistence.

"I sure do wish Chuck hadn't sold his property," Val told Burke. "That idiot who now owns the ranch is already causing problems."

"You mean Denton Franks?"

"Yeah. He used to be all hat and no cattle. Now he's big hat and too many cattle. I got a good look at his feed lots—he's not even trying to rotate pastures or anything like that. The stench is getting really bad from too many steers being crammed into those spaces. We've called the Sheriff multiple times about the conditions the cattle are in, but nothing gets done. We've called other county officials, too, but got the same results. I've called Denton a time or two myself. If you really want to piss him off, criticize his hat and mention greenhouse gases."

Ari drew in a breath at the mention of Denton Franks' name. Since she'd kept an eye on Denton's father all these years, she knew exactly who that was.

"Revisiting the scene of his father's crime?" Ari hissed at Val.

"Hey, I'm sorry. We didn't mean to," Burke tried to apologize.

"It's a little late for that." Ari dropped her napkin on the chair after scraping it backward and standing. "Janie, the meal was excellent. Excuse me." She turned quickly and stomped out of the dining room.

"Burke, I thought you knew better," Janie said, rising to follow Ari.

"Yeah." Burke ducked his head under Janie's glare.

"Some humans are nothing but tainted meat, too poisonous to feed on," Ari's father told her many times. *"They're not worth your time or trouble,"* he'd add.

It was the only reason Mitchell Franks was still alive. Night had fallen as Ari dropped into the comfortable chair she'd occupied earlier in the game room. Still, she could see clearly enough outside. Nothing moved, and only the faint sound of night insects filtered past the double-paned glass.

A half-moon shone high over the Jordan Ranch; Ari would have to find someplace to turn in two weeks' time. It sure as hell wouldn't be here, in case Denton Franks wanted to take a shot at *her*.

Please say his father isn't living with him, Ari sighed. Mitchell's wife had died three years earlier—she'd read the obituary in the Dallas newspaper. As for Val's wolves—he ought to be worried about their safety on the full moon, too.

"Ari?" Janie had found her.

"Val's wolves won't be safe on the full moon, with that family living next to the Jordan Ranch," Ari blurted.

"They've already worked that out—that they'll either run on the northeast side of the ranch, or go elsewhere," Janie sat on a matching chair opposite Ari's.

"But," Ari began.

"They've been warned to stay off our property," Janie attempted to calm Ari. "Val's already said he won't vouch for their safety if they trespass."

"But if they get in a lucky shot, they'll walk away free men. Again."

"Ari, listen to me carefully. If they harm anyone on this ranch, they will die on this ranch. Even if I have to drag them out of that house and onto our property to do it. I don't care what kind of shifter or human is staying here with us; if the Franks trespass, they die. One way or another. Mitchell Franks claimed your father was killed on Chuck Danforth's property instead of Jordan property. We know different, because we found the place where he died. If Brett had been given permission by the Grand Master, he'd have gone after him."

"Mitchell Franks is a liar," Ari hugged herself.

"Arianne?" Lance stepped off the elevator.

"If you need to speak privately," Janie started to rise.

"Stay," Ari held out a hand. "I don't think Lance will say anything that you can't hear."

"If that's what you want."

"I do."

Lance pulled a chair away from a nearby game table, setting it between Ari's and Janie's. "I have some news," he said. "About the home invasion in Austin, and about the man who attacked Ari at her house."

"Are they related?" Ari asked.

"I'm worried that they are, although the FBI is now involved, and so far, they're just as shocked and puzzled as the rest of us."

"Then start at the beginning, because right now, you're not making sense, Lance Elliott," Janie demanded.

"Well, the man who broke into Ari's house really was declared dead in Corpus Christi," Lance said carefully, as if he still didn't believe those words himself. "His body disappeared shortly after he was taken to a funeral home. Three days later, he breaks down Ari's door and tries to get past her, but she doesn't allow it. She nearly severs his head in the process. He is then tagged and sent to the ME's office, for forensics to examine.

"This afternoon," Lance hesitated for a moment, searching for the proper words to describe the events at the morgue, "they had to evacuate the ME's office because the perp rolled off the table and started destroying everything within reach, his head wobbling on top of his neck the whole time. Right now, he's full of bullets, strapped to a gurney and still twitching." Lance closed his eyes and drew in a deep breath.

"What about the guy in Austin?" Ari whispered.

"Same type of break-in," Lance opened his eyes and blinked at her. "Homeowner ended up shooting the guy several times to bring him down. Sent the body to the ME's, just like we did. Once we found out about it, we sent a warning to Austin PD. They tied the guy down, even though they were skeptical about it. Turns out, they were glad they listened to us."

"And the homeowner?" Janie prompted.

"He got banged up in the altercation. Went to the hospital. Got released. Three hours later, he's back at the ER, and now he's in an isolation ward, because they can't figure out what's wrong with him. Texas Bureau and the FBI were called in, and now Austin and the ME's office here are crawling with agents. I gotta ask, Ari—are you feeling well?"

Ari felt the blood drain from her face. She'd been far from well after waking earlier. She understood that Nico didn't want to talk about what had happened. "I did have a headache when I woke up, but Nico came looking for me and it cleared up shortly after that."

"You're fine, then?"

"I think so. I don't feel bad, if that's what you're asking."

"We'll keep an eye on her, but she doesn't smell sick," Janie told Lance.

"I keep forgetting about that," Lance sighed and shook his head. "You'd know, wouldn't you? Speaking of scent," he turned back to Ari,

"Did you smell anything off about the one who broke into your house?"

"Do you remember what I told you—that he smelled awful?" Ari replied. "He smelled—rancid. Like rotted meat," she shrugged.

"I recall your comment that he smelled as if he'd rolled in roadkill," Lance agreed.

"Yeah. Except *he* may be the roadkill. How is that even possible?"

"We don't know. I worry that whatever the FBI and the state bureau find, they won't give us the full picture."

"What about the officers who were doing surveillance?" Ari thought to ask.

"Oh. That." Lance shifted uncomfortably.

"They're dead, aren't they?"

"We pulled the car with both bodies still inside it from the Trinity River a few hours ago," Lance looked down at his hands, which were dangling between his knees. "No word on how they got there, yet, or whether they died by drowning or in another way."

"All of this is far from normal," Ari rose and paced away from the window. "Is Nico talking to Burke?"

"Yes. Mona gave his phone back," Lance tossed over his shoulder. "They're going over the insurance policies and everything that needs to happen from now on."

"Keep Nico's name out of the press," Ari turned back to study Lance. "I think you and I know how much danger he's in, and we can't even describe who or what his enemies are at this point."

"My question is why he has enemies in the first place," Janie slapped a hand on the arm of her chair. "This makes no sense at all. No previous threats—no ransom notes, no accusations, just death and destruction."

"Now that you put it that way," Ari nodded. "Why wouldn't somebody make demands if they had problems with Nico's parents—or with him?"

"He says they weren't acting different, like they were hiding something," Lance rose and stretched. "They were going about their business as they normally did. And, to find out we've got zombie-like symptoms in two attackers, now? The homeowner in the Austin case—his last name is Garcia," he added. "Nico says he has no idea who the man is, and Garcia is a common name."

"Do me a favor, if you can," Ari rubbed the shell outline in her palm, which refused to smooth out.

"What's that?" Lance lifted an eyebrow.

"See if anyone in Spain has been murdered under unusual circumstances."

"I'll ask, but we may not get results."

"Ask some of those FBI agents. I'll bet they can get answers. Besides, they'll come looking for Nico before long, don't you think? To ask him questions?"

"I figure they will. Val will ask Burke to be with Nico if that happens."

"I want to be there, too, if it's possible."

"What about Mac?" Janie rose from her chair.

"I think the less the FBI knows about Mac, the better, don't you?" Lance turned a concerned gaze on his aunt.

"Probably. Still, you ought to talk to Mac about this. That bird knows more than he lets on; I'd bet money on it. I also think that had Mac met any other detective, he may not have fared so well," Janie observed.

"Do you think there are any of our kind in the FBI?" Ari asked.

"It's possible," Lance appeared thoughtful. "But finding that out? It would take one to know one."

"Another reason to let me go with Nico if they question him."

"I'll see what I can do. Now, if you start feeling bad, let Aunt Janie know. She'll get a doctor here right away."

"I'm fine," Ari reassured him.

"Come on, then. Let's see if Burke is done with Nico yet."

"I had no idea how complicated all this is," Nico's voice betrayed sadness and a bit of confusion. He and Ari sat at the kitchen island again, having a dish of cobbler and ice cream. Mac had some of each on a small saucer and was enjoying his dessert.

"What did Burke tell you?" Ari asked.

"He had me sign a power of attorney, and he says he can take care of everything from here, but he has to talk to me before he accepts any settlements or makes major decisions on my behalf."

"That's good, I guess," Ari told him.

"Ari, since this has gotten so complicated," Lance and Mona walked into the kitchen after having a private conversation with Burke, Val and Janie.

"What Lance is trying to say is that we can list you as missing under suspicious circumstances, and pack and bag up the contents of your gallery as evidence." Mona placed air quotes around the word *evidence*. "Janie says there's plenty of room in the basement to set up a studio, if you want to finish your painting."

"It won't have natural light, but it's a workspace," Nico sent Ari a hopeful glance.

"Fine," Ari agreed. "Say I'm missing, then. Nico and I can paint together. The lease is paid through the end of next month, anyway."

"Stay. Here," Mac croaked, sounding as wise as any raven might who had blackberry cobbler clinging to his beak.

Claudio studied the email he'd received from First Scholar. Once, when he was human, his fingers would have shaken while opening such a message.

Now, he was no longer subject to those rushes of adrenaline, but he did view the email with trepidation. Seventh seldom received a message from First, generally because Seventh—Claudio's designation —lived in the inhospitable wilds of North America.

That hadn't been *his* description of his homeland; Third had stuck that clever insult on his back, like a *kick me* sign he couldn't reach to remove.

Working up his courage, Claudio tapped the message to open it on his laptop. Only three words appeared. Three words that held an encyclopedia of hidden information, and none of it good.

First had sent a terrible warning—a warning to him specifically, because it would inevitably spread terror across his homeland.

That knowledge sent a numbing fear through Seventh.

Find the Raven, the message read.

CHAPTER FOUR

"*D*o you think Val is right—that we could be followed if we come this way often?" Mona asked.

"We come this way a couple of times a month, at least—it's nothing new," Lance replied. They'd gotten on the road late, and both had an early morning ahead of them.

"But this new faction may not know that," Mona began. Lance, paying attention to his driving, forced down growing irritation.

"Have you gotten much sleep since this mess started?" He changed the subject.

"Not really. I wish we could have gotten the security images from that electronics store. I get the idea that our original perps came through the back door of the restaurant, since we didn't find anything on Ari's security recordings."

"I think we can consider those recordings lost forever," Lance replied. "Those were stolen, plus the employees and Norm were killed over it."

"Where's Norm's body?" Mona asked.

"Still in the morgue," Lance began. "Shit," he muttered angrily and increased his speed.

"What?" Mona demanded, before turning to look behind them. She didn't see anyone close enough to look like a tail.

"No. We know where Norm is. What about those two store employees? Where are they? Are they going to crawl out of their morgue drawers and cause a riot?"

"Oh, for the love of," Mona shuddered. "Please, don't let that happen," she whispered.

"Call Belwether," Lance directed. "See if he knows what's going on. How long does it take for whatever this is to take hold?"

"That one from Corpus—they said he'd died three days earlier," Mona hauled out her cell phone and tapped Belwether's number.

"How long did it take him to get from there to here?"

"Captain," Mona said when Belwether answered. He didn't give her time to speak—Lance could hear the captain's voice from where he sat.

"All hell is breaking loose at the morgue," Belwether snapped at Mona. "We've put up barriers and every tactics team we could find is already there, surrounding the building. Get ahold of Lance and come to the station as quick as you can—the FBI is here and they have plenty of questions. I don't have answers."

"On our way," Mona said before ending the call.

"Fuck." Lance's hands gripped the steering wheel tightly while his gut churned. "We don't know what's happening, either," he reminded Mona.

"Yeah. I doubt that sleep is gonna be in the forecast for a long time to come."

Lance and Mona were forced to show their badges before entering the station. Outside, regular uniforms guarded the perimeter, some armed with rifles.

"Is Belwether expecting a coup?" Mona hissed as she and Lance walked through the door.

"The same situation is happening in Austin," Officer Gray met them at the elevator. "The Governor is considering calling out the National Guard."

"How did this get so out of hand—and this fast?" Mona asked him.

"Whatever disease these perps are carrying—it's really contagious," Gray replied. "I was raked over the coals by an infectious diseases doctor before I was hauled in here to talk to the FBI."

"You didn't touch the body, did you?" Lance asked.

"Nope. Thank goodness. I heard a rumor that those two officers, plus Norm and the electronics store employees, are involved in this mess, now. I'm not an alarmist, and I'll be the first guy to say zombies don't exist—but this? Who the hell understands any part of it?"

"We don't," Mona agreed as she and Lance boarded the elevator. "Take care, all right? Make sure you're not followed. Call us if you have problems."

The elevator doors dinged shut, blocking their view of Officer Gray.

"You like him," Lance accused.

"And what if I do?" Mona barked.

"No reason. I know nothing. How's the weather?" Lance attempted to lighten the mood.

"Get in here," Belwether bellowed as they stepped off the elevator and onto the third floor.

Exchanging a quick glance, Lance and Mona hurried into the Captain's office. A man and a woman were already there, having coffee and talking with Belwether.

"Lance, Mona, these are Special Agents Del Reeves and Laronda Abrams of the FBI," Belwether introduced his guests.

Del Reeves was pale and thin, with brown-hair-going-gray, and in his early fifties, in Lance's estimation. Laronda Abrams was as dark as Reeves was pale, appeared to be in her early thirties, and looked as if she worked out in the gym twice a day.

Lance found that he and Mona were under a great deal of scrutiny from both agents before Reeves held out a hand to shake.

"I hear you work in forensics," Laronda Abrams shook with Mona.

"I do—mostly computer work, file recovery, cell phone messages, security camera recordings, that sort of thing."

"You've gone through the boy's phone, then?" Reeves asked.

"Yes. I have a copy of everything, if you'd like to take a look."

"We'd appreciate that," Abrams nodded. "We'd also like a look at the security recordings from Leone's gallery."

"Not a problem," Mona told her. "All of that is in my lab."

"We'd like to ask questions, first, since you're the ones who found a place for the boy and the woman after her home was compromised," Reeves began.

"I'll bring in more chairs," Belwether offered, before going to the door and motioning for an officer outside to do it for him.

"What's your connection to the Jordan Ranch?" Abrams began her questioning while Lance and Mona waited for extra chairs.

"We're related to the family," Mona replied. "I'm sure you've discovered that already—it's no secret."

"Yes—we ah, checked when Captain Belwether told us where the boy was."

Inwardly fuming, Lance kept a retort behind his teeth. So far, FBI Special Agents Abrams and Reeves weren't making friends or playing nice.

"Do you honestly believe the boy doesn't know anything about why his parents were killed?" Reeves took up the questioning. "Or why those killers appear to be hunting him and the Leone woman, too?"

"He doesn't know anything," Lance said as a uniform carried two chairs into Belwether's office. Lance thanked the officer and took the chair, positioning it so he could stare directly at his interrogators.

Taking her cue from him, Mona did the same. Belwether took his seat behind the desk, leaned his elbows on it and waited for the next question.

"You know we can make your life unpleasant if we find you're withholding evidence or information?" Abrams' eyes bored into Lance's.

"I have no doubt you could do almost anything you wanted," Lance agreed. "It won't change the fact that the boy and the woman have no idea why the Garcias died or why their house was bombed or why Ari's house was broken into by a fucking zombie. Now, can you explain any of this zombie shit to me? Because I sure as hell would like to understand how that's even possible."

"Calm down," Belwether's voice was low and threatening.

"Right," Mona took up Lance's argument. "We haven't found a shred of evidence in any of the recordings and information we've gotten so far, and yet the ME's office is having a riot involving dead people even as we speak. And, the last I heard, Austin PD is experiencing the same thing. I don't see you down there, belittling them over any of this."

"Corpus is ah, dealing with the same situation," Reeves admitted.

"Fucking hell." Lance rose from his seat and stalked out of Belwether's office.

Mona watched as Belwether cursed under his breath and strode out of his office to go after Lance. "You shouldn't piss Lance off," Mona pointed her words at Reeves. "He's the best detective on the force. Belwether knows it, too."

"We heard that," Reeves turned away from Mona's accusation. "We're under fire because people in DC are demanding answers, and we don't even have the right questions, yet."

"Anything else happening other than Corpus' morgue being overrun by zombies?" Mona asked with false sweetness.

"Two tankers dead in the water outside the ship channel. And I mean dead—as in there's nobody alive onboard either one," Abrams admitted. "And a cruise ship that left Houston two days ago was found drifting about five miles off the coast. Everybody on board died of some unusual disease. We're keeping it out of the news for now, and higher ups are working on a more plausible excuse for families of the deceased and for public consumption."

"Where are the tankers from?"

"One is registered in the UK—the other in Spain."

"Ah. You should have led with that one," Mona pointed out. "The kid's parents went on a trip to Spain last year—in September. They may have upset somebody. There's nothing on the kid's phone to indicate that and he says they only did touristy things, but somebody, somewhere, got their britches in a bunch. Whatever this is, they're hunting people named Garcia, now."

"We can't say for sure it was these Garcias, and we don't know that it originated in Spain," Abrams said. "Maybe they were hunting the guy in Austin all along."

"Sure is a strange way of going about it, then," Mona sniffed. "Have you checked to see if anything is happening in Spain?"

"We've got feelers out," Reeves acknowledged as Lance and Belwether walked back in.

"That means you've heard a rumor or something, and it just doesn't make sense," Mona surmised.

"How much do you know about Spain?" Reeves asked. "About their folk tales and such?"

"Not much. Enlighten me."

"There are tales there about ghosts that wander crossroads at night," Abrams shrugged. "There've been more sightings than usual lately and not just at crossroads, but that's all they can tell us for now."

"Ghosts? That doesn't fit with zombies here," Belwether returned and sat heavily on his chair with a sigh.

Lance, his face set and expressionless, took his chair again and refused to take the bait.

"One has to believe in ghosts to begin with," Reeves observed. "I doubt one has anything to do with the other."

"Maybe we should find an expert," Mona suggested.

"A ghost hunter? You're joking," Reeves frowned.

"No—somebody who knows about Spanish myths and legends. We've already seen the impossible in the last two days. What can it hurt?"

"I can get someone to do research. Maybe a professor or two here in the States can help us out," Abrams told Reeves.

"You get on that, then—after we talk to the boy."

"The boy is in bed," Lance growled. "You can talk tomorrow. He's been through enough already, without having to look at your sour faces tonight."

"Touché, Detective," Reeves huffed. "Tomorrow morning, we'll meet here at oh-seven hundred, and we'll go see Nicolas Garcia and Arianne Leone."

"Fine." Lance didn't bother to get up or see the Agents out of the Captain's office.

"Since you're both related to the Jordan family, I'm putting both of you on this case until further notice," Belwether waved them out of his office. "Be here at six-forty-five in the morning for a brief meeting before you leave."

"Right." Lance was first out the door, leaving Mona frowning at Belwether. "They could have been polite, and they weren't," she said before following Lance.

"Duly noted," Belwether said to her retreating back.

Val called while Lance drove Mona home. "Val?" Lance put the call on speaker.

"The kid insists that you and Mona have guards, or come back here tonight," he said.

"We're bringing two FBI agents tomorrow morning to question Ari and Nico," Mona said. "I wouldn't turn down a guard, though."

"Stay in one place or the other, then, and I'll arrange it," Val agreed.

"Lance can stay at my place; it's neater than his," Mona said.

"Good. I'll send two your way."

"Tell them not to confront an attacker," Lance said before Val could end the call. "Just tell them to get us up and we'll get the hell out of there, okay?"

"Any suggestions on how to identify the one you're talking about?"

"They'll smell like rotted meat. Ari described it as roadkill."

"I'll give them specific instructions. If you have to leave, make sure you have a secure place to go and take the guards with you."

"We'll do that," Mona agreed. "Good-night, Val."

Ari stood under the warm water of her en-suite shower, staring at the scallop shell imprint on her left palm. More and more, she'd become convinced that had Nico not placed the shell in her hand, she could be worse than dead at the moment.

The evidence on her palm didn't look as if it were going to fade, either. The ridges and outline of the shell were sharp and perfect, as if it had branded itself on her palm.

Nico hadn't mentioned it again and neither had she, as if it were a shared secret they'd take to their graves. Shuddering at the thought, Ari turned off the spray and stepped out of the walk-in shower, grabbing a towel from a nearby rack.

While drying herself, she considered everything Nico had been through. She worried that he was keeping his grief to himself, now. Should they consider a therapist—somebody he could tell his troubles to?

Under normal circumstances, it would be a reasonable thing to do. Nothing about any of this could come close to normal or reasonable.

"Ari?" Nico knocked on her door shortly after she'd dressed in her pajamas. Grabbing a thin robe out of her bag, she went to the door to let Nico in.

"What's up?" she asked as Nico, Mac clinging to his right shoulder, walked in.

"Remember when I told you earlier that I had a dream about you?"

"Yeah."

"I didn't tell you the whole dream," he said.

"You want to sit down? There are chairs over by the window," Ari invited.

"Sure." Nico and Mac followed her across the bedroom until they reached the chairs in question. Nico took one and made himself comfortable; Mac hopped onto the high back and did the same.

"What else happened in your dream, Nico?" Ari settled onto the other chair to listen.

"I saw Mama and Papa first," he said. "We were walking down this long road, until we got to a rocky cliff by the ocean. We didn't say anything while we walked, but when we reached the ocean, they told me things."

"What things?"

"They said they would always love me, and a part of them would always be with me. Then, they said that Mac would help guide me, and that you and Mac would guard me. But first, I had to help you. Mama told me that I needed to help you, Ari. She said you had to hold the shell."

"Nico," Ari clenched her hands for a moment. "I uh, need to show you something." Holding out her left hand, she opened her fist to show him her palm. "I don't think it's going away," she whispered. "You and your mama really did save me. I was sick, Nico. I know that, now."

"You and I—same," Mac croaked at Ari while eyeing her palm. "We stand. At. The end."

"At least one of us knows what's going on," Ari pulled her hand back and rested it on a knee.

"Ex. Plain. Late. Er."

"Okay. Nico, do you need anything? I think I can sleep on the floor if you want to stay in the same room tonight."

"Mac and I will be okay, I think."

"All right, but if that changes, let me know."

"I will."

Waffles and news waited for Nico and Ari when they woke the following morning. Janie's regular cook, Mary Kate, was back after her regular days off. Janie was having a cup of coffee at the island while Mary Kate put waffle batter together and turned sausages and bacon in a big iron skillet.

"Lance and Mona have to bring out two FBI agents to talk to both of you," Janie said as Nico and Ari sat at the island. Mac hopped onto the back of an empty barstool next to Nico.

"You didn't like that, did you?" Nico asked Janie.

"No, hon, and neither do Lance and Mona." Janie wore an uncharacteristic frown as she spoke. "They won't learn anything they haven't already read in the reports, so this is just a useless trip—except somebody could be watching them by now."

"You think they could be followed?" Ari asked as Mary Kate set a cup of coffee in front of her and a glass of juice in front of Nico. Mac, who got a small glass of water and a napkin, croaked a thank you.

"We don't know, do we?" Janie shook her head.

"Maybe we ought to go somewhere else, then. I don't want you to be in danger," Nico said.

"We'll see about that," Janie said. "I'm just not in any mood to play nice with rude FBI agents. Mona and I talked about it this morning. At least we have two guards who will be following Lance and Mona today, in case somebody does try to tail them."

"Morning," Val walked in to join them. Ari knew he'd already been working; he smelled like he'd gotten extremely close to cow patties and a newborn calf.

"They all right? Mom and baby?" Ari turned toward him.

"They are. Just needed a little help, that's all. They'll be kept in the barn for a day or two, to make sure everything stays that way before joining the rest of the herd." He grinned at her; it was the first time she'd ever said anything nice—or spoken voluntarily—to him.

Mary Kate filled plates and set them on the island in front of everybody; Ari found her appetite over eggs, bacon, sausage and a waffle.

"When are those agents supposed to be here?" Val asked his mother. Ari watched as he filled every square on his waffle with syrup before cutting into it.

"I figure around nine," Janie replied. "Will Burke be here before then?"

"Should be here anytime," Val said, stuffing a chunk of syrupy waffle in his mouth and chewing in a determined fashion.

"Good," Ari felt her shoulders sag. She hadn't known how tense she'd become after hearing the agents were coming. At least Burke could back them off Nico if it became necessary.

"F. B. I." Mac croaked. "Can't live. With. Them. Can't lure. More. Than. One with. A. Doe-nut."

Val turned his head. Ari watched as his shoulders began to shake. He was laughing at Mac's joke.

"High feathers," Nico held up a hand. Mac brushed it with a wing.

"Great. We have the police and the FBI on the way, plus a raven doing stand-up." Ari broke a piece of bacon in half and bit into it. "Makes perfect sense," she added.

Val guffawed.

"This place is big," Agent Abrams said, peering out her backseat window as Lance drove over the cattle guard and onto Jordan Ranch property.

"Our Aunt Janie is one of the best people I know, and if you're not polite, I'll haul you both out of here myself," Mona told Abrams and Reeves.

"Is that a threat?" Reeves asked.

"It sure is. Aunt Janie's special. If you feel the need to be rude, remember you're on private property and by invitation only. Violate that and you'll be asked to leave."

"As long as we're allowed to speak with the boy and the woman. We're only doing our job," Abrams attempted to soothe Mona's ruffled feathers.

"And we're doing ours. This is family land we're driving across, don't forget that."

"We'll try to remember our manners," Reeves said. "Although the dead jumping off three ships in Gulf Coast waters overnight may overwhelm our sensibilities during questioning."

"You think Ari and Nico have anything to do with that? Please," Mona huffed as Lance pulled into the driveway and stopped the car.

"They don't even know about it, yet. Nobody does, present company excepted."

Lance stepped out of the car as the front door opened. He recognized Francine, Janie's housekeeper. She and Mary Kate, the cook, were sisters and had worked for the family for nearly three decades.

"They're waiting in the kitchen, if you'd like coffee or breakfast," Francine said as the agents followed Lance toward the door. Mona, still in a bad mood, followed behind.

"Coffee sounds good," Agent Abrams said as Francine stepped aside to allow them to enter.

"I'll take them to the kitchen, Francine," Lance told her.

The dishes had been cleared away and Ari was drinking another cup of coffee when Lance led the agents into the kitchen. One was human—the other—*wasn't*. Ari's eyes narrowed at the female agent, who was probably a coyote in her other form—*had to be coyote*, Ari decided. Ari's nose was good enough to tell that much.

The coyote shifter had stopped dead in her tracks the moment she'd stepped into the kitchen—she'd finally understood that she wasn't the only shifter on the premises, and the shifters around her were all larger predators.

"Have a seat," Val slid off his barstool, eyeing Agent Abrams with a frown. "Time to get down to business, eh?"

"You're ah, Ari Leone? Laronda Abrams," Agent Abrams held out a hand to shake with Ari. "It's okay—Agent Reeves knows what I am."

CHAPTER FIVE

"Who knew that meeting bigger predators would bring out their best manners?" Mona whispered to Lance as they watched Nico and Ari talking to Abrams and Reeves in the family room, while Burke listened in.

"I had no idea the FBI had manners," Lance shrugged, lifting his coffee cup for another sip. "All of them I've met have been abrupt at best, and downright nasty at their worst."

"Janie says Abrams is a coyote. Maybe our esteemed agent knows a mountain lion could have her for breakfast."

"Except Ari wouldn't."

"Abrams doesn't know that."

"Ari does."

"You always did have a knack for reading people." Mona fist-bumped Lance.

"Where do you suppose those dead people went after they jumped off those tankers and the cruise ship?" Lance asked.

"I don't know, but I sure as hell wouldn't go fishing down there right now. I wouldn't board one of those ship without protective gear, either—not for ten million dollars. You think they'll just walk ashore come nightfall, and wander down the street looking for more victims?"

"No idea, although if somebody played *Thriller*, maybe they'd all start dancing."

"Well, nothing else appears to be working," Mona drawled.

Lance's phone vibrated in his pocket; pulling it out, he saw the call was from Belwether. "I'll take this outside," he said and walked away.

Mona heard his voice fade as he spoke with their Captain and walked toward the back door.

"We're just as confused as anyone else about all this," Ari told Reeves. "Until one of them kicked down my back door, I'd never thought it possible."

"So far, the only way to stop them is by decapitation," Laronda Abrams admitted. "The one you ah, attacked, finally lost his head at the ME's office. He's out of commission, but there are three others there now, causing problems."

"All three were members of Dallas PD," Reeves explained. "They apparently came in contact with the first one, or another we haven't found, yet. The store clerks—their case has been handled already."

"Have you looked into passenger manifests—for anyone traveling here from Spain?" Burke asked. "Mona thinks all this is connected, somehow."

"We're going through those, now," Reeves said. "So far, our team hasn't gotten back to us with the information."

"I'd look at those who came and didn't go back," Nico observed. "I mean, that would make sense, that somebody who can still think is running this show."

Reeves and Abrams exchanged a look before turning back to Nico and Ari. "We've come to the same conclusion," Abrams admitted. "None of these zombies can speak or think. That means they're following orders. Somebody else really is behind this."

Seeing movement from the corner of her eye, Ari turned to watch as Mac rubbed his beak on the back of Nico's chair, as if he were doing whatever he could to keep it shut. Then, he lifted a leg and scratched behind his ear before ruffling his feathers. He knew something; she was sure of it.

How did one go about bribing a bird to talk?

"What we've seen, too, so far, is that whatever affects these—zombies," Reeves said the word as if he found it outside the realm of anyone's reality, "is highly contagious. How did you avoid being affected by it," he asked Ari. "Can we assume that others like you can also avoid it?"

He was asking her if shifters were immune. "Agent Reeves, I consider myself extremely lucky in this regard. Do not assume others like me will be unaffected," her voice and her eyes were hard as she stared at him.

"All right," Reeves made a note on a small pad. "Do you have further questions, Laronda?" He turned toward Agent Abrams.

"Not now. I would like to give you our direct cell phone numbers, in case there's anything else you need to tell us."

"Okay." Ari accepted cards from both agents. Burke rose to see them to the door. Ari saw Lance sidle into the room after Burke and the agents left, rejoining Mona before approaching her and Nico.

"We have to take them back, or we'd stay for lunch," Mona said. "Thanks for doing this—we really couldn't wiggle out of it."

"Not a problem," Nico shrugged. "I don't think they know the proper questions to ask about any of this, yet."

"Neither do we," Mona confessed. "Look, take care of yourselves. If anything happens, we'll let you know."

"Thank you," Ari said.

After they left, Nico released a pent-up breath. "Do you think they'll have to decapitate those dead officers?" he asked.

"Yes," Mac croaked.

Claudio read through several messages from trusted sources. As of now, there were incidents confirmed in Corpus Christi, Austin and

Dallas. More could crop up at any moment. So far, there was little information from mainstream media, but that wouldn't last long.

Once word got out, along with images, the madness would engulf the entire country. There wasn't any way for local law enforcement or the FBI to keep a lid on this; it was designed that way.

In the past, strange events such as these tended to be regional, long before modern technology came along. Now, with live feeds constantly reaching viral status, it couldn't be contained within a region.

And, since all events in the past had occurred on foreign soil, Claudio had no idea whether the power which held the enemy partially in check would unravel completely.

The last reported sighting of the raven had been in France—until things began to happen in Texas. Somewhere, in the second largest state of the US, a black bird was likely searching for something important, just as Claudio did.

As long as the raven remained a raven, Claudio wouldn't panic.

No, panic was reserved for the unusual circumstances which allowed the raven to become a man.

"Let's see," Claudio seldom spoke to himself, but it seemed like a good idea on this night. "The first incident was reported in Dallas. Shall we study those events while we arrange a flight to DFW?"

"Yes. That is a fine idea," he replied.

"Apparently the FBI is going along with the idea that you're missing under suspicious circumstances," Janie told Ari at dinner. "They're clearing out the gallery and packing it up as evidence. You should have all your canvases and art supplies delivered here in the next two days."

"Thank goodness," Ari said. "I need to ship that commission in the next three weeks or I won't get the rest of the money."

"I hope you're officially found by then," Val said.

"Officially found would be awesome," Nico sighed. "I'm worried that won't be the case."

Ari turned a worried look in Nico's direction. "Just a feeling," he said. "I didn't mean to upset you."

"If you have concerns about your business or expenses, Burke can handle it for you," Val told Ari. "He can hold off the people on the commission, telling them the painting is in the FBI's possession."

"That's not a good thing," Ari replied. "It could damage my reputation as an artist, too, if that information gets around."

"I'm sure it'll work out," Janie said sympathetically. "Let's not worry about that until we have to, all right?"

"All right." Ari went back to her dinner. It was good advice; Ari didn't know whether her mind would accept it, however, and allow her to sleep at night rather than obsessing about it.

"I'm just looking forward to painting with Ari," Nico said. "I learned more from her than from my college art professor. She gave me good advice on the composition for my final project."

"Nico started working in my studio on weekends when he was sixteen," Ari said. "Since the gallery was across the street from Blue Taco, he'd come in all the time and we'd talk about the work on the walls. When he mentioned that he'd gotten paint on his bedroom carpet at home and was in trouble with his mother, I told him he was welcome to work in my studio. There's plenty of space, and the concrete floors in the back are perfect for an artist."

"The basement has concrete floors," Janie said brightly. "We'll just roll up the area rugs and the space is yours."

"Normally it's only used as a tornado shelter," Val said, grabbing another roll from the basket. "We made it comfortable; it has a radio and television down there, along with a fridge, a bathroom, a sofa and some extra chairs."

"That's in case we ever got stuck down there," Janie explained. "If the house collapses above us, the basement is reinforced to hold up under that until somebody can dig us out."

"We only had one of those garage shelters," Nico said. "It was tiny, but we could all fit in there if we needed it."

"Those save lives," Val agreed. "And they're better suited for people in cities."

"I had nothing," Ari wrinkled her nose at Nico. "Except a bathroom in the middle of the house. It was built in the seventies, and only has a carport instead of a garage."

"Haven't housing costs just skyrocketed?" Janie complained. "I remember when a three-bedroom house in Dallas was actually affordable."

"Burke couldn't believe what Mona paid for her house," Val nodded. "It's nice, but nothing fancy."

"Zom-bees run down. Prop-er-tee price-es," Mac predicted.

"Master Scholar," the co-pilot dipped his head respectfully to Claudio as he stepped aboard the private jet. "You honor us," the co-pilot added.

"Are my guards aboard already?" Claudio asked.

"Of course."

"Thank you for your service on such short notice," Claudio told him. "The Scholarium are grateful."

"Honor and duty," the co-pilot dipped his head again. Claudio mumbled a reply and made his way toward the back of the jet, where two guards waited. He recognized them from last time; one was originally from Spain, the other from France.

Wise of the First to send those two, Claudio thought as they rose to greet him. The flight from Tulsa to Dallas wouldn't be a long one; he hoped to pull *Insight* from at least one of his guards on the way.

Once Claudio was settled, Renault exchanged a glance with Alejandro. *Which would be chosen to deliver insight first?* The physical pain involved concerned neither. The picking through of old memories, however, was another story.

"How old are you, Alejandro?" Claudio asked as the jet taxied along the runway.

"Three centuries, Master Scholar," Alejandro replied.

"And you, Renault?"

"Nine centuries, Master Scholar."

"This is a short flight," Claudio observed. "I will draw from Alejandro during that time, as he is the younger."

"It will be so," Alejandro dipped his head to Claudio, before opening his shirt for Claudio's invasion.

"I apologize for the discomfort—and the mental anguish," Claudio murmured as sharp claws formed on his right hand. Alejandro's body went rigid as Claudio's talons pierced his chest.

The other Scholars had learned to separate themselves from the fear and turmoil of the times they investigated through *insight*. Claudio found himself struggling with many of Alejandro's memories as they walked across the tarmac to a waiting vehicle.

Externally, Alejandro appeared fine. Claudio could only imagine what bringing these memories back and making them fresh again had done to his guard. A second apology could make them both appear weak, so he held it back.

How did one deal with finding many times great-grandchildren among the ruins of the attack on Guernica?

Alejandro had done just that, and he'd wept over their broken bodies. And, while he and Alejandro were connected, Claudio had felt those tears as if they were his own.

Had the *et Inpaenitens*—the Unrepentant, gained new members during that volatile time—prior to and during the course of World War II? Had even more been added during wars and terroristic attacks since then?

That had yet to be determined.

How will they strike this time? Who will the targets be? Claudio couldn't venture a guess as yet. Soon enough, new demagogues would rise, victims would be chosen, and the cycle would begin again.

Could the world, already in chaos and torment, defeat the rise of evil, or would its population accept and bow before it?

Claudio had never been so terrified that it would come down to the latter.

~

"Tai Chi?" Ari asked Nico after breakfast. "We haven't gotten any exercise lately."

"I could go for that," Nico agreed. "I feel—restless, I guess. Unmoored."

"There's the proper word—unmoored," Ari agreed. "Mac, you want to do Tai Chi?"

"Watch," Mac said.

"He could probably do *snake creeps low* pretty well," Nico observed.

"Snake. Gets. Pecked," Mac grumped.

"Can you show me? I've always wanted to learn," Janie said. "We can go to the backyard—past the pool and under the shade trees."

"Dress in loose clothing," Ari said. "We'll meet in the backyard in fifteen."

~

"What are they doing?" Lance frowned when he and Mona found Ari, Janie and Nico in the backyard, doing what looked to be a slow dance. The raven, perched on a bench, watched from a nearby gazebo.

"Looks like Tai Chi," Mona said. "Wish I'd gotten here sooner, to watch from the beginning."

"No, I meant, what are they doing out here in broad daylight, with no guards?" Lance turned toward Mona. Both wore sunglasses, which reflected the morning light bearing down on the Jordan Ranch.

"We're here, now," Mona said. "Besides, they're in the shade."

"And that makes it all better?"

"I think it's calming. We could all use some calming, you know. Getting some sunlight isn't a bad idea, either."

"I suspect they haven't seen the news, then."

"Aunt Janie's never been a big TV fan."

"That probably ought to change—at least until this is over."

"How long will that take? Do you know?"

"No idea."

"You think they ought to hide in the basement for who knows how long, then?"

"If it will save their lives. The truck with Ari's painting and supplies will arrive tonight. They can paint in the basement and ride this out."

"Laronda says the family in Rockport had Spanish grandparents," Mona said. "Thank goodness the kids were visiting family in New Mexico, or it could have been a lot worse."

"What's worse is willfully decapitating two dead officers and one dead detective to keep them from terrorizing the morgue."

"If I get exposed to one of those things and it kills me, don't hesitated to do what needs to be done," Mona said. "I mean it."

"Burn-ing works. Too," Mac turned his head to croak at them.

"Maybe we need flamethrowers instead of guns?" Mona lifted an eyebrow at Lance.

"Yes," Mac said before turning back to watch the Tai Chi lesson.

"If I didn't already know she was a big cat, I'd suspect it after watching her do this," Mona followed Ari's movements as Nico and Janie worked to copy her.

"Where can we get flamethrowers? That we won't have to explain to anybody?" Lance asked.

"Let me talk to Laronda."

"You best buds, now?"

"Better buds, at least. Once she found out we're not as human as she originally thought, she's come around."

"Reeves still has a stick up his ass."

"I think Reeves was born with a stick up his ass."

"Belwether says we have to work with them, so we're working with them," Lance grimaced. "I'm surprised they didn't force us to travel to Rockport with them."

"Way out of our jurisdiction," Mona pointed out. "We'll get more information when they have it in hand."

"Here's my question," Lance began. "Why go after others, if Nico and his parents were the real target? Killing others, either with the same name or with Spanish ancestry doesn't really make sense. Does it?"

"They're not reporting any of that in the news," Mona sighed. "For now, it looks like random killings. What I really want to know is this— why was Blue Taco bombed, when everybody else is attacked by zombies? Forensics is still working on who could have made the bomb, you know. If they can pinpoint a source, I'll be interested to know whether he or she is a zombie, and or someone who died in the blast."

"It's a cinch that nobody who got blown up in that restaurant will turn into a zombie," Lance appeared thoughtful. "You think that was by design?"

"Who the hell knows at this point?" Mona shook her head. "Look, they're done." She indicated Ari and the others.

"I need a towel—that was more exhausting than I thought it would be," Janie walked up the steps to join Lance and Mona on the deck.

"Water and a towel," Ari said, as she and Nico followed Janie.

"I have water and lemonade in the kitchen," Mary Kate called out the back door.

"I hear the sound of heaven," Mona grinned before turning to follow the others into the house.

Ari watched Nico, who drank lemonade and avoided eye contact with Lance. Mac also appeared to be watching the same two with interest. Finally, Lance rolled his shoulders uncomfortably and spoke.

"There was another attack in Rockport last night," he said. Nico turned toward Lance, then, his face set as he listened carefully to the report.

"You think some of the dead from those ships came ashore in Rockport," Nico said.

"Did we tell him about those ships?" Lance turned his head toward Mona. "Did the FBI agents tell you about them?"

"It doesn't matter how I know," Nico absently turned his glass of lemonade on the granite kitchen island. "If it hasn't made the news, yet, it will soon, I think."

"We're trying to figure out a pattern in their attacks," Mona said. "The current theory is they're attacking people with family roots in Spain."

"But there are a lot of those people in Texas, many by way of Mexico and other countries in South America, right?" Nico asked. "Why choose one family in Rockport, when there could be dozens in the area?"

"We've considered that," Lance acknowledged.

"Agent Abrams and Agent Reeves are in Rockport now, aren't they?"

"Yes, they are," Lance admitted.

"They should practice caution. I think I'll get in the shower; thank you for the lemonade, Mary Kate. It was perfect."

Ari watched Nico shuffle out of the kitchen, heading toward the hallway leading to his bedroom.

"Your stuff from the gallery will be delivered late tonight," Mona said.

"Thank you," Ari replied.

"Ex-cuse me," Mac said and flapped out of the kitchen to follow Nico.

"What just happened?" Lance asked, his gaze locked on Mac's avenue of exit from the kitchen.

"I think Nico may be upset over all this," Ari said, rising from her seat. "Has there been any news on reclaiming his parents' bodies?"

"They're still working on that," Mona said.

"It may not have come as good news that his parents could have been randomly targeted," Janie sighed.

Ari suspected that wasn't true, but she didn't stop to argue. Instead, she followed Nico and Mac, whose bedroom was along the same corridor as hers.

"There's something else, too," Lance said.

"What's that?" Janie sipped her lemonade.

"The man in Austin died. So far, he hasn't come back as a zombie or anything else. They're hoping that whatever the zombie passed along took him down completely."

"Maybe you ought to start doing an analysis of blood, then, to see which ones are affected and which ones die," Mary Kate suggested.

"I think they may already be working on that," Mona hedged.

"Good." Mary Kate turned out a bowl of rising yeast dough to knead, her hands tossing a light dusting of flour onto the dough and then pushing and folding the mass with a surety only years of practice could produce. "There has to be a reason—and a way—for these zombies to target the ones they're hunting, don't you think?"

"We agree," Lance told her. "Look, we ought to get back—we have work to do. Thanks for the lemonade, Mary Kate."

"Any time."

Ari found Nico, head down and sitting on the side of his bed, the scallop shell in his hands. Turning it over and over without seeing it, he stared at the polished wood floor at his feet instead.

"You've had more dreams, haven't you?" Ari sat next to him.

"Yes," Mac croaked from Nico's headboard. "The best. Dream."

"I don't want to be the best," Nico whispered. "I want my life back."

"I know," Ari placed an arm around his shoulders. "You keep thinking they're still here, and you catch glimpses from the corner of your eye."

"And then you have to remind yourself that they're gone."

"Yeah."

"We're not strong enough," Nico said. "Not yet. Maybe not ever, and the foes haven't really made themselves known, yet."

Ari's brow wrinkled at Nico's statement, before her left palm, where the imprint of the shell lay, began to tingle.

"Hold. It. Out," Mac commanded. Blinking, Ari held out her hand, only to find the shell imprint emitting light.

"What the?" Her eyes widened in shock.

"When you can blind somebody with the light from your hand, you'll be ready," Nico breathed. "Until then, we're not strong enough."

"Find. Skaw-lerrs," Mac croaked. "Need them."

"Yeah." Nico agreed.

"Did he say scholars?"

"Not the kind you're used to," Nico added.

"What kind are they, then?"

"Kind. Who. Drink. Blood."

"We need vampires?" Ari squawked. "How do you even know about vampires?"

"I know I'm protected here by werewolves—and one mountain lion," Nico sighed, sounding as if his patience was wearing thin. "We'll need vampires—and a bunch of other things unless a miracle happens."

"Need. Nooz-pay-purrs," Mac said.

"Of course you do," Ari's sarcasm was waking. "Why wouldn't a raven need newspapers?"

"Master Scholar," Renault held a pint of blood in his hand. Claudio looked up from scanning the want ads in the Dallas newspaper.

"Thank you, Renault." Claudio accepted the blood gratefully. "I've found two of our advertisements. I'm still searching for the third."

"Alejandro made sure they were entered properly, and the amounts paid online," Renault assured Claudio while the scholar consumed the offered blood. "Are you sure this method will work?"

"This is how he was found last time. Newspapers still exist. The only other way to make a connection is through the internet. Let us hope it does not come to that."

"What if the third ad was omitted?" Renault was worried, although he kept his voice even.

"The third one holds the last part of the number." Claudio handed the empty blood bag to Renault. "They need all three parts. How long are the ads set to run?"

"For one week."

"Good. Let's hope we find the third part and get a reply to our fishing expedition, then. It isn't often that one fishes for birds, is it?"

"No, Master Scholar."

"Call me Claudio. We're working together and may do so for a while. First names are preferred from now on."

"Of course. If we find the raven, how long will it take to find the Custodian?"

"That I cannot say. Pray that it will be soon, so that the protectors the Custodian chooses may come to full power before the *et Inpaenitens* turn against us."

"For the survival of our race," Renault nodded.

"For the survival of bloody everything," Claudio grumbled and went back to searching the newspaper.

"They really packed this stuff up like they meant it." Ari found yet another screw in the wooden crate bearing her commissioned painting.

A truck arrived at the ranch after midnight; several of Val's werewolves helped unload it. Everything was in the basement shelter in less than an hour, leaving Ari to uncrate everything.

The crate she'd chosen to open now was the unfinished commission. She wanted it done as quickly as possible, because Nico's words had haunted her since he'd said them earlier in the day.

She had no idea what kind of war Nico prepared for, but she'd eventually determined that's exactly what he meant.

How did he know? Mac said dreams. Actually, he'd said *the best ones dream.* The best *what?*

A few days earlier, she'd have thought her sense of reason had deserted her if she'd known about a talking raven and a war that nobody else knew about.

She felt foolish enough asking Janie to buy an online subscription to the Dallas newspaper, just so Nico and Mac could read the personal ads.

Nevertheless, Janie had charged the six-month subscription to her card and offered her laptop to Ari, with the understanding that neither she nor Nico would log into their email or social media accounts.

Ari was too afraid to do either; Nico refused to even think about it. She had no idea what sort of ad they were looking for in the newspaper; she was too afraid to ask.

Too afraid to know more than she already did.

"What is. Wrong?"

Mac had joined her, and she'd been too focused on her thoughts to hear or scent him. Realizing her cheeks were wet, she hastily wiped the moisture away before turning toward the raven, who perched on a tall crate near the stairs.

"I don't really know." Lifting the electric drill, she studied the screw in the crate.

"Life. Change in. Flash."

"Then I've had too many flashes already," she set the drill bit over the screw and pulled the trigger. The screw came out with the screeching sound of metal grinding through stubborn wood.

"Thank goodness that's the last one." Setting the drill and the screw on the box containing her brushes and paints, Ari pulled the top off the painting.

"At least it wasn't damaged," she sighed as she looked it over. "Maybe I can finish it tomorrow, and hand it to Burke to send away."

"Where this?" Mac flapped closer to take a look.

"Palo Duro Canyon. It's my favorite place to go on a full moon."

"Moon no. Long-er hold. You. If you. Are. Strong e-nuff."

"What's that supposed to mean?"

"Eh," Mac made a gesture she could only assume was a raven shrug.

"Right." Ari took a seat on the basement floor and began unloading the box of brushes, paints, gesso and medium. "Crap. They didn't load my paint platter. Probably thought it was trash, because I left it covered in paint. Damn. My father gave that to me."

Ari found tears dripping down her cheeks again.

"Doon't," Mac attempted to stop the tears.

Ari sobbed once before leaping to her feet and running for the stairs.

CHAPTER SIX

"I need to understand Ari's story—involving your family," Nico said as he and Mac arrived in the kitchen. It was quite early the following morning, and they found Janie there, having a cup of coffee by herself.

"She. Won't tell. Us," Mac said.

"It's funny that you're asking about that now," Janie said. "We had a bit of a run-in with our new neighbors right after sunset last night. They swear they mistook the heifer for a deer, but it was shot on our property, with other heifers nearby. They claim the animal was on their property—that they weren't trespassing or shooting across the fence. The Sheriff was called out; so far, he hasn't done anything other than tell the fool not to do it again. *Pending investigation*, he says," Janie hmmphed and sipped more coffee.

"This neighbor—he's involved in Ari's problem?" Nico prompted.

"He shot Ari's father on a full moon, when he shouldn't have been anywhere near here. He was told not to start hunting until the following night. He killed Ari's father, in mountain lion form, with a night scope and long-range rifle, from the property his son now owns next to ours. The worst part is human law can't hold him accountable, because his prey wasn't in human form. And he skinned and beheaded Ari's father and kept the trophies. I'm sure the head is still hanging on a wall, somewhere."

"Fuck," Mac cursed.

"We tried to pay restitution, because that idiot wouldn't have been anywhere near here if my husband hadn't hired him to kill a bobcat that was taking down calves. Ari's mother refused the money. I don't think she ever recovered from that tragedy. She died four years ago, far too young for a normal shifter's lifespan. Ari still grieves for both of them."

"That's horrible." Nico sighed, ducking his head.

"Fuck-ing. Awe-full," Mac agreed.

"Ari knows how you feel, Nico," Janie reached out to pat his hand. "Losing parents, and then knowing their killer is still out there, unpunished."

"I won't stop until they're dead," Nico said as Mary Kate bustled into the kitchen to make breakfast.

"Yours or Ari's?"

"Mine for sure. Ari's? Who can say?" Nico slid off his barstool. "I'm going to take a quick shower. How long until breakfast, Mary Kate?"

"Half an hour," she smiled at him.

"I'll be back in half an hour."

Mac hopped onto Nico's shoulder and the two of them left the kitchen.

"When do we ever stop hoping that life will be fair?" Janie asked Mary Kate.

"Probably when we die," Mary Kate replied.

"Yeah. You're probably right." Janie stood and stretched before going to the coffeemaker to pour another cup.

"Look, he's an old man, and he likes to remember his glory days," Denton Franks held out a check to pay for the heifer his father shot. "He really did think it was a deer."

"Right. Maybe it's time to take the gun or the bullets away, Franks," Val hissed. "I'm not taking that money. He killed one of my prize heifers. I hope the Sheriff remembers how to do his job."

"You're still pissed because he disobeyed your father's orders all those years ago," Denton accused.

"Damn right I am. He got a trophy and left the real culprit out there to kill again. Then he refused to return the money. Yes, I'm still pissed."

"You can't say the mountain lion wasn't responsible for any of those kills; my father eliminated a predator," Denton's voice rose.

"Yeah. Actually, I can say that. If I were you, I'd keep your old man far away from Jordan land. Should a future incident occur, I'll go straight to the media with this. I don't think you want the animal rights activists breathing down your neck, either."

"Fuck you, Jordan," Denton shouted.

"Get off my land, Franks," Val snapped.

Denton turned on his heel and strode toward his brand-new, outsized truck, which he'd paid extra to have raised farther off the ground.

Val froze when he heard the soft sound of large paws running on the paved road near the cattle guard on his property.

"No!" Val turned to shout as the mountain lion raced toward the truck, leaping at it the moment Denton Franks shut the door. The mountain lion thumped against the truck's door like a compact, tawny-furred tornado, hissing and growling as she ripped off the side mirror and tore out the windshield wiper on the driver's side.

Terrified, Denton put the truck in reverse and backed up, causing the mountain lion to slide off the truck, but not before putting deep scratches in the paint and metal. Denton's back wheels flung out dust and gravel as the mountain lion gave chase. She only stopped when Denton's vehicle jarred its way across the cattle guard and onto the highway outside the entrance.

"I. Got. This." Mac settled on Val's shoulder for a few seconds. "Go. Back."

"You sure?" Val asked, not taking his eyes off Ari for a moment. She stood at the edge of the cattle guard, her tail twitching angrily.

"Yes." Mac flapped off Val's shoulder, flying toward a very angry mountain lion.

~

Ari was so angry, she wanted to kill something. Wanted to claw its throat. Wanted it to suffer.

Wanted Mitchell Franks and his spawn to suffer.

"Not. Cool." Mac dropped to the ground beside her.

Turning her head, Ari yowled at Mac, making sure he saw her large, impressive teeth.

"Don't. Let. Them. Know. You are. Coming," Mac advised. "Sur-prize. Attack. Best. Come. Back. Now."

Ari yowled at him again, before turning and stalking toward the house, her tail twitching, extreme anger in every movement.

"Time for. Tie. Chee?" Mac settled for walking beside her rather than flying, his legs stretching into quick, wide hops to keep up with an angry mountain lion. Ari growled low in her throat. If Mac thought he could distract her with sarcasm, he was seriously mistaken. Plus, the fact that he was baiting her irritated Ari further.

"Hrrrmmmm," Ari growled and kept walking.

"You. Ig-nor-ing mee?"

"Hrrrmmmm," she repeated, turning her head away.

"You. Are. Curr-sing. Mee?"

"Hrrrmmmm."

"Call-ing mee. Stoo-pid bird?"

By this time, they'd reached the spot where Val had stopped to wait for them, roughly a hundred feet from the driveway.

"May-bee. You are. Just. Bee-ing. Catt-ee."

Ari chose that moment to snarl in indignation at Mac and Val, before loping away. "You can't blame her," Val shook his head. "I'd have done worse if that had been me all those years ago. And, there wouldn't have been a scrap of evidence left behind for anyone to find."

"Missed. Op-or-tune-it-ee."

"I was too young," Val mumbled. "And too stupid. The Grand Master at the time wasn't a strong leader and was afraid of the race being outed. He was challenged fifteen years ago and lost the fight. If that had been a werewolf who died instead of Ari's father," Val shrugged.

"Be-ware. The one. Who en-joys the. Kill too. Much." Mac croaked and lifted off the ground to fly after Ari.

"You just described Mitchell Franks perfectly," Val mused as he watched the raven fly toward the house.

Texas State Senator Darnell Cheatham strolled into his office feeling invigorated. He'd had some ideas come to him while he and his family were away on vacation. Ideas that he intended to put forth in committee for possible legislation.

"Hello, Senator," his chief of staff, Gerri Dean, greeted him with a smile. "I didn't think you'd be back before tomorrow."

"I just wanted to drop by and check in—I had a few thoughts while I was on vacation. I think I'd like to put a plan together on my computer before I'm officially back in the morning."

"I'll see you're not disturbed, then," Gerri said. "How was it? Your trip to Spain."

"Enlightening," Darnell replied, enthusiasm lighting his features. "I learned a lot while I was there."

"I wish I could go, sometime," Gerri said. "So many things to see."

"I have a few historical facts you may want to read about," Darnell said. "I'll be in my office. You don't need to bother letting me know when you're done for the day. I can take care of myself."

"Of course. Good to have you back, sir."

"Good to be back."

Darnell walked away from Gerri's desk with a spring in his step. Gerri hadn't seen him that excited about anything in the six years she'd worked for him.

"Maybe we all need a vacation in Spain," she mumbled and went back to work.

~

"Yes, it was stupid," Ari slumped on the sofa in the sitting room where Janie sat, thumbing through a magazine.

"You could have hurt yourself, too," Janie quietly pointed out. "Flesh, no matter how fit and muscular, is still no match for metal machinery."

"I tore off his rearview mirror after he was rude to Val."

"Val doesn't need you to fight his battles."

"I know."

"Your fight isn't with Mitchell's son, either."

"Yeah." A heavy sigh followed Ari's admission.

"Having said that," Janie set the magazine aside, "we still have an ongoing feud with Mitchell, who shot one of our prize heifers last night. The nerve of Denton, trying to wave a check at us as if that would make it go away. I don't care how old and senile Mitchell is, Denton needs to take the guns away and put a tighter rein on that old man."

"Like that will happen in this state," Ari huffed.

"Well, he wouldn't be the first trophy hunter—or the last—to go down trying to make another kill."

"Let him come near me," Ari growled.

"Ari, I'm not sure you should be the one, if it comes down to that. Overkill will invite other hunters in to deal with a rogue."

"I get that." Ari sounded defeated.

"Timing is everything," Janie went on. "For now, it's too soon to act on this. That stunt you pulled earlier is fresh in Denton's mind. We'll let this go for a while, unless Denton's father gets away from him again. Mountain lions aren't a protected species here. We don't need somebody hunting one—especially on our property, without our permission."

"I'm sorry," Ari apologized. "I wasn't thinking past the heat of the moment."

"I know. It's an understandable reaction to something that could result in deadly consequences—for us."

Darnell found what he looked for after nearly two hours of searching through his computer—the email from Benny Killebrew, pastor of the Eternal Flame Church in Swindall, Texas. It was dated nearly two years earlier, and the senator had ignored it when it first arrived in his inbox.

Dear Senator Cheatham, the message began. *You have spoken urgently in the past regarding the very topic I write to you about today. Your efforts in the past have fallen upon deaf ears, but now, I have the proof you need to go forward.*

I implore you to watch and act upon the video I am enclosing, which shows real witches casting spells in our great state. They are in the act of turning people into zombies, werewolves and other abominations.

I know this may be hard to believe, but two of my own church members have been taken by that crowd and converted against their will. They have refused my offer of help to cast out their demons and will not come near the church because of their possession.

We deserve legislation, not only banning these blasphemous ceremonies, but our government should call upon every righteous soul in our state to eliminate the problem, using whatever means necessary. This includes those who have fallen victim to their spells, and are demon possessed or turn into werewolves or worse at night. Don't let them fool you—they call themselves wiccans, but they are witches, plain and simple, and we know what the Bible has to say about that.

Yours in Faith—the Most Reverend Benny Killebrew.

Underneath was the Church's address and telephone number. Darnell shoved a thumb drive into a slot, copied the email and associated video, shoved the drive in his pocket and rose from his desk.

Sunday was in four days, and it was high time he made an appearance at a church outside Austin. He'd watch the video at home after pouring himself a stout glass of bourbon.

Things were falling into place far easier than he'd ever imagined they would. The recent outbreak of whatever it was that had set several morgues into emergency mode would play into his hands. And, if he could find others like Killebrew—his mission, which had never gained traction in the past, would be assured of success.

"I called, but there was no answer. I left a message," Nico frowned at Mac.

"Night. Fall." Mac said, before fluffing out his feathers. The ruff of red ones beneath his chin stuck straight out for a moment before falling back in place.

"We need to tell Ari. I went looking for her earlier, but she was getting a talking to from Janie," Nico blew out a frustrated sigh.

"Mis-take. She made."

"Yeah. I understand it, though. I don't think I'd have let that guy drive away."

"That one. Not. Gill-tee yet."

"You think that will change?" Nico asked.

"Yes. Soon. Have. Fee-ling." Mac walked carefully across Nico's bed so his talons wouldn't pull threads from the comforter, then hopped onto the footboard and made himself comfortable. "Bad. Biz-ness. May-bee Ari not best option. For you. Too im-pull-sive."

"I'm not taking it back," Nico frowned at Mac. "Ari and I," he didn't finish. "Besides," he continued with a sigh, "the dreams are terrible, but you know that already."

"Yes. Burr-den. Sorr-ee."

"You don't make the choice. You just have to guard the choice."

Mac ruffled his feathers again and croaked softly. Both knew, in their own way, that Nico's mother had already sacrificed herself for that choice.

"You have green paint on your face." Ari jumped and held back a shriek as Nico made that comment. She'd been so engrossed in finishing the commissioned painting that she failed to hear him come down the basement steps.

Mac stood on Nico's right shoulder, wisely holding back any comments. "Janie says dinner is almost ready. Is it done?" Nico studied the painting. "It's beautiful, Ari. It doesn't need another thing."

"I'll text Burke and tell him it can be shipped in the next two days. I don't have crating supplies here—he'll have to make arrangements."

"I'm sure he'll do fine," Nico said. "There are places in Dallas that can crate it for him."

"I know. It's just hard not doing it myself, to make sure."

"Yeah. Go wash the green paint off and come eat. Mary Kate made chicken and dumplings. It smells great. I promised I'd show her how to make tamales tomorrow."

"Were you asking for tamales?" Ari frowned at Mac.

"May-bee."

"Ari, it will be a shame if my parents' recipes are lost," Nico said. "So I'm sharing them with Mary Kate. She's been good to us, just like Janie and Val."

"I know. I'll go wash off the paint." Ari walked into the basement powder room and shut the door. "I'll meet you upstairs," she called out and turned the water on before looking at her face in the mirror. There it was—a smudge of green across one cheek. She recalled wiping a tear away as she painted, and it had left its own kind of evidence behind.

"Your captain has given permission for you to travel with us next time."

Lance accepted the thumb drive from Del Reeves as he digested what the FBI agent told him. "That was quite the mess in Rockport," Reeves continued. Lance sat across the table from the FBI agent in a

Dallas restaurant. They'd met there to have dinner and discuss recent events.

"I heard that tissue samples were being tested," Lance said, holding the thumb drive as if it were as dangerous as the information it contained.

"We're waiting on results," Reeves grimaced. "You think they've been in the ladies' room too long?" Turning his head, Reeves glanced toward the hallway where the restaurant's bathrooms were.

"I'm sure they're fine," Lance waved off Reeves' concern. "Besides, they both have guns and I, for one, wouldn't want to get into a fight with either."

"Here they come," Reeves visibly relaxed as Mona and Laronda walked toward the table.

Lance finally understood that Reeves had seen things in Rockport that made him wary. *Did the thumb drive contain that information, or would he have to ferret it out of the agent?*

Mona leveled a look in Lance's direction as she took the chair beside his, letting him know she had information to share. *Had Laronda given her what Reeves was hinting at?*

"I'm starved," Laronda lifted her menu and opened it. "Want to share an appetizer?"

"Get what you want, Laronda," Reeves said. "We'll help you eat it."

"If you like street tacos, their appetizer here is awesome," Mona said.

"I'm sold," Laronda said. "I want a steak, too. Are they any good?"

"Decent. Not the best you can get in Dallas, but good enough for the money," Lance told her.

"Decent is fine. I need red meat."

"I'm with you," Del set his menu down and closed it. "And another glass of Scotch. A double, at least."

"Are we ready to order?" Their server arrived as if she'd been called.

"Sure are," Lance drawled. "I'd like the T-bone, medium rare, please, with baked potato, everything on it and green beans, please."

"I want the same," Mona handed her menu over.

"We'll make it easy," Laronda said. "T-bone here, rare, please, with the same sides."

"Make it four, medium rare, same sides," Del handed his menu to the woman.

"So that's four T-bones, three medium-rare and one rare, with baked potato and green beans?"

"I think that's it, and he needs another Scotch—a double this time," Lance nodded toward Del.

"I'll have your drink right out," the server smiled brightly before walking away to turn in the order.

"Lance, there's a baby in isolation at a hospital in San Antonio," Mona said quietly. "The next-door neighbors asked the family to babysit and left the baby with the woman before going out for the evening."

"Fucking hell," Lance breathed. "They think the baby is infected, now?"

"They do," Laronda said, moving the salt and pepper shakers to the center of the table so all could reach them.

"What in damnation can you do with a zombie baby?" Mona's voice broke. "Her parents were screaming when the baby was placed in a plastic bubble and taken away."

"Somebody is watching them, now, to make sure they weren't infected, but they'd left the baby with the neighbors overnight and hadn't touched her," Laronda explained. "Once the police were called when the couple didn't answer the door, their bodies were found, in much the same shape as the victim in Austin. The baby had a single scratch across her forehead, but for now, she's still alive."

"We figure the attack happened shortly after the baby was left with the victims," Del took up the tale. "It allowed enough time for the incubation period for whatever this disease is. Still doesn't account for the baby, though."

"Have you gotten a handle on the incubation period?" Lance asked.

"Six to eight hours before it appears to kill them—that jives with the victim in Austin. It takes another twelve to twenty-four before the zombie effect falls into place."

Lance let that information settle as he focused on the Dallas street he could see through a nearby restaurant window. It was still daylight; the solstice was approaching, bringing the longest day of the year with it. New age people would be out celebrating the event.

By that time, a baby could turn into a zombie, more attacks could come and who knew what the fallout would be from all of it if they didn't find a cause and a cure soon.

"Have your forensics people released anything yet on their tissue analysis?" Mona asked Laronda.

"Only that the tissue has the same sort of decay that normal, dead tissue exhibits."

"Only this isn't normal, dead tissue."

"Yep. They're scratching their heads, only they won't admit it. They just say more testing has to be done."

"Do the tissue samples reanimate?" Lance asked.

"Not that they've seen. I think it's the standard brain connection with the rest of the body," Del replied. "Although they're studying the brain tissue, too, with the same results."

"So it has to be an intact brain and body?" Mona made a face as she considered her words.

"It looks mostly that way for now—Arianne almost decapitated the one who broke her door down. He didn't let up at the morgue until his head was severed completely. Still don't know yet about missing limbs affecting anything."

"Please, don't spoil dinner," Lance complained.

"We can discuss this later," Del said as the bartender placed a double Scotch in front of him. "How's the kid doing?" he asked when the young man walked away.

"The kid is fine. Ari made a blunder, though, according to Aunt Janie," Mona answered.

"What happened?"

"She tore the rearview mirror and a windshield wiper off the dumb neighbor's truck and left some pretty big scratches in his compensating-for-small-equipment vehicle."

"She turned? In front of him?" Laronda almost dropped her water glass.

"No. Just came running out of nowhere when the fool threatened Val."

"After Val refused the check Denton Franks offered to pay for Val's prize heifer that Denton's asshat father shot the night before—on Val's property. Val told him to leave. Denton wanted to argue. Enter a full-grown, pissed-off mountain lion," Lance took up the story.

"Has the Sheriff been called?"

"The night it happened. Denton says his father's senile and didn't know a half-grown heifer from a deer—across a fence and on somebody else's property," Mona huffed. "That man doesn't need guns within reach, sounds like."

"Mitchell Franks hasn't endeared himself to anyone in our family, and he's certainly got history with Ari's."

"In what way?" Laronda asked.

"Mitchell Franks used to hunt game, not only in Texas but across the country and even in a few foreign ones. Used to get his name and picture in the newspaper regularly for it, too. Uncle Brett started losing calves one season. He knew it was a big cat of some kind—probably a bobcat, although the tracks were pretty big. He and his ranch hands could never get close enough to kill it, so he hired Mitchell. Told him to come out on a specific date to look for the culprit. That date happened to be the day after a full moon. Mitchell jumped the gun, went hunting the night of the full moon and shot Ari's father, who had permission to be where he was that night."

"Not only was his picture in the paper, he had the head and the pelt of his kill in it with him. As you can imagine, Ari and her mother were devastated. Mountain lion shifters aren't that common," Mona sighed. "It was a big mess for the family. We offered compensation; Ari's mother refused it. Ari's hated Mitchell Franks all this time. She figures it put her mother in an early grave, too. Aunt Janie explained it all to us—after we took Ari and Nico to the ranch."

"You didn't know until then?"

"Nope."

The server was back, bearing a huge tray and a tray stand. Setting the stand and tray down, she placed steaks in front of the proper guests, all of them sizzling hot and fresh off the grill.

"This smells heavenly," Laronda sniffed in appreciation. "Thank you."

"Is there anything else I can get for you?" the server asked.

"I'd like a glass of pinot noir," Mona said.

"Do you have a preference?"

"Bartender's choice," Mona replied.

"Anyone else?" she asked as she lifted the tray and stand.

"I think we're good," Lance smiled at her. "Thanks."

"I always wondered how that sort of thing was handled," Del went back to the previous discussion as he cut into his steak.

"It's not always handled that way," Laronda said.

"We won't tell you, so you can maintain plausible deniability," Mona pointed a fork at him. "A lot depends on who's in charge at the time."

"Are you saying that Mitchell Franks is lucky to be old enough to turn senile?"

"Maybe. Who wants to know?"

"You know—I'm on Ari's side in this," Del shook his head. "People can be too stupid to live, sometimes."

"Except he did. Live, that is," Mona said. "My steak's good. How's yours?"

"Mine is more than acceptable," Laronda said, cutting another piece.

"We have a message," Claudio breathed as he turned on the burner phone. "Let's hope it's authentic."

"Shall we check the number, Master Scholar?" Alejandro waved a tablet, waiting for Claudio's command to search the source.

"Yes. Here it is," Claudio showed the phone to his younger guard, who had the number tapped in in a matter of seconds.

"Ah. This is strange," Alejandro's brow wrinkled in an uncharacteristic facial expression.

"What is strange?" Claudio asked immediately.

"The number. It's listed to someone that the police have reported as deceased."

"Let me see," Claudio held out a hand. Alejandro set the tablet in Claudio's grasp, so the Master Scholar could see for himself.

"This is the son of the restaurant owners—the restaurant that was bombed?"

"Yes, Master Scholar."

"Well, then. Before we listen to the message, which could be a trap, we will investigate this bombing."

"Of course, Master Scholar." Renault, who'd remained silent until now, agreed with Claudio's assessment. "Should I bring the car, or will you be doing research from here tonight?"

"I'd like to speak with the lead detective on the case," Claudio replied. "Once we find him, we shall ask questions."

"We will find him quickly, then," Renault responded.

"His name is Lance Elliott," Alejandro informed Claudio. "Shall I find his number?"

"Yes. I wish to speak with him very soon. Time grows short I fear, and this may already be spiraling out of our control."

"I have his number, from the Council database," Alejandro said, after only a few moments passed.

"Call the number. Tell him we have information and are willing to meet with him in a public place."

"Of course." Alejandro lifted another burner phone and dialed Lance's number. It was answered on the second ring.

"Detective Elliott," came the answer—more than audible to all three vampires listening in.

"Detective Elliott? This is Reynaldo Alverez, from Grand Prairie," Alejandro gave an assumed name and hometown. "I have information on the Blue Taco restaurant bombing, if you are interested." Alejandro's voice was smooth, with only a hint of a Spanish accent.

"I'd be willing to listen," Detective Elliott replied after a few seconds passed. "Can you meet me at the police station?"

"I would prefer to meet in a public venue," Alejandro said. "Your choice, of course."

"I'm at a restaurant at the moment," Elliott said, intending to say more before Alejandro cut him off.

"I can meet you there," Alejandro offered.

"It's downtown Dallas, and I have three officers with me."

"That will not be a problem. Tell me where to meet you, and I will bring the information."

"Can you tell me a little beforehand, just to let me know you actually have the information you say?"

"Of course. This bombing—and the disease which appears to bring the dead back to life—are connected. Now are you willing to meet with me?"

"Yes. How soon can you get here? No weapons—I'm warning you now. All of us are armed, as a precaution."

"I understand this. I will carry no weapons upon my person."

"Good. Meet me at the Cow's Nest restaurant, on Breaker Street."

"I will be there within an hour."

"I'll be waiting." Elliott hung up first.

"He will search for the name you gave immediately," Claudio smiled and steepled his fingers. "Alejandro, you are an asset of the highest order, to create aliases for all of us."

"I couldn't do it without the Council's assistance," Alejandro shrugged. "They make it all appear legitimate you know."

"Bring the car, Renault," Claudio said. "With your memories and Alejandro's expertise with electronics, we will solve this mystery very soon."

"Belwether, we need some plain-clothes officers at the Cow's Nest in the next hour," Lance spoke into his phone. "Someone who says he has information on the bombing is meeting me here."

"I'll send two cars out," Belwether said. "I may come myself—I haven't had dinner, yet."

"Steak's good tonight," Lance said before ending the call.

"This is what I found—he has a Facebook account, is on Twitter—appears to be a Rangers fan." Mona turned her phone so Lance could see what she'd pulled up on Reynaldo Alvarez from Grand Prairie, a city located between Dallas and Fort Worth. "Owns a tire and battery place."

"Anyone want dessert while we wait for the informant and our backup to arrive?" Mona asked.

"I want chocolate cake," Laronda said. "Today is the day for chocolate."

"I'm with you," Mona agreed.

Half an hour later, while he was sipping a cup of coffee after dessert, Lance watched Belwether stroll into the restaurant, dressed casually in slacks and a polo. Sidling up to the bar, the Captain accepted a menu from the bartender and looked through the selections while keeping a discreet eye on the door.

Lance's back was to the door, so Laronda and Del were watching the entrance for him. "Three walking in," Del reported as the door opened.

Could my informant have company? Lance fought the urge to turn around.

"Walking this way," Del mumbled, toying with his coffee cup.

Laronda drew in a deep breath before gripping the table hard and appearing to panic. "Vampires!" she hissed, causing Lance's heart to stutter in his chest.

CHAPTER SEVEN

"*W*ill it help if we offer the standard, *we mean you no harm?*" Claudio asked as Alejandro pulled up chairs for the Master Scholar, Renault and himself at Lance's table. Laronda and Del had moved to a nearby table after Renault politely asked them to do so.

Laronda still stared at the three vamps with wide eyes, however, so the compulsion hadn't been meant as anything other than a request with a small amount of persuasion.

Lance understood compulsion, although he'd never seen it until now. "How do you know anything about the bombing?" Lance began uncomfortably. "I suspect none of you actually live in Texas."

"I reside in Oklahoma," Claudio said. "You are quite correct. What you don't know is this—the bombing may only be the beginning of many things, most of which will be far, far worse than these death walkers."

"What can be worse than that?" Mona asked.

"Do you have a strong grasp of European history? I am Claudio, of the Septum Scholarium. I suspect you have no idea what that means, eh?"

"Septum—seven," Mona said, pretending indifference. "Scholarium? School—or scholar, maybe?"

"Yes, very good," Claudio nodded at her. "Since your colleague at the other table named us as what we are, we assume you also know what she is?"

"We do," Lance admitted.

"Good. This is far better than I hoped. May I ask how you know this?"

"Well, she told us," Lance said, working to keep his hands and his voice even. For his first meeting with a vampire, he felt he was doing well enough so far.

"Shapeshifters must trust before they reveal," Claudio pointed out.

"We ah, have family who are also, well," Lance didn't finish.

"You are half." Claudio stated flatly.

"Yes. Nobody else knows, not even our captain," Mona said.

"You are related?" Claudio looked from Mona to Lance.

"Yes. Cousins."

"I see. Now, tell me about the boy."

"Boy?"

"Did he survive the bombing? Much depends upon your answer, and the truthfulness of it."

"Why do you want to know?"

"Because we are in a position to help him."

"How?"

"If he is alive, he is in grave danger from terrible enemies—the ones responsible for the bombing and the walking death now plaguing this state."

"You're saying the vamps want to protect a human?" Mona didn't bother hiding her skepticism.

"I understand that you may not believe this. You would be very wrong," Claudio said.

"Do not offend the Master Scholar," Renault growled.

"Threatening us is also offensive," Lance countered.

"I take it the boy is alive?"

"I didn't say that."

"How many officers are in this restaurant?" Alejandro asked. "I count five besides you and the two nearby, but my judgment could be off."

Lance swallowed hard. "Are you threatening all of us?" he asked.

"No. Not yet. You do not grasp the gravity of the situation. We must know if the boy is alive, that is all. If he is, that is the only information I need."

"Why go to all this trouble, then?" Mona asked.

"To make sure the one who called and left a message for me earlier is indeed Nicolas Garcia, rather than the enemy laying a trap for us. There is one more thing, however, if you don't mind."

"What's that?"

"Have you, by chance, seen the *Eques Corax*—the Raven Knight?"

I can't believe I'm driving vampires to my cousin's ranch. Lance's face was set as he drove along the highway toward the Jordan Ranch. Behind him, in Del's rental, Mona, Del and Laronda followed. He'd been ready for a standoff with his fanged guests until they mentioned Mac.

It wasn't until he dialed Nico's cell phone and Nico answered that he'd learned that Nico had, at Mac's urging, placed the call to Claudio the vampire earlier. Nico put Mac on the phone, Lance handed his phone to Claudio and the two—vampire and raven—had held a conversation in Spanish.

His Spanish was rusty, but he understood the word *impenitente*—it meant unrepentant. He hadn't asked Claudio what the significance of the word was, or how it was connected to what was happening, but felt he'd learn soon enough.

Not long before he reached the ranch, Val called.

"They can hear you," Lance said as he spoke to Val.

"I understand. I merely want a guarantee of safety for every living thing on this ranch."

"You have my word, as a member of the Scholarium," Claudio

replied before Lance could relay the message. "If you have doubts, contact your Grand Master. He knows of us."

"You know what we are." Val said it flatly. Lance knew that tone. Val didn't like it one bit.

"Our Council has already contacted your Grand Master. He relayed to us that the Jordan Ranch may be considered a place of refuge, should we need it. It turns out that you have also become a refuge for those we seek to find. I have hopes that this proves advantageous for both our species."

"I did get a call from the Grand Master, but he was intentionally vague. Therefore, I'll be waiting for your explanation," Val gruffed and hung up.

"Well," Claudio sighed. "I suppose you would call that our *Lucy, you got some 'splaining to do* moment."

His quote, delivered in a creditable impression, was the last thing Lance expected any vampire to say.

It made him laugh.

～

"I can't believe you're not terrified of vampires," Ari stared at Nico.

"Ari, I've been having nightmares that are far worse than any vampire, I think." Nico's gaze was steady. He'd grown far older than his nineteen years in the space of a few days.

"I'm sorry, Nico. I just can't—wrap my head around this. That somehow, I'm tied up in all of it."

"You didn't expect to be involved in this train wreck," Nico nodded. "Neither did I."

"These. Vam-pires. Friends," Mac croaked at Ari. "Not be. A-fraid."

"So you've met them before?" Ari snapped at Mac.

"No."

"Great." Ari stalked out of the media room, where Nico and Mac had retreated after dinner. There, they'd broken the news that she needed to meet the vampires, just as Nico and Mac did.

"She'll be back," Nico told Mac, who looked ready to fly after her. "She's my friend. Even if she doesn't come to trust these vampires, she'll stand with me in case I need protection. That's just the way she is."

"You. Don't. Know. That."

"She was ready to give her life when that monster broke into her house—to save us," Nico went on.

"I. Know."

"I saved her life and enslaved her at the same time. How do you explain that to a friend? She can't ever be the same again. Just like I can't." Nico's words were bitter.

"I. Know. Still. Have. Doubts. About her."

"Your visitors have arrived," Janie walked out of the elevator when the doors opened. "Want to ride down or walk?"

"Walk," Nico said, sounding weary as he rose from the chair beside the window. "Thank you, Janie. I'm sorry if this makes you uncomfortable."

"Honey, we have to get this sorted, according to Lance and Mona. This is bigger than any of us thought, I imagine."

"It. Is." Mac concurred.

"Come on, Mac." Nico tapped his shoulder. "Let's go meet our vampire scholar."

Claudio stepped into the werewolf's home after Val invited him and his guards inside. Lance had gone in first, letting Val know right away that he was safe and unharmed.

"Your home is lovely," Claudio complimented Val.

"The boy and the raven are on their way. Ari is somewhere."

"Ari?"

"You'll know when you meet her," Lance said. "I'll go find her," he nodded to Val as Mona, Del and Laronda came inside.

"May get rain later, Mr. Jordan," Laronda said. "I smelled it when the wind changed direction."

"We could use some rain," Val told her. "Ponds are getting low."

"It will be a thunderstorm," Nico said as he walked in with Mac clinging to his shoulder.

"At least we see you before the *Manus Malo* have revealed themselves," Claudio dipped his head reverently to Nico and Mac. "As yet, we have only seen victims of *et Inpaenitens*, and not their living servants."

"Who are you talking about—what do those words mean, and are they not living? Are they people or something else?" Mona asked.

"Ah, forgive me. We speak of the Unrepentant, and no, they are not living as you think of living. Their flesh rotted—or was burned—long ago. Only their spirits remain, and those are exceptionally malevolent. You will learn that they have a particular agenda, and once freed from their bonds, they will stop at nothing to achieve it."

"Can you explain it better?" Val asked. "Because at this point it sounds like ghosts."

"That term is far too innocuous for what they are," Claudio shook his head at Val. "As terrifying as a ghost may be, a multitude of human shades cannot compare to even one of the Unrepentant."

"I'm having difficulty believing any of this," Del rumbled.

"Be grateful that you have not yet encountered evil like this."

"I work for the FBI. I don't deal in roses and chocolate," Del said as Laronda nodded at his words.

"We understand this," Claudio replied. "You have not seen the memories and visions that I have seen. I assure you; they are terrifying."

"When will these—what did you call them—show up?" Mona asked Claudio.

"Evil hands? It will be very obvious, but that day is unknown, and the harbinger to the event is a tale that is not mine to tell."

"Can we be more cryptic? So far, I know less than when we started," Laronda complained.

"Here's my question," Ari walked in with Lance. "Where do we go from here?"

Claudio drew in a breath as Ari came near. He'd always heard that the scent was unique, but he'd never experienced it firsthand.

And, as it was layered over the natural smell of her mountain lion shifter, Claudio could only gape and fall into stunned silence.

Renault and Alejandro hadn't spoken until then. "Incredible—the scent," Alejandro breathed.

"If you had ever known for yourself the difference between the scent of a *Manus Malo* and a *Manus Lux*, you would kneel down," Renault sighed and knelt before Ari. "I will guard you with my life," he pledged.

"What is he talking about?" Ari hissed at Claudio.

"We are pledged to serve the *Luce Signiferum* and his *Manus Lux*. We may not turn aside from that duty, even if it costs us our lives," Claudio said softly. "We follow the guidance of the *Eques Corax*—the Raven Knight—who has performed this duty many, many times."

"So we're supposed to hang out together—like a band of merry men—and one woman?" Ari demanded. Mac, whose feathers remained ruffled after she'd asked to speak with him alone, hadn't said anything yet.

"You are. First. Wo-man," Mac finally replied. "On-lee men. Bee-fore now. Ni-co chose you. I did. Not."

"I don't think you're getting the point," Ari grumbled, ignoring the insult. "I don't want to hang out—and do—whatever it is I'm supposed to do."

"Pro-tect. Ni-co."

Ari went still. "Fuck." Pressing fingertips to her forehead to stall an oncoming headache, she walked away from Mac until she stood in front of her bedroom window. She hadn't shut the plantation shutters, so she stared through the window at the yard bathed by waxing moonlight. Her eyesight—that of a large cat even in human form, saw better at night than most. The moonlight wasn't needed, and to her sharp vision, the side yard was perfectly visible to her.

"The full moon is in a few days," she sighed. "What the hell is going on?"

"Will tell you. Late-er," Mac said. "Sorr-ee."

"Are you going to tell me that my life will never be my own again?" Ari whirled as she accused him.

Mac ducked his head. "Don't. Know."

"Should I go ask that vampire? Renault?"

"He. Does not. Know. Ev-ree-thing."

"When will you tell me what I need to know?"

"Soon, per-haps."

"Ari?" Nico tapped on her bedroom door.

"Come in." Ari shut her blinds as Nico walked in and closed the door.

"Val is letting the vampires use the basement until we can find a safe place for all of us," Nico said as he flopped onto a chair beside her bed. "Claudio has funds to provide for that and anything else we need. Plus, he has access to other ah, vampires, if we need their help."

"Why are they helping us?" Ari snapped. "I don't understand this at all."

"What do you think will happen if all humans are either dead or have become zombies? Where will the vampires get their blood supply?"

"This is self-preservation?"

"Half of it is self-preservation, yes. The other half is this—as bad as you think vampires are, what we're dealing with is far worse. Most vamps aren't evil; we've just been conditioned to believe they are."

"So, suddenly you're a vampire expert?" Ari retorted.

"He has. To. Learn. Fast," Mac cautioned. "Not the. Time to. Fight each. Oth-er."

"Nico, may we come in?" Claudio tapped on the door.

"Come in, Claudio," Nico called out. Ari sighed and shook her head as their vampire guests now walked into her bedroom and shut the door.

"I understand you have misgivings, Ms. Leone," Claudio said. "I would feel the same if I were in your situation. I hope you can give us the benefit of the doubt until you see for yourself what is coming, and how important your role will be in stopping the horror."

"Lady Lionesse, you have not witnessed the purges of the past," Renault spoke. "I have."

"Purges?" Ari crossed arms tightly over her chest.

"When the old gods meet the new, the aftermath is often unpleasant," Claudio supplied. "Nico and those who came before him are the wall—and sometimes the gate—between the two."

"I don't understand any of this," Ari snapped.

"You don't understand the creatures you call zombies, either," Claudio explained. "Yet you were willing to fight one to save Nico and the raven. It would have cost you your life. You know this, do you not?"

"I do." Ari paled and ducked her head at Claudio's statement.

"Ari is trying to come to grips with her life changing so drastically, and in a way she can't reverse, just as I am," Nico sounded weary. "It's late. Some of us need sleep. Ari, will you help us move your paintings and supplies in the basement, so Claudio, Renault and Alejandro can have a safe place to stay?"

"Nico, you know I'd go to the ends of the earth for you," Ari dropped her arms with a sigh.

"Fun-nee. You say that. Now," Mac croaked.

"We'll get to that later," Nico cast a worried frown at Mac. "Come on, Ari. We'll get the basement sorted, and then we can go to bed while our new friends watch the night."

"How beautiful," Claudio breathed as he studied Ari's finished commission. "If this one is not yet sold, I will buy it for myself," he declared.

"It's sold, but I have to get it to the buyer in Virginia or I won't get the rest of my payment," Ari muttered as she packed her paints and brushes into a box.

"I can make that arrangement for you," Claudio offered. "Alejandro is quite adept at making these things happen."

"Could you?" Nico spoke as he set two of Ari's finished works in a corner where they wouldn't get damaged.

"I will see it done," Alejandro replied directly to Nico. "All I need is the address."

"Here," Ari pulled a slip of paper off the back of the painting. "It needs to ship by the weekend."

"We will see it taken care of," Claudio assured her.

"I think that's the last of it," Ari set the box of art supplies near the paintings Nico stored. "Janie probably has extra beds upstairs."

"We will be fine," Renault said. "Chairs and sofa are fine for us; we won't feel them once we fall into the rejuvenating sleep."

Ari went still. As much as she felt vulnerable to these vampires at night, they were also vulnerable during the day. "I promise to guard you through the day," she told them.

"We all do," Nico agreed. "Come on, Ari. We need to sleep if we can."

"You have our gratitude," Claudio beamed. "Thank you."

"Well, I'll be gawd-damned," Darnell Cheatham mumbled as he replayed the same section of Reverend Killebrew's recording. He doubted the man was intelligent enough to tamper with the images like that, so they had to be real—right?

The boy couldn't be more than fourteen or fifteen. Those witches—vermin, in Senator Cheatham's mind—were gathered in a circle, casting a spell on that boy. There was no other way to describe it.

Overhead, a full moon shone, and before his eyes, the boy changed. Not painfully, like all the movies claimed, but morphing from one shape to another in a fluid motion—like a spell had been cast.

The wolf then howled at the moon, and the witches celebrated. One witch was so bold as to hug the wolf, who howled again. The recording ended after that; Cheatham wondered if that's when the spy stopped recording or if Killebrew had cut off the copying process at that point.

"I'll bet they had sex with that wolf," Cheatham grumbled, and he felt as if he'd been shortchanged, somehow.

Killebrew had to have more information on these people—he'd all but said the same thing. Yes, Cheatham would definitely be in Killebrew's congregation come Sunday, and together, they'd put a stop to this sort of behavior everywhere.

"If it can happen in Texas, just imagine what they do in New York." Cheatham pulled the thumb drive from his computer and rose to lock it in his wall safe. Soon enough, if he had his way, everybody depicted in that video would be dead, and the video itself would be broadcast from one end of the country to the other.

In fact, he knew of a few social media sites that would be perfect to present these images to the world. Who cared if they were short on facts or fabricated scandals on most days? They had an audience, and that audience was exactly the type of people he wanted to reach.

Lifting his cell phone, he dialed a number he'd contacted once or twice to spread rumors about an opponent or two.

"Senator," Ralph Hooten sounded happy to hear from him.

"Hey, Ralph, how ya doin'?" Cheatham pulled out his false enthusiasm and dusted it off. It would work perfectly for this conversation.

"Just great. Say, you don't have some more ah, advertising for us to spread to the good followers of Hooten and Hollerin', do ya?"

"I may have something guaranteed to knock your boots and socks off," Cheatham replied. "How about we meet for lunch next Monday? I'm tied up this weekend, I'm afraid."

"Whatever is good for you," Ralph agreed. "Just let me know where and when."

"I'll shoot you an email in the next few days," Cheatham said. "You're gonna love this, Ralphy boy. Guaranteed."

"I like the sound of that," Ralph said. "See ya on Monday."

"Yep."

Cheatham ended the call as a shiver ran through him. He was

beginning to feel it—the historical significance of his actions in the next few days would have worldwide repercussions. His name would be printed in the history books for sure, and, good or bad, it wouldn't matter.

Either would suit him just fine.

~

Nico dreamed.

Only this dream wasn't like the others. No—this one held a significance that terrified him more than all his previous nightmares combined.

A name came to him in the fog of his dream, as terror-filled screams sounded and a faceless villain turned toward him, his hands soaked in blood.

"Nicolas! Wake now," a deep voice shouted at him, while strong hands shook him awake.

"Mac," Nico shouted, as the hands pulled him off the bed and set him, stumbling, on his feet.

"I'm here, Nico," the deep voice rumbled. "The Adversary's human puppet has set his feet on the path and none are safe now."

"Huh?" Struggling to push away the remnants of the terror that gripped him, Nico blinked into the eyes of the stranger that held him up with a firm grip on both arms.

In the dim light of a very early morning, Nico recognized those dark eyes, although they'd been much smaller on the raven.

With only a towel wrapped around his waist, Mac had become the knight, sworn to protect him until he could protect himself.

The Adversary had declared his presence, and nothing would ever be the same again.

CHAPTER EIGHT

ri, feeling disoriented and sluggish, forced her feet to the floor. Normally, she'd appreciate the softness of expensive carpet beneath her feet, but not today. It would take a supreme act of will to rise from the bed on this morning.

Sleep hadn't come for a long time, while worried thoughts chased themselves in her mind and morphed into nightmares during a troubled, half-doze.

"Ari?" Janie tapped on her bedroom door.

Was it later than she thought? Ari jerked her head toward the clock on the nightstand; it read seven-forty-five. It wasn't that late; something else was going on or Janie wouldn't disturb her like this.

"Come in," Ari called out.

Janie walked in and shut the door behind her. "You didn't have a good night by the look of things," Janie observed.

"Did anybody have a good night?" Ari stood and felt a momentary unsteadiness.

"I'm not sure," Janie said. "But I need your help."

"Whatever you need, I'll do," Ari said.

"Well, we have to run into town and buy a few things—for Mac."

"What's wrong? Is he sick?"

"Nooo," Janie shook her head. "He's fine, health-wise."

"What does he need, then?"

"Get dressed—wear something suitable for shopping and I'll show you. Meet me in the kitchen. We'll have breakfast, then go out."

"All right. I think I need about a gallon of coffee to wake up, though."

"We have coffee in the kitchen. Take a shower—it'll help." Janie walked out of the bedroom, leaving Ari with plenty of confused thoughts.

What the hell do ravens need? Had he been eating too much human food? Did he need mealworms or corn? They sold those things at feed stores for chickens. Maybe that's what Mac needed.

Her stomach felt sour enough after meeting vampires the night before. *They don't often bother shifters*, her father told her not long before his death. *Most go about their business without causing a fuss. If you ever scent one, act like you didn't notice and the vamp will probably do the same.*

A vampire had sworn an oath to protect her life with his own the night before. What the hell was she supposed to do with that?

"Shower. Dress," Ari reminded herself aloud before walking toward her bathroom. Jeans and a nice top ought to do well enough for a local feed store.

"Coffee," Ari begged as she walked into the kitchen, before coming to an abrupt stop as a new scent hit her.

Not human.

Not werewolf.

Not any shifter she'd ever come across.

A shirtless man sat next to Nico; both were hunched over and engaging in a soft, private conversation. Nico's neighbor suddenly straightened and glanced in her direction.

He needed a haircut.

He was stunning.

His black hair and eyes gave him away. Ari felt light-headed for a moment.

It took several seconds before she realized he was only dressed in a pair of sweatpants. Val's probably, because he was the only one tall enough to lend this one clothing.

Muscles rippled on his torso and arms as he scooted his barstool back and rose. "I'm sorry if this troubles you," he said, his words betraying a slight accent.

She couldn't place it, as she was still staring—well, gaping might be a better word.

"We're going to Abilene to get him some clothes to wear," Janie broke the spell as she thumped a cup of coffee on the island. "Drink this, Ari—I think you need it."

"Oh. Right." Ari moved past the human-looking Mac and lifted the coffee cup with a murmured, "Thanks." She didn't take the seat next to Mac's.

No.

Ari settled on a barstool two down from his. Deliberately, she avoided his gaze while sipping coffee. Turning to look at him could cause her to choke, and embarrassment wasn't anything she wanted for herself at the moment.

"No sleep, eh?" Mac rumbled.

"It's not a good idea to talk to Ari before she's had her first cup," Nico advised.

"Oh. Right."

At least he doesn't struggle with the words, like raven Mac, Ari thought as she drank more coffee. The warm brew slowly woke her brain and cleared away the cobwebs from too little sleep.

Janie said Abilene instead of Fort Worth for the shopping trip. Didn't matter; the ranch was roughly halfway between, with an hour's drive east or west.

"We'll be okay going to Abilene for the day," Nico said. "We need burner phones and a few other things, too."

"Janie, you are not paying for this," Ari rose to pour more coffee in her mug.

"I'm not. That vampire gave Nico a credit card last night, and a list of things to get for him and the others, too," Janie told her.

"Never thought I'd see the day when vampires would be staying here with our blessing," Mary Kate met Ari halfway with the coffeepot. "I admit, having one of them out there watching for the Franks was more than welcome."

"Somebody guarded the western fence line?" Ari didn't hide her surprise.

"Sure did. Watched the Franks house all night, to make sure nobody sneaked out," Mary Kate filled Ari's mug, gave her a tight smile and went back to making breakfast.

"Val was grateful, actually," Janie said. "He just had to warn the ranch hands to stay away from the area."

"Val's hands have been patrolling that fence, haven't they?" Ari settled on her barstool.

"Yes, and it's tiring. Last night, Renault gave them a break."

"Here's to Renault, then," Ari lifted her coffee mug in a toast to the vampire guard.

"If anything came out of that house, Renault would have called for Alejandro," Mac said. Ari briefly considered that his voice reminded her of warm caramel, poured over the best pecans Texas could produce.

"I'm starved," Ari sighed as she drank more coffee. It was evident from the way her thoughts had turned to food.

"It's good that your appetite is back," Janie smiled at her. "Earlier, you looked green around the gills."

"I felt that way, too."

"I've only been in the States since last November," Mac answered Janie's question as Ari, who'd volunteered to drive Janie's SUV, pulled into a parking space at a busy shopping center in Abilene.

"Shoes or clothes first?" Janie asked, opening her door to climb out of the front passenger seat.

"Haircut?" Mac asked.

"There's a salon and barbershop halfway down," Janie pointed. "Let's see if we can get you in."

Ari didn't say anything as she stepped out of the vehicle. The key fob was in her pocket already, so she grabbed her purse and shut the door. The Cadillac would lock itself in a matter of seconds after they stepped away.

In fact, Ari had only answered direct questions on the trip. Janie had all sorts of questions for Mac, who answered as best he could. Ari knew when he was being evasive, although she couldn't quite say how it was that she knew.

Nico had known Mac would turn; Ari felt that in her bones. Why keep it from her, though? *What was the big secret, that they felt they couldn't tell?*

She was a shapeshifter—this was nothing new to her. Maybe humans would freak when it happened, but she wouldn't.

"I think we can fit him in," the salon's receptionist smiled widely at Mac, although Janie was the one who'd asked about his haircut. "Maybe ten minutes?"

"That sounds wonderful," Janie replied, although the receptionist was already heading for the back to let someone know about the walk-in.

"I guess we'll have a seat, then," Janie buried her annoyance behind a bright smile. They found four adjoining chairs and settled down to wait.

"Janie?" Nico leaned forward so he could see her around Mac's impressive bulk.

"What is it, Nico?"

"Have you ever heard of someone named Hunter Pace?"

Janie's eyes widened in surprise, while Ari drew in an audible breath.

"Old or young?" Janie said after several seconds passed.

"Young. Maybe sixteen?"

"Hunter Junior," Ari leaned back in her chair with a sigh.

"I know of him," Janie replied. "Why? Where did you hear that name?"

"In a dream," Nico said. "He's in danger. Do you know where he is?"

"Is that who you saw when I woke you this morning?" Mac asked quietly.

"Yeah."

"He's serious, Mrs. Jordan," Mac said. "The boy is in very real danger if Nico sees him and learns his name in a dream."

"Call it what it was—a nightmare," Nico muttered.

"I can find out, I suppose," Janie pulled her cell phone out of her purse. "Ari, will you come outside with me while I make this call? Nico, will you be all right?"

"I'll take him back with me. He'll be fine," Mac assured her.

Ari followed Janie out the door as the receptionist returned to take Mac and Nico to a stylist in the back of the shop. A strange pain hit Ari between her shoulder blades as she followed Janie down the sidewalk until they reached an empty storefront.

"I think Burke knows where the boy is," Janie said as she tapped Burke's number on her phone. "He took care of a few legal obstacles when Hunter Sr. died."

"We have no love for Hunter Sr.," Ari mumbled as her sharp hearing registered Janie's phone ringing Burke's number.

"Hunter Jr. has no idea what happened," Janie began when Burke answered.

"Burke, I know this may sound strange, but we have the idea that Hunter Pace Jr. may be in danger. Do you know where he is?"

There was hesitation on Burke's end, before he said, "Yes. I do. What kind of danger?"

"I get the feeling it's in the mortal category," Janie explained.

"I can get a message to his Aunt," Burke offered. "Does this mean a visit, perhaps?"

"Maybe. Can I get back with you on this? I don't know how urgent this is, so hold off contacting her until we know for sure."

"How soon will you know?"

"Maybe in an hour or two. I'll call back whenever I have the answer."

"All right." Burke ended the call.

"I had a feeling he'd know," Janie's shoulders slumped. "His father may have been *lupus non grata* while he was Grand Master, but the boy had nothing to do with any of that."

"I hope Nico knows what he's doing, setting this in motion," Ari frowned.

"If you knew the boy was in danger, wouldn't you save him?" Janie dropped her cell phone in her bag.

"Yeah. I guess I would," Ari admitted. "He didn't let Mitchell Franks go. Hunter Pace Sr. did."

"Well, we've all paid for that mistake," Janie huffed and started walking toward the salon. Ari followed, then slowed as they passed a coffee shop. "I need a coffee," she said, opening the door.

"You have cash?" Janie turned to ask.

"Yeah."

"Get me a vanilla latte, then, if you don't mind."

"Sure thing." Ari walked into the coffee shop while Janie strode toward the salon. After turning in her order, Ari took a seat at a tiny table near the window to wait for the barista to make their drinks.

Mac barely noticed his reflection in the mirror or the stylist who moved about him, measuring with her fingers and snipping off long and uneven hair.

No.

His thoughts were on the woman, Ari—and whether she presented more danger to him than to Nico. That danger was wrapped in the ancient curse that forced him to serve the Custodian of the Hermit's Stone—which wasn't an actual stone and had only once been in the hands of a hermit. Many other hands had held it, but that single name had stuck with the artifact through the centuries.

Ari—the only woman chosen to be a Custodian's chief protector, could be the death of him if he didn't hold himself—and his emotions —away from her. Better for Nico to let her go and find another.

You mean better for you, a small voice reminded him.

❧

"That looks great," Nico studied Mac's haircut from every angle while the receptionist ran the card Nico handed over.

"It does look good," Janie agreed.

"Here we go," Ari walked in with a drink carrier. "Nico, I got root beer for you. I didn't know if you wanted anything else, so it's black coffee for you," she handed a lidded cup to Mac.

"Black is fine," he said, his dark eyes narrowing as he searched her face for a moment. "Thank you."

"Janie," Ari handed off the vanilla latte before removing the last cup for herself.

"What did you get?" Nico asked her.

"Caramel mocha. This day needs chocolate. And caramel. And coffee."

Nico added a tip to the ticket, signed it and stuffed the receipt and credit card in a pocket. "Where to now?" he asked.

"Shoes," Mac said. "Please."

❧

"I'm glad Nico is buying things, too," Ari whispered to Janie as they watched Mac and Nico trying on athletic shoes.

"I think they'll need the boots they found at the first store, but these are good for most days," Janie agreed. "Although Val would be upset to hear that they bypassed the cowboy boots altogether."

"Not everybody looks good in cowboy boots, and certainly not in a cowboy hat," Ari nodded.

"That fool, Dalton Franks has no idea how idiotic he looks—his hats sit right on top of his big ears and pushes them out farther, if that's possible."

"Funny. I would have pegged him for the all hat and no cattle variety, but Val says he has too many cattle penned up in too small spaces."

"You haven't gotten the stench from a strong west wind yet; give it time," Janie grumped.

"How did he buy that place? I figured Val would at least bid on it, since it's right next to you."

"He would have, but the place was never listed. I get the idea that Franks approached Chuck, and made an offer Chuck wouldn't refuse," Janie said. "Therefore, we get Fool One and Fool Two next door, who don't know the first thing about managing a real cattle ranch. It's not healthy to leave your cattle standing knee-deep in muck twenty-four-seven. I'm surprised they don't have the vet on speed dial by now."

"Idiots," Ari snarled.

"At least Denton's kids are in college, and don't bother to come home except for Thanksgiving and Christmas. I don't blame them; I don't know how they deal with the smell that close to the house."

"How did you find all this out?" Ari asked.

"Mary Kate runs into their housekeeper at the grocery store sometimes. She's thinking about quitting—their housekeeper, not Mary Kate. Couldn't pay me to breathe that mess every day, but then our noses are more sensitive than theirs."

"By a lot," Ari said. "Those look good," she called out as Nico studied the shoes on his feet. "Make sure they're comfy."

"They are," he grinned at her while walking back and forth. For a moment, he was the Nico she'd known, from *before*—before everything had gone wrong and their lives had skidded into a wrong turn, flinging them in a direction they'd never expected.

Would there ever be a time for a memorial for his parents?

Had he lost his youthful joy forever?

And for what? Mac knew things. Nico knew things, too. They weren't telling her everything—not even close. Most of the time, too, she had the vibe from Mac that he was judging her—and didn't like what he saw. He was polite enough—but then he was polite to everyone.

"Your expression just changed—like clouds obscuring the sun," Mac suddenly stood before her, a box of athletic shoes in his hands. "Is something wrong?"

"No," she lied.

"Nico, have you made your decision?" Mac turned to ask.

"I'll take these two pairs," Nico lifted boxes from the floor and rose from the bench where he'd sat to try on shoes.

"Good enough. We need clothes, next, and then we ought to go back."

"Nico, I forgot to ask earlier—do you know how soon we need to reach the young man you mentioned?" Janie asked.

"Before Sunday," Nico replied as Mac lifted the boxes away from his hands.

"I'll let Burke know," Janie told him.

"How important is he?" Mac asked softly.

"He must be protected," Nico sighed. "He may be in a position to return the favor sometime."

"I'll make the call. Meet me outside after you pay." Janie headed for the door.

"I'll go with her," Ari said and followed Janie toward the store entrance.

"I've never seen it this full." Janie studied the back of her Escalade before Ari tapped the button to shut the hatch.

"You told them to get enough clothes to last two or three weeks," Ari said as they walked around the vehicle to get in. Mac and Nico had loaded everything in, then ran to a nearby ice cream shop for a cold treat.

"I did tell them that," Janie agreed, climbing into the passenger seat in the front. "I guess I wasn't thinking about how much space all that would take."

The air conditioner was running full blast, cooling the interior while they waited for Mac and Nico's return. "Summer in Texas always makes me grateful for the folks who figured out how to put AC in cars," Ari leaned back in the driver's seat.

"I second that," Janie agreed. "I sure hope they have bottled water at that ice cream parlor. I'm thirsty."

"Me, too," Ari agreed. They'd both requested water when Nico asked if they wanted anything. She shifted in her seat—the strange prickling along her back had returned, making her uncomfortable.

"Ari," Janie's hand suddenly gripped Ari's arm as she stared straight ahead.

Ari drew in a breath; Denton Franks, with his father, Mitchell, were walking toward Janie's vehicle.

"Let me handle this," Janie hissed as she opened the door and stepped out of the SUV.

Ari, angry in an instant and worried that Denton didn't have the best intentions toward Janie, also climbed out of the Escalade.

"Denton," Janie said as he approached. Ari's gaze stayed on Mitchell as a growl formed low in her throat.

"I need your car insurance information, to fix my truck," Denton told Janie. "There's at least three thousand in damage done."

"If you'll let me onto your property, I'll take care of that mountain lion for you," Mitchell said. "I did it once before, you know."

"You will never be welcome on our property again," Janie snapped at the older man. "You failed to kill the actual predator, and you know that."

Ari seethed as Mitchell attempted to convince Janie to let him hunt on the Jordan Ranch.

"Problem?" Mac and Nico arrived, carrying ice cream and bottles of water.

"Denton and Mitchell want to hunt the mountain lion on our property," Janie folded arms across her chest as she glared at Mitchell.

"Janie, will you take this?" Mac handed his dish of ice cream to her, while Nico took the bottle of water. On the other side of the vehicle, Ari vibrated with rage. He had to stop this debacle before she turned and tore both human men to shreds.

"Now," Mac turned toward Denton and Mitchell. "You should

never have killed the first mountain lion," he began. "Let me assure you, too, that if you threaten this mountain lion, someone will certainly take it amiss." Then, Mac turned toward Denton. "The heifer your father killed, mistaking it for a deer, was worth five thousand because of her breeding and potential to birth good stock going forward. You can write a check to Val for the difference between the damage to your truck and the cost of the heifer. Or, you can wait for this to play out in court, and I'm sure your father's questionable eyesight and judgment will be brought into the public eye."

"Well," Denton sputtered.

"How dare you question my judgment," Mitchell raised his voice. "That was a deer, I swear it."

"A deer on someone else's property is not yours to shoot," Mac slowly turned back to Mitchell. "You do not get to hunt on any property not your own, unless you have permission. You did not have permission in the past, either for the mountain lion or the heifer. I warn you now; do not approach the Jordan Ranch again. If you do, and especially if you carry a weapon of any kind, I cannot guarantee your safety."

"Is that a threat?" Denton huffed.

"No. It is a warning," Mac shot back.

"I suppose you're the one who'll do something about it if I do cross the fence?" Mitchell demanded.

"You will never know what hit you, but it won't be me."

"Dad, let's get out of here," Denton grabbed Mitchell's arm to pull him away.

"I'm still a marksman," Mitchell shouted at Mac as Denton pulled him away. "I'll kill anybody coming my way."

"Believe what you want, old man," Mac said quietly. "You can't fight vampires if a gun is all you have."

"Let's go," Janie handed Mac's ice cream back to him. "I think we've had enough excitement for today."

Ari unclenched her fists as she watched Denton and Mitchell disappear into the coffee shop. "Murderers," she muttered in their direction before sliding into the vehicle.

"Are you okay to drive?" Janie asked after getting a good look at Ari's face.

"Yeah."

"Water," Nico passed a cold bottle of water to Ari between the two front seats.

"Take your time," Janie soothed as Ari nearly ripped the cap off the bottle to drink.

"We need to have a conversation with the vamps when they wake," Mac told Ari later as they pulled bags and boxes from the back of the Escalade. "Renault needs an update on the Franks." He gave Ari a meaningful look as she followed him into the house.

"Maybe I should patrol the fence line with Renault," Ari muttered.

"Ari, revenge seldom turns out the way you want," Mac advised. "Renault has been a guardian for the Scholars for centuries. He knows his business. I will guarantee this, however. If he is forced to destroy Mitchell Franks, you'll have your revenge, I promise."

"How?"

"You'll have to trust me on this," Mac replied. "Just have a little patience, Lady Lion."

"Patience? My father was murdered years ago. How patient should I be?"

"Wait until your power manifests," Mac sighed. "It's coming, or it should be. If not, the stone will choose another."

"Drop the jeans off in the laundry room," Janie said, interrupting the conversation as they walked into the kitchen. "I'm sure you don't want to wear those stiff, dye-stinky things until afterward."

"He doesn't," Ari answered before Mac could. "I smelled that all the way home."

"Then most certainly they will go in the wash," Mac agreed, pretending amiability.

"Come back to the kitchen after you do that," Janie called out. "We have sandwiches."

"Your shipment arrived earlier," Mac informed Claudio. "It's stored in the refrigerator in the laundry room."

"Very good," Claudio nodded. "We always worry about such things."

"We also have new information, and a concern," Mac went on. "I've arranged for Ari and Nico to join us in half an hour."

"Do you need all of us?" Renault asked.

"Yes, and you especially," Mac replied. "It concerns a dispute earlier today."

"I see much has happened while we slept," Claudio said.

"Nico has begun to feel the growing power of the human Adversary, unless I miss my guess," Mac continued.

"Never a good sign, when it happens this quickly," Claudio mused. "This Adversary must be powerful already."

"That's my guess," Mac agreed. "As for Ari, her power isn't manifesting as it should, and that is a concern. She should be much farther along, now. Also, we may be needed to go on a rescue mission before Sunday."

"At Nico's request?"

"Yes."

"The pulling dreams are never comfortable."

"I have seen this before," Renault admitted. "I have also witnessed the refusal of help—and what came afterward."

"I remember you now," Mac dipped his head to Renault. "During the Basque witch trials."

"Yes. We lost the Custodian, who only used the stone to heal. He refused our warnings, De Lancre arrived and the Custodian was put to death, along with his trusted disciple."

"Holy men, as I recall," Mac sighed.

"Yes. They thought themselves safe enough. More would have died, had we not sent a rescue party."

"Who only rescued others like themselves," Mac shook his head. "They left many more behind to be tortured and killed."

"Sadly, that is also true. The *auto de fe* is a horrible thing to witness."

"I searched for two years before the next Custodian arrived," Mac noted. "Much had to be accomplished before the witch trials were ended in the area."

"It takes years to stop it completely," Claudio said. "Only to have it flare up again when the stone is between Custodians."

"One of my concerns is that the country is already experiencing instability and division," Mac pointed out. "This will only make things worse."

"My worry is that the *Unrepentant* will cross the sea."

"They send their human minions—I have never seen them cross before," Mac countered.

"The Custodian has never been given the stone in another country."

Mac closed his eyes for a moment as if this piece of information didn't sit well. He knew the Scholar was correct—before, in every case, the transfer had occurred on Spanish soil. Never had it traveled so far, and then been transferred to another afterward.

"This bears thinking about," he rolled his shoulders as if attempting to find a more comfortable way to accept what Claudio said.

"The stone came to the boy's mother, did it not? On Spanish soil. I feel she was pulled to stay there and was caught between it and her love of Nico and his father."

"Did she know, then, that she would pass the stone to Nico upon her arrival in Texas? He says she gave the stone to him shortly after her return."

"She is dead; we cannot question her."

"The boy is the youngest Custodian on record."

"I know that well. Ari is also the first woman chosen as a Protector. I hope this is a good sign."

"As do I, although I have doubts as to her suitability."

"Arianne is also the first chosen shapeshifter," Renault observed. "She may bring something new to that role."

Mac exchanged a glance with Claudio; it was obvious he also had doubts but didn't disagree aloud with Renault.

"You bought enough phones?" Claudio changed the subject. Ari and Nico were walking down the steps into the basement for the meeting.

"Yes. From three shops, so as not to appear suspicious," Mac said, turning to watch Nico and Ari enter the room.

"Please, sit," Claudio invited the new arrivals to make themselves comfortable. "Mac says you have news for us regarding events earlier."

"I doubt they got a good look at me; they were focused on Janie and Mac," Nico sighed as he flopped onto a chair. "Still, the Franks may recall that I was there, and someone out of the ordinary to be with Janie."

"Never a good thing," Claudio acknowledged. "Was there a confrontation?"

"Yes," Mac replied. "Denton Franks demanded that Janie give him her automobile insurance information, to pay for the damage to his truck on Jordan property. I made a counteroffer."

"What was the counteroffer?"

"That Denton write a check for the difference in the cost of the heifer his father killed, minus the amount to fix his truck. He wasn't pleased," Ari supplied.

"Ari was so pissed, I think she could have ripped both men apart with her bare hands," Nico mused.

"Did you join the conversation?" Claudio asked Ari.

"No. Janie told me she'd handle it. Turns out, Mac handled it."

"How do you feel about that?"

"Frustrated."

"I see."

"Are you pissed that I handled it?" Mac asked coolly, turning dark eyes in her direction.

"No. You did the best thing possible. It's just that every time I see either of those men, my blood boils."

"Understandable," Claudio dipped his head. "You did the right thing, by remaining silent."

"I'll try not to read too much misogyny into that statement," Ari snipped.

"There was none intended," Claudio sighed. "You have been wronged by one of those men, and now have his son to deal with as well. Protect yourself, Lady Lion. You know firsthand how dangerous humans can be to all of us in this room."

"I'm sorry I called you a misogynist," Ari mumbled.

"It is forgotten already," Claudio waved off her apology. "We must work together to combat what is coming. A division in the ranks will kill us all."

"Should we relocate, Master Scholar?" Alejandro asked.

"Not yet. I believe Nico has a mission for us."

"Yeah. We have to find Hunter Pace Jr. He's in danger."

"Are there time constraints?" Claudio asked.

"We have to get him away before Sunday," Nico replied. "After that, it will be too late."

"Burke Jordan knows where the boy is," Mac said. "We'll have that information soon enough. I suggest we go Saturday evening to warn the boy and his aunt."

"Will they believe us?" Renault asked.

"I sure hope so. This may be our first clash with the Adversary, and we need to stay out of his sight as long as possible. We're not ready, yet, as you are well aware."

CHAPTER NINE

"**I**s this the best copy you have?" Senator Cheatham spoke with Reverend Killebrew on his private cell phone.

"It's the best copy we could make of the original."

"Do you have the original?"

"I can get to it."

"I'd like to speak with the person who recorded it—might they be the same source?"

"Oh, yeah. I can arrange a meeting for sure. He may want a little cash, you understand."

"How about I buy it from him for a thousand. Will that do? I want full rights to it, so he'll have to sign a release."

"He'd do it for a hundred," Killebrew said.

"I'll offer a thousand—and no questions asked."

"Good enough. When can I get the two of you together?"

"Sunday morning service? I'd like to join the congregation for your sermon."

"Then we'll look forward to meeting you in person, Senator."

"See you Sunday, Reverend." Cheatham ended the call.

"You think the zombie thing has run its course?" Lance handed a coffee to Del Reeves, who sat at a borrowed desk at the precinct. "We haven't had a new attack in two days."

"I wouldn't bet on anything in this mess. Two days sounds like a reprieve, in my estimation," Del replied.

"Giving us enough time to get some paperwork done before the next round?" Lance sat heavily on a nearby chair.

"That's one way to look at it."

"There you are," Mona walked in with Laronda, each carrying a specialty coffee from a shop down the street.

"Croissant? We got enough for all of us." Laronda held up a paper bag.

"Don't mind if I do," Lance grinned.

"How's the kid doing?" Mona asked as she bit into her croissant.

"Janie says things are okay, but Nico may have been seen by the neighbors yesterday," Lance mumbled around a mouthful of food.

"How did that happen?" Del asked.

"Long story," Lance replied. "Turned into a bit of a mess. And, speaking of turning, we ought to go back to the ranch this afternoon."

"New development?" Laronda turned an inquisitive gaze on Lance.

"You could say that. I want to ask Mac a lot of questions."

"You're going to interrogate the bird?"

"In a manner of speaking. If you want to tag along, Janie says we're invited to dinner."

"Dinner sounds heavenly," Mona stuffed the last corner of her croissant into her mouth.

"Barring a new zombie attack, I'm in," Laronda agreed.

"Me, too," Del said.

"I'll let Janie know." Lance pulled the cell phone from his pocket to make the call.

~

"Renault said there was no activity from the Franks' house last night, and that the stench from the cattle shifted with the wind," Mac reported at breakfast.

"Lance, Mona and the feds are coming for dinner tonight," Janie told him. "Lance wants to talk to you."

"Of course he does."

"I think you should tell him about Hunter Jr." Ari sipped her coffee. "Just in case."

"There's an idea," Mac considered Ari's suggestion. "Janie, do you think Lance and Mona would go with us? It may be difficult convincing the boy and his aunt."

"You can ask—I have no idea what their answer may be," Janie told him.

"Even if they don't go, I think it's better that somebody with authority knows where we went, just in case," Ari explained.

"Not a bad idea. Val will go with you if you ask him. The boy should recognize his own kind, after all," Janie said.

"Good idea," Mac nodded at Janie. "I'll ask Val."

"The other thing is this—the full moon is Sunday night. I get the feeling the kid needs a pack around him this time," Nico spoke up.

"You think he's had to go out on his own?"

"For around two years," Nico nodded. "I've never been a fan of coffee, but it's growing on me now," he lifted his cup to Janie.

"Mary Kate makes the best," Janie grinned.

"I'm worried."

Hunter whirled to face his Aunt. He'd lived with her ever since his mother passed, two years after his father's death.

He barely remembered either of them and was still unclear about how, exactly, his father died.

His mother—nobody ever said it directly to him, but his sharp hearing had caught the word suicide on several occasions. He'd come into his heritage, or so Aunt Catherine called it, two years earlier.

He was a werewolf. Aunt Catherine homeschooled him and told

him many times that he should never be ashamed of what he was or who his parents were.

He felt isolated most of the time, and, upon occasion, understood completely the path his mother chose for herself.

"What are you worried about?" Hunter asked.

"Just—strange vibes," she shivered.

She shouldn't be shivering—not in this heat.

"The moon makes me feel troubled, and it shouldn't," she added. "I have a new wand set out to charge, and it needs positive energy. Right now, I feel exactly the opposite."

"What do you think it is?"

Hunter sat on the edge of the front porch, swinging his legs in the shade of a tall elm. Aunt Cathy sat on the porch swing nearby, looking worried.

The breeze lifted low-hanging elm branches, bringing a familiar scent to Hunter's sensitive nose. "Joe's on his way," he announced.

"I hope he knows what this is," Cathy hugged herself. "I hope he's read the cards and can tell me something."

Joe walked into view; Hunter could see him down the rutted, dirt road leading to Catherine Charles' rural home.

Joe spoke to spirits, according to Catherine, but he'd never spoken to Hunter about his parents. Joe also read tarot cards and was accurate in his readings—if they were interpreted properly, that is.

"Want iced tea?" Catherine stood and made the offer the moment Joe could hear her question.

"I'd take tea," he said and continued walking toward the porch.

The storm door slammed as Catherine went inside to get tea for Joe.

Hunter watched as Joe settled into the rocking chair near the front door, content to wait for the offered cold drink.

"Yard looks good," Joe said.

"Mowed and trimmed yesterday," Hunter replied.

"Went past Erly's place—he needs a machete to get to his car, looks like."

"Erly's not crazy about mowing. Or unannounced visitors—or

going to town. I think he's still eating off that deer I brought him six months ago."

"Meat and beans, that's Erly," Joe made himself more comfortable in the rocking chair.

"He just needs looking after, now and then."

"Hmmph," Joe rocked himself for a few seconds. Catherine returned with his tea, which he took and drank deeply.

"You need me for this conversation?" Hunter dropped off the porch.

"I doubt it," Catherine told him. "Why?"

"I'll go help Erly with his yard work." Hunter loped away before his aunt could stop him.

"He's bored silly," Catherine sighed as she watched Hunter travel down the driveway at a swift pace.

"He's why I came," Joe said. "I had an itch to read the cards this morning. I think he may be in some kind of danger. I think he ought to leave, Cath."

"And just where will he go?" Catherine demanded. "He's sixteen. He needs schooling, still, and because of what he is," she didn't finish.

"He needs to be with his own kind," Joe pointed out.

"I don't see a pack of wolves banging on the door, do you? What, exactly, did you see in that reading?"

"That he's in danger, and that danger will include us, if he stays."

"Right. Are you sure you interpreted the message correctly?"

"That's the best I can do for now."

"If I remember right, you didn't want to include him in the circle two years ago."

"I've changed my mind about that," Joe admitted.

"But now? You say he needs to leave? What am I supposed to think? That a year from now, after he's gone to who knows where, you'll say you were wrong again?"

"Catherine, I came to tell you what I saw in the reading. I can see you're not ready for any truth I can give you." Joe set his empty glass on the porch beside the rocking chair and rose to leave.

"How soon?" Catherine called after him as he stalked away from the house.

"Soon." Joe continued his journey with a half wave.

Catherine's landline rang, pulling her away from the porch. Muttering to herself, she went into the house to answer it.

"Hello?" she said.

"Catherine? This is Burke Jordan," came the reply. "I'm calling about Hunter."

Here was the pack of wolves she'd dismissed earlier. Years ago, when she took Hunter in as his closest kin, there were other offers.

Offers from his own kind, that she'd refused or ignored. After Joe's warning, she still didn't want to listen.

"Catherine? Are you still there?" Burke's voice broke her away from her thoughts.

"I'm here." She wiped a tear from her cheek and forced herself to listen carefully to Burke's words.

"Burke's done what he can," Janie said. "The rest is up to you," she told Mac. "He told Catherine Charles that he'd find a place for her, too, if she wanted to come along. He doesn't think she will."

"She's in danger, too," Nico shrugged. "All her neighbors are."

"Then you'll have to tell her that," Janie said.

"Lance and Mona are here with those FBI folks," Francine poked her head through the game room door. "Cars just pulled in."

"I'll be down in a minute," Janie said.

"We'll come with you—they have questions," Mac pulled Nico to his feet and followed Janie to the elevator.

"Is Ari downstairs?" Nico asked as they loaded into the small elevator and pressed the button to take them to the ground floor.

"She was in her bedroom when I came up," Janie replied as they traveled downward.

"Try to reach her," Mac suggested.

Nico closed his eyes while Janie watched, fascinated. "What is he doing?" Janie whispered to Mac.

"He and Ari should have a connection already. It's time to start testing whether she can hear him—telepathy, you'd call it."

"How is that possible?" Janie frowned. "Wait; never mind." She held up a hand to stave off the explanation—or the excuse for not providing one.

"Mac and I have been able to connect recently," Nico turned toward Janie. "Ari still can't hear me."

"I'll be honest," Janie said as the elevator came to a stop and the door opened. "Lately, I feel as if I'm living in an alternate reality."

Nico and Mac exchanged a glance before following Janie toward the front door.

"Ari, good to see you," Lance greeted her. "Val, thanks for inviting us," he nodded to his cousin, who stood beside Ari at the front door.

"Come on in," Val invited Lance and the others. "Dinner will be ready in a few. Would you like a drink beforehand? We have lemonade and a variety of the harder stuff."

"A drink sounds great," Del said, shaking hands with Val. "Thank you."

"This way, then." Val led them into the area to the left of the front door, where the wet bar stood at one end. Built with a western theme, the bar had ranch-related antiques on the walls and leather barstools lined up along its length.

"What will it be, then?" Val stepped behind the bar.

"I can help," Ari followed his lead.

"Scotch if you have it—on the rocks," Del requested.

"We have Johnny Walker, Glenlivet and Macallan," Val said. "Your choice."

"I'll take Glenlivet," Del said.

"Glass of wine?" Mona asked Ari.

"Red, white or blush?" Ari asked.

"What would you recommend?"

"Pinot noir, maybe. It's on the dry side, though. If you want something sweeter, Janie has some Moscato and some Riesling."

"I'll have the Pinot," Laronda said.

"I'll take some of that, too," Mona agreed.

"Lance wants an old fashioned, unless I'm badly mistaken," Val set a glass of Scotch in front of Del.

"You got it," Lance agreed. "Hard to find one better than what you make."

"Aren't you going to join us?" Mona asked Ari as she set two glasses of Pinot noir out for Mona and Laronda.

"No—I already feel like I'm losing my mind—alcohol would probably make it worse."

"Losing your mind in what way?" Mona sipped her wine and nodded. "Good choice," she told Laronda.

"I could have sworn I heard Nico's voice in my head, earlier, telling me to answer the front door. Weird, huh?"

"Can't argue with that, I suppose," Laronda said. "I've never heard anybody talking in my head except me."

"Lara," Del shortened her name in a familiar way, "there's no room in there for anybody else," he teased.

"Says the man who irons his boxers," Laronda teased back.

"My mother always told me to wear clean underwear in case I was in an accident," Del grinned. "*Neat and tidy* was her motto."

"She was an awesome woman," Laronda held up her glass to toast with Del.

"Yes, she was," Del agreed, clinking his glass against Laronda's. "She adored you."

"When did she pass?" Val asked quietly.

"About eighteen months ago. Sudden," Del shrugged. "She always said that's how she'd want it, so I guess she got her wish. Stunned the rest of us, though."

"I'm sorry for your loss," Ari poured a club soda for herself and added a slice of lime.

"There you are," Janie walked into the room, followed by Nico and Mac. "Want a drink?" she turned to ask both.

"I'll take a Coke with lime," Nico said.

"I'll have what this man is having," Mac nodded in Del's direction.

"I'll fix Nico's if you'll do the Scotch," Ari told Val.

"Coming right up," Val lifted the bottle of Scotch to pour into a glass.

"I hope you know how strange this sounds," Del told Nico over dinner. "It would be difficult for anyone to take your word on this, you know."

"Burke already called the boy's aunt," Val said. "Nico says she and her neighbors are also in danger, although I'm not sure why at this point."

"A young shifter in the middle of humans is never safe," Laronda observed. "I speak from experience when I say that, too."

"I agree with that part," Val gave her a brief nod. "The boy needs a pack around him at this age. There are things that he can only learn from being with a pack, because that's how wolves survive."

"Every shifter needs someone to watch their backs," Janie said. "A support system makes you safer. I've always felt far better when I'm on the ranch and know there are others of my kind around me."

"Laronda won't tell you, but she was an orphan," Del said. "Someone killed her parents on a full moon. Neighbors found her in the house the following day and, since they never found her human-looking parents, put her in foster care."

"I'm sorry," Ari turned toward Laronda. "That was horrible for you, I know."

"You've had a taste of the same thing," Laronda agreed. "It's one of the hardest things I've ever had to deal with."

"Do you remember them? Your parents?" Nico asked.

"I was four, so there's not a lot I do remember," Laronda sighed. "Dinner is excellent, Mrs. Jordan."

"Mary Kate has a way with lamb," Janie smiled.

"The chops and sauce are wonderful," Lance agreed.

"Back to the werewolf boy," Mac began. "Are any of you four interested in going with us to pick him up?"

"I'll go," Mona offered.

"I think the boy should have a chance to see that there are other shifters interested in his wellbeing," Laronda said. "I'll go with Mona."

"I'll go," Val offered. "With you, Nico and Ari with us, I think that should be enough, don't you?" Val spoke to Mac.

"More than enough, and I'm grateful for the offer," Mac acknowledged Val's, Mona's and Laronda's agreement.

"I'll need some time with the kid before the full moon, too," Val said. "To get him ready to run with the pack."

"Will this journey occur after dark?" Claudio floated into the kitchen, his feet barely touching the floor. Ari imagined it was only a formality—to appear as if he were walking to reassure the mortals in the room.

"I suppose it can," Val said. "Would you like to join us?"

"Yes, if you don't mind, although I've already fed."

"Please, sit," Val indicated an empty chair at the end of the long, formal table. "I wouldn't mind if you came with us Saturday evening."

"We'll need two cars," Nico said. "And we should let them know a crowd is coming."

"A crowd isn't a bad thing," Mac said as the table fell silent. "Just in case we need multiple witnesses later."

"Witnesses for what?" Mona frowned. Ari nodded at Mona's question—it was something she also wanted to know.

"In the past, people have been whisked away from harm, only to be accused of terrible crimes afterward," Mac replied, his eyes hooded.

He remembers things from the past, Nico's voice sounded in Ari's mind, making her jump.

Did she hear me? Ari heard Nico's voice again, only this time, Mac answered in her head.

I think she may have, Mac agreed, turning his full gaze on Ari.

Dear Jesus, make it stop, Ari begged mentally.

Mac's laughter exploded, startling the entire table.

✧

"You could have warned me," Ari accused as she glared at Nico and Mac. Dinner was over, Lance and the others had left the ranch and Janie and Val had gone to bed. Mac asked Ari for a few minutes of her time before she retired for the night.

The telepathy that they now shared was the topic for discussion.

"We didn't know if or when it would show up," Mac attempted to defuse the situation. "There have been some who didn't get it until much later, and a handful who didn't get it at all. Those weren't the best of times," he added.

"Does this mean you're going to be in my head all the time?" Ari demanded, feeling angry and betrayed.

"It's telepathy, not mind reading," Mac explained. "I can't read your thoughts, and I'm grateful you can't read mine I assure you. If I don't specifically send a message to you, you won't hear from me."

"Are there any more surprises coming?" Ari frowned at Mac.

"I've asked for discretion," Nico sighed. "You're displacing your anger, Ari. It should be aimed at me, not Mac."

"Right. This is exactly what I was afraid of. It's a boys' club, and the woman gets left out."

Before Mac could stop her, she'd turned swiftly and ran toward the door of the media room.

"That went well," Mac rumbled.

"I just—I just can't tell her some things. Not yet," Nico sighed.

"Because it would scare the hell out of her?" Mac crossed his arms as he studied Nico.

"I know what my nightmares are like," Nico responded. "I want to spare her as long as I can."

"She may or may not appreciate that in the long run," Mac pointed out.

"I know. I'll live with her being mad at me."

"She's mad at both of us; don't delude yourself."

"Yeah."

Hunter sat on Erly's porch, studying the neighbor he'd known for most of his life. Erly was the only black man living in the area—that Hunter knew of, anyway. He'd mowed and trimmed Erly's lawn during the day; darkness had fallen, he'd had supper with Aunt Catherine, then sneaked back to see Erly.

Fireflies winked in and out of the trees surrounding Erly's small cabin, bringing fairy tale settings to life around them.

"I've known for a while that you shift," Hunter said, breaking the silence.

"You think I didn't smell the wild on you after you shifted the first time?" Erly hmmphed at Hunter's statement. "I even know what kind of shifter you are. Can you say the same about me?"

"No." Hunter hung his head.

"Nothin' to be ashamed of," Erly said. "But it is somethin' you should learn. It's a good idea to be with your own kind—at least for a while. Catherine can't teach you the lessons another werewolf can."

"Will you tell me? What you are?"

"Not a lot of us left," Erly shook his head. "Kinfolk all dead, I believe."

"Tell me, in case I run across another, someday," Hunter wheedled.

"All right, but keep it to yourself. I'm a black jaguar, and those are rare in both natural and shifter forms. I've been mistaken for everything from a giant housecat to a *chupacabra*," Erly chuckled.

"Sounds like you're lucky to be alive."

"We're both lucky, in this day and time."

"Aunt Cathy refuses to come with me," Hunter's voice betrayed his loneliness.

"I'd come with you, if I could. It'd be nice to be surrounded by shifters for a change, where I didn't have to hide twice—once for being a shifter, and twice for being black."

"Are there black werewolves?" Hunter asked.

"Some," Erly replied. "Shifters are more accepting than other folk, most times."

"I'll ask if you can come, since Aunt Cathy is dead set against it," Hunter said. "Be nice to have a familiar face, you know?"

"I know what you mean," Erly agreed. "I'll pack a bag, just in case."

"I hope you don't have to unpack it until we get where we're going," Hunter told him. "I gotta go before Aunt Cathy starts looking for me."

"Take care of yourself, boy, in case I don't see you again."

"You do the same, Erly."

Hunter dropped off Erly's porch and made his way across the lawn, toward his aunt's house. He had no idea what the future held for him, and he wanted answers.

Ari felt out of sorts as she drank coffee in the kitchen on Saturday morning. She'd offered to help Mary Kate fix breakfast; Mary Kate told her to take a seat and have some caffeine.

"Ari," Janie walked in, her cell phone in her hand. "Lance wants to talk to you." She held the phone out so Ari could take it.

"Hello?" Ari said, holding the phone to her ear.

"Ari, there's been another outbreak of zombies in the Houston area," he reported. "That means Laronda and Del have to fly to Houston. I'm going with them this time, but Mona is still going with your bunch to get the boy."

"I think we'll be okay," Ari told him. "Val, Claudio and I should be enough protection—if it's needed."

"Mona will have a weapon with her if she needs one," Lance said. "I don't anticipate trouble, but it's always best to be prepared."

"You're right. Thanks for letting us know, Lance. I appreciate it."

"Take care, then, and we'll see you when we get back."

Ari handed the phone back to Janie after Lance ended the call. The pain flared between her shoulder blades again, as if in warning. She ignored it.

"I can't believe they're finding more of those creatures," Janie shoved the phone into a pocket of her jeans. "Val and I were hoping that part had run its course. Oh, there's something else. Last night, Renault sent a text to Val, with some pictures he took of the Franks hauling dead cattle off the property. Renault says he could smell the disease in them as they were loaded. He said he recognized it. I called Lance this morning—Del offered to get the Department of Agriculture involved and go around the worthless Sheriff we have. Val's moving our herd to the east side of the ranch as of this morning."

"What disease?" Ari asked, although she was afraid of the answer.

"FMD," Janie said. "You probably know it by Foot and Mouth disease."

"And with all those cattle penned up in small spaces," Ari sounded grim.

"Yep. The best way is to put all of them down and clean every bit of equipment, clear out stored food supplies and get rid of any rodents in the area. If Franks thinks he'll go ahead and get the live ones to market, well, the authorities should be on their way now."

"This could hurt your business," Ari began.

"This could hurt the entire cattle industry in Texas," she huffed. "Exports could be shut down, too, and that will cripple the state's, if not the country's, beef supply."

"Idiots," Ari growled.

"We'll have to wait this out, and have our herd checked for the disease," Janie said. "Clueless assholes."

"What happened?" Nico walked into the kitchen, with Mac close behind.

"Foot and Mouth, more zombies, only Mona tonight," Ari counted off the latest.

"Ari's still pissed," Nico turned toward Mac.

"I get that." Mac moved around the island to get coffee.

"I think I liked the raven better," Ari grumped.

"I can turn freely, now, and only when I want," Mac leveled a hooded stare in her direction. "It's easier to communicate like this, and I can hold my own coffee mug."

"I'm not asking you to change." Ari turned her head away from his uncomfortable gaze. *You're asking* me *to change, without warning me of what's coming*, she snapped mentally.

That—is true. My apologies.

Right. Apologies not accepted.

We are *in a bad mood today.*

The full moon is coming. Most shifters are in a bad mood. I call it PMSS—pre-moon-shift-syndrome. The males get it too. You're welcome.

Janie looked from Ari to Mac and then back to Ari. "I hope Mona and the vamps can keep you two from killing each other tonight." She thumped her coffee cup on the island and stalked out of the kitchen.

CHAPTER TEN

"Haven't been on a military plane since I left the military," Lance said as he, Del and Laronda walked across the tarmac to climb aboard the C-12 Huron waiting for them.

"I hate prop planes," Laronda complained, hefting her overnight carryall onto a shoulder.

"It's a short flight," Del said, reaching the bottom step first.

"Short and bumpy, guaranteed," Laronda followed him up the metal steps. "And after this, no doubt we'll board a small coast guard cutter to take us to the yacht in question."

"How did they get infected? Do you know?" Lance ducked his head to step onto the aircraft, going from bright sunlight into the dim, cooler interior of the plane.

"We don't have that information, yet. We're still trying to track all stops on their logs."

"You think they made some not-so-official stops?" Lance slid into a seat across the aisle from Del's. Laronda chose the seat in front of Lance's so she could easily talk to both men.

"It's possible. There's one theory that they may have been in contact with one of the tankers that showed up outside Corpus Christi."

"Offloading drugs?" Lance asked.

"That's part of the theory, yes. They found cocaine aboard the yacht, so they're waiting for our arrival before removing anything— except for the catatonic zombies."

"Who called it in?"

"Fishermen. The boat wasn't moving, so they trawled close to it and saw two bodies lying on the deck."

"Have heads been removed?"

"That's in the works, if it hasn't happened already."

"Six bodies on the boat; all of them in the same shape," Laronda turned in her seat to speak with Lance. "We're working on IDs, too, but if they're from Mexico or points south, that may not be easy to do."

"Laronda and I think they may have dropped anchor, waiting for another mode of transport for the drugs, then succumbed while they waited. If somebody else did show up and they boarded the boat before getting the hell away from there," Del shook his head as he left his thoughts hanging.

"Then we may have others infected. Is forensics examining the boat?"

"They've combed every inch of it and took samples and fingerprints. That's how they know the bodies were infected."

"We'll go onboard in haz-mat suits, just like they did," Laronda said. "Don't need to take chances with this shit."

"Too damn contagious," Lance agreed. "Sure would like to know what it is and where it came from. Since no official announcements have been released, Dallas media is speculating that all this suspicious activity could be anything from a government experiment gone wrong to an attack by a hostile foreign faction to a virus from aliens—the outer-space type."

"I'm guessing that last one's from the stations that don't fact check their reports," Laronda sighed.

"You guessed right."

"Buckle up, we'll be taking off soon," the co-pilot informed the plane's three passengers. "ETA is fourteen hundred."

"What's it like—this close to the full moon?" Nico asked as Ari shifted in her chair and sighed for perhaps the twentieth time.

"Skin feels wrong," Mac replied when Ari appeared unwilling to answer the question. "Itchy. You just want to become—your other self. It's not comfortable."

"Feds showed up at the Franks' ranch," Janie walked into the game room upstairs. "I hope they get that mess sorted out."

"You feel the same?" Nico asked her. "Mac says that Ari wants to shift; it's why she keeps moving restlessly and sighing."

"It's the same for all of us, and the day before, the day of, and the day after a full moon isn't the best time to ask personal questions," Janie told him.

"Oh. Okay."

"I know you're curious. Practice patience. We'll answer your questions next week."

"Good enough," Mac gave Nico a pointed look. "Next week it is."

"Sundown is at eight-forty-nine tonight—I think we can leave at nine or shortly after," Janie said, changing the subject. "We'll need Mona and Claudio's assistance, since the boy's a shifter, too, and will be as itchy as we are."

"Are we prepared to take on additional passengers, if his aunt changes her mind?"

"We are. Burke is bringing his van and will meet us there. We'll be able to carry several away if it's necessary."

"Good." Nico shifted in his overstuffed chair. "They're all in trouble—everybody who lives around Hunter and knows what he is."

"More people than just his aunt knows?" Janie asked, her voice sharp as she stared at Nico. "You're just now telling us that?"

"Yeah." Nico made himself smaller in his seat.

"Then I'm really glad the vamps are coming. I dislike walking into what could turn into a massacre. We keep this secret for a reason. That child has placed himself and us in mortal peril." Janie, clearly angry, stalked out of the room.

"But we're in mortal peril anyway, aren't we?" Ari rose from her chair and followed Janie's path out of the media room.

"I told you they're hypersensitive around the full moon," Mac sighed. "Back in the day, shifters of all kinds would disappear for at least three days and go back to the wild just to feel more comfortable. Nowadays, they can't vanish—it would draw too much attention."

"Sounds like a tough life to live."

"It is and always has been—in this universe of existence."

"I should have realized that."

"You're still learning. Give it time."

"Were you there—during the uh, *event*?"

"No. I was born a few centuries later. Cursed not long afterward."

"You're not going to tell me, are you?"

"Not if I can help it. I warn you—it has never appeared in anyone's dreams, either, because it's not relevant."

"Look at you, being all private and stuff."

"I deserve the privacy, kid. Just like you do."

"And Hunter doesn't understand how private he should have been."

"I believe it's his aunt who owns that faux pas. She should have taught him better and she didn't. She's placed his life in danger, probably without realizing that even your best friend can let something like that slip. Humans tend to misunderstand these things."

"I guess that's why Janie's worried about a massacre."

"With the myths and legends about werewolves, not to mention books, television shows and movies freely available to spread misinformation, most people will shoot first and ask questions later. Not that shifters wouldn't be a danger to humans, if their lives are threatened," Mac qualified his statement. "Human meat is still meat, but it brings too much trouble with it. Easier to feed off deer, rabbits and other wildlife that nobody else will miss or send out a hunting party to find. Humans have developed weapons to kill shifters from a distance."

"Like Ari's father."

"Yes. It's safer for shifters to blend in with the human population; it ensures that they're able to survive in places with shrinking wild country, although a few reside in large cities. They prefer more open spaces if they can afford it, or suburbs if they can't."

"Is it weird that Janie's family raises cattle?"

"You'd be surprised at how many shifters raise meat animals," Mac replied. "I once knew a fox shifter who owned a poultry farm in Spain."

"Irony," Nico snorted a laugh.

"He liked his chickens more than he liked people, and not necessarily in the culinary sense," Mac grinned. "Had a clever sense of humor, that one."

"Aren't foxes known for that?"

"That's the rumor I've always heard."

"Mona, thank you for volunteering to go with Val and the others," Janie told her. "Take a seat. Ari and I are having an afternoon snack."

Mona nodded to Ari and took a seat near hers. Janie set a fresh cup of coffee at her elbow, then joined them at the kitchen island.

"What's the latest on the Franks' cattle?"

"Word is they'll have to be destroyed—they're all infected from being packed so close together."

"Idiots," Mona echoed Ari's critique of Janie's neighbors. "Is that gun-happy old man going to do the honors?"

"I don't know what the plan is," Janie sighed, staring out the kitchen window toward the back yard. "I just want it to stay away from our side of the fence."

"Will you have some of the hands guarding the fence tonight, while Val and the vamps are out?"

"He's already made arrangements," Janie nodded, holding her coffee mug in both hands to sip its contents.

"Good. Every time I think of those people, I get the willies."

"I just feel soul-burning anger," Ari muttered.

"I'm pissed and worried at the same time," Janie admitted. "If they cost us our herd, you can bet Burke will get involved and a lawsuit will be filed. There's an attorney in his firm that specializes in this sort of thing."

"You think the Franks have insurance?" Mona asked. "I doubt they have enough money in the bank to handle a loss like this."

"I have no idea. They sure weren't spending money on ranch hands to tend their cattle properly. They have plenty of land—they just didn't want to travel more than a few hundred yards to feed and water any of them. Val says their windmills aren't working and the ponds are mostly dried up. Penning the animals was Denton's way of dealing with the situation, instead of looking for somebody to do repairs or dig new wells."

"You're saying those animals have stood in slop and feces, packed in like sardines?" Ari growled.

"Yes. We probably should have asked the Feds or an animal rights group to check the place before now, but we didn't want to get any closer to them than necessary," Janie made a wry face. "Calling the Sheriff and the county was a waste of time. Neither Val nor I have any sympathy for the men in that family."

"I've never met Denton's wife, but I have only anger and condemnation for Mitchell and Denton." Ari's hand shook as she lifted her coffee mug to drink.

"Ari, if you'd like to change for a while," Janie offered.

"Thank you. Will it upset you?" She pointed her question at Mona.

"Not unless I'm on the menu."

"You're not. I'm not hungry—just mad, and you'd never be on the menu anyway."

"Then we're good." Mona sipped coffee.

"I'll be back in a few," Ari said and walked out of the kitchen.

"Mac, we may have trouble," Nico called out from his chair by the window. "It looks like the neighbor's truck just pulled into the driveway."

"What the hell?" Mac reached the game room window in three long strides, pulling back the curtain to see the truck parked in the drive. It still bore the damage that Ari had done to it only a few days earlier.

"We should probably get down there," Mac let the curtain fall before turning and heading for the door and the stairs beyond.

Nico rose and hurried to follow, clattering down the stairs in Mac's hurried wake. He nearly slid off the bottom step when Mac shouted—*at Ari's mountain lion.*

Her tail-tip curving and whipping in anger, Nico could see she was more than agitated as he held onto the bottom newel post to regain his balance.

"Arianne, I don't need to tell you what kind of trouble this will bring if you go to the door," Mac lectured.

Ari growled, her tail whipping faster after the scolding.

"Janie and I will handle this," Mac snapped, before stalking toward the front door.

"Ari, you need to stay back here," Nico hissed at her. "Janie doesn't need them accusing her of having a wild animal in her home."

"Grrrr-owlllll," Ari argued, the sound deep in her throat as she bared large, sharp teeth at Nico. Nico's eyes widened in shock. Ari turned away after seeing her friend become fearful. With tail still curling in anger, she padded toward the hallway where her bedroom lay. *Bite them if they upset Janie,* Ari instructed Nico. *Claw them if they try to come in the house.*

I'll leave that to Mac, Nico replied, his sending shaky. *I hear his kind like eyeballs.*

Sounds great. Tell him to do that with my blessings.

I'll—be sure to let him know.

"What do you want, Denton?" Mac watched as Janie crossed arms tightly over her chest. He could feel the waves of anger coming off her; her wolf wanted out to tear into this idiot human, who had no clue how close to death he could actually be.

"I know it was you who called the feds," Denton snapped. "We're gonna lose all our cattle because of it."

"You think you could pass those steers and yearlings off as healthy at a cattle auction?" Janie huffed. "You're pretend ranchers, you know that? You and that joke masquerading as your father. You're lucky nobody was following the trail of dead cattle you've been hauling out of here at night. Did you think the auction service wouldn't notice sick animals when they came out to video your livestock for sale? Or, were you hoping you could pay a bribe or two and get past that?"

Denton's mouth hung open in shock. "I think you hit the nail square on the head," Mac told Janie as he gently pulled her out of the way. "I believe you'll be hearing from the Jordan's attorneys regarding compensation, should any of their herd become infected," Mac told Denton, as he took a step toward the other man. "And we'll certainly pass on information that a bribe may have been offered. My suggestion is that you don't make this worse by overstaying your welcome here today."

"This isn't over," Denton pointed a finger at Mac as he backed away from the door.

"Of course it isn't—how long before you lose the property, Franks?" Mac demanded.

"Shut the hell up. You'll be sorry for this, I promise you," Denton shouted as he jerked his truck door open and climbed in.

Denton slammed the truck door. The rearview mirror, barely hanging on after Ari damaged it, dropped with a crash of metal and broken glass onto the concrete driveway.

"Idiot," Janie snapped as Denton put the truck in gear and squealed away.

"Is it too much to hope his transmission falls out going over the cattleguard at that speed?" Mac mused.

"He'll just blame us for that, too," Janie snapped. "Shut the door. I need a drink."

Ari, still in mountain lion form, paced and growled inside her bedroom. Every time she thought of Janie, the pain formed between her shoulder blades.

Was Janie in danger? She was planning to stay at the ranch while Val went with the others to find Hunter Pace.

Ari growled low, until she envisioned Janie going with Val while she stayed at the ranch. The pain between her shoulders faded.

Janie needs to go with Val tonight, Ari sent to Nico. *If she doesn't, I think she'll be in danger here.*

Why do you think that? Mac entered the conversation.

Because of the pain I get when I think of her staying here. I should stay here instead. You're an asshole, by the way.

Because I kept you from making a fool of yourself again?

My assessment still stands, whether I make a fool of myself or not.

Look, I understand that the full moon is close. Just—keep your wits about you if you stay here tonight.

Fine.

Maybe Renault should stay here, too, Nico pointed out.

Well, it couldn't hurt, Mac agreed.

You don't trust me, do you? Anger was evident in Ari's mental voice.

So far, we haven't seen much restraint, Mac's sending was dry.

You can fuck right off, Mac Flynn.

We shouldn't be fighting amongst ourselves, Nico warned. *It will give the Adversary an advantage he shouldn't have.*

Right now, the Adversary is Denton and Mitchell Franks.

The real one will arrive soon enough—he's already out there, Ari, Mac retorted. *While I understand this is all strange and new to you, I've been fighting this same battle for centuries.*

Just—leave me alone, all right?

We'll leave you alone for now, Nico ended the mental argument.

Mac hated how guilty he felt every time he argued with Ari. *Can't be because you have you have an ulterior motive for shoving her away from Nico—and from you, too*, the small voice reminded him.

Shut up, he told himself and followed Janie to the bar for a drink.

"Will you be okay if we ah, have to stay through the full moon?" Lance asked Laronda quietly as they boarded the stranded yacht.

"We'll make arrangements if we have to," she replied. "This isn't our first rodeo, and probably won't be our last."

"All right. If you need help or a guard or something," he said, stepping across the deck where the evidence markers lay. They'd dressed in haz-mat suits before boarding and doubled up on the gloves required.

"How long were they dead on the deck?" Lance squatted next to Del, who studied the outlines of body-shaped red slime on the surface.

"Not sure," Del replied. "So far, this is the first time we've seen anything like this."

"You think it's because they were in direct sunlight?"

"I can't even speculate about that," Del grunted as he rose from his crouched position.

"Got a report," Laronda handed her phone to Del.

"Looks like somebody had the same thought," Del passed the phone to Lance, who'd also risen to his feet. "They exposed one of the bodies found on the deck to a sunlamp—looks like the body is turning to red jelly."

"That's—sick," Lance thumbed through the text and images on Laronda's phone. "Do you think the sunlight is neutralizing the disease —or making it easier to spread around?"

"They're still working on that," Laronda replied. Lance handed her phone back with a nod.

"Ready to go below deck?" Del asked.

"I thought you'd never ask," Laronda sniped sarcastically.

"Can you send that information to Mona?" Lance asked as they made their way toward the steps. "Maybe she'll see something we don't."

"I can do that." Laronda tapped on the cell phone for a few moments before Lance heard the swooshing sound of a message sent.

"You got good reception out here—my phone may as well be dead," Lance told her.

"We have good reception in a lot of places," Laronda offered a tight smile. "Come on, let's go see if the former residents left anything behind that will help us out, here."

~

"Gone native?" Val asked as Ari's big cat walked past him on his way to the kitchen.

A tail twitch was her only reply.

"Wish I could do the same," he called out after her. "I've been itchy and out of sorts all day."

"Because Denton Franks decided to pay us a visit," Janie greeted him in the kitchen. "No, she didn't get involved—Mac and I handled the fool and sent him packing. Val, I think he may have paid a bribe to get those cattle sold at auction," she added.

"I'll mention that to the USDA agent. They're pretty pissed about this. Wish we'd known it sooner."

"You have Renault to thank for finding it when he did."

"What do you buy a vampire who has everything? As a thank you?" Val mumbled as he lifted a stack of mail off the counter and leafed through it.

"The vet has the bullet that killed our heifer—pulled it out during the autopsy. He's waiting for the Sheriff to pick it up," Janie said.

"Clint McCullough is famous for losing evidence and turning a blind eye," Val grumped as he dropped the stack of mail back on the counter. "Appears to be letting his son run wild—I heard the kid was picked up with two other students at their high school for destruction of school property. All three were released afterward, without even a slap on the wrist."

"No surprise there," Janie sniffed. "The vet sent pictures and as much information as he could in an email. I think he expects the bullet to get lost, too."

"He's had dealings with Clint before. No idea how the man keeps getting elected."

"I do. He pays and then takes kickbacks," Janie said. "Any election is for sale, if you have enough money."

"True enough. What's this I hear about you coming with us tonight?"

"Ari and Nico think I should. Ari will stay here, and I hope Renault stays with her—in case Denton or Mitchell want revenge of some kind."

"The Franks better stay on their side of the fence," Val growled. "Penning up our herd on the east side wasn't easy, and that grass wasn't ready for them to graze again this soon. We're just now getting hay baled in the northwestern fields—we need that for the winter months."

"They had no idea what they were doing, and they've not only killed their herd because of it, they've put ours in danger, too. I asked Mary Kate to cook chicken fried steak for us tonight—may as well have our favorite meal—it's the only thing that could go well on this day."

"Have you heard anything from Lance?"

"Laronda sent some pics of red gunk left behind after zombies were left in direct sunlight. I have no idea what they walked into with this new breakout. Laronda will need someplace to change tomorrow night. I hope she's able to find a safe place if they have to stay through the full moon."

"I'm sure she's dealt with this before, and her partner is used to it—he said so."

"I hope the vamps have taken care of—you know."

"Claudio did it himself—nobody in that group will reveal what or where we are, Mom."

"Good. I should have known you'd take care of things."

"Do I have time to clean up before dinner's ready?"

"If you can do it in fifteen."

"I'm heading for the shower now."

"I'm not upset that they're leaving me here," Renault assured Ari. She'd changed back to eat dinner with the others; now, she and Renault watched as Janie's SUV and Burke's van drove toward the ranch entrance. "Alejandro and Claudio can deal with this easily enough."

"I hope Nico can make the boy feel safe enough leaving his aunt—if meeting other werewolves doesn't convince him of that."

"Once he scents them, I think it will go smoothly," Renault reassured her. "Now, it is time for me to walk the fence between this ranch and the neighbors', eh?"

"I'll keep my phone with me in case there's trouble," Ari told him.

"I don't expect trouble—the visit earlier was only bravado and idiocy wrapped together," Renault said. "Nevertheless, I will let you know if anything out of the ordinary occurs. I also believe that Val's wolves will be placed strategically between the divider fence and the house."

"Barbed wire is a good idea—until it isn't," Ari shook her head. "I'd go with you tonight, but."

"It is too dangerous," Renault agreed. "Rest assured, I will only notify you if things have gone beyond my talent to rectify."

"Renault," Ari placed a hand on his arm as a familiar pain struck between her shoulders. "Don't wait. If something doesn't look right, send the message fast."

"If you insist." Renault surprised her by patting her hand, rather than removing it. Most vamps didn't like being touched unless they invited it, and Ari hadn't realized it until she'd already done just that.

"Stay safe," Ari called out as Renault faded quickly into the darkness. Then, pulling the front door shut, she bolted it, patted the phone in the pocket of her jeans to make sure it was there, and went to find a book to read in Janie's library.

"Swindall is a wide place in the road between Comanche and Blanket, north of Highway 377," Val explained to Claudio, who sat in the front passenger seat. Janie had chosen to sit in the back while Mac, Nico and

Alejandro rode in Burke's van, which traveled the road in front of them.

"I take it the boy's home is in a rural area?" Claudio asked.

"Very, according to Burke. He says it's confusing, unless you're a local—or a wolf."

"Some choose a rural life for that very reason," Claudio agreed.

"I don't know about your kind, but my kind definitely prefer a rural existence," Val responded.

"As do many of mine, although they are always near a post office or mail facility. We must eat, you know."

"We do, too," Janie spoke from the back seat. "There are many of us who raise meat animals—it's insurance against lean times, if they come."

"A wise decision."

"You're worried about what's coming, aren't you?" Val gripped the steering wheel tightly for a moment.

"Yes. It will become much worse before it gets better. In all the knowledge that I have gathered, these—zombie-like creatures have only appeared once before, and then only for a short time. This is not a good omen, my friend."

"When did this happen?" Mona asked. She'd chosen to sit in the back seat with Janie on the trip to Swindall.

"Most recently in the seventeenth and eighteenth centuries. For now, these creatures are being beheaded to keep them from becoming —something worse."

"Something worse? What could possibly be worse?" Mona breathed.

"Ghouls are what we call them—demon-like beings that feast on living and dead flesh. They can become monstrous, true demons, if they are not stopped," Claudio replied. "I feel you should know this, should any zombie escape notice long enough to evolve."

"*How* do you know this?"

"Vampires were instrumental in destroying the ghoul outbreak last time. We also took a handful of those still active—for the scholars to study. I did not witness these changes personally; I am not old enough.

The eldest of us did witness the evolution. These creatures were very difficult to kill, once they reached demon status."

"Do you think some of them may have escaped capture this time?" Janie's voice betrayed worry and concern.

"Undoubtedly. Too many bodies have not been accounted for. Vampires are searching diligently to find them before it is too late. If even one escapes capture, the resulting damage and death can be —catastrophic."

"Are those vampires keeping in touch with you—to let you know if they find any?" Val asked.

"Yes. So far, only a handful of the ghouls are accounted for, and that is most concerning. There is something else you should know, too."

"What's that?"

"These—demons—will answer to a single master. That master is now among us; we knew it when the raven became a man. Soon enough, the human Adversary will make his presence known, although his identity may remain a mystery. It is our task to help Nico, Mac and Ari find him or her before the world changes."

"Changes? In what way, other than the dead coming back to life?"

"You have heard enough for tonight," Claudio cautioned. "When the full moon has come and gone, I will tell you more."

"This place really is hidden," Nico observed as they traveled along a driveway consisting of two dirt strips with mowed grass in-between.

"I suggested that she move away from Waco, for the boy's safety," Burke explained. "The farther away from larger cities, the better, since she's a half-blood and doesn't really know how to teach a young wolf."

"That must be hard for him—not knowing," Nico leaned his head against the headrest with a sigh.

"Not too different from you in that respect," Mac reached in from the backseat to pat Nico's arm.

"Yeah. Nightmares are cruel teachers," Nico agreed. Burke glanced quickly in Nico's direction before pulling to a stop outside a small cabin with a wide front porch. A single, uncovered bulb served as a porch light, illuminating the space surrounding the front door.

"I'll get out first," Burke held up a hand as Nico reached for the door handle. "I know Catherine, and she knows me." He shut the driver's side door and walked toward the cabin.

"The others just pulled in behind us," Mac announced after turning in his seat to look.

"That must be Hunter's aunt," Nico said as a woman opened the front door before Burke could mount the porch steps and knock.

"Those are custody papers," Mac explained as Burke pulled folded papers from his suit coat. "Hunter's aunt will have to sign those before he comes with us. Keep your fingers crossed that she does just that."

"Claudio says no coercion in this," Alejandro agreed. "We will place an order for her not to reveal where Hunter is without Burke's approval."

"Is Burke his guardian if she signs?" Nico asked.

"That's right. He offered years ago, with the idea of leaving him with Val and Janie," Mac replied. "Val told me about it. It's how Janie knew to contact Burke after you saw Hunter in your dreams."

"He's offering her a pen," Nico sounded breathless.

"She's signing," Mac's shoulders slumped in relief. "I think we can get out of the car, now."

Val, Janie, Mona and Claudio stepped out of Janie's SUV at the same moment Mac, Alejandro and Nico climbed from Burke's van.

That's when Hunter made his presence known. Even Nico heard the audible, indrawn breath; Hunter recognized Burke's scent immediately. What none of them expected was what the boy did next; he begged Burke to allow him to bring a friend with him—someone named Erly Graham.

∼

"There is activity next to one of the Franks' cattle pens," Renault reported. "I hear cattle lowing—and sounds of moving hooves over firmer ground."

"What the," Ari felt a sharp pain between her shoulders as Renault spoke to her over her cell phone. "Renault—I think they're trying to stampede the cattle," Ari's breath caught as the vision hit her. "Get the wolves out of the way—hurry."

Shoving the phone back in a pocket, Ari raced for the back door. The house stood on a knoll of higher ground—she could see better from the vantage point of the eight-foot wall surrounding the backyard.

With a leap that betrayed her shifter heritage, Ari landed atop it, balancing perfectly as she rose to her full height to listen and sniff the wind.

Renault was correct—the sound of cattle pounding on solid ground came to her only a moment before the scent of diseased animals reached her nose. Shots rang out in the distance.

Get out of the way, she shouted at Renault and any wolves still standing their ground. *They're being stampeded deliberately. The cattle have broken through their enclosures and are heading for the fence.*

Ari had no hope that any of them would hear her, but there was little else she could do to warn them as the pain in her shoulders intensified.

Then, against all expectations, a bright light appeared in the hand where the shell shape had been embedded.

It spoke to her.

Showed her.

"Now," she shrieked, blasting a light so intense it crackled like lightning.

The subsequent boom echoed a strike so powerful it rocked the wall she stood upon. Just west of the separating fence on the Franks' property, a wide crack in the earth split open.

The stampeding cattle, urged on by gunshots behind them, tumbled into the depths of a deep crevasse that hadn't been there only seconds before.

An aftershock hit; Ari leapt to the ground on the outside of the wall, hoping that she hadn't killed anything other than a cattle herd doomed to die anyway.

Only then did she realize her cell phone was ringing in her pocket. Renault was calling. "Renault?" Ari held the phone to her ear.

"Arianne—I've—been shot."

CHAPTER ELEVEN

*A*ri didn't know the werewolf ranch hand who helped her get Renault back to the house, but she thanked him just the same.

"Want help?" he asked as she settled Renault onto a kitchen chair and ran to get a towel. Renault's head wound was bleeding sluggishly; the bullet had entered his forehead just above his left eye. Ari was terrified he'd die.

"Just stay with us and call Val, if you don't mind," Ari told the man as she placed the towel over Renault's wound. "Here's my phone," she handed her cell phone to the man who dialed quickly.

"Renault," Ari said, "Please tell me you're alive."

"Bullet—must be removed—soon."

"Val, this is Henry," the ranch hand spoke on the phone. "The Franks spooked their own cattle and stampeded them our way. Renault got hit with one of their bullets. We don't know if he's going to make it —the bullet is in his brain, and there's no exit wound. He needs help. How far away are you?"

"He's an hour away," Henry told Ari after listening to Val's reply.

"Too long," Renault mumbled.

"Renault, we won't let you go, all right?" Ari told him. "Henry—I have to try something. Don't be shocked, and stay on the phone with Val, just in case."

"I'll stay on the phone," Henry nodded. "You hear that, boss?"

"I heard it." Val's voice was clear to Ari's sensitive ears.

"All right," Ari set the towel aside and gripped Renault's hands in one of hers. Lifting the palm with the shell image on it, she held it inches above Renault's wound. "Come on—you can do this," Ari gritted her teeth as light emanated from the shell indention.

Renault's eyes opened wide as the light grew brighter—until it was so bright he had to close them in self-defense.

Henry yelped when the slug and several fragments slapped into Ari's palm with a solid thwack.

"What happened? Tell me," Val shouted on the other end of the call.

"I uh, think the bullet's out, boss," Henry replied as Ari slid down Renault's chair and thumped onto the kitchen floor, exhausted.

"Towel?" Renault blinked at Henry, who only hesitated for a moment before grabbing the towel off the island and pressing it to the wound.

"I should heal, now that the bullet is removed. Arianne, are you all right?" Renault tried to move his head. Henry barked at the vampire to stay still.

"I'll be okay. I've been better," Ari replied.

"That's a big ravine on Franks' property," another werewolf ranch hand walked into the kitchen. "Reckon it was an earthquake?"

"Boss? Kev's here. Want to talk to him?" Henry spoke into the phone. "Here." Henry handed the phone to Kev.

"They're all right I think," Kevin studied Renault and Ari. "She's holding a bullet slug in her hand, if that means anything. Yeah—we'll stick with the earthquake theory if anybody asks. At least the split ain't on our property. Yeah—I'd say it's at least thirty feet wide, forty feet deep and runs the length of the property. Right now, it's full of dead cattle."

❧

Mac listened shamelessly as Burke spoke with Janie on his cell phone. Nico told him mentally that Ari had used her talent in some way, but so far all he'd understood was that the Franks had stampeded their own cattle in the direction of the Jordan Ranch. Somehow, Ari kept them from breaking through the barbed wire fence.

In the chaos, Renault had been shot by one of the Franks, and Ari was attempting to help him.

Mac turned in his seat; in the third row of Burke's van, Hunter Pace and Erly Graham sat, silent and listening carefully to Burke's conversation with Val's mother, Janie. Val was on the phone with one of his werewolf ranch hands, who was at the house with Ari and Renault.

"If the bullet and fragments are out, Renault should be fine," Alejandro thought to console Nico, who appeared upset.

How much power do you think she had? Nico sent to Mac.

I don't know, but it must have deflected the cattle somehow—nobody's died yet, if Burke is correct.

I guess we won't know for sure until we get back.

Stop worrying. She'll either have enough or not. If you're forced to choose again, what she has will disappear, along with the shell indention. She can go back to her life. Maybe it's for the best. Besides, she still won't be at full power for a while, yet. We'll see what she has, how she handled this, and go from there.

I'd feel better if Ari was with me the whole way, Nico grumbled.

We need a solid team; you know that. Name calling and arguing back and forth won't make that happen. I thought she'd be a good fit at the beginning, but that was before she did stupid stuff. We may find more of the same when we get back.

Then we'll look at what she did and decide soon.

Good.

"Unless they drive around and come through the gate to the house, they're not getting across that ravine," Ari stood beside Henry as they watched the flashing lights of emergency vehicles at the Franks Ranch from the top floor of the house.

"I'd give a lot to know what they're talking about," Henry said. "I'm sure it'll be on the news soon enough. I wouldn't know where to begin to describe what happened, other than calling it a simultaneous lightning strike and earthquake, so I'd just as soon they stay on that side."

"I figure somebody will be pissed when they get home and find out about it," Ari grimaced.

"It's not on our side, and I sure as hell don't have a problem with it. If that diseased herd had gotten anywhere near ours, might be hell to pay."

"I hope Val and Janie get back before they come over here, then. I don't want to talk to anybody about this."

"What did you see? Anything?" Henry turned toward her.

He doesn't know, Ari blinked at him. *Renault may be the only one who knows what I did.* "Just a flash of lightning—and then the sound of the ground splitting and cattle running."

"I'd say we saw a miracle tonight, then," Henry squared his shoulders. "Coulda been a lot worse. I think I'll have a cup of coffee in the kitchen while we wait for Val to get back."

"Yeah. I'll be down in a few," Ari told him.

Henry took the stairs; she heard his footfalls on the treads as he made his way down. Ari refocused on the emergency vehicle lights she could see in the distance. *Mac will be pissed for sure*, she sighed and hugged herself. At least Renault had allowed Henry to carry him to the basement after she'd removed the bullet; he said he wanted dark and quiet to recuperate.

She'd put the bullet and fragments in a plastic bag, labeled it and left it on the kitchen island for Val to find.

You have to talk to them, she derided herself. *You have to explain what happened, even if it does piss Mac off.*

Who am I kidding? Everything *pisses Mac off. He wasn't like that when he was a bird. What happened?*

~

"Nice," Erly walked into the kitchen with Nico and the others, taking in the size of the house and all its amenities.

"Take a seat," Janie invited as he and Hunter stopped at the island. "We'll find drinks and snacks if you want them."

"Kev, Henry, will you come to my study?" Val asked both men, who rose as he entered the room.

"Sure thing, boss," Kev nodded.

"Where are Ari and Renault?" Claudio asked as the men headed for the door.

"Renault is in the basement—don't worry, once Ari got the bullet out, he seemed to be fine. Ari's upstairs, watching the media circus next door."

"There's a media circus?"

"After the lightning and the earthquake, I guess it was inevitable," Henry shrugged. "At least it's all on the other side of the fence."

"Nico and I will ah, go up and talk to Ari," Mac said, edging toward the hallway and the stairs beyond.

"If you find out anything, let us know," Janie said.

~

Ari heard them on the stairs long before they reached the room. "What sort of trouble have you caused this time?" Mac demanded.

"Well, I formed lightning, created an earthquake, killed about a thousand head of diseased cattle that were spooked by gunshots and running this way, then pulled a bullet out of Renault's brain. If you want more information, I suggest you ask nicely." Ari stalked out of the room and ran down the stairs before Mac or Nico could call her back.

"Ah, Arianne," Claudio stopped Ari as she headed for the front door. "Thank you for taking care of Renault. Might I ask how you removed the bullet?"

"With this." She held up her left hand, displaying the scallop shell imprint.

"Only a few could ever heal with the stone, and never any with just the imprint," Claudio took her hand in his own and studied the imprint curiously.

"Well, tell that to Mac. I'm going for a walk."

"Do you wish for Alejandro to accompany you?"

"I can take care of myself, thank you."

Ari opened the front door, walked through it and shut it behind her. There was one way to find out what was going on and learn what the Franks were telling the news crews. It only took a few steps for her to become invisible, and only a few more seconds to transport herself to the Franks Ranch to investigate.

She'd learned a great deal by asking the stone shell questions, even if it were only an imprint in her hand.

"It had to be a bomb," Denton Franks said for perhaps the tenth time as the Sheriff attempted to write notes for his report. "The Jordans are behind this; I'm sure of it."

"No bomb did this—earthquake for sure," a state trooper shook his head. "Has he seen the pile of cattle in that crack?"

"Those are his cattle," the Sheriff snapped. "Go clear the reporters away or something."

"That's your department, not mine," the trooper replied. "We're here to help investigate, not run interference."

Ari ghosted invisibly around the men as they quarreled, studying the Sheriff, Denton Franks and the trooper.

It was an act of nature, she breathed into the Sheriff's mind. *Write that down. Earthquake. Lightning. Look, it's starting to rain.*

Thunder rumbled overhead as rain began to drum on the hats worn by law enforcement.

"Fucking hell," Denton swore as heavier rain pelted him, soaking his clothing in seconds. "Where's the old man?" he whirled about, searching for his father.

"Denton," Mitchell Franks strode toward his son, his rifle gripped tightly in his hand, barrel pointed upward rather than down.

Good-bye, murderer, Ari whispered at him as lightning coursed downward from a roiling storm cloud, the metal barrel of his gun acting as a lightning rod and burning Mitchell to a swift, fiery crisp. *That's for my father,* she added, *and for Renault.*

The strike flung Denton through the air, dropping him into the mud fifteen feet away. The Sheriff hadn't escaped unscathed; the left side of his uniform was charred as he gaped at Mitchell's burned corpse, which crumbled and fell as he watched.

My work here is done, Ari mused. *Time to go back, now.*

No. Mac wanted to get rid of me. I understand that, now. I'll make it easy for him.

Ari sent herself back to the house with no trouble at all.

Mac felt her presence before she materialized. "You wanted to get rid of me. Problem solved. I'm leaving," Ari snapped at him. "Good luck with the Adversary."

"Ari," Mac shouted as she disappeared. "Bloody hell," he ranted.

"What's wrong?" Claudio flew into the room, not bothering with touching the floor.

"I made a mistake," Mac dropped his face in both hands. "A really big mistake."

"No logs, no indication they met with anyone, but their fuel tanks are full and that shouldn't be. There are no records of the boat being in port since they were in the panhandle of Florida more than two weeks ago," Del slapped his report on a desk at Houston's FBI Headquarters.

The woman behind the desk frowned at Del. "You've seen the other sites—what do you make of this?"

"I don't know, but I don't trust those red, slimy bodies one bit."

"They're holding them in special bunkers and exposing them to more sunlight before beheading—just to see if it kills the disease."

"And if it's something else? Something unexpected?"

"We've taken precautions. That part is out of your hands, Agent Reeves."

"Are there other reports coming in?"

"Not yet."

"Don't you find that unusual—for bodies whose brains aren't functioning properly? How do they suddenly know to hide from us? Wait," Del hesitated. "Are we needed here any longer?"

"I suppose not."

"Is there a flight we can catch back to Dallas?"

"If you can find one with enough empty seats." The woman flipped open the report folder.

"Thank you. We'll be in touch."

"You'd better be ready to go if we find more bodies."

"Of course." Del was already heading for the door.

"I put Erly and Hunter in bedrooms across the hall from one another on the third floor," Janie told Val as he settled on a barstool and lifted the bag containing the bullet and fragments. Ari had labeled it carefully.

"Mac upset Ari, and now she's gone. Nico's trying to reach her," Janie went on.

"You think any of this is on TV yet?"

"I'm afraid to find out."

"I'll do it. I figure we'll look at the ravine tomorrow morning. I think Ari may have saved our cattle and eliminated the task of putting Franks' herd down at the same time."

The doorbell rang at that moment; Alejandro rushed into the kitchen. "The Sheriff and the media are here," he breathed.

"I'll go let them in," Janie said. "Put that bullet somewhere safe."

"We weren't at home when it happened," Val told the Sheriff, whose clothing looked scorched on the left side. "What's this about Mitchell Franks getting hit by lightning?"

"It's how my uniform got singed," the Sheriff snapped. "Denton got thrown a few feet; had to get the paramedics to take him to the hospital. His father was hauled to the morgue looking like burned barbecue. Denton has a broken leg, at the very least."

"You think it was really an earthquake?" Janie asked.

"That's what it looks like. USGS is still fussing about it, so we'll probably have more information in the morning."

"Perhaps fracking may be to blame?" Alejandro suggested.

"Hmmph. Don't say that out loud around here—too many oil and gas wells are feeding the economy. You're fighting a losing battle if you start on fracking," the Sheriff huffed.

"Earthquakes from fracking are very real and very dangerous," Alejandro said. "I suggest," he added, placing compulsion, "you should remember that if anyone asks."

"I'll remember," Sheriff McCullough nodded. "I'll add that to my notes."

"Mr. Jordan," a reporter held out a microphone as the Sheriff turned to leave. "What was it like? Did it shake the house?"

"I heard that it did shake the house. Unfortunately, I was away from home at the time. Good-night," Val said and shut the door in the reporter's face.

"Have you tried contacting her?" Mac asked. Nico, sitting on the side of his bed with head in hands, didn't bother looking up at Mac's question.

"No," Nico mumbled. "I guess things were further along than I thought."

"You mean than *I* thought," Mac sat heavily beside Nico. "This is my fault. The stone is speaking to her through the imprint, and I didn't have a clue. No wonder she's been out of sorts—the stone is always agitated this early in the war. It's from showing you the dreams and—other stuff."

"Yeah. I wonder if she'd come back for Renault, if he asked. She saved his life, using the imprint."

"Nobody's ever done that before, and there have only been a few who were able to ghost from one place to another. Vamps are hard to kill, but a fragmenting bullet to the brain can do it," Mac said.

"How many have been able to ghost?"

"She's the third."

"We really need that talent, don't we?"

"I'm afraid we do. The stone certainly thinks so. It's teaching her, when I should have been doing it. I decided to wait instead, and that could have turned deadly tonight."

"I think we need her help with Hunter and Erly," Nico dropped his hands and turned to blink at Mac. "They're feeling out of place, and I worry it will get worse before it gets better."

"Then maybe you should try contacting her," Mac let his shoulders sag. "She won't listen to anything I have to say—that's for sure."

Ari, tucked inside her favorite cave in Palo Duro Canyon, surveyed the park lying below. She'd changed to mountain lion shortly after ghosting to the park—it was one of her favorite places to spend a full moon.

Nearby, her clothes were folded and piled neatly out of the way; she'd need them again but for now, she was content to enjoy the night breeze caressing her fur, the sounds of nocturnal animals and birds, and the scent of far-off rain.

Ari? Nico's voice reached her, startling her from a peaceful reverie.

Ari, I need you, he told her. *I know you don't really need or want us, but,* he floundered for words.

I doubt very much that Mac needs anybody, Ari responded. *Unless it's to verbally abuse in some way.*

He messed up. We both did, okay? He thought you weren't progressing—that you were too tied up with your personal life. I guess you had foresight the rest of us didn't. The stone can make you irritable when the future is this unstable. Deep down, you felt it, and the onset of the full moon made it worse, I think. Will you give us another chance? We really need your help. Mac thinks the zombies have gone into hiding so they can, uh, transform.

Into what?

Demon servants for the Adversary.

They'll answer to the enemy?

Claudio says the same thing.

How is Renault?

Alejandro says he's healing. They're afraid to tell him you're missing—or whose fault it is that you're missing.

Don't tell me feather butt is worried about that.

He messed up and he knows it, Nico responded.

Then I'll think about coming back—after the full moon.

Hunter and Erly may need your help. Val will do what he can for Hunter, but Erly—he's a black jaguar. Do you know how rare that is? He said he hasn't seen another cat shifter in years.

You want me back for the full moon, don't you?

It would make me feel better, Nico admitted. *Where are you, anyway?*

Palo Duro Canyon.

I should have known. Will we see you tomorrow?

Probably.

Thanks, Ari. I owe you.

Mac owes you. You don't owe me anything.

~

"She's coming back tomorrow, and she called you feather butt," Nico told Mac.

"She really cares about you," Mac rose from Nico's bed to stretch and yawn. "I'm going to bed. You should, too. Tomorrow's gonna be a long day."

"Mac, Ari's the only family I have left. I know I'm young. I understand she's a woman and not the type you've worked with before. Stop pushing us, okay? We're doing our best not to let you down."

Mac had gone still for a moment, listening to Nico's words. "Yeah," he nodded, then turned and walked out of Nico's bedroom, closing the door softly behind him.

"Honestly, they should cover this ravine with dirt and let it go," Val told Mac the following morning as they stood at the fence separating the Franks property from the Jordan Ranch.

Bloated cattle filled half the ravine, all of them dead either from the lightning or the fall into the ravine's depths.

"Any word on Denton?" Mac asked, while he mentally considered the amount of power Ari expended to create the enormous crack in the earth. The lightning strike required even more power; no doubt she wanted to kill the herd quickly and avoid lingering deaths.

"Still in the hospital this morning—they fixed his leg and kept him for observation. I can't say I'm sorry at all about Mitchell."

"Carrying a mostly metal object during a thunderstorm isn't the wisest thing to do."

"Is that Denton's wife?" Mac asked as a woman walked toward the opposite side of the crater.

"Yeah. That's Maurine."

Mac and Val watched as she approached the yellow tape tied to stakes along the western edge of the ravine. Although it was quite a distance between them, Mac's sharp eyes watched her pull a cell phone from her pocket and tap on it before putting it to her ear. Seconds later, Val's cell phone rang.

"Maurine?" Val sounded surprised as he answered the call.

"Yeah—I'm sorry to hear that," Val said after listening for a few moments. "Are you sure that's what he wants?" he asked after listening again. "All right. Have him call Burke if he's serious," Val said. "Thank you, Maurine. Let us know if there's anything we can do."

Val pocketed his cell phone with a heavy sigh. "She said Denton doesn't have the will or the strength to keep the place up. I interpret that to mean he's broke and can't afford to clean up the mess. She told me he wants to sell the place and said to offer it to me first."

"For a quick sale, no doubt," Mac grunted.

"Because I offered to buy it from him once before," Val replied. "Shortly after they moved in and started taking short cuts in handling the cattle."

"Which are now all dead," Mac said.

"Yeah. The stock pens are a wreck, and will drag the price of the place down, and not only because they're too close to the house and carry such a stench."

"Well, provided he doesn't change his mind, he'd be a fool not to take any offer you make."

"I'll make a fair offer for what he has left," Val scuffed his boot against a clump of grass beneath the fence. "Deep ravine full of dead cattle included."

"Ari," Janie rushed forward to hug Ari when she walked into the kitchen close to lunch time. "Are you all right?" Janie asked as she pulled away.

"I'm fine. I just needed to think about things after last night."

"Mac says you pulled Mitchell's bullet out of Renault," Janie lowered her voice to a whisper.

"I left it in a bag on the counter for Val," Ari reminded her.

"Oh, my goodness. It's in a kitchen drawer," Janie hurried to the drawer in question and pulled the bag out.

"I think it will match the bullet that killed Val's heifer," Ari said. "Can I make some coffee? I haven't had any yet."

"I'll have some with you. You have no idea how thankful I am that you were able to help Renault. I shudder to think what would have happened if the old bastard shot Henry or Kevin."

"He was a crazy old man who should have had his guns taken away long ago," Ari said, moving toward the coffee maker and pulling out the pot to fill it with water. "You'll never convince me that he mistook Renault for a deer, and that would have been his second murder—that I know of."

"And one that wasn't on his property—again," Janie agreed as she watched Ari scoop ground coffee into the filter.

As the scent of fresh-brewed coffee permeated the kitchen, Ari pulled two mugs from the cabinet and set them beside the coffee maker.

"Lunch will be ready in a few," Mary Kate told Ari as she checked a pan of lasagna in the oven.

"Want coffee?" Ari asked her.

"No—I've had four cups already," Mary Kate said.

The back door opened; Ari scented Val, then—*Mac*.

"Mom, Maurine called while we were checking the ravine," Val said. "She says Denton wants to sell the ranch, and is offering it to us, first."

"It'll take a lot to put it back to rights," Janie sniffed as Ari set a cup of coffee in front of her.

"Want coffee?" Ari asked Val.

"I'd take some." He settled on a barstool next to Janie.

"Want coffee?" Ari turned to Mac after she handed the cup she'd intended for herself to Val. He refused to meet her eyes.

"I'd take coffee," Mac dipped his chin in agreement while choosing a barstool for himself.

Ari poured two more cups, setting one in front of Mac, before taking the barstool on Janie's other side. It left a barstool between her and Mac, putting distance between them.

"If Denton doesn't cover that ravine, the stench will get worse really fast," Janie said.

"Which will drive the price down further and prolong the sale. Nobody will want to buy it as is," Val pointed out. "I'm not willing to do anything about it until I have a signature on papers," he added.

"No realtor will consider offering that mess until something is done about rotting, putrid cattle," Janie agreed.

Can you do something about covering up that mess? Mac asked Ari.

If I have to. Ari sipped her coffee, refusing to look in Mac's direction.

Good. I hear Lance and his FBI groupies are on their way out, Mac continued. *Mona spent the night here. I figure we'll be having a conference after lunch. They have news—we have news. I think Laronda should stay here for the full moon shift tonight.*

I hear Erly is a black jaguar, Ari said.

He is. He may be interested in meeting you and Laronda. He says Hunter is the only shifter he's had contact with in years.

Cats are generally loners—certainly not as social as other shifters, unless they're a family unit, Ari said. *I used to take my mother to Palo Duro Canyon all the time.*

Look—I'm sorry, Mac apologized. *We've all been on edge, and I didn't realize my concerns were affecting my judgment and my interactions with you—and with Nico. He pointed it out to me last night.*

Nico is the only family I have left, Ari finally turned to lock eyes with Mac's. *No matter what you say or do, I will protect him as long as I can.*

That, oddly enough, is exactly what I'd ask you to do. I should have known you'd be willing to stand between him and danger, no matter what.

That's right.

Nico also said you called me feather butt. I deserve that.

And not just because it's true?

At least you didn't call me featherbrained.

I'll save that one for later.

Mac snorted a laugh, causing Janie and Val to stop discussing the sale of the Franks' ranch and turn toward him and Ari in pointed curiosity.

"It's nothing," Ari waved a hand and smiled.

"Janie says lunch is ready," Ari walked into the game room. She'd volunteered to let Nico and the others know, since she hadn't met Erly and Hunter yet.

"Hear that?" Mona rose from the sofa and smiled at Hunter.

"I'm ready for some lunch," Erly rose to his feet.

"You must be Erly," Ari held out her hand to him. He shook with a grin.

"Haven't seen another big cat in a while," Erly told her. "Pleased to meet you."

"Same here," she told him. "Haven't seen another since my mother passed a few years ago."

"Sorry to hear that. Hunt, you hungry?" He turned toward Hunter.

"Yeah," Hunter rose. "You're Ari? Nico says you're family to him."

"He's the only family I have left," Ari replied, shaking Hunter's outstretched hand. "Mary Kate has lasagna ready. It smells like heaven," Ari told him, letting his hand go and urging him and Erly toward the door. "Wash up and join us in the kitchen. You, too, Nico."

"You don't have to tell me twice," Mona said, rising from the sofa. "I'll be there in two shakes. Glad to have you back," she said softly as she walked past Ari.

"Yeah. Things are sorted for now."

"Come on, Ari," Nico called from the stairway. "We'll eat it all if you drag your feet."

"That sounds like a threat," Mona said. "Come on, Lance should be here any minute, and he loves lasagna. If we waste too much time, we could lose out on Mary Kate's specialty."

"I'm coming," Ari declared, following Mona out of the room.

CHAPTER TWELVE

"It looked like pale, red jelly," Del described what was left behind on the boat deck after two bodies had been removed. "Have you seen anything like that before?"

"I haven't," Mac replied. Everyone, including Del and Laronda, were sitting around the formal dining table, enjoying a lasagna lunch. In minutes, the conversation turned to the yacht investigation.

"Did it have a scent?" Ari asked Laronda.

"It smelled like rotted gym socks," Laronda made a face. "I let Del get close to it, since his nose isn't as sensitive."

"It did sort of smell like gym socks—the kind with mold growing on them," Lance nodded at Laronda's assessment. "I guess that means it was a whole lot worse for you, huh?"

"Every time—you being mostly human and all," she teased.

"You have no idea how good it feels to lay that out in the open and be comfortable in your own skin," Erly gave Lance a nod. "Thank you for letting me come with Hunter," he told Val.

"It's no trouble—I was worried Hunter would feel alone, after his aunt refused to come with him."

"If she'd known there was gonna be lasagna this good, maybe she woulda changed her mind." Erly's smile lit up his eyes, turning them to a golden brown.

Ari noticed; the full moon pulled on every shifter at the table. Erly's eyes would be gold when he shifted.

"I've never met a black jaguar before," Janie held up her glass of iced tea. "Good to have you here—and Hunter, too."

"I can make myself useful," Erly offered. "I have carpentry skills."

"He does, and he put Aunt Cathy's new roof on last year," Hunter agreed.

"Then we'll talk salary next week," Val told Erly. "We have to hire outside help if we need building repairs done, and there's always something that needs doing."

"If we buy the Franks' property, he could help with that, for sure," Janie told Val.

"They're selling?" Lance sounded surprised.

"After last night, I think they're desperate," Val said.

"What happened last night?"

"You haven't heard? It's all over the news," Nico said. "There was a freak earthquake on the Franks' ranch last night. Happened to coincide with Mitchell Franks stampeding their sick cattle in this direction. The earth just split open and swallowed all of them before they could set foot on this property. The Sheriff's Department seems to think fracking caused it."

"There's a lot of that going on," Erly pointed his fork at Nico. "Nothing good ever comes of that, mark my words."

"Denton's wife called Val this morning. After Mitchell was killed by lightning in that thunderstorm last night, Denton wants to get rid of the property and fast," Janie explained.

"He was carrying his rifle, barrel pointed upward," Ari said. "Lightning just fried him to a crisp. Threw Denton across the yard and singed the Sheriff's uniform. Everybody headed for cover after that happened."

"To divine intervention," Mac held up his glass of wine. He winked at Ari as the others echoed his toast.

~

"How dangerous will it be if I hop back to my house for more clothes?" Ari asked Mac and Nico. They'd gone to the game room after lunch. "I didn't know we would be gone this long," Ari mused. "Is someone watching the house?"

"Burke hired someone to take care of the outside—the lawn and flower beds," Nico said. "I asked him to. I haven't heard that the lawn service has been attacked."

"As long as you transport yourself inside and don't go outside—and the locks haven't been tampered with," Mac replied after thinking about it for a moment.

"What if they come looking for sign of her later?" Nico turned to Mac. "Will they be able to scent her?"

Mac considered that for a moment. "If they become demon, they can tell a fresher scent from an older one, but that will only occur inside the house. They will realize, however, since there's no scent following you out the door, that you arrived and departed in an unnatural way."

"So they'll know that I'm alive and helping Nico?"

"Yes."

"Are we sure there will be demons?"

"I think we can guarantee it at this point. The stone has left Spain. That, in itself, spells trouble for all of us. The demon strain will not be held back by the safety net constructed there by prior holders of the stone. On this continent, no such spells have been laid, leaving the victims to become what they were intended—first the creatures you call zombies, and then demons, if the zombies aren't beheaded in a timely manner."

"Then I'll have to keep washing clothes every few days," Ari sighed.

"I think Janie will order for you," Nico suggested.

"I'm already taking advantage of her hospitality. I don't want to ask her to spend money on me, too."

"That's not what I'm suggesting," Nico pulled a card from his pocket. "Claudio gave us emergency funds—there's plenty left on this bank gift card that we didn't use before."

"Just consider it money well spent by the vampire council—we're helping to protect their food source."

"You've had dealings with them before?" Ari studied Mac's face.

"Several times, beginning with the time I had to tell them what was happening when it only looked like the precursor to a World War."

"Please don't ask him about it—I've seen the visions in my nightmares. It's horrible," Nico begged.

Someday, I'll tell you, Mac mentally told Ari. *The boy's right —none of this is pleasant conversation.*

All right. "Card, please," she held out her hand for the gift card. "I'll ask Janie to order a few things."

"Order a pair of hiking boots, too," Mac advised. "Something sturdy, just in case."

"On it." Ari waved the card as she walked out of the game room.

"Janie would pay for anything Ari wants, and she's worried about overstaying her welcome," Nico shook his head.

"Ari hasn't had the best childhood, with a murdered father and a grieving mother," Mac said. "She's been forced to carry that burden for a long time and doesn't want to dump it on somebody else that she cares about."

"You think she had anything to do with Mitchell Franks getting fried?"

"If she did, it was quick and relatively painless—more so than her father's death."

"Has anyone controlled lightning before?"

"A couple of times, and none this early in the game."

"I'm grateful my mother told me in a dream that Ari needed to hold the stone," Nico remarked.

"Your mother held the stone for a short time—before she gave it to you. I can't help but think she knew exactly what she was doing."

"I miss her. And Papa."

"I know." Mac draped an arm around Nico's shoulders. "They still watch over you, kid. I can feel it."

"It was her roots in Spain that she went looking for," Nico pulled away from Mac. "Papa's family—most of it, anyway, came from Mexico."

"He still may have had Spanish ancestry—you know that. The stone has a stronger connection to you than most I've seen."

"I haven't dreamed a reason why, yet."

"The stone knows what to tell you and when. Have patience."

"How much patience do you think the Adversary will have?"

"Very little, but he has to pull the population to his side to do his worst. Don't worry, that will happen fast enough, if experience has taught me anything. Set the people against themselves, and then sit back and watch while the minions jump on his command—then blame it all on the opposition."

"So it's like the witch blaming Dorothy for the flying monkeys in *The Wizard of Oz*?"

"That describes it perfectly," Mac agreed.

"Get what you know will wear well and hold up," Janie advised as she and Ari flipped through clothing choices on the Internet. "Something may look great in the pictures and be nothing but cheap crap when you get it."

"I hate that you can't feel fabric through a screen," Ari smiled at Janie. "I'll go with brands I've bought before and shoes and boots I know will fit."

"We'll return what doesn't work," Janie nodded.

"On another note," Ari said as she dumped five T-shirts into her cart, "I'm kinda worried about tonight—like something won't go right, somehow."

"You feel that about the ranch?" Janie now looked worried.

"No—it isn't local, whatever it is," Ari explained. "I don't know what it is, it just worries me."

"Val was contacted by a realtor right after lunch—the Franks are serious about selling, looks like."

"Have they named a price?"

"They're still working on that—I think the realtor has to go out and look at the property—to see everything that's wrong with it before making a suggestion."

"Have the cows started stinking, yet?"

"Henry says he can smell them very well."

"Maybe the realtor will be able to smell them too—when he gets there."

"I have no idea when he'll get there—Val says it's somebody from Fort Worth who specializes in farms and ranches—he doesn't know the man. Burke usually goes through another realtor he knows, and he may be in the loop already."

"I hope they suggest a fair price, then," Ari mumbled, adding several pairs of her favorite jeans to the online cart.

"Don't forget socks—for your boots and athletic shoes," Janie tapped her computer screen.

"Oh, yeah." Ari entered *women's socks* in the search box.

"And a wheeled suitcase or duffle to hold it all—just in case. Mac said some traveling may be required; I have a feeling our FBI agents are going to ask for help soon enough. Laronda and Del belong in a special division of the agency—a lot of shifters and a few vamps already work there. They have human partners a lot of the time."

"How did you find out about that?"

"Mona—she asked Laronda. That girl has always been the direct sort."

"Whatever works," Ari added socks to her cart. "Shortest distance between knowing and not knowing."

"They're enjoying the pool this afternoon," Janie said. "Lance told Del and Laronda to pack swimsuits. Hunter and Erly had something with them in their bags."

"I think I'll buy one for myself," Ari breathed and tapped the request in the search box.

"Good idea. Buy for Nico and Mac, too."

"Is that really Mac?" Hunter asked Nico. Both were watching Mac's raven dipping in and out of the waterfall feature, bathing in bird fashion and flinging water droplets around him as he fluffed and flapped.

"I think he's enjoying himself," Nico nodded. "We don't have swimsuits, so this is the only way he can get in the water and still be decent."

"I ordered swimsuits for you and Mac," Ari took a patio chair near Nico's. "Should arrive in the next two days."

"Thank you," Nico turned a bright smile toward Ari.

"Thank Janie. She suggested it."

"You didn't get anything embarrassing, did you?"

"Not for you," she teased. "You'll look good in red and black, I promise."

"Did you get Hawaiian shorts for Mac?"

"I thought about it—flowers and everything. Instead, I got him a suit with a Ravens logo—for the ice hockey team."

"They did okay last season," Hunter supplied. "I watch minor league hockey with Erly now and then. Since the team is from his hometown, he keeps up with them."

"He's from New Orleans?"

"Don't let him catch you saying it like that. Say *Nawlins* instead."

"I heard that," Erly called out from his float at the center of the pool.

"Sorry, Erly," Hunter grinned. "You know I have to educate whenever it's required."

"Then you need to follow me around. Plenty of folks need educatin'."

"It's my goal and life's work," Hunter slapped a hand over his heart. Erly snorted a laugh.

~

"That was a mighty fine meal, Mrs. Killebrew," Darnell Cheatham patted his belly. "And a fine sermon, too, Reverend," he complimented his hosts, who'd invited him to their home near the church.

"Bobby Ray is on his way, now, with the original recording," Reverend Killebrew pushed his chair back from the table and stood. "Senator, would you like coffee in the living room?"

"I sure would."

"Phyllis," Killebrew turned to his wife, who looked frazzled after putting a full meal of fried chicken, mashed potatoes with gravy, and homemade green beans with bacon on the table after church.

"I'll have it ready in a minute," Phyllis promised, as Killebrew led Darnell toward the sanctuary of the living room so Phyllis could get on with the chore of making coffee and then cleaning up the kitchen.

A knock sounded on the front door shortly after coffee was served, and Darnell was introduced to Bobby Ray Gentry, who carried a video camera case in his left hand while shaking hands with the right.

"Just happened to be out that night, huntin' raccoons," Bobby explained as he settled on the sofa and opened the case. "Here's the original recording—sorry it's so grainy, but it was late at night."

"I have people who can fix those problems," Darnell waved off Bobby Ray's concern. "I have cash, if that's acceptable."

"That, and the promise that these people will get what's coming to 'em. Not a Christian in the lot, for damn sure. No idea why the woman and the boy showed up for church afterward—maybe they were checking out the enemy standing between them and sending everybody to the devil."

"No doubt," Darnell murmured as he took the small plastic case containing an SD card. "This is for you." He pulled an envelope from his pocket and handed it over. "The Lord always helps those who keep the faith and fight his battles."

As Darnell spoke those words, Bobby Ray blinked—had he seen a righteous glint in the Senator's eyes? Whatever he'd seen, it made him want to do exactly what the Senator said; fight the Lord's battles. Destroy the Lord's enemies. He'd consider that—and the best way to do just that, making the Lord and the Senator happy at the same time.

"Yes, sir, Senator," Bobby Ray stuffed the envelope in his back pocket, half-rising from his seat to do so.

"Want coffee, Bobby Ray?" Killebrew asked.

"No, thanks, Rev. I have plans with my cousin Billy this afternoon, but we'll be at the service later."

"I'll look forward to seeing you then," the Reverend replied.

"Well, I better get going—that motor won't fix itself," Bobby Ray rose and shook again with Darnell. "Nice to meet you, Senator. Will we see you in the congregation again?"

"It was a fine sermon," Darnell said. "I may become a regular."

"Good to hear. Thanks again."

Killebrew saw Bobby Ray to the door; a few words were exchanged between the two before Killebrew rejoined Darnell. "Tell me how the proposed legislation is going on the new immigration bill."

"Before we get into that, do you have information on other friends like Bobby Ray? I think I'd like to speak with them."

"Phyllis," Killebrew called out. "Bring me that list of websites from my desk."

Phyllis rushed in with a folder in less than two minutes, presenting it to Killebrew without a word.

"Kitchen clean yet?" Killebrew narrowed his eyes at her.

"Just about. Only have to wipe counters and it's done."

The reverend waited until his wife was back in the kitchen before handing the folder to Darnell. Then, he settled in for the Senator's report on the immigration bill.

"Because I hate picking bunny fur out of my teeth the next day," Ari poured a glass of iced tea to go with her sandwich.

Erly had asked her why she was eating dinner before the moon rose for the evening. "I do the same thing, sometimes," Hunter confessed.

"Is that why you bring me the whole deer when you take one down?" Erly asked him.

"Yeah. I go hunting when I know you need meat," the boy

shrugged. "Deer are more of a challenge, but I know you like rabbits and squirrels, too."

"Haven't bought meat in two years," Erly grinned at Ari. "Kid keeps me supplied."

"I think I figured out why you like hockey," Ari told him, changing the subject.

"Why's that?" Erly asked, curious.

"It's the puck, isn't it?"

A slow grin spread across Erly's face. "Damn straight. I could bat that thing around a lot better than they can—if they'd let my cat play."

"Any cat shifter would be an excellent goalie," Ari said.

"I like the way you think," Erly laughed. "May as well have a sandwich with you." Erly pulled the bag of bread across the island. "Want one?" he asked Hunter.

"Sure. I'll grab the mayo."

~

"I feel it too," Mac told Nico. "A turning point, I think. From now on, the battle will be fully engaged, and it will happen faster than most will believe."

"How long does it take for a demon to form?" Nico asked. He sat on the floor in Mac's bedroom, looking up at Mac, who'd taken the bedside chair.

"Days or weeks—a lot depends on who they were before and where they hide during the change—they grow faster if they're in a safe place."

"You think they'll strike the first blow?"

"I don't get that vibe—not yet, anyway. I believe this first strike will be all too human."

"What if it involves Hunter's aunt? I still think she's in a lot of danger."

"We gave her as much information as we could. There's a point where you have to step back and let them make the final decision, good or bad, without giving too much away. We must keep our names and natures out of this. Staying alive to fight the coming war is far more important."

"We don't need the entire country going nuts because they just found out there are werewolves, vampires and other shifters among the population. Imagine what the Adversary could do with that kind of information," Nico sighed.

"That's exactly what we want to avoid—handing them a convenient enemy to wage war against. Once they've formulated their plan, they'll add their demons to the enemy list, while controlling them to destroy swaths of the population."

"Beginning with the ones they don't like?"

"Got it in one, kid."

"How long before we join forces with Lance, Mona and the FBI agents?"

"Soon, I think—while their bosses are still capable of rational thought. If that rational thought ends, we may be forced to break away and form our own army, including more vamps. Claudio will call them in when we ask. He also has a few places set aside to house and feed an army, if it becomes necessary."

"Ari and I—will we be strong enough by then to help you shield that place?"

"That's the big question, isn't it? If the Adversary moves quickly, well." Mac didn't finish—he didn't have to. "We've never fought against all the weapons the Adversary can use; they've been prevented in the past, purely by the spelled location or lack of resources. Here, it's open warfare, with every option on the table."

"What are you not telling me?" Nico asked.

"It won't happen—the gateway is blocked."

"Gateway?"

"It's nothing to worry about; once that gateway was blocked, none who are on the other side of it have gotten through. They won't either, unless we lose this war. And, if we lose this war, all is lost anyway."

"How did all this land on us, Mac?" Nico whispered.

"I'm cursed—that's how I'm involved. You and Ari? Fate often chooses the ones everyone else overlooks. The stone evidently saw something in you—that's the best explanation I have."

"What kind of stone is this?" Nico drew the carved shell from his pocket to study it.

"Jet. It's from an ancient tree and not a stone. A tree that never grew on this Earth."

"Then how?" Nico turned a puzzled gaze on Mac.

"No more questions. It's almost sundown and I need to speak with Claudio before the others go out for the full moon."

"I have healed perfectly," Renault responded to Mac's question. "Arianne's talent saved my life."

"That, and the fact that a vampire's flesh is harder to penetrate than a normal human's," Mac agreed. "Had that bullet exploded farther in your brain, even Ari couldn't have saved you."

"My would-be killer is deceased. Should I thank her for that, too?" Renault asked.

"I think she'd prefer that you keep that between the two of you," Mac replied dryly.

"Very well. You wish us to watch the neighbor's house?"

"Yes, but from a distance. I know the stench is getting worse the longer those cattle are exposed," Mac told him. "Claudio wishes to stay here at the house with Nico and me. He's already asked Alejandro to keep an eye on Val's herd while he and the hands shift."

"I will do this gladly. Are you expecting anyone? Is the wife still at home?"

"She's staying at the hospital in Abilene with her husband. The property should be empty and temporarily abandoned. Something bothers me about that."

"Of course I will watch it carefully," Renault said. "I will have my cell phone with me and let you know if anything out of the ordinary happens."

"Please do. I can fly out to help if it becomes necessary."

"You mean, if others arrive with weapons?"

"That's possible, I suppose. For now, I don't feel that as a pressing matter. Just let me know if you see anyone coming onto the property."

"It could be messy out tonight—rain is coming up from the gulf coast and is expected to arrive in Dallas and Fort Worth shortly," Alejandro remarked after checking his cell phone.

"That would certainly make for a messy night," Mac conceded.

"Alejandro and I are used to poor conditions," Renault said.

"Not that we like them—we're just used to them," Alejandro gave a tight smile.

"Yes. As he says," Renault agreed.

"The others are ready to go out," Nico turned toward Mac.

"We will go," Renault said and floated swiftly toward the back door. Alejandro followed closely.

Ari watched as Val, Hunter and Janie's wolves trotted toward the small pack that waited for them atop a knoll at the north end of the ranch. A forested area that most ranchers would have cleared for more grazing land, the Jordan family had nurtured the trees instead, making it a good place to hunt rabbit, deer or other prey. To the south, it was fenced off to keep the cattle away from hunting werewolves.

Ari had never been here as a mountain lion. Her father had died somewhere on the property, but she'd never been shown the place. Her mother had gone out during the trial, but she'd stayed at the house with Janie, who'd made chocolate chip cookies and kept a nine-year-old safe and busy.

Would her father's remains be in the Franks' house?

Later, perhaps, she'd investigate. Tonight, the moon called, although its pull wasn't as strong as it was in the past. In fact, she wasn't sure she had to shift, but the others expected it of her.

Besides, Erly's black jaguar and Laronda's coyote were close by; they would be hunting with her. Erly hadn't hunted with anyone else in a long time, so she intended to give him that experience tonight.

Laronda yipped and trotted away, nose to ground. Erly and Ari were content to let her take the lead; a rabbit had left fresh tracks—it was time to hunt.

~

"There are three of them with video cameras. The logo on their shirts is that of the Texas Animal Rights Federation," Renault informed Mac over his cell phone. "They are wearing masks over their faces and recording images of the dead animals in the crevasse."

"Too bad they didn't show up months ago," Mac rumbled. "They might have saved some of the herd. Now, it's all diseased, wasted meat."

"What do you want me to do about this?"

"It's TARF," Mac held a hand over his phone as he informed Del of the interlopers on the Franks ranch.

"I'd leave them alone," Del shrugged. "Just make sure they don't come on this side of the fence."

"Keep an eye on them, but don't interfere unless they come onto Jordan property. I do suggest you record them with your phone, if that's possible."

"Of course."

~

Laura McGrady stuffed her video camera back in its bag while Mark and Renata did the same. The scene was just as bad as her informant in the Texas Highway Patrol said it was. Piles of dead cattle in the ravine —all of them diseased before the ravine magically opened to swallow them.

Who knew how many suffered from injuries before dying? Why hadn't someone reported this mess before now?

"We're going to the ranch next door to ask them why they never reported this," Laura set her camera bag in her car's trunk.

"I think that's a good idea. I don't care if it is nearly eleven at night," Renata agreed. "If they knew about this and didn't report it, they're almost as guilty."

"Maybe you should let me do the talking," Mark reasoned with both women. "We may be able to get more information if we don't go in with guns blazing."

"Don't mess it up, then," Laura warned as she slammed the trunk of her car. "Do we know who owns the ranch next door?"

"I can find out." Renata pulled her cell phone from a pocket before climbing into the front passenger seat.

"The car is approaching the house now," Renault informed Mac.

"They wish to ask questions, perhaps?" Claudio suggested.

"I can get rid of them easy enough," Del said, pulling his ID out.

"Perhaps a joint effort?" Claudio asked.

"Shall we meet them at the door—before they have the opportunity to knock?" Lance asked.

"I'm all for it," Mac agreed. "Mona, will you stay with Nico in the kitchen?"

"Sure," Mona herded Nico toward the back of the house.

Mac opened the front door just as one of their three guests was poised to knock, surprising all of them.

"We ah, are from TARF—Texas Animal Rights Federation," the man stuttered.

"Is there something we can do for you?" Mac asked.

"We have questions about the dead cattle on the uh, adjoining property," the man gulped as Mac stared him down.

"We know you were there earlier—one of my employees reported it and recorded your presence," Claudio said.

"We ah," the man was at a loss for words.

"We want to know why that whole debacle wasn't reported—before it came to this," one of the women demanded.

"But it was reported. Several times—to the Sheriff and several other local agencies. Nothing was ever done about it until we called in the Department of Agriculture," Del opened his ID badge and presented it to the woman. "Now. I would like your names and your position or affiliation with TARF, the name of your supervisor if you have one, and appropriate phone numbers," he added.

"Jesus, Laura," the man whispered, sounding terrified.

Catherine and the rest of her Wiccan coven had gathered for an Esbat, a ceremony held at the full moon to honor the goddess. Tonight, they would also seek healing for one of their own, recently diagnosed with skin cancer.

The last time they'd used this particular clearing, Hunter had changed for the first time. Catherine's mind wandered back to that event as she and four others waited for three more members to arrive.

That night, after Hunter's change, he swore that he'd heard someone running away. Granted, his werewolf hearing was quite sharp, but his nose told her someone had definitely been there.

The scent led to tire tracks a quarter mile away; Catherine had been frightened that someone had seen Hunter change. They'd even visited a local church the following Sunday, to see if Hunter could identify the scent belonging to the trespasser.

If he were a member of the church, he hadn't attended that Sunday. As the days and weeks passed and nothing came of it, Catherine began to relax until she'd blocked it from her mind. And, until tonight, the coven hadn't met in that same place again.

Tonight, she'd brought her favorite purple amethyst rock crystal to mark the northern compass point, representing Earth. Three others would also place symbols, one for Air on the eastern point, one for Fire on the southern point, and the last for Water on the western compass point, to cast their circle.

Three hooded figures approached, one holding a candle, another a chalice of water, and the third held three long, white goose feathers.

"Let us cast the circle," Joe called, bringing the coven together, his robed arms held wide.

Everyone approached their proper places; Catherine set down the amethyst crystal and prepared to thank Earth for its presence.

Gunfire erupted around them; bullets sprayed the coven and surrounding trees. Someone screamed. Catherine turned to run; she fell at the sudden pain in her back. The last thing she heard before final darkness came was the sounds of men whooping and shouting in celebration.

CHAPTER THIRTEEN

ico! Ari's mental shout echoed Nico's calling of her name by less than a second. She knew—and *he* knew.

Hunter's aunt was dead, along with several others.

We can't save them all, and we'd have been targets, too, Mac pointed out moments later. *This is the first volley—somehow, the Adversary chose these as his first targets. His followers will flock to him, now, and his demons will surely arrive with them. Nico tried to warn them; they did not listen.*

I'm coming back to the house, Ari growled.

No. We're dealing with the TARF animal rights group who chose tonight to visit the dead cattle and poor conditions on the Franks ranch, Mac replied. *Now is not a good time, Ari. Stay there with the others; they need you.*

Damn, Ari sent a mental sigh. *When it rains, it pours.*

Pray that the Adversary doesn't know how to make it rain, or any tracks and evidence left behind by the killers could be destroyed.

Ari was stunned into momentary silence. *He—can do that?*

Some have done it in the past. I cannot say yet what this one's strengths or weaknesses are. You did it, too, remember—when you created the earth-rift?

You're not reassuring me at all, Ari countered.

Being reassuring isn't my job—I have to give you the reality of the situation, or we will fail.

I have to go—Erly found a giant rat to chase. Thanks for the reality check.

Her sarcasm wasn't lost on Mac, who turned back to the conversation between Del and the animal rights trespassers.

"Thank you for the coffee—and the information, Agent Reeves," Mark Hall said as Del saw them out the front door.

"What do you suppose will happen to the dead cattle? Will the Franks try again?" Laura asked.

"The Franks are already looking for a buyer to cut their losses," Del replied, his voice a deep rumble. "After Mitchell Franks was killed by lightning that night, I doubt they want to stay and face charges for the way they handled everything."

"You think they'll try to leave the state?" Laura demanded.

"I'm not a mind reader, young woman. I have no idea what their plan is. Good-night."

Del, with Claudio standing behind him, made sure the three got in their car and drove off the ranch. No doubt, Renault would watch carefully to make sure they didn't return.

"That was a difficulty we didn't need," Claudio said as Del shut the door and locked it.

"Hunter's aunt was killed a few minutes ago," Mac reported as Del and Claudio walked into the kitchen. Nico, sitting at the island, looked pale, but didn't speak.

"Why would they target her? Do they know we took Hunter?" Mona asked quickly.

"I have no idea why they targeted her, and I doubt they know we have Hunter or Erly. I figure we'll have more information tomorrow."

"Where did the murders happen?" Del asked, frowning.

"In a clearing about half a mile from Catherine Charles' house, outside Swindall," Nico mumbled. "You can check to see if anybody reported gunshots or a disturbance in the area."

"Thanks, kid." Del pulled out his cell phone and dialed a number. He put the call on speaker so the others could hear. Lance and Mona listened carefully as the call connected.

"FBI, Director Smith speaking."

"Ray, this is Del. We may have a situation near Swindall, Texas. Can you check for any local reports of gunshots or disturbances?"

"I'll check. Hold, please."

While they waited, they were regaled with information about contacting the FBI for specific crimes or occurrences, plus a message that someone would be with them shortly. Roughly three minutes passed before Director Smith was on the line again.

"Have a report of gunshots, but no other information," Smith said. "What would you like us to do?"

"Do you have two or three to send out?"

"I can arrange it, but it may take a couple of hours, including transport time."

"If you would. I have reliable information, I think, that murder is involved."

"I'll put a rush on it, then. Do you have a specific location?"

"What I got is that it happened half a mile from Catherine Charles' home outside Swindall, and there may be more than one dead."

"I'll send for a helicopter. That'll make the travel time shorter."

"Thanks, Ray."

"I'll let you know what we find." Smith ended the call.

"That was fast," Mona breathed as Del pocketed his cell phone.

"That was a vampire," Del replied. "All the wolves are off tonight, so they'll send vamps to investigate. Even if there are armed humans in the area, they won't get a good shot at any vampire before they're put down."

"Ray Smith won't be his real name," Claudio remarked.

"No. The other Director, a werewolf, calls himself Jay Jones. They help run the special division that Laronda and I belong to. That's why we were sent to investigate the zombies popping up in Texas. Lara has a good nose; she can smell when they're lying. I'm good at annoying people and forcing them to answer questions. We know when they're telling the truth ninety-seven percent of the time."

"And you can go about your investigation, no matter what time of day it is," Claudio nodded. "Vampires are relegated to night hours only."

"What the vamps lack in daytime constraints, they make up for in other areas," Del said. "I hope we have answers on this one in a couple of hours."

"What will they do if they find something?" Nico raised his head. "Vampires can't stay past daybreak."

"They'll call in the Rangers, if it looks like a mass shooting." Del didn't sugarcoat his words. "Locals might be pissed when we go around them, but if we're dealing with multiple murders, they need to step out of the way."

Del's cell phone rang. Del put the call on speaker as he answered. "Ray?" Del sounded puzzled to hear from the vampire so quickly.

"Locals already on the scene," Ray reported. "All over it, in fact. I won't say this whole thing stinks of evidence tampering, but from what I've heard so far, there are eight dead and civilians all over the crime scene, messing it up."

"Call the Rangers, if the locals haven't done it already," Del said.

"Already did that—they're on the way, but I have no idea whether they'll have any uncontaminated evidence to collect. There's something else you should know, too."

"What's that?"

"Looks like the victims were a group of Wiccans, out on the full moon. Do you have information on who could have done this?"

"No—all I have is that it happened," Del cast a glance in Mac's direction. Mac's hands were clenched in tight fists, his eyes held an angry glint, and his body language expressed a desire to explode. "If I get anything else, I'll let you know," Del added and ended the call quickly.

"Fucking, bloody," Mac began to curse, first in English and then in a language the others couldn't understand.

"We should have asked Hunter some pointed questions earlier, and we didn't," Nico sighed after Mac stormed out of the kitchen while continuing to curse. "We weren't thinking."

"Nico, is this going to get worse?" Mona asked gently. His miserable expression worried her greatly.

"Yeah. I can't say yet just how, but it'll get worse fast. I'm going to my room—I need to think about all this." Nico slipped off his barstool and headed for the hallway outside the kitchen. Mona, Lance, Claudio and Del watched him walk away.

"I haven't seen the kid this dejected since his parents died," Lance mumbled.

"Wiccans—witches—will be targeted from this point forward. Whether other groups will be added to that list remains to be seen," Claudio said.

"Are we in the dark ages again?" Lance demanded.

"Yes," Claudio replied. "I must speak with Alejandro and Renault. Excuse me." Claudio lifted a cell phone from a shirt pocket and left the kitchen, not bothering to let his feet touch the floor.

He should have let her go.

Hell, he should have gone with her.

Mac chastised himself. Somewhere, outside Swindall, Texas, an innocent group of people had been gunned down—murdered because of their religious choices.

Another religion would lay claim to the deed—if not now, then very soon. Had he and Nico been so distracted by the events at the ranch that they'd completely forgotten who—and what—they were dealing with?

As bad as this was, would tomorrow bring worse news?

Mac cursed again.

"Well, I'll be damned." Darnell couldn't hold back the grin as he opened the email from Reverend Killebrew. There was a video attachment, which served to delight the Senator.

He'd gotten up early; his wife was still in bed, as were his teen children. After getting a cup of coffee from the housekeeper, he'd taken a seat in his study to read emails while breakfast was prepared.

The video was perfect; it showed the forming witches' circle, and the beginning of an incantation, before gunfire erupted. If Bobby Ray recorded this, then he'd upgraded his video camera.

"Look at that—got 'em all," Darnell crowed, then jumped when the housekeeper knocked on his door, telling him his omelet was ready.

"Damn," Darnell spilled hot coffee on his hand in his haste to shut down his email. "I'll be right there," he snapped, jerking tissues from the box on his desk. If things went well, he'd have two videos to deliver to Ralph Hooten, along with a list of other websites to share them with.

Ralph wouldn't appreciate not being exclusive on this, but Darnell knew the man too well—if enough money were offered, Ralph would sell his soul and his grandchildren to the highest bidder.

Plus, he now had ready slaves for new projects; Bobby Ray wouldn't like jail one bit, and Darnell had incriminating evidence.

Bobby Ray, Reverend Killebrew and anyone else he'd involved in this crime belonged exclusively to Senator Darnell Cheatham, and they'd damn well better ask how high when he told them to jump.

He needed a new base of operations for this developing venture—his wife and kids needed to stay out of this. They sure didn't need to know anything, in case somebody asked questions. Right after breakfast, he'd start looking for a suitable rental—or maybe a place to buy.

Yeah. Something rural, where he could set up a compound. He had connections in real estate; somebody could find a place large enough—and get him a good price on it, too.

~

"You're joking." Val spoke to one of Burke's associates at the law firm. At the man's urging, he lifted the remote and turned on the television in his bedroom while getting dressed, to watch the video the TARF animal rights group had recorded at the Franks ranch.

"The stench is horrible," the woman, identified as Laura McGrady, told the reporter. "Apparently the County Sheriff was called multiple times regarding the condition of the animals and the way they were treated, and nothing was done. We've tried to contact his office, but nobody will talk to us. The Agriculture Department says they can't provide information on an active investigation, so we have no other information to go on."

"Who reported the conditions?" the reporter, a young woman with shoulder-length, dark hair, asked.

"A neighbor, who has asked not to be identified."

"Did you see evidence of the lightning strike and the earthquake?"

"Of course. Even with the rain that night, there are marks where the bolt hit, and you can see for yourself what kind of damage the earthquake caused."

"They've done nothing to clean up or dispose of the dead cattle?"

"No. They're all still there, and it has to be a health hazard by this time. I know it may be hard on the owners, having a family member die by lightning strike, but word has it that he was hit because he was carrying a rifle, and he was the one who was shooting to spook the cattle in the first place. This, of course, was after the Department of Agriculture discovered that all the animals were infected with foot and mouth disease."

"You believe this was planned by the owners?"

"I think so, yes."

"We'll follow up on this developing story," the reporter spoke directly at the camera. "Thank you, Laura, for being here with us today."

"Damn." Val hit the power button on his remote and tossed it on the bed. "Gonna be a long day after a long night."

"Well, the Franks ranch made the news—again," Val dropped onto a barstool. He'd had no sleep—his wolf had been out most of the night with the pack, and now, shortly after showering and dressing in clean clothes, he had a new serving of trouble to deal with.

"Mona told me some TARF people were there last night," Janie sat wearily at one end of the island, sipping coffee.

"Well, they and their video were on the Dallas news this morning. At least the full moon is over if the place gets swamped with gawkers and news crews."

"There's something else," Janie set her coffee mug down with a sigh.

"What's that?"

"Hunter's aunt was killed last night, along with seven other people. We didn't know that she was Wiccan—and didn't know to ask about anything like that. She was out with her friends last night for the full moon, and it looks like they were killed because of their religion."

"You think it's a hate crime?"

"I do, and so do Lance, Mona and Mac. No idea whether it can be officially described as a hate crime, but that's what it was."

"Has the boy been told?"

"Not yet. I think Mac and Erly got him in bed. He's asleep, but who knows how long that will last?"

"Well, this day is off to the worst possible start," Val mumbled as Mary Kate set coffee and a plate of food in front of him.

"I don't know the status of the investigation. Del's division called the Rangers after they learned the locals, including civilians, were all over the crime scene," Mac explained to a more-than-exhausted Ari.

"I feel sick," Ari mumbled as she sat on the side of her bed, refusing to look at Mac.

"So does Nico. I have no idea how Hunter will react when he finds out. Erly and I got him into bed. I told Erly afterward; he was pissed."

"And so am I."

"I know. Look," Mac knelt down and placed a hand over one of hers. "Maybe I should have listened to you last night. We could have tracked the murderers. Instead, their crime will likely be impossible to investigate, because of the local fiasco afterward."

"Has Del gotten any updates?" Ari finally lifted her eyes to Mac's.

"Not much, and he's dead on his feet. Everybody needs sleep, including you. If you want something to eat before you turn in, Mary Kate is in the kitchen."

"Food isn't going to make this better, I don't think. Hunter will be devastated. That's the only family he had left."

"I know." Mac patted her hand after letting it go. "Try to sleep, Ari. I don't think things are going to get better from here on out, so rest while you can."

Ari watched him walk out of her bedroom and close the door. Her hand still tingled and felt warm from his touch. The rest of her, however, felt a chill she couldn't cast away. *Ari?* Nico sent.

I'm here, Nico.

I feel cold. And scared.

I do, too. Will it help if my lion sleeps in your room?

Will she sleep on the foot of my bed?

If that's what you want.

Yes. Please.

Minutes later, Ari's mountain lion padded silently into Nico's bedroom. She found raven Mac already there, perched on Nico's headboard. Ari leapt onto the end of the bed while Nico watched, then made herself comfortable, curling up in a large, tawny ball.

"Sleep," Mac croaked.

"Yeah." Nico pulled covers up and dragged his pillow into a better position. Mac fluffed his feathers and settled down to nap, too.

"There are three videos on this," Darnell slid a thumb drive across the table to Ralph Hooten. "There's a list of websites on it, too. I want you to share—discreetly, of course, all three with those websites."

"But," Ralph reached for the thumb drive.

"I have a little incentive for you if you do as I ask," Darnell grinned. "Just not here. I put a check in the mail this morning, addressed to you—to take up the mantle in this cause."

"There's a cause?" A light appeared in Hooten's eyes as he took the thumb drive and stuffed it in a pocket.

"When you see those videos, you'll know exactly what the cause is," Darnell replied. "I'll be checking all those websites, too, just to make sure the cause is being represented."

"Damn, this sounds exciting," Hooten said. "But my site gets them first."

"Of course. Order a steak—they're good here and we'll have a small celebration for a better world to come."

"I was able to change sheets on Mac's and Ari's beds, because they're all asleep in Nico's room," Francine told Mona as she settled on a barstool in the kitchen. "Mary Kate and I are off the next two days, and I wanted to get as much done as possible before we left."

"What are they doing in Nico's room?" Mona frowned as she offered Francine a cup of coffee.

"Ari's lion is asleep on the end of his bed. Mac's bird is asleep on the headboard. The door was open slightly, so I peeked in. I didn't know birds could snore."

"Neither did I," Mona said. "On any other day, that would make me laugh."

"Has anything been on the news, yet?"

"I'm afraid to ask." Mona set a mug of coffee in front of Francine. "I doubt anything good will come out of this. I hope Del and Laronda can wiggle their way into this investigation. No doubt they'll be looking for Hunter and Erly as possible suspects. When Burke has his human head back on his shoulders later, I want to ask him about keeping both of them off the news and out of the public eye."

"Wouldn't it be better if we just flat out say they were with us?" Francine sipped her coffee.

"I don't want the media anywhere near this ranch, or near Nico, Ari and Mac. The public thinks Nico and Ari are dead; they're still targets of whatever this is that's happening. If people learn otherwise, it will drag all of them into the spotlight."

"In addition to Val and Janie," Francine sighed and set her cup down.

"Yeah. Having the video of the Franks ranch mess on television is bad enough. Lance is checking in with our Captain right now, but we're still assigned to help Del and Laronda, in addition to keeping Nico safe."

"Will Lance tell him we have Hunter and Erly?"

"He's leaving that up to Del and Laronda."

"Sounds reasonable. The FBI probably knows what's best."

"It's not the first time that less than human involvement has been hidden by their Department," Mona explained. "Most of the government doesn't know about their division, and they're thankful for that."

"Did you leave any coffee for me?" Lance walked into the kitchen.

"There may be a cup or two left," Mona said. "Help yourself."

"The baby from Rockport—the one that was quarantined—she died," Lance said as he poured a mug of coffee and joined Mona and Francine at the island.

"Was she infected?" Mona asked.

"She was. Things were ah, handled, during the autopsy."

"Damn. How did the parents take it?"

"Not well. I'm worried that this could go viral in very little time. I mean, there are rumors everywhere, but no solid evidence to back any of it up, yet. Now that those murders happened last night outside Swindall, who can guess what the next shock will be?"

"There's no guessing to it. Not anymore," Del walked in, with Laronda close behind. "I've got videos on my phone, but we need to watch them on a bigger screen. It ain't good, as my mother used to say."

"We need to wait for the others—I don't want to watch any of this more than I have to," Laronda countered. "The Department is attempting to track down who released the zombie recordings—only somebody close to the investigation could do that, and it sure as hell wasn't us."

"Videos? Where?" Lance asked.

"They're on every conspiracy theory website out there, take your pick," Del said. "Three separate videos. One may have had some enhancement, but the damage is done. If they haven't hit the mainstream media yet, it won't be from lack of availability."

"Cue widespread panic," Mona lifted her cup and drank.

"That's not the half of it," Laronda warned. "Trust me."

"What in the name of all that is holy were they thinking?" Val's words were hissed through clenched teeth as he watched the recording of Hunter's first turn to werewolf. "That woman should never have had custody—she's exposed him—and us—to the entire world."

"She's dead," Mona reminded him. "Because of what she did. If Nico hadn't warned us, Hunter would be dead, too."

"They're treating Erly as a suspect already—at least the locals are," Lance handed Val a glass of Scotch.

"Of course they're looking for the closest black man to pin it on," Laronda snapped. "Typical."

"Lara, we know the truth of what you're saying," Del told her. "We're in a position to help—and to protect Erly."

"I know." Laronda's shoulders sagged.

"It's not right," Mona said. "It never is. I think I need a hug after watching those murders."

"What do we tell the boy?" Val stared at Lance. "How do we tell him that not only can the world recognize him for who and what he is, but that his only remaining blood relation is now dead?"

"I hope Mac and Nico can help us out with this," Mona said. "This —Mac said it would get bad in a hurry. Well, this is really, really bad."

"Don't show these videos to Hunter." Val rose from a chair in his study, where they'd gathered to watch the videos.

"Not a problem. He didn't have a cell phone, so he can't see them that way, either," Lance replied.

"We need a temporary alias for Erly—and Hunter," Mona suggested.

Del exchanged a glance with Laronda. "We can take care of that," Del said. "Just give us a day or two to get it done. Our division is already working on debunking the zombie and the werewolf videos—they're claiming they're computer generated images."

"How long do you think that will last?" Val asked.

"The ones who visit those websites will believe it anyway—you can't change their minds no matter what. I'm hoping to reach everybody else and introduce doubt. Many are already skeptical of what they're seeing, anyway."

"So it's made its way to the mainstream media?"

"Some sites are carrying it. It's only a matter of time before they all do."

"It's time to show this to Mac and Claudio," Lance said. "I'll be interested to hear what they have to say about it."

Mac's shoulders ached from the tension he felt. Ari had awakened first, dropping off Nico's bed so quietly that she hadn't alerted either.

He'd asked her mentally where she was when he woke; *in the shower*, she'd replied. Nico woke with a start from yet another nightmare. Mac, already dressed and waiting, understood the pain in Nico's eyes.

Something bad had happened. The Adversary was on the move and beginning to flex his power.

"I know you feel like you've been dragged over jagged rocks," Mac said. "But Hunter needs to hear about his aunt from us—and Erly needs to be with him."

"I'll get dressed." Nico slid off the bed.

"There are two ranches available for a quick sale. One just came on the market yesterday. There's an interested party, but I still think you can get it for a bargain price."

Darnell Cheatham sat in a realtor's office in Austin. Marlon Keating owed him a favor, so he was calling it in.

"Where are they?" Darnell asked.

"The one that was listed yesterday is west of Fort Worth. The other is about an hour and a half west of where we're sitting—in Hill Country. The first was a working cattle ranch—the second is a hunting ranch. The price on the first is considerably less than the second, because the owners fell on hard times recently."

"Bankruptcy?"

"Not yet, but all their cattle were killed in a bizarre accident."

"Oh. You're talking about the one hit by the earthquake? The same one that was on the news this morning, after those animal rights assholes made a video? No, thank you. That one has too much notoriety for me. Let's look at the other one."

"Here's the information, with pictures and descriptions," Marlon pushed a stack of papers across his desk. Darnell lifted them and leafed through the pages. "This looks good," he nodded. "House and outbuildings look to be in good repair. You think we can talk them down on price a little bit?"

"I think we can talk them down a lot."

"Good. Make them a low but reasonable offer, and keep my name out of it, all right? This will be a purchase made by a new organization."

"All right. Do you have a name for it, yet? What about financing?"

"No financing. This will be a cash sale. That should help with talking them down, eh?"

"It certainly will," Marlon agreed.

"You'll be representing Bane Noir Enterprises," Cheatham noted.

"Interesting name," Marlon began.

"I have a particular—fondness for it," Darnell replied. "Get this started. I want that property in my possession as quickly as possible."

"Shouldn't be too difficult—it's sitting empty right now. Owners live out of state and they have a cash flow problem."

"Even better."

~

"They're looking for you and Erly as persons of interest, but we're trying to intervene without giving your location away," Del told Hunter as gently as he could. For now, the boy looked stunned and in disbelief.

Erly sat beside Hunter in the game room, wearing a grim expression. "They killed 'em because they said 'blessed be, or love and light,' instead of God bless?" Erly finally spoke. "Not a mean bone in Catherine Charles' body, or the others, for that matter."

"It's not a character issue," Mac, who stood behind Del, offered. "It's a war of religions, because it's the easiest way to rile people up and force them to choose sides."

"May as well say it's a species issue, too," Erly muttered. "They suspect there are werewolves. What about vampires and the rest of the shifters?"

"We're trying to keep a lid on that," Del replied. "I just don't know how well-informed the enemy is, or how much proof they can produce or manufacture."

"In this day and age?" Erly asked. "They can make or manipulate anything. Tell me it ain't so."

"We know that," Mac sighed. "We're trying to protect what we can; we just can't protect everybody."

"Erly, I don't feel good," Hunter mumbled before rising and hurrying toward the bathroom.

"I don't care if they come hunting me—I can disappear," Erly tossed over his shoulder as he followed Hunter. "Hunter don't deserve what he got, and he sure as hell wasn't involved."

CHAPTER FOURTEEN

"Just lay low for now," Darnell snapped at Bobby Ray over the phone. "If the Rangers come snooping around, I'll see if I can't deflect their investigation. We'll have a new base of operations soon, and you can move in there with your cousin. Did you get rid of the rifles?"

"Yes, sir. We ain't stupid."

"When the move takes place, I'll have more work for you," Darnell told him. "I warn you, though, talk about this to anybody, or speak my name, and you're as good as dead, got it?"

"I got it."

"Good. I'll have a new phone and phone number for you soon, and we'll look into buying a new arsenal for your use. Keep your mouth closed about this, and only discuss it with Reverend Killebrew."

"Got it."

"Good."

"His wolf is shivering in a corner of his room," Erly reported as he filled a dinner plate for Hunter in the kitchen.

"If you can get him to eat, I think I can help with the rest," Val said. "Wolves belong in a pack. We can drop him off at the barn, and Henry and a few others can den with him."

"Val's right," Janie said. "Having others around him will soothe the wolf."

"I'm willing to try anything," Erly said. "I just hope he eats, first."

"Erly, he'll eat when he's hungry," Val sighed. "We'll do whatever we can to help the boy."

"All right, then. I'll get this to him and tell him we'll help if he'll let us."

"Take a plate for yourself," Janie suggested. "If you eat, maybe he'll eat with you."

"Why didn't I think of that?" Erly flashed Janie a quick grin.

"I'll find a tray while you fix your plate," she offered. "We're about to put the food on the table, anyway. Ari makes good pot roast."

"Where is she?" Erly asked.

"She went to change shirts—she splashed brown gravy on the one she was wearing."

"I love brown gravy," Erly said. "Can the boy and I have extra?"

"I believe so. Give me a second and I'll put some in a covered dish."

"I made plenty of gravy," Ari walked into the kitchen wearing a clean shirt. "Enough for extra all around, including what I ended up wearing."

"Don't be wastin' gravy," Erly teased. "It makes mashed potatoes tolerable."

"I'll file that away for future reference," Ari laughed.

"I hate to interrupt, but we've been called to investigate disappearances at a wildlife refuge not far from Port Aransas," Laronda strode into the kitchen wearing a worried frown.

"Disappearances?" Ari asked.

"People go in—they don't come out. Two park rangers went in to search for missing tourists, and they haven't been seen or heard from since."

"That doesn't sound good," Janie put a lid on a container of gravy and added it to Erly's tray.

"It's not good—especially since they never found all those dead people who jumped off the boats down there. We're adding to our team, Ari, and we've already notified the Department. You, Mac and Nico are going with us, this time."

"When?"

"Tomorrow morning. It's the first flight we could find to carry all of us together. We've made arrangements for Claudio and his guards to come after nightfall, if they want to."

"I think one of them should stay here—to guard the ranch," Ari said.

"Mac said the same thing."

"What if I can get us down there, ah, faster?" Ari sent a guarded look to Laronda.

"Mac said you might offer. He says it's unwise at this point."

"Fine. We'll go the conventional route, then."

"We'll have new IDs and passports for you before we fly," Laronda continued. "And it wouldn't hurt to dye your hair before we submit a new photo to the Department."

"I've never dyed my hair." Ari didn't like the idea.

"It can be temporary, don't worry. Sometimes, I buy the kind that will wash out completely the next time you shampoo."

"Well, if you know what you're doing," Ari assented.

"I do. We'll get you fixed up. Want black or brown?"

"Brown, please."

"That should cover your honey-blonde very well," Laronda nodded. "After dinner, we have a hair appointment."

"What about Nico?"

"Haircut," Laronda said. "Then a few stylish purple streaks and he's a new man."

"Did we get enough new clothes washed for you to take if you need to overnight?" Janie asked.

"Yeah. I'm good," Ari replied.

"Then let's sit down for supper before it gets cold. Erly, get that boy fed, and we'll get him to the barn after dinner."

"Will do." Erly lifted the tray and walked out of the kitchen.

"Good-night, Senator," Darnell's Chief of Staff called out as he walked out of his office to go home.

"Gerri, if I get a fax from Marlon Keating, just put it on my desk, okay?"

"Of course. Is there anything else?"

"Not tonight. See you tomorrow." Darnell hefted his leather satchel over a shoulder and walked toward the door. Tonight, rather than taking the stairs to the first floor of the capitol, he decided to take the elevator down.

The marble floor echoed with his footsteps as he made his way toward the elevator, then stepped aboard when the doors opened with a soft ding.

With the first-floor button pushed, Darnell watched absently as the door shut. Halfway between his floor and the next, the elevator stopped abruptly, with a jerk and a bounce.

Darnell reached out to push the call button when the light went out, leaving him in complete darkness.

"Dammit," Darnell cursed, feeling his way toward the buttons at the front of the car.

"You're not trapped."

The voice sounded as if it were echoed from far away, until two, ember-bright eyes blinked open before him. Darnell swallowed a shriek.

"You have no need to fear me," the voice grated, as if it were attempting to soothe the Senator.

"Who?" Darnell's voice was a husky, frightened whisper.

"You may call me Belhar," the voice now sounded amused. "I present myself to you in this way, so as not to frighten you further.

Eventually, when you recognize my worth, you will not be afraid. We are allies, you and I. We want the same things."

"What things?"

"Death to witches. Death to werewolves and those who love werewolves. Vampires. Other things not quite—human."

"What makes you think I'll take your word for any of this?"

"I know what happened in Swindall, and all involved. I know many things, Senator. I am in a position to help you greatly."

Darnell began to sweat. Someone knew he was involved in that mass murder. "I could have you killed," he threatened.

Belhar's laugh filled the elevator car and echoed through Darnell's mind. "Oh, you amuse me so," Belhar was quite gleeful. "You see, I cannot be killed. I am eternal."

The lights came on, temporarily blinding Darnell and forcing his eyes shut until he could deal with the sudden brightness. When he finally blinked them open, his back hit the rear of the car as he hastily retreated from Belhar's form.

Tall, black horns curved atop the face of a demon. A muscular chest, covered in dark hair, made Darnell's eyes widen in fear. At least Belhar had covered his legs and privates; he wore dress pants that appeared to be made of the finest black silk.

There were no shoes; shiny, black cloven hooves were Belhar's feet. "I have already made arrangements for you to take possession of the ranch you are negotiating to buy," Belhar continued. "You will receive a call from your friend, and for half the money up front, you may move your operation there immediately. I am very much looking forward to this, you understand."

"Wh-what?"

"You will have an army soon—I have been building it for you. This army will move on your command, and you will lay blame for all they do upon the opposition. Have you not always desired such?"

"I don't understand."

"I told you I can be quite useful. And, whenever you need me, you only need to call my name and I will appear. Do not hesitate, or much could be lost to the enemy."

"The witches? That enemy?"

"Ah, still naïve as yet. You have so much to learn, Senator. So, so much. Until we meet again." Belhar disappeared before Darnell's eyes as the elevator lurched into motion.

"Are you sure Hunter will be all right if Erly comes with us?" Laronda asked Val the following morning. "He wants to come, but he's worried about the boy, too."

"Hunter will be fine, I think," Val replied. "He wants to work with Henry and Kev today. They're repairing fence on the east side. We didn't offer—he asked them if they'd let him help."

"Erly said he was used to hard work," Laronda sighed. "Thank you for putting us up and for looking after the boy. I have no doubt that we'd have bigger trouble in Swindall than we already do if you hadn't taken the boy out of there when you did."

"His wolf could be dead, and a few more humans could be dead, too," Val nodded. "I can't help but think that Erly would have tried to protect the boy, and that may have meant his death as well."

"Just what Claudio said last night," Laronda agreed. "He and Renault will be flying down tonight to join us, unless we can solve this mystery before then. I truly doubt that will happen."

"After Swindall, I don't think anything will be easy to solve from now on," Val nodded. "We'll be fine with Alejandro here to help at night, I think."

"How's the land sale coming along?"

"Burke is meeting the local realtor today; if things go well, we could have papers signed by tomorrow. Depending on how long it takes to get the abstract updated and all, we may ask to go ahead and start covering up that rift right away. I don't want rotting cattle to draw vermin in, and the stench in this heat is almost unbearable."

"Then I hope things go like you want them to," Laronda said. "We need to leave, now, but I'm sure Lance and Mona will keep you updated on our return."

"You're welcome here when you get back," Val told her.

"As long as we don't put you and yours in danger, we'll take you up on that offer."

"You and Del have helped us out—you're like family, now."

"Awww—I really want to hug you right now."

"I'd take a hug," Val grinned.

"Haven't been on a plane in years," Erly said as he buckled up next to Ari. "Never been in first class before."

"First time in first class for me, too," Ari told him. "Mona says these were the only seats available."

"Would you like something to drink before we take off?" The first-class flight attendant asked.

Ari exchanged a wide-eyed glance with Erly before saying, "Coffee, please."

"I'll have what she's having," Erly grinned.

"Coffee all around, I think," Del said from across the aisle.

"I'll have it right out, and I'll bring menu cards for you to look over," the flight attendant smiled.

"Not bad for a two-hour flight," Ari sighed as she ate another grape off her plate. "I'm not sure I can ever be satisfied with coach again."

"This would make a long flight bearable," Erly agreed, putting his feet up and leaning his seat back. "In the war, I flew on a military plane to Korea. Felt like three-day-old roadkill afterward."

"Erly, tell me you didn't serve in the Korean War," Ari whispered, leaning close so the attendant wouldn't hear.

"I did. I'm older than I look, you know."

"Damn." Ari leaned back in her seat before reaching out to pat Erly's hand. "Thank you for your service, Erly."

"You're welcome."

"These oak savannas give way to fresh-water marshes, and eventually to the saltwater marshes," a park ranger explained as he drove an open-air bus down a narrow trail. "Unfortunately, the first abandoned vehicle was towed away before we realized the people hadn't left the park, as we originally suspected."

"Can you show us where it was?" Del asked as the bus bumped along the uneven terrain of the Aransas Wildlife Refuge.

"I'm taking you there, now. Another vehicle is about half a mile away—the first two rangers who went to investigate that one are also missing. Agent Reeves—those are friends of mine, as well as coworkers. I sure hope you can find them for us."

"We'll do what we can, but we can't make promises, you understand."

"Yeah. We understand."

He doesn't understand, Mac sent to Nico and Ari. *None of this makes any sense to him and his fellow rangers. Ari, if you'll sniff around when we get there—you, Erly and Laronda should be able to tell whether the worst has happened.*

What are you expecting us to smell? Ari asked.

It'll have a hint of something you've smelled before, but—changed. A lot.

Can you describe it?

The best way I can describe it after talking to Claudio is a hint of decayed roadkill, with smoke and evil thrown in, Mac responded.

You're describing the demons, aren't you? Nico said.

Yes. I don't have a sensitive nose like Ari and the others, but other vampires who experienced this in the past have made similar comments.

"Here we are," the ranger interrupted the silent conversation. He'd parked several yards away from an area where crime scene tape had been tied to metal stakes stuck in sandy soil.

"Ari, if you and Erly will go with Laronda to check on the ground first," Del said after stepping off the bus.

"We're on it," Laronda replied as she followed Del. She stepped aside, waiting for Ari and Erly to join her.

The others disembarked and gathered around Del and their ranger guide, waiting for the shifters in their group to sniff for evidence.

Let me know what you find, Mac told Ari.

"Those ain't deer tracks," Erly stopped several feet away from the crime scene, after noticing animal tracks on the sandy road.

"You're right," Laronda agreed, studying the tracks Erly pointed out.

"Too big for a cow, too," Ari noted. "Hold on. I need to kneel down, I think." Ari squatted next to a set of cloven-hoofed prints but leapt up almost immediately with a short, half-scream. To Mac's ears, it sounded far too close to a yowl from Ari's mountain lion. She'd smelled something, for sure.

"Del, come with me," Mac pulled Del away from the group. "Mona, stay with Nico." Mac rushed toward Ari's position, hauling Del with him.

"Damn," Erly repeated Ari's movements, kneeling next to the prints before rising again swiftly. "I don't know what that is, but I don't think I like it."

"Lara, tell me what you smell," Del arrived with Mac, wearing a concerned expression.

"All right, but you owe me, Del Reeves." Laronda knelt beside the prints and drew in a breath, before her coyote yipped in distress. Mac had to grab her arm to keep her from running away from the site.

"Demons," Ari hissed. "Don't ask me how I know, I just do." She cradled the hand with the shell imprint—it burned and ached at the same time.

"I think we're going to need help," Mac said. "Del, how many can you pull in from your Department of the fanged and furred variety—before sunrise tomorrow?"

"Maybe a handful are close enough," Del said. "I can put in a call."

"Do it. I'll leave a message for Claudio, to see if he has any friends to bring along. I also need to know how many dead people are unaccounted for."

"Has to be several hundred at least," Del said. "But I can tap into the Department's official records to get a better idea. How do we kill these things?"

"Vamps have the best chance against them," Mac replied. "Beheading them is safest, just like in their zombie phase. There's a catch, though."

"What's that?" Laronda asked.

"These will have fangs, claws and a really bad attitude," Mac responded. "That information is from Claudio, by the way. Vampires are far more familiar with this version of the enemy than I am."

"What do we tell the park ranger?" Del asked.

"That we need to bring in help—to fan out and wade through the marshes if necessary. I don't want to upset him at this point and tell him his friends aren't coming back—not in human form, anyway."

"I'll have some of our people come in and secure the area. The park is already shut down until the investigation is over," Del shook his head. "I'll tell him that we're taking over for now, and to send all employees home this afternoon. I'll clear it all through the Department."

"Del, do you think they ought to shut down access to Matagorda Island, too?" Laronda asked.

"Maybe. Got any feelings on that one?" Del turned to Mac.

"Not without seeing it, first," Mac told him. "Nico may have a feeling about it, though."

"Then let's go ask."

"Not in front of the Ranger," Ari cautioned.

"Yeah," Erly agreed. "We don't need to draw attention to the boy."

"Let's get out of here for now—this place doesn't feel safe," Ari said. "I feel—cold, and it's in the nineties." *I don't want anything sensing Nico*, Ari informed Mac silently.

"Come on—we'll get out of here for now," Mac began walking toward the bus.

"Yeah. I'm gettin' the willies," Erly agreed.

"This place is for sale, but they're still renting it out until a buyer comes along," Del dropped his duffle in the foyer of a large beach house. "We don't need to be holed up in a hotel—in case somebody becomes suspicious when the vamps come in."

"Well, if I had a million or two stashed away, I'd buy this place," Ari said, looking around.

"What she said," Mona walked in behind Ari.

"Wow," Nico's eye lit up as he saw the view of the gulf straight through from the foyer. "Can you imagine waking up to that every day?"

"You say that now," Mona called after him. "Wait until the next hurricane comes along."

"Don't rain—or blow wind at over a hundred miles an hour on that kid's parade," Erly said. "Let him enjoy it now."

"You've been through a hurricane?"

"Katrina," Erly nodded. "House was completely destroyed; that's why I moved to Texas. Still like the gulf when it ain't blowin' up a hurricane, though. Fresh fish and shrimp—man, those were good times."

"Ari, come look," Nico called out. Ari grinned and went to see what fascinated Nico so much. She found him on the balcony stretching across the back width of the house. Wind blew in from the gulf; seagulls flew past, some so close Nico could almost reach them. Down on the beach, a couple were walking on the sand while the waves piled up close to their feet.

"That looks spectacular," Ari breathed in the salt air. "I'm not sure I've ever stayed this close to the water."

"I hope we get to spend some time on the beach," Nico sounded wistful.

"Me, too. It looks like fun."

"Some days, I feel like the word *fun* has been removed from our vocabulary," Nico shook his head.

"If there is any way, I swear we will have fun again. Paint together again. Wake up in the morning with no worries again." Ari draped an arm around Nico's shoulders and hugged him. "We're family, remember?"

"Yeah." Nico's arm went around Ari's waist. "It's up to us, now, whether any of that happens."

"I'll bet there's a spectacular view when a full moon rises over the water," Ari breathed.

"I think so, too," Laronda joined them on the wide balcony. "The others are discussing whether to cook in or go out for dinner. Erly says there's a Cajun restaurant in town, so he's voting to eat out."

"Or we could order to-go and somebody could go pick it up," Ari suggested. She and Nico broke apart to turn toward Laronda.

"I think I like that idea best," Laronda said. "There are plenty of chairs out here—we could have our dinner and watch the water at the same time if we want. Come back in—we can look at their menu online and place the order. We can strategize while we eat."

"They just looked at the ground and then rushed you out of there?" Teresa Moore, an investigative reporter from San Antonio, sat across from Jeff Walker, the park ranger who'd driven FBI agents through the wildlife refuge earlier. They'd chosen a popular beer and burger restaurant in Corpus Christi to have their meeting.

"Yep. Didn't say a thing about what they saw or what they were looking for—they just ran back to the bus, told me to get everybody out of the park and shut the place down," Jeff replied.

"Are they planning to go back later?"

"That's the idea I got," he shrugged. "I really shouldn't be talking to you about this, but we lost two of our own to whatever this is, and it pisses me off that they really didn't go any farther than the first crime scene."

"Do you think it has anything to do with those zombie attacks?" Teresa pushed Jeff for an answer.

"Those zombies will leave human footprints behind. We didn't find anything like that, and neither did the police."

"What do you think they saw, then, that spooked them so much?"

"I didn't say spooked," Jeff lifted a thick-cut French fry, loaded it with ketchup and stuffed it in his mouth.

"What do you think they saw?"

"No idea. Nothing around there but animal tracks, you know. Maybe a cow or two wandered in—we saw their tracks."

"What happened to the cows? Did you find them?"

"Wasn't looking for any, and nobody reported them missing. Maybe afraid to. Don't worry—if they travel into the marsh, they'll end up as alligator bait."

"You think they'll go back tonight? The FBI agents?"

"No idea. I did hear them discussing reinforcements—to do a wider search."

"How many did you take into the refuge?"

"There were eight. One was barely old enough to be an agent, I think. They all had badges though, so I didn't ask questions. The lead agent—he looked like he'd snap my head off if I asked the wrong questions anyway."

"I don't suppose you got any pictures?"

"No. Why the hell would I?" Jeff sputtered.

"Never mind. Did they close off Matagorda Island, too?"

"Yep. The whole refuge is shut down until they say it's safe to open again."

"What about boats—are they keeping boats from passing by?"

"They didn't say anything about that. I figure somebody could rubberneck from a boat, but they'd need powerful, night-vision binoculars or a good video camera with a telephoto lens and a night mode setting to see anything worthwhile."

"Is there someplace close by that sells those things?"

"There's a sporting goods store just west of here, off South Padre Island Drive."

"Know anybody who'd rent a boat to me?"

"I do. A close friend of mine has a big fishing boat. He'll drive it, too, because he knows where he's going. He fishes around there all the time."

"Good. We'll take my car. I'll drive; you call your friend. We'll go on a night fishing expedition, to see if the FBI shows up at the refuge tonight."

～

"Now that was a decent low-country boil," Erly said, patting his stomach. "Dirty rice was real good, too."

"It was all good," Lance said. "I'll have to remember that place if I'm ever in the area again."

"Claudio and Renault are on their way," Del stepped onto the balcony, closing the sliding glass door behind him. "They're flying on a private jet and bringing a few friends with them. Should be here in less than two hours."

"Gonna be a late night, then," Erly said, rising from his chair. "Think I'll take a cat nap before they get here."

"Lance, I need to see you, Mona and Ari for a quick meeting," Del continued as Erly made his way past Del and into the beach house.

"Where?" Mona asked.

"There's a study off the kitchen. We can go in there."

"All right." Lance rose; Ari and Mona stood, too, ready to follow Del.

"Tight fit," Mona said as the four of them crowded into the small study, most of which was taken up by an empty computer desk.

"Two of you will have to stand," Del apologized.

"Don't worry about it—I've been sitting too long as it is," Ari replied.

Mona ended up with the extra chair, while Del occupied the one behind the desk. "We have news about where the bomb came from that destroyed Blue Taco," Del said. "Lara already knows about it."

"What's the news, then?" Lance asked.

"We found the bomb maker," Del stated flatly. "After his rotting corpse drew flies and the neighbor's dog."

"He supplied the bomb and got knocked off afterward?" Mona asked.

"That's the current theory."

"How did he die?"

"This is the weird part," Del said. "His torso has a big hole in it. Like he was gored to death by a longhorn."

"Huh?" Ari frowned at Del.

"Forensics is working on the body now. They'll let me know if they find any foreign material in the wound and what it's made of."

"Anybody we know?" Lance queried.

"I figure you've heard of Louis Breckinridge."

"Damn. He's been off the grid for how long?" Lance leaned in to catch Mona's eye.

"At least fourteen years," Mona nodded. "Asshole."

"Dead asshole, for three weeks or so, as best we can determine," Del said.

"Right around the time the restaurant was bombed," Ari breathed.

"So they got enough to bomb the restaurant and the house—do you suppose they have more bombs than that—to use later?" Mona demanded.

"No idea. Breckinridge's house looked as if a hurricane went through it and blew every scrap of evidence away."

"So we couldn't tell how many bombs he made. What about supplies and receipts? Is there a money trail?" Lance asked.

"I guess it was all cash or stolen," Del shrugged. "No credit cards used or receipts anywhere, but we're checking sales of the proper components locally, and looking into reported thefts."

"It still gets us no closer to who actually commissioned all those bombs," Ari pointed out.

"We can't go around asking about beings who kill with horns, now can we?" Mac stepped into the study and shut the door. "Laronda brought me up to speed," he added.

"Does Nico have any ideas?" Ari frowned at Mac as she crossed arms defensively over her chest.

"He suspects the horn theory may be correct, whether they find evidence of it or not. I figure he's right."

"As do I," Ari snapped.

"We don't need conflict within the ranks," Del warned.

"I know." Ari dropped her arms and turned away from Mac.

"We're still working out why certain people were targeted by zombies," Del went on. "So far, we have no theories about that."

"Removing the competition," Mac replied. "Nico and I have discussed that, and it's the only logical conclusion we could find. The people who were attacked? All of them were potential replacements if Nico goes down."

"Nico will not go down," Ari hissed at Mac.

"Fucking hell," Lance swore. "Are you kidding me?" he added.

"As long as Nico or a replacement holds the stone, the gate will remain closed. If the Adversary gets his hands on it, then we're all doomed." Mac jerked the door open and stalked out of the study, shutting it hard enough that a photograph of seagulls trembled on the wall.

"Nico will *not* go down," Ari repeated through clenched teeth, before exiting the room right behind Mac.

"What the hell are we even talking about?" Mona demanded. "What gate? Where?"

"No idea," Del sighed. "Rest up if you can. We'll go back to the wildlife refuge right after the vamps arrive."

CHAPTER FIFTEEN

"Arianne, we have not spoken since I was injured," Renault said softly as he sat beside her in the back seat of the van the vampires arrived in.

"You don't have to thank me," Ari began.

"No, you misunderstand. How good is your night vision in this form?"

"Much better than a human's," she replied.

"Can you see this?" Renault held up his right hand.

Ari could see it, all right. She looked from the shell imprint to Renault's face and then back to his hand.

"How?" she whispered.

"I cannot say. I have guarded two others who have held your position in the past. Neither of them passed the image to another."

"Did either save your life?"

"No. In those cases, I saved theirs."

"Maybe that's the difference."

"Perhaps. I feel as if it is—a badge of honor, I believe you would call it."

"Then wear it proudly," Ari bumped her shoulder with his, before recalling that vampires as a rule didn't like to be touched.

Rather than being offended, Renault chuckled. "We are friends, yes?"

"Yes."

"Then we may bump shoulders or fists," he smiled. "Whenever warranted."

We'll stop outside the visitor's center and get out there. No need to alert anyone to our presence by driving in, Mac informed Ari.

Right. Will Nico be with you or me?

I'll take him in with me, but he'll know if we're close to the enemy's minions. We'll give a warning, so be ready.

What do you want me to do?

Find demons. Kill as many as you can.

Good. That's what I want to do.

The vamps will go in first—you can stick close to Renault if you want. He may need protecting again.

I doubt the demons will have guns, Ari replied dryly. *That was Mitchell's last shot. He got lucky, hitting Renault like that.*

You got lucky when you removed the bullet. I didn't think your power had developed that much, and Renault could have died anyway from a half-formed effort.

Are we back to that again? Look. Just—send a warning if it's necessary. Otherwise, stop talking to me.

"Something wrong?" Renault spoke to Ari quietly.

"No," Ari lied. "Just—thinking about what we may find in the wildlife refuge."

"We are seven vampires, in addition to the others. We will strike a blow against these enemies and show them we are not helpless."

Renault, tell me if you can hear me, Ari sent a silent message.

"Ari?" Renault's eyes widened.

You have the shell imprint. I think it recognizes you and this is part of its power, she told him. *We will tell Nico after tonight's battle.*

We must tell Claudio, too.

That's your decision to make.

"You ready for this?" Lance handed Mona a Colt M4 Trooper rifle and extra clips before taking one of the weapons for himself. Del already had one slung over a shoulder.

Laronda and Erly had shucked their clothes and were now coyote and jaguar. Both waited patiently for their human counterparts to lead the way.

Ari, on the other hand, remained in human form and stood near, but not next to, Mac and Nico. Beyond those three, Claudio spoke quietly with six vampires, Renault included.

"Am I imagining things, or does the air feel—heavy?" Mona asked Lance as she shouldered her weapon.

"Something's up, that's for damn sure," Lance whispered. "Shoot first, ask questions later, okay?"

"As long as you do the same."

"Shouldn't feel this hot," Del stepped back to talk with Lance and Mona. "Wind's off the gulf and should be fresher than this."

Lance watched as Mac and Nico walked toward him. "It's a hatching ground," Mac breathed. "That's why the air feels like it does."

"That doesn't sound comforting," Mona muttered.

"Come, the vampires are ready. They'll lead us in," Mac explained. "Make sure to hit demons and not vampires."

"I think we know that," Lance said.

Renault, if you see anything, let me know—I'll help if help is needed, Ari sent to the vampire.

Of course. Claudio and I have already decided that it would be appropriate to inform you if we find our enemy. We are about to move, now. Keep a safe distance unless you hear from me.

You got it.

Ari watched as seven vampires lifted lightly off the ground and floated toward a stand of oak trees. Ari understood their mode of travel and choice of direction—the scent coming from there put all of them on edge.

We were right to shut down the refuge—things would have gotten much worse, Nico told Ari.

The itch between my shoulders is like fire, Ari replied.

Be ready, Nico warned.

Demons! Renault shouted.

The night sky exploded with shrieking, flying creatures.

Ari relocated in an instant.

"What the hell?" Jeff Walker rushed to the front of his friend's boat to get a better look at the creatures erupting above the trees in the wildlife refuge.

Behind him, Teresa recorded the event with her new video camera. Neither were prepared for the flash of light and resulting boom that shook the boat. Teresa was knocked off her feet by a swell of water that nearly capsized the vessel. Jeff grabbed the railing and hung on as another swell hit them.

"We need to get out of here," Mike Rafferty, the boat's owner, shouted as he revved the engine and turned the wheel, steering the boat around and into the gulf. Another swell lifted the back of the boat as Teresa struggled to rise.

Jeff turned around as the boat raced at full speed away from the wildlife refuge. The boat's engine drowned out the shrieking sound as he watched another explosion of flying creatures rise above the distant trees.

"Bullets aren't slowing them down," Del shouted at Lance, as they fired into the night sky at screaming, angry demons.

"Nobody told me they could fly," Mona took aim at another over her head.

"I'm not sure they knew," Lance shouted back as another flash of light and subsequent earth-shaking boom tore monsters apart overhead.

"Get out of the way," Del turned and began running as chunks of demon began falling among the trees.

Mona and Lance ran with Del; limbs and trees were damaged behind them by the grisly fall of demon flesh.

~

"Your army is dying," Belhar's glowing red eyes bored into Darnell's. "You need to do something about it before they are all destroyed and I am forced to make new ones. Time is short."

"What am I supposed to do?" Darnell had been lifted from his bed by Belhar, and now faced him in the dimness of his own kitchen.

"Call them. Send them to your new compound."

"I have no idea how to contact them."

Belhar breathed an annoyed sigh. "I see I must teach you everything," he growled. "When I say the words, you repeat them mentally. Do you understand?" Belhar's eyes glowed brighter.

"Fine," Darnell snapped. "Tell me what to think."

"Ah, now you understand," Belhar sounded pleased. "Repeat these words. *I command my servants to rise and come to me now. I have a new kingdom. You will meet me there. Together, we will make a new world.*"

Darnell thought each sentence as Belhar instructed, until he reached the end. "There. All done. Did anything happen? I didn't feel a thing."

Belhar reached out with a clawed hand and sank the tips of his nails into Darnell's chest, surrounding his heart.

Darnell drew in a ragged, pain-filled breath as the visions hit him.

~

Ari stood beneath a third stand of oaks while Nico reached out to mentally search for more monsters. Nico and Mac had caught up to her, while vampires had taken a protective stance and now stood in a ring about them. Ari had no idea where Erly and Laronda were and hoped they were safe—from both the monsters and the fall of their flesh after she blasted them.

There are more here, Nico sent a mental image to Ari, who dipped her chin in understanding.

Are we close enough for you to target them? Mac asked.

Yes.

We must hurry—I feel, Nico didn't finish.

Nearly a quarter mile away, another legion of demons burst into the sky. Ari aimed her blast and launched, only to have it explode into empty air. Nico fell to his knees with a cry.

A burning pain hit between Ari's shoulders at the same moment, doubling her over in agony.

"The Adversary has taken his first soldiers," Mac hissed as the air around them became so cold Nico shivered. "Nico, we've done as much as we could. Come, we will go back, now." Mac lifted Nico to his feet and pulled him away, leaving Ari to fend for herself.

Renault stepped forward to help Ari. "How many?" Ari breathed as she straightened with Renault's help.

"My guess is that three hundred or so escaped. There were three legions festering here. We destroyed two of them," Claudio came forward to report. "Without your help, that would not be true, and more would have escaped to join their master."

"Let's go back." Ari turned to watch Mac and Nico walk away. She could have gotten all of them back to their vehicles with no trouble; Mac chose to walk. "We need to find Erly and Laronda," she added, shoving thoughts of Mac from her mind.

"Spread out," Claudio indicated three of his vampires, who quickly dispersed.

"They will find our colleagues," Renault told her. "Shall we?" he gestured toward the visitor's center, which was far away from where they stood.

"Yeah. Let's go." Ari hunched her still-aching shoulders and began the long trek to the van.

〜

219

It's better if I push her away. And keep pushing her away, Mac reminded himself on the long walk back. He'd been rude and he knew it—and felt bad because of it.

He had to keep her at arm's length, or the prophecy would manifest. It was easier at first, thinking that she wasn't qualified and another would be selected. That theory had been proven wrong. *Why did Nico have to choose a female? Why was that female Arianne Leone?*

"You're angry with yourself," Nico observed. He'd walked silently beside Mac for half their journey before speaking up.

"I," Mac began.

"Stop mistreating Ari. She doesn't deserve it," Nico said. "You've said yourself that we have to work together. Tonight, Ari and I worked together. We took down two-thirds of the enemy's demons. What did you do, other than upset her—and us?"

"I'm sorry."

"Tell that to Ari." Nico disappeared, just as Ari could. Mac knew he'd find Nico with their van; he broke into a trot to get there faster.

~

"I'm sorry I hurt your neck," Erly apologized to Laronda. "But getting you up that tree was the best choice I could make."

"Don't apologize—you were right," she rubbed her neck. "No puncture wounds, so that's a plus. Who knew those—things—were going to burst out of the ground around us? We could have died."

"The tree and limbs protected us," Erly sighed as he pulled on his shirt. They'd ran for the van shortly after the demons left the ground around their tree and launched themselves into the sky.

"I have to tell you, that's the spookiest situation I've ever been in," Laronda nodded. "Do you hear something?" she jerked her head around.

"Somebody's here," Erly nodded toward the van's door. He tensed, ready to make the change and defend himself when Nico opened the door.

"Thank goodness," Laronda breathed.

"You guys okay?" Nico asked.

"We're fine," Erly replied. "How about you?"

"We got two-thirds of what was out there. The Adversary pulled the last third away. Who knows where they are now?"

"We need to hunt 'em, don't we?" Erly frowned.

"Yeah. Claudio thinks there may be around three hundred. That many can do a whole lot of damage before we find them again. Plus, more will be in the making—bet on it."

"Do you know what happened to the missing people?" Laronda asked.

"Those demons need a food source," Nico ducked his head. "Live humans are meat to them, just like the alligators and other wildlife in the refuge."

"Those things eat people?"

"They want meat. Doesn't matter what the source is. The only thing they want more is to serve the Adversary, who will no doubt tell them to feed on his enemies."

"That don't sound good," Erly muttered.

"How do you know this?" Laronda asked Nico.

"I have dreams. Well, nightmares, actually—of what has happened in the past, and what can happen in the future. Sleeping hasn't been exactly restful—not for a long time."

"Is there anything you can do about it?" Erly asked.

"The only time I went without nightmares is when Ari's lion was sleeping at the foot of my bed. The minute she left, the nightmares came back."

"Damn shame," Erly shook his head. "Sorry to hear that."

"You're exhausted, aren't you?" Laronda said.

"Kinda. Maybe I'll ask Ari's lion to curl up on the bed again tonight."

"I figure we'll leave tomorrow after breakfast—I'd say you need your sleep," Laronda observed.

"Well, well, glad to see you two safe," Del, Lance and Mona arrived. Del poked his head in the open door to give Laronda and Erly a tired grin.

"Erly had to drag me up a tree, but we made it," Laronda told him.

"Where's Mac?" Lance, who leaned in behind Del, noticed Nico wasn't with his constant guardian.

"He's walking and fuming," Nico shrugged. "I already told Ari where I am; she'll be here with the vamps any minute."

"I see them," Mona called out.

Mac's bad mood continued as he swung into the van and found a seat. Everyone else was already loaded in and waiting for his arrival.

Nico sat in the back row, surrounded by Erly and Laronda. Mac was forced to sit with Mona and Lance in the center row. Claudio had taken the front passenger seat, no doubt to discuss what he and the other vamps had seen and done when nobody else was with them.

He watched as the bus containing Ari and the other vamps pulled out first; Del put the van in gear to follow them.

"We killed some, but that was before they took flight," Claudio told Del. "Once that happened, we were helpless to follow them."

"In your past experience, did any of the demons have wings?" Del asked.

"No. Sadly, this is a new development. I have no idea what could have changed to produce this twist in their creation."

"Somehow, they've increased their power," Mac didn't sound happy. "Perhaps it's because the world has become unstable and deeply divided."

"Certainly something to consider," Claudio agreed. "I will discuss this with the other scholars when I make my report."

"It won't be easy telling the families of the missing that their loved ones are gone for good," Mona said.

"The Department will assist in handling it," Laronda said. "Did anybody else get the willies when those things started shrieking?"

"Every part of them is designed to instill fear," Mac said.

"You are worried," Claudio turned in his seat to look at Mac.

"More than ever before," he admitted. "It's like the game changed without our knowledge, and we no longer understand the rules."

"We are different, too, Mac," Nico said. "You know it's true. Ari—have you seen anyone do what she did tonight?"

Mac rolled his shoulders uncomfortably. "No," he admitted.

"Can the Adversary find us?" Erly asked. "I mean, if he could call that vermin away from here," he didn't finish.

"As long as you're near enough to Nico, Ari or me, he can't," Mac replied. "Just as we can't locate him—for the same reason. We have power to protect us against his second sight, just as his protects him and his—what did you call them? Vermin?"

"Vermin," Erly confirmed. "Ugly, flying vermin."

"We weren't close enough to the vermin the Adversary called away," Nico offered quietly. "I'm just glad you and Laronda survived their rising."

"Erly put us between two thick limbs on an oak. If they'd risen next to us, they'd have brained themselves on the tree," Laronda explained. "Erly saved us both."

"It's a cat's natural defense to climb," Erly said. "Instinct saved us."

"Then we'll drink to instinct when we get back," Laronda told him.

"Will these creatures pass on the disease, like their uh, previous selves?" Mona asked.

"These will eat you first," Mac rumbled. "You need to let your captain know that more zombies will likely be in the offing, since we killed two legions of demons tonight."

"We'll alert our Department, too. Any idea where the strikes will occur?" Del inquired.

"They'll be looking to replace a lot in a short amount of time," Nico sighed. "I expect crowds of people to be exposed to the disease."

"That's awful," Erly breathed. "Can't go anywhere or do anything anymore."

"If you wish to wait until the vampires rise in the evening tomorrow, you are welcome to return to Dallas on our jet," Claudio offered. "This way, the young man can visit the beach while he is here."

"I think that's a good idea," Del turned briefly toward Claudio. "Thank you."

~

"What the hell are those things?" Jeff Walker squinted at Teresa's laptop screen, trying to make sense of what he was seeing.

"They look like biblical images of demons," Teresa mumbled, attempting to zoom in and edit the images to make them larger and clearer. "See—they have horns, bat wings, they're naked—and loud," she added, turning up the sound.

"Too bad the clip is only fifteen seconds long, and nearly half of it is just empty sky after you fell on your ass," Jeff observed.

"It's enough," Teresa snapped at him. And leave my ass out of this. What I want to know is this—we saw a bright light, and then those things were just—gone. Does the FBI know what those things are, and do they have a laser or something to kill them?"

"Now I know why they wanted everybody out of the refuge," Jeff shook his head as he studied the still image Teresa paused. "Those things look evil."

"If they killed your friends, they're exactly that," Teresa said. "I need to get this to my boss. I think he can sell this to the national networks with no trouble."

"You think this has anything to do with those zombie videos—you know the ones on the conspiracy websites?"

"I don't think that's a conspiracy any longer," Teresa's brow furrowed in a frown. "This sure as hell isn't a conspiracy. We saw it. I wonder if anybody else saw it?"

"All the more reason for you to put this out first, I guess," Jeff suggested.

"I couldn't agree more. Look, if you're willing to go on camera to answer questions about this, I think I can make it worth your while," Teresa told him. "You and Mike, both."

"Sure. Whenever you want. I don't figure I'll be asked to go back to work for a day or two, at least."

~

"Ari, would your lion sleep in my room? When you're that close, I can sleep without nightmares," Nico asked as their crew trooped into the beach rental.

"If it helps you sleep, then of course," Ari told him.

"Thank you."

"If you need me, I'll be in the doghouse," Mac said behind Nico. "Why didn't you tell me that Ari can keep the nightmares away?"

"I didn't know until she slept on the end of my bed. The nightmares came back the minute she left my bedroom."

"I—none of the others had this much trouble, even the ones who dreamed," Mac blew out a ragged breath. "Nico, I owe you an apology. Ari, too."

"Apology accepted," Nico told Mac. "I'm exhausted and I just want to sleep."

"I'll take a quick shower and be in right after," Ari said, turning toward the stairs and the bathroom where her toiletries were.

"Thanks, Ari," Nico called out as she went up the stairs.

"Now," Nico turned toward Mac. "Don't you think it's time you told me why you keep pulling her in and then pushing her away?"

"This I would like to know also," Renault now stood beside Nico. "You upset Arianne almost daily, when there is no need for it."

"It has to do with the curse laid on me centuries ago," Mac's shoulders drooped. "I've never been this pressed to struggle against it before."

You're jealous of Renault, Nico's words breathed into Mac's mind. *I don't know why I didn't see it before. It's still not the reason you're upsetting Ari, though, is it?*

Nico, it's—my life will end if I give my heart, Mac forced himself to admit.

Some things may be worth your life, Renault broke into the silent conversation, before lifting inches off the floor and gliding away. *I will keep watch tonight. Sleep well, young Nico*, he added.

"How the fuck," Mac's words exploded in a forceful hiss. "How did he get telepathy?"

"Ari," Nico shrugged. "Renault has an imprint on his palm. If he didn't deserve it, it wouldn't be there. Go to bed, Cormac Flynn. Tomorrow, we begin our search for the Adversary—and his vermin."

"I recognize the wisdom of your words," Mac dipped his head to Nico. "You have become more than wise."

"Tormented into it," Nico replied grimly. "I'm going to get in the shower, then I'm going to bed. See you in the morning." Nico relocated, leaving Mac alone in the tiled entryway of the house.

"I have to go. There's work to do," Darnell whispered to his wife, only half-waking her. "I'll call later."

Striding quickly from his bedroom, carrying a small bag with a few articles of clothing and his toiletries inside, Darnell went downstairs before making a call to Bobby Ray.

"Huh?" Bobby Ray's voice betrayed his waking state as Darnell pressed the phone to his ear.

"It's time. Meet me at the new compound. You got the address I sent you, right? Bring your friends and cousin. Anybody who wants in on this, bring 'em. We have work to do."

"I'll get right on it," Bobby Ray replied, sounding more alert.

"Good. I'll be there, waiting when you get there. My eyes are open wide now, Lieutenant. We'll build our army together, and we'll strike down our enemies together."

"Want me to bring the Reverend?"

"If he wants to come. If he does, tell him to bring his wife, too. She's a decent cook, and we need that. In fact, bring wives and girlfriends if you want. It's a big place. We'll need somebody to cook and clean."

"I'll let them know."

Darnell hung up the phone before sending a mental summons to Belhar.

"You called?" Belhar's arrival was sudden. Darnell didn't fail to notice the wisps of fog (or was it smoke?) drifting away from Belhar's grotesque form as he solidified.

"Get me to the compound. We have work to do."

"It will be as you say, Master." Belhar didn't hide his glee as he transported the Senator to the recently-purchased hunting ranch in Texas' Hill Country.

"They'll be back late tonight," Janie told Hunter, who'd asked about Erly and the others. "How are you doing, sweetheart? Want scrambled eggs or over-easy?"

Janie already had a soft spot in her heart for the young werewolf; Val did, too. "I'll take scrambled. I can cook 'em, you know. You don't need to wait on me hand and foot," Hunter said.

"It's been so long since we had a young one in the house," Janie smiled as she cracked three eggs into an iron skillet while Mary Kate pulled a pan of biscuits from the oven. "Makes me feel young myself."

"Happy to be of service," Hunter grinned. "I feel better—some. Working with Kev and Henry has helped a lot, and I learned stuff I didn't know before. Erly can patch that leak in the barn when he gets back. I can help."

"Val will certainly appreciate that. The orphan calves will, too."

"Hunter, how's it going?" Val walked into the kitchen after being out moving cattle to a new pasture.

"I'm good," Hunter said. "Kev told me that if I learned to ride a horse, I could help move the cows next time."

"I think we can work on that," Val nodded. Janie handed him a cup of coffee. "Thanks, Mom," he said and sipped from the cup. "We have an ATV for emergencies, but the horses don't spook the cows like that contraption does."

"That reminds me," Janie said. "Hunter, do you have a driver's license?"

"No," Hunter admitted. "Aunt Cathy always said we'd get to that after I turned sixteen, but," he shrugged.

"Once we have your new ID from Del's Department, we'll work on that, too," Val said. "That way, you and Erly can drive into town and buy supplies to fix the barn."

"Erly does have an aversion to driving anywhere," Hunter nodded. "He had a car, but I don't think he drove it for more than a year."

"I heard that both houses were searched for evidence," Val took a seat beside Hunter. "I hope you took everything you wanted, because it's considered a crime scene, now."

"That pisses me off—that they think Erly and I are capable of," Hunter stopped for a moment before wiping angry tears off his face.

"You're an easy target," Janie soothed while placing a plate of food in front of him. "I don't doubt for a second that a nearby bunch of prejudiced hooligans are responsible for those murders."

"Burke says at least three weapons were involved—I wonder how they're explaining that," Val said. "Since they're only looking for two people. Rangers may have other information, but they're not sharing. Burke got this from a friend of a friend who knows the Sheriff down there. On a brighter note, Burke gave the down payment to the realtor listing the Franks Ranch yesterday. I sign papers tomorrow and closing will be in three weeks. The best news is that we have permission to cover up that ravine."

"Thank goodness," Janie breathed. "I can't walk outside without getting a whiff of that mess."

"Val, Janie, I think there's something on television you need to see," Francine walked into the kitchen.

"What's that?" Val set his coffee cup on the island and turned toward the housekeeper.

"I think it's what our bunch had to deal with last night. It's my guess they didn't know that somebody recorded those—things."

"Here," Mary Kate turned on the television that sat in a counter corner. "Which channel?" she asked her sister.

"Local news—they all have it."

"Holy cow," Hunter exclaimed as he leaned forward to get a better look. "Those things look like," he didn't finish.

"Like demons," Janie gasped. "Mac said demons. I didn't believe him. Those things are loud, too—can you hear that?"

"How do they kill those things?" Hunter asked, awe and terror in his voice. "They fly. We don't fly. None of us do."

They watched as the same short video clip was shown over and over, while a news anchor droned in the background. "Val, is this what's in our future?" Janie turned a frightened gaze toward her son.

"Pack up every pan and scrap in this kitchen, woman," Benny Killebrew growled at his wife. "Can't you see I'm in the middle of writing my resignation letter? We have a higher calling now, and you're gonna like it. Understand?"

Phyllis sniffled as she began opening cabinets to pull everything out of them.

CHAPTER SIXTEEN

"I don't believe this." Mona sat next to Lance in the beach house family room, watching demons rise from the wildlife refuge.

"Had to be recorded from a boat in the water," Del said. He and Laronda walked in carrying mugs of fresh-brewed coffee. "Erly and Ari say breakfast will be ready in ten."

"It's only a matter of time before the same websites start harping that this is revenge from witches for killing some of their own," Mac strode into the room and took a nearby chair to watch the recording on the local news.

"Oh, look—it's our very own park ranger," Mona snarked as Jeff Walker appeared on the screen.

"We were on a boat in the gulf last night, and saw those things," Jeff confirmed. "I'm terrified that my friends—all those missing people in the refuge—are dead."

"You're saying that the FBI was on the scene last night?" A female journalist, off-camera, asked.

"That's what I heard. They shut down the entire refuge yesterday, and there were flashes of bright light last night while those—creatures

—were flying. I hope they have a weapon that will kill those things. They look evil to me."

"Have you spoken to your supervisor, or the head of the Fish and Wildlife Service?"

"No. You're the first one I've talked to."

"Will this place your job in jeopardy?"

"Maybe. I don't know. What I do know is whatever those things are, we have to get rid of them—and whoever made them. That can't be natural."

"What the hell?" Ari snapped as she caught sight of Jeff Walker on television. She and Nico had walked into the family room together. "People do stupid stuff," Nico replied quietly.

"Breakfast is ready," Ari announced. "Stop watching that crap. It'll just make you crazy."

"Breakfast sounds great. Turning off the TV even better," Del agreed, rising carefully with coffee cup in hand. "Lead the way; I'm starved."

Ari walked next to Nico on the beach after breakfast. Gulls took flight as they approached, while the surf washed over their footprints, convincing the sand to forget they were ever there.

"The sound of the water is a good filter," Nico observed as they walked along. Occasionally, he stopped to watch in fascination as colorful coquina clams, uncovered by lapping waves, burrowed back into the sand to hide themselves from predators and the sun.

"It's an allegory," he pulled his eyes away from sand-buried bivalves and squared his shoulders before walking away.

"An allegory?"

"For everybody, everywhere," Nico replied. "We're constantly struggling to survive, aren't we?"

"Well, when you put it like that. Is Mac still trailing us?" Ari refused to turn around and look.

"Yes." Nico bent over to lift a shell. "This is beautiful, but it's dead." He turned the shell over to reveal a small, round hole. "The shell is protection, and it's relatively thick, but it still fell victim to a predator." Nico pocketed the shell and continued walking.

"Did you sleep all right last night?"

"Yeah, with normal dreams, but they were still chaotic."

"I sleep better when I'm in mountain lion mode. The cat rests better than the human does."

"Sometimes I wish I had another form—a disguise, to disappear into and free myself from the constant bombardment of the negative energy the Adversary is creating. There was negative energy—a lot of it—already swirling around. Half his work has been done for him."

"I used to tune out the news, because it was all bad, seems like. Now, it's worse, and we're stuck in the middle of it. How soon do you think the Adversary will turn his vermin loose on innocent people?"

"Soon. I'm sure he's already preparing his manifesto against the witches, who he'll blame for creating the monsters. He may add to that list, too, because of those videos showing Hunter's change to wolf. In the past, people were tortured and burned for being witches or lycanthropes. It's only a matter of time."

"Lycanthropes? They were burning people for being werewolves? If they'd had a *real* werewolf, anybody who tried to capture him or her would lose a hand at the very least."

"Check the history of the inquisitions—all of them. Some list that as the sin or heresy committed by the hapless victims. You're right, though. All those people tortured and or burned to death were human."

"Or half-human, as Mona and Lance are."

"Yeah. It's easy to stir up the general populace, once they have an enemy to point a finger at. With the video of the vermin on every news channel, they'll be stirred up for sure."

"Maybe we ought to tell all of them that guns are of no use against these things," Ari said, toeing a clump of seaweed out of her path.

"You honestly believe that will work?" Nico turned toward Ari, a deep frown marring his youthful features.

"No." Ari shook her head and kept walking.

"They want to destroy the stone," Nico said after a while. "They'll have to kill me to get it."

"Nico, they'll have to kill me first," Ari said. "And, if it's nighttime, they'll have a bunch of vamps to get through before that."

"They'll figure out that attacking during the day is their best bet."

"Then we ought to do our best to root them out before it comes to that."

"Ari, that will take a miracle."

Mac berated himself; he had nobody to blame but himself for the fact that he was trailing far behind Nico and Ari on the beach, instead of walking beside them.

He also berated himself for admiring Ari from behind. She was dressed in a sleeveless tank top and shorts, and she'd chosen to walk the sandy beach barefoot. She was tall, lithe and fit, her calf muscles presenting themselves well at every step she took.

She and Nico were talking, and he should have joined that conversation. He should be privy to Nico's thoughts and musings.

My fault, Mac reminded himself. It was time to admit that he was drawn to Ari like a moth to a flame, and, like the moth, risked losing his life in the process. He could recall the last of the curse laid upon him, after his path in this world had been laid by another.

Should you ever become presumptuous enough to give your heart completely, your curséd life will end. She'd laughed after pronouncing his doom, and then disappeared.

Through the centuries, he'd wandered in and out of the lives of those chosen by the stone. Most he had little affection for. A few he'd served with devotion, but never loved.

Until now.

Nico had drawn a response from him that no other had; he felt— fatherly. Nico was so young. Had been so unprepared. Mac couldn't help caring for the boy.

Ari—even in raven form, his heart had lurched the first time he saw her. He'd ignored that reaction, focusing only on Nico. Whenever he found himself responding to Ari after that, he'd pushed her away. Been rude and hurtful, when it wasn't warranted.

All to protect his own ass.

She was devilish in her own way—the one who'd carefully laid the curse upon him. He was facing what could be the worst Adversary of them all. Mac needed to form a bond with Nico and Ari, to combat the Adversary's strength.

He'd done just the opposite.

You have to fix this, he chided himself. *Get up there and apologize.*

Except he couldn't. Ari would hiss at him and he'd deserve it. When had the raven knight become such a coward?

When I chose to love, came the simple reply. Who knew how fragile the heart could be, when the hard shell he'd built around it was breached?

Are you ready to come walk with us? Nico invited.

Hold up, I'll be right there, Mac replied and broke into a trot.

"Here," Nico handed the lettered olive shell he'd picked up to Mac. "The shell wasn't enough; the creature needed protection from those around it. Left on its own, it perished."

Mac turned the buff and brown shell in his hand until he saw the hole that another creature, known as a drill, had created to feed on the mollusk inside. What was left behind was a beautiful shell, but it was empty of life.

Mac sighed and pocketed the shell. He was determined to carry it as a reminder—an allegory for his life.

"Nico, I know you can sculpt as well as paint," Ari said after the three of them walked in silence for a few minutes.

"You want me to create a false stone, don't you?" He turned toward her in understanding.

"Yes. I think we can give it a bit of a spark—maybe enough to fool someone?"

"Yes," Mac nodded. "I think that's a good idea. Only make more than one. Ari will carry one, I will carry one, and Renault will carry one. The fourth one you make should remain with you, Nico."

"Yes," Nico agreed. "That's a fine idea."

"We'll work on that when we get back to the ranch," Ari said. "We need to find some jet, Mac."

"Yes. I'll look into it. Perhaps Claudio can help."

"They can do research while we sleep tonight," Ari said. "Look, there's a great blue heron."

The tall bird was wading through shallow water ahead of them, searching for small fish or crabs. Ari pulled her burner phone from a pocket to snap a photo. "I've never been this close to one," she breathed.

"Should we turn back and leave him to his breakfast?" Nico asked.

"I think so," Mac replied. "We're three miles from the beach house."

"How long is that going to last?" Darnell grumbled as Reverend Killebrew's wife, Phyllis, sniffled while filling the lodge's cabinets with canned goods, bowls, and pots and pans.

"She'll get over it, or I'll help her get over it," Benny grumbled. "You wanted to talk?"

"Yeah, but I only have folding chairs in my study right now."

"That'll be fine. Are we getting more furniture soon?"

"I asked Bobby Ray to scrounge. It doesn't have to be fancy; it just needs to be functional." Darnell led Benny away from the kitchen. "It's just through here," they walked along a hallway before turning left into a study lined with bookshelves. A TV tray was set up near the window, and Darnell's laptop was there, plugged into the wall.

"I already got the ball rolling on the utilities and stuff, but we need funds. Don't want the Justice Department interfering because I diverted campaign funds, if you know what I mean," Darnell explained.

"If you need funds, then I can take care of that," Benny offered. "I can have those websites that carry our video messages ask for donations to further the cause. It's the least they can do for us since we put them on the national media map."

"We did that, for sure," Darnell pointed Benny toward one of two folding chairs near the laptop. "Once the money starts coming in, we can do whatever we want with this place. How soon can you get that set up?"

"Maybe tomorrow. I think we can pull in some big donors, too, if we handle it the right way."

"Whatever it takes," Darnell said. "I just need names—and their wish list."

"Wish list?"

"Enemies? We can take them down—just tell us who. We'll tell you how much."

"Seriously? I mean, Bobby Ray's good, but he ain't that good."

"We don't need Bobby Ray for this—we have other allies."

"What do you mean?"

"Let me introduce you to Belhar."

"You called, Master?" Belhar appeared and bowed his head to Darnell. "I must tell you that I have been searching diligently for the ones who destroyed much of your army last night. Should they be found, I will act on your behalf. I have also looked into replacing those destroyed. I will keep you advised on my progress."

Benny Killebrew, who'd been too shocked to speak at first, took in every bit of Belhar's features, from the tips of his curved, black horns to the pointed, cloven hooves at the end of furred, goat-like legs.

"Ah, Reverend Killebrew, so nice to finally meet you in person," Belhar smiled.

"The Governor is considering a special legislative session," Del sat heavily at the kitchen table next to Lance's chair. The detective leaned both elbows on the table, morosely consuming a cup of coffee.

"No doubt to discuss the vermin we flushed out of the refuge?" Lance asked.

"He considers it an emergency," Del commented dryly.

"It is an emergency. Too bad he can't do a damn thing about it," Mac set a cup of coffee on the table and joined the conversation.

"Whatever they do, it'll be stupid and ineffective," Lance agreed. "They'll demand information, which up to now only the Governor and a few high-ranking senators have been privy to. Once it gets out to the entire legislative body, there'll be hell to pay."

"Our Department has warned him and other state law enforcement that they may come across more zombies-in-the-making," Del said. "Which can turn into demons-in-the-making if we don't handle it appropriately. We may have to call in the regular FBI, because we don't have enough agents to spread throughout the state."

"Humans will be more vulnerable," Erly arrived in the kitchen to rifle through cabinets for a snack. "Laronda and I aren't helpless, but we felt that way when those things popped out of the ground last night."

"Few are invulnerable to those things, in my estimation," Mac shook his head. "Humans will become food if they get in the way."

"If the regular FBI gets involved, then they need to start looking at places where a lot of people congregate," Lance suggested. "Music festivals, outdoor fairs, popular shopping malls—that sort of thing."

"I've already passed that message along," Del said. "Mac, do you suppose Claudio can pull in more vamps for night events?"

"I can ask. I'm sure their Council will see the sense in bringing more in."

"What about werewolves to combat demons? If they won't pass along the disease, that is," Lance asked.

"Some of ours went in to collect samples from what got killed in the refuge," Del admitted. "We should know for sure after they run tests."

"You had a cleanup crew ready to go in?" Erly found a box of cheese crackers and carried it to the table.

"Yep. Better safe than sorry," Del replied. "We don't need demon alligators, if that stuff can be transmitted."

"You had to ruin my appetite, didn't you?" Erly made a face at Del. Mac snorted a laugh.

"Why didn't I ever think of doing this before?" Laronda wiped her face with a towel after, she, Mona and Nico did Tai Chi with Ari.

"It's good to work out the kinks and force the worries back," Ari said. "I usually do it every day—until recently. Nico used to show up at my studio and exercise with me."

"I learned a lot from Ari, and it sure helped when the semesters got stressful," Nico said. "It's worth the effort."

"I want to learn enough to do it on my own," Mona admitted. "That was a workout, even if it looks slow and effortless."

"I'm all for a shower and then food," Nico said.

"Should we get something delivered, or can we go out?" Laronda asked.

"I think we should go out," Nico said.

"What he said," Ari leaned her head in Nico's direction. "I'm hungry, and I always heard this is a good place to get shrimp or locally-caught fish."

"I'll let the others know, and then head for a shower myself," Mona said. "Last one out pays."

Ari ran upstairs, following Nico. Once there, she turned toward one of three bathrooms located on that floor.

Ari, there's something I need you to help me do, Nico sent.

Not a problem, Ari said after Nico told her what he wanted. "Get in the shower. I'll have it finished by the time you're out."

"Best idea today," Laronda grinned as a server placed a margarita in front of her.

"I agree, and I'm not old enough to drink," Nico told her. "Shrimp cocktail is awesome, though."

"Best view in Port A," their server said as they watched a sailboat dock right outside the open-air restaurant.

"It sure is," Erly said.

"I think you'll like the red snapper you ordered—we got it fresh this morning."

A distant, booming sound interrupted the conversation. Nico exchanged a glance with Ari, while Mac looked from one to the other.

We moved the vamps—they're back at the ranch, Nico told him. *Ari and I—we had a feeling that the Adversary was honing in. That's why we wanted to go out to dinner.*

Ari waited for their server to leave the table before telling everyone the news. "I hope you didn't have anything important back at the beach house," she sighed.

"Why?" Del's forehead creased in a frown.

"Because it just blew up," Nico replied.

"Weapons are in the back of the van," Laronda said. "I have my purse and my sunglasses—I can replace everything else."

"I'll let the Department know," Del stood and pulled out his cell phone.

"Good idea," Lance said. "I'll come with you." Del and Lance walked toward the front of the restaurant to find a private place to hold a conversation with Del's superiors.

"Ari, do you think you can move a vehicle?" Mac asked quietly.

"Maybe."

"We can drive away from here to a secluded spot, and then you can get us out of here. Nico, please don't leave me out of this conversation again, I beg you. I would have agreed with your decision, I promise."

"I told Janie the vamps were back in the basement, and left notes for Claudio and Renault to find when they wake," Ari said.

"We may be back there before they wake," Nico mumbled as their server, bearing a tray and a tray stand, approached the table.

"Thank you," Laronda told Nico. "I appreciate what you and Ari did."

"Governor just called a special session," Mona lifted her cell phone when it chimed. "Captain wants to see us when we get back, too."

"Tread carefully from now on," Mac warned after their server walked away. "The enemy has the talent to pull many to his cause. He managed to find the beach house, likely because it was a recent rental large enough to house a bevy of agents. Don't trust anyone outside this circle."

"Because that wack-job ranger spilled the beans to a reporter that we were there, no doubt," Laronda sniffed. "Asshole."

"One may wonder if he's still alive—or wholly human if he is," Mac grimaced.

"I can check," Laronda said, lifting her cell phone and sending a text.

"Let's eat, I'm starved," Lance said as he and Del returned to the table. "Then we need to get the hell out of here."

"You're all on the Department payroll going forward," Del said as they loaded into the van to drive away. "Lance and Mona are on loan from Dallas PD until this is over. Your pay will go into bank accounts under a brand-new alias. The alias you used here will officially be retired, because you'll all be officially reported as deceased.

"Going forward, if you need supplies, we can have money diverted from your pay to cover expenses, and the packages will be delivered to a single Post Office box in Abilene, under the names of Kirk and Scottie Shipman. That includes anything from shampoo to sneakers. Agents posing as Kirk and Scottie will pick up the packages, and they'll be delivered to the ranch."

"I get a paycheck," Nico bumped shoulders with Ari.

"We get a new alias, too?" Laronda asked Del.

"Officially, yes. I can't say how glad I am that we used one this time. That fool ranger may have given the names he could remember to the enemy."

"Is he missing?" Mona asked.

"I haven't gotten a reply to my text," Laronda said. "Somebody will be checking on him, and that may take time."

"In other words, he isn't answering his phone," Mac observed.

"Got it in one," Laronda agreed.

"Where are we going?" Lance asked as Del drove the van toward the ferry, rather than going back toward the beach house, which was in the opposite direction.

"Across the ferry, and toward Rockport. I think we can get lost somewhere in between."

~

"Long as they think you have information, they'll keep you alive," Phyllis breathed as she slid plates of food into Jeff's and Teresa's cages. The expansive, dimly-lit tornado shelter, built to house numerous guests at the hunting lodge, had turned into a makeshift prison.

"Who are they?" Teresa whispered, her words trembling and confused.

"You saw what brought you in," Phyllis gave a soft snort. "If that ain't the devil, then he don't exist."

Jeff waited until Phyllis left the large tornado shelter behind the main house before speaking. "Mike's in trouble, if he isn't dead," he muttered, naming his boat-owning friend. "We may as well be."

"Maybe we can get that woman to help us," Teresa hissed.

"You didn't get a good look at her, did you?" Jeff demanded. "Her face is black and blue. She won't help us because she can't even help herself."

"It's not just us in trouble," Teresa said flatly. "Anything that comes in contact with what took us is in trouble, too. I recognized one of those men. If I can get out of here," she left the threat hanging.

"Who was it?"

"Senator Darnell Cheatham," Teresa said. "Now do you understand?"

"Great. The state has made a deal with the devil."

"Let's hope it's only this one part," Teresa snapped. "Eat before they come back and take it away."

~

"That was fast," Val shook his head as he and Janie watched the news.

"The park ranger and the journalist who reported on those monsters are both missing, now. Probably because the ranger saw our bunch and was involved in recording the mass rising of those undead creatures."

"At least Ari got the vampires away safely before their rental was destroyed," Janie said. "This is terrifying."

"I'm thinking about letting them have the Franks house—to use as their base if they want to bring in more agents," Val said.

"That's a good idea, hon. A really good idea. There's plenty of room, although they may have to fumigate to get the smell of Mitchell Franks out of there before Ari will step foot in the place."

"Very true," Val appeared thoughtful. "They included some of the furnishings in the sale; all they want is a few things off the walls and such."

"Val, what if Ari's father," Janie didn't finish.

"We need to get over there and find out," Val said. "And demand that it stay so we can have a proper funeral here on the ranch."

"All those years," Janie shook her head. "It must have been beyond frustrating—and sad at the same time."

"Yeah."

Val's cell phone rang. He answered.

"Val, it's Lance. We're at the front door."

"Be right there." Val ended the call, leapt from the game room sofa and ran toward the stairs.

"The beach house barely made the news, once word was out that Jeff Walker and Teresa Moore were missing," Mac spoke with Claudio and Renault.

"We are grateful that Ari and Nico performed a rescue," Claudio dipped his head to Mac. "We are in your debt. The others we brought with us have gone home, but they asked me to thank you on their behalf."

Renault didn't comment that Ari had carefully placed him and his vampire associates in the same position she'd found them, once she transported them to the Jordan Ranch.

The notes helped greatly, too, when they awoke in a strange place and to different scents. She and Nico had saved their lives. Renault carefully touched the shell imprint on his palm.

Could he do some of the things Ari could—eventually? He already had telepathy, and that was a wonder in itself.

"The Governor of Texas has called a special session, no doubt to deal with the unusual activity we've already witnessed," Mac went on. "We should watch carefully, to note what their suggestions are. If the Adversary has already gotten to a few," Mac shook his head.

"Ah. The usual tactic. Get the law and the government and your religion on board, and things become even more horrific," Claudio observed. "I've asked two of our additional crew to keep track of those websites, where the recording of the first killing of witches took place. I will be very interested to see which legislators bring that up first."

"Del and his Department are feeling out the Texas Rangers investigating that crime," Mac said. "It should be easy enough to see if any of them have been compromised. He's been given permission to brings some on board, but Nico has to approve them before they're read in. We may need a lot of help when crowds of people are attacked to create more zombies and demons."

"We can send vampires to night venues, if we suspect an impending attack," Claudio offered.

"Nico needs to be involved in those choices, too. I'll ask if he's had any feelings on the matter."

"They will act soon, will they not?" Renault's imprint tingled the moment Mac mentioned zombies and demons.

"We believe so. Del's Department is working its way through potential targets."

"Do you think the journalist and the Park Ranger are dead, or being kept alive in case they have vital information?"

"Could be either. If they get reliable descriptions on any of us, then our alias won't protect us any longer."

"You expect this to happen?"

"In this day and age, yes. At least Ari and Nico colored their hair. They may be more difficult to pin down. As for Erly and Laronda, they have other guises, as do I. My worry is for Del, Mona and Lance."

"We will protect them at night," Claudio said. "You must find a way to do so during the day."

"Ari will protect them as much as she can," Renault offered.

"I'm worried about when they're not close to Ari, Nico or me," Mac admitted.

"Very true. I understand that Mona and Lance have a meeting with their captain tomorrow?"

"Yes. I think Ari should go along; I can stay here with Nico, unless he says otherwise."

"Then I suggest making another hair color change for Ari, only this time it should be a more permanent solution."

"She'll love that," Mac's words betrayed sarcasm.

"Renault, will you place a call to Everette? If she is available, ask her to visit us tonight, and bring a friend to act as security."

"I'll do that now." Renault excused himself and floated away.

"Everette?" Mac was curious.

"One of us, although she is ah, quite different, too. Everette will do Arianne's hair, so she can go out tomorrow with Lance and Mona."

"I figure Del and Laronda will go, too, but Ari can help Laronda keep an eye on everybody. Where is Everette, by the way?"

"Dallas. She can be here shortly, if she's available. She will also be instructed not to reveal any information, should she be asked."

"Pick your color. I'd suggest platinum or auburn, girl. You'd look good either way," Everette told Ari, framing Ari's face with capable hands.

Everette, dressed in a slinky, glittering silver top and tight-fitting black pants, wore size ten platform heels from a well-known designer. Her honey-gold complexion was set off by a carefully styled pink wig and long, thick, false eyelashes.

Ari, fascinated by Everette, watched her every move. "Your nails are amazing. Are they real?" Ari asked, staring at the pink and black zebra-striped designs.

"Oh, these? Pffffff," Everette waved a graceful hand. "You don't want me doing your hair with my real nails. You know I'm a vamp, just like I know you're a shifter."

"Still looks great," Ari shrugged. "Why don't you choose which color—platinum or auburn. If I have to color my hair, then at least one of us will be happy."

"You'll be happy, too, once I'm done," Everette ran her fingers through Ari's hair. "I promise."

"May I make a suggestion?" Renault walked into the bathroom where Everette had set up.

"You can do whatever you want," Everette smiled at Renault.

"Ari, I think I'd like to see the platinum first," Renault said. "And if you have to revert to the auburn, it may be an easier transition."

"You get a gold star," Everette pointed a finger at Renault. "Platinum it is."

CHAPTER SEVENTEEN

"I haven't been here since Lance talked to Nico after his parents were killed," Ari followed Laronda and Mona into the police station the following morning.

"You look completely different with that hair color," Mona said. "We can get visitor passes and go upstairs while Lance and Bill park the car, Leah," Mona used Del's and Ari's new aliases as they passed two detectives on their way to the front desk.

They were helping themselves to breakroom coffee by the time Lance and Del caught up with them.

Ari followed the others to Captain Belwether's office, and shut the door behind them.

"Who's this?" Belwether studied Ari.

"Security," Lance said, taking a seat at the far end of the desk. "I assume you want to ask us about the vermin at the refuge?"

"Yes, that's exactly what I wanted to talk about," Belwether waved Del, Mona and Laronda to the other chairs in his office, leaving Ari standing by the door.

"We can tell you right away that our usual weapons had absolutely no effect against those things," Mona said. "Like they didn't even feel the bullets."

"Did you kill any of them?" Belwether didn't sound happy.

"We killed two-thirds of what was there," Del replied evenly. "Or, I should say our security killed them."

Belwether's head jerked toward Ari. "You killed those things?"

"This is where you have to trust us, Captain. It's better if you don't know how it was done. For your protection and for ours," Del said. "My Department is currently testing the remains of what was killed. I hope we have a report soon. We'll share as much as we can with you."

"You know the Governor has called a special session?" Belwether turned toward Lance.

"We do."

"Well, I, along with several others from Dallas PD, have been called to testify before a committee. The Governor wants to know what's going on."

"We'll have someone contact the Governor," Del said. "Meanwhile, you can give the information you have."

"Which isn't much—by design," Belwether complained.

"I'm sorry we can't be more forthcoming," Del apologized. "We have a job to do, just like you. Hand over information on the zombies and say with a clear conscience that all you know about the vermin in the refuge is what you've seen on television."

"Carefully leaving the FBI out of it," Belwether didn't sound pleased.

"We're officially dead, remember?" Del reminded the captain.

"Hmmph." Belwether didn't appreciate Del's ready answer.

"But you're the ones behind the request for extra security at festivals and concerts, aren't you?"

"Yes. This is of extreme importance."

"Right. Well, if that's all you plan to give me, then we'll talk later, perhaps."

"How soon do they want you to testify?" Mona asked.

"In three days. I'm supposed to have all my ducks in a row by that time, along with the people summoned from Corpus and Austin."

"Good luck. I hope they feed you well while you're there," Lance rose first.

"That makes two of us," Belwether gruffed as they walked out of his office.

~

"He hates not being in the loop," Mona explained as they walked toward Lance's car. "He can get really grumpy about it, too."

"We've seen what a little bit of knowledge did for Jeff Walker and that journalist," Del pointed out. "Belwether could be walking into danger, with what little he knows."

"A lot of people know what he knows," Ari said. "We know more. He doesn't need that extra target on his back, especially if those hearings are televised."

"I'll find out," Del said as he opened a car door for Laronda. Mona and Ari got into the back seat from the other side, leaving Del and Lance up front.

"Where to now?" Lance asked.

Del gave him an address. "What's that?" he asked.

"A Department motor pool, where we can switch vehicles," Del replied. "We need something bigger than this, and it won't hurt if your car goes in a different direction and lays low for a while."

"Can't be too careful," Laronda said.

"Yeah."

~

"Thomas and Sons Used Car Parts?" Mona read the sign over the brick façade.

"They actually sell used car parts out of the front," Laronda explained as Del instructed Lance to drive into an adjoining, covered parking garage marked for employees only.

"It only looks small on the outside," Del grinned as Lance found himself going down one level, and then another level as Del instructed. "Park over there by the black Lincoln Navigator," Del pointed toward an empty spot. "We'll be taking the Navigator and the Mercedes parked next to it."

"Damn, we've moved up in the world," Lance said, pulling to a stop in the designated space and shutting off the engine.

"The Navigator has dark windows, so you'll get that one," Del told Lance. "Lara and I will take the Mercedes."

"Who'll drive mine, and where is it going?" Lance asked.

"Here they come," Del grinned. "Ari will know, but you won't. They're werewolves, and they'll take a jaunt around the city before parking it at a house leased by the Department."

"Aren't we efficient?" Mona grinned.

"It saves lives," Laronda shrugged.

Lance waited a full ten minutes after the werewolf agents drove his car out of the underground garage to venture out. Mona and Ari rode with him; Del and Laronda would follow within a few minutes.

"Anyplace you want to go before we head back to the ranch?" Lance asked as he pulled onto the street.

"I think I'd like a strawberry shake," Mona said. "It's been that kind of day."

"I'd take one," Ari said from the back seat.

"All right, but don't nag me if I want a root beer float," Lance responded before heading toward the nearest ice cream and dairy store. "Okay if we go to the drive-through?"

"Fine with me," Mona said.

"When do you think we'll get the list of events and venues for Nico to look over?" Ari asked.

"Probably have it by the time we get back to the ranch," Lance said. "Why?"

"The spot between my shoulder blades is twinging," Ari told him. "That spells trouble."

"Is there something specific you can focus on?" Mona turned in her seat to ask.

"Not yet," Ari shook her head. "If the pain gets bad, then the danger is close. The first time it happened, I had no idea what it was."

"When was that?"

"When we went to Abilene to buy clothes for Mac. I got a sudden pain then. Had no idea that it was warning me that Mitchell and Denton were now in the area and watching for Janie to get back to her car."

"That's some kind of warning system, then," Lance said, turning off the road and into a drive-through, where he joined a line of other cars waiting to place their ice cream orders.

"Yeah. It took a while longer for me to realize exactly what it was and how to read it. Nico has a warning system, too, but I think his works differently."

"Let us know if we need to get out of here in a hurry," Lance said, inching the SUV forward as the line of cars moved ahead.

"I will."

∼

"Something doesn't feel right." Nico rose from his deck chair by the pool. Mac, sitting nearby, was on his feet a blink later.

Ari? Nico sent. *Something feels—off.*

I know—I'm already feeling tightness and discomfort between my shoulders. Do you have an idea on the location?

Toward Austin? Nico sounded as if he were struggling to get a better feel for the discomfort he'd experienced. *There's a crowd, and I,* he hesitated. *Motorcycles?*

Oh my gosh, it's the motorcycle rally they hold in Austin every year, Ari moaned. *Nico, we need to get down there. Thousands will be at that rally.*

Take me, Mac demanded.

I'll meet you there, Nico said before hauling Mac with him to Austin.

"Tell Laronda and Del that the motorcycle rally in Austin is under attack," Ari told Lance and Mona before disappearing from the back seat.

"Fucking hell," Mona cursed before hauling out her cell phone and calling Laronda.

~

"I thought you'd like to watch the replenishment of your army," Belhar stood beside Darnell, looking out a floor-to-ceiling window upon the crowd of people below them. A parade was winding its way along the street, filled with motorcycle clubs, individual bikers, girls riding in bikinis, convertibles carrying celebrities and a few floats. Musicians played music at intervals along the sidewalk as the parade passed by.

Darnell licked his lips. "You think we can haul in a few of those girls—for other activities?"

"Of course," Belhar grinned. "I was only waiting for you to ask. Give the word, Master, and I will bring your army."

"The word is given," Darnell smiled. Only a moment passed before the air above the parade was filled with flying, shrieking demons, diving in and out of the crowd and methodically pulling away humans, while others around those taken screamed and fled in terror.

~

"Protect Nico," Ari yelled at Mac as she lifted a hand and began blasting demons who weren't carrying humans.

They'd landed atop a three-story business on Congress Avenue in downtown Austin, just blocks away from the Texas capitol building.

Nico had his own way with the enemy, although it took longer. He employed his power to snuff demons into powdered dust, before floating the humans they carried gently to the street below.

Some had already gotten away, he knew; he and Ari could only save so many in the time they had.

"Incoming," Mac shouted as a demon took notice and raced in their direction, folding its wings and reaching out with viciously clawed fingers to destroy the three who were bold enough to fight with his horde.

Holding out both arms, twin blades appeared in Mac's hands as he prepared to defend Nico. The demon shrieked as it approached, as if affronted that someone was foolish enough to oppose him with mere blades.

Leaping up, Mac whirled his body in midair as the demon came into range, slashing off the head with his first strike, then slicing through the abdomen with the second.

Ari turned swiftly to blast another demon following the first, while Nico continued to save as many humans as he could.

Sirens filled the air, their shrill warnings echoing off buildings as first responders arrived amid the pandemonium. Mac hoped desperately that they were armed with something larger and more serious than guns or rifles as he waited for another demon to make an attempt on Nico's life. If their only weapons were rifles or guns, the police could become additional targets for the demons swirling around the street below.

"I am here," Renault appeared, before leaping off the building and removing a demon's head in mid-flight, only to twist his body and return to the rooftop.

Mac blinked—there were half-formed, leathery wings on Renault's back; he'd used those to help him return to the safety of the building before launching himself after another demon flying too close. Except this one bore a screaming woman in its arms.

Mac blinked again as Renault removed the demon's head, then pulled the woman away while the monster's body dropped toward the street below.

"Here," Renault shouted at Mac, before tossing the woman toward him. Nico, rather than Mac, managed to catch the woman with his power and drop her gently onto the roof.

Meanwhile, Ari shouted in rage as the remaining demons, many still carrying humans, abruptly disappeared.

"We have to leave," Nico shouted.

"Not yet," Renault dropped onto the rooftop and approached the woman, who'd fallen to her knees and wept.

"You will remember none of this," Renault told her, holding her face gently in his hands.

"Let's go," Ari snapped and transported the four of them back to the ranch.

❦

"Why couldn't we see them?" Darnell shouted at Belhar, who bared his teeth at the presumptuous human.

"Our vision was blocked," Belhar hissed. "They always hide themselves behind the light. We have retrieved many slaves for you; be satisfied with that." Belhar disappeared in a huff, leaving Darnell to find his own way back to the capitol.

❦

"I woke and knew you needed help," Renault said. "I'd been dreaming before my waking, and in the dream, I stood in daylight. Vampires do not dream in the rejuvenating sleep," he added.

"Things are changing," Nico told him. "I believe that the stone had restrictions where it was before, as did the Adversary and his minions. Once it was away from those bindings long enough," Nico shrugged.

"So the gloves are off? Is that what you're saying?" Mac asked Nico.

"I suppose you could put it that way. We must believe that the stone knows what it's doing, and who to choose for its army to combat an unbound Adversary."

"None of this sounds comforting," Ari said.

"Very true," Renault agreed. "May I have some water? I feel—thirsty."

"I'll get it," Ari rose from her seat at the kitchen island. "Want ice?"

"I will try it," Renault said.

Ari set a glass of ice water in front of the vampire, who lifted the glass carefully before taking a sip. In moments, when there was no adverse reaction, he drank the entire glass before setting it down with a rattling of ice cubes.

"The stone has never been capable of anything like this before," Mac breathed. "And, for now, I believe we should keep Renault's transformation secret."

"I must tell Claudio," Renault countered.

"Of course. Only those of us currently fighting this battle will know," Mac agreed. "We need your help. We don't need the Council hauling you away to poke, prod and test. I fear what it could lead to."

"We will consult Claudio. He will know how to proceed," Renault argued.

"All right, but we need you until this is over. The stone has decreed it," Mac said.

"Where do your wings go? When you don't need them?" Ari asked, pulling the conversation to a safer topic.

"They become a part of me, I suppose. I wasn't thinking about it while I was fighting those creatures."

"It troubles me that the demons can just disappear, leaving no trace or trail behind," Nico grumbled. "I hope Del's Department can give us information on how many were taken. It will give us an idea of how many demons the Adversary will create."

"You're acting as if they're already dead," Janie walked in, wearing a troubled expression.

"Janie, except for the ones Nico was able to save, they are pretty much dead," Ari rubbed her forehead. "Those things—I can't begin to explain the hate rolling off them, along with that evil scent they carry."

"That is an apt description," Renault dipped his head in agreement. "The stench alone convinces me they are evil."

"How can normal humans become something like that?" Janie asked. "That is what they were—before they became zombies and then turned into demons. Or did I misunderstand?"

"You didn't misunderstand," Nico explained. "It appears that in addition to the disease that turns these people into zombies, they're getting a good dose of hate to go with it. This sort of hate is like a virus; it spreads rapidly among those who aren't immune. Eventually, it's the only emotion they're capable of expressing. There's nothing human left of them—it's all hate."

"Their goal is to infect the entire state, and then the whole country, before spreading it around the globe," Mac said. "Again, like a virus that has no cure."

"This is more terrifying than I could imagine," Janie shook her head.

"We got the dozer crew filling in the crater," Val strode in before stopping abruptly and staring in wonder at Renault, a vampire, not only awake but sitting in the light shining through a nearby kitchen window.

"Something's different," he drawled after a moment's silence.

"Renault helped us fight our first battle with the enemy's vermin," Ari turned in her seat to face Val. "Think of it as a kind of miracle."

"Kind of? It's a flat-out miracle," Val shook his head in amazement. "Welcome to sunlight, Renault."

"Thank you," Renault dipped his head to Val. "Perhaps I will try food later. Who can tell?"

"He has wings if he needs them," Ari grinned at Val. "So it's an even bigger miracle. He needed them in Austin, because we were fighting from the top of a building."

"I see I'm behind on current events," Val said. "Mom, is there anything to drink?"

"Lemonade in the fridge," Janie replied. "Or do you want coffee?"

"Lemonade first," Val said, taking the barstool next to Ari's. "Where are our human compatriots?"

"On their way here," Nico replied. "Should arrive in half an hour or so."

"Where are Erly and Hunter?" Ari asked.

"Patching the roof of the calf barn," Val said. "Erly's doing a really good job. Hunter's learning the ropes."

"Erly was one of the first black engineers in a desegregated army during the Korean war," Renault said. "He won't tell you this himself, you understand."

"How do you know?"

"I asked him."

"Simple. Straightforward. I like it," Ari bumped her shoulder against Renault's and smiled at him.

Mac suddenly looked as if something he'd eaten disagreed with him. Nico nudged Mac's elbow, forcing him to sit straighter and school his features.

～

"They took a bunch of others somewhere else. I have no idea why I'm down here," the newcomer hissed at Teresa Moore's pointed question. "What the hell are those things, anyway?"

"Whatever they are, and as ugly as they are, what's pulling their strings is worse, or so I've been told," Jeff's words conveyed defeat. "We're never getting out of here alive. Trust me."

"Your name?" Teresa asked the stranger.

"Friends call me Big John."

"Your real name?" Teresa pressed.

"Will remain a secret," Big John huffed. "I have no idea who you are, or where we are. Not ready to give out personal facts, you understand."

"He's just another biker motorhead," Jeff snapped at Teresa. "Look at his outfit, for Pete's sake."

"Just because I'm dressed in my leathers doesn't mean I fit that description," Big John argued. "Shut the hell up. I don't belong in here."

"Yet here we are," Jeff tossed out a hand. "In separate cages, waiting for somebody to come feed and water us, like animals."

"Animals in a lab experiment, you mean," Teresa said. "Shut up, Jeff. I've had enough negativity today."

"You got me into this, remember?" he accused.

"Right. If I recall correctly, you volunteered."

"Shut up, both of you. I need to think," Big John snapped.

"Like thinking will help," Jeff sneered. All three froze when they heard the lock on the outer door pop open. Sudden light streaming into the shelter temporarily blinded them. When their vision cleared, they didn't recognize the man who'd come down the steps, brandishing a Glock pistol in his right hand and dangling a ring of keys in his left.

"Boss wants to see you," he pointed at Big John. "He thinks you're special. Come along peaceful-like, and I won't shoot you."

"Who are you?" Teresa demanded. "We haven't seen you before."

"Oh, they call me witch-killer," he grinned. "I kill other things, too. Like people who piss me off." He pointed the gun at Teresa's head.

"This is connected to those murders in Swindall?" Teresa searched her memory for the information she'd heard on the subject.

"Say that town's name again, and you're dead," Bobby Ray said, then laughed. "All I gotta say to the boss is that you were uppity. An uppity woman around here is dead meat."

"Come on, you," Bobby Ray turned to unlock Big John's cage. "come out of there with your hands up, or I'll shoot." The gun was now pointed at Big John as he made his way through the narrow door of the cage.

"Go on up the steps," Bobby Ray motioned with the pistol.

"Huh?" Big John turned as if he hadn't understood. Bobby Ray started to repeat himself when suddenly a furious eagle was in his face, flapping wings making him close his eyes in defense as the eagle began clawing and biting the hand with the gun.

The gun dropped to the concrete floor as Bobby Ray cried out in pain. A naked Big John rematerialized, grabbed the gun and shot Bobby Ray as he attempted to rise.

Two more bullets broke the locks of Jeff's and Teresa's cages, before Big John dropped the gun, became an eagle again and flew out of the shelter, heading for open sky.

"Help me," Bobby Ray's voice was barely a whisper as he reached toward Teresa's cage.

"You're asking the uppity woman for help?" Teresa emerged from her cage, lifted the gun and fired two bullets into Bobby Ray's head before running up the steps toward the open door.

Wait for me," Jeff shouted and ran after her.

A terrible shriek and a horrible vision stopped Jeff in his tracks the moment he exited the storm shelter. Teresa's bloody remains were being gobbled up by one of those—*creatures*—they'd seen rising from the wildlife refuge.

"Get back inside," Phyllis grabbed Jeff's arm and shoved him toward the shelter door. "Before they eat you, too."

Once inside, Jeff didn't argue as Phyllis locked him inside Big John's cage, since it held the only working lock. She'd stepped over Bobby Ray's body as if she barely noticed it. "Where did the other man go?" Phyllis asked. "The one in this cage?"

"He went out first—I guess he didn't last long," Jeff whimpered.

"Who killed Bobby Ray?"

"Teresa—out there," Jeff's voice shook. "She managed to get the gun."

"I'll have to let Benny know. He won't be happy," Phyllis muttered. "I'm sorry about your friend."

"Yeah." Jeff slumped into a corner of his cage before dropping his head in trembling hands.

Big John stepped out of the shower, after an attempt to remove the feel of the creature carrying him away from Austin. The whole thing was sick—in the extreme. He still didn't know what they were or where they'd come from. Besides, he needed to get back to the business; stolen bikes and other vehicles would be coming in. And, as he had a criminal record, there was a warrant out for his arrest. He'd be stuck in a human jail the minute he approached the authorities to tell them where he'd been; therefore, he had no plans to tell anyone anything.

"You're a lucky fuck," Big John stared at his image in the mirror before moving out of the bathroom to grab some clothes to wear. He had work to do, and maybe it would help clear his mind.

"Images were recorded of the rooftop in question, but only a bright light can be seen from any of three separate camera angles," a national news journalist reported. Del, Lance, Mona and Laronda had finally arrived at the ranch, and had chosen to turn on the news in the game room upstairs.

Ari, Nico, Renault and Mac joined them.

"Huh?" Del squinted at the screen as one camera angle was displayed. Yes, it was brightly lit, but he could see Ari, Nico, Mac and eventually Renault, or their outlines, at least, as they fought invading demons.

"Most people can't see what you're seeing," Nico told Del. "They only see what looks like sunlight—similar to looking straight into the sun. They have to look away after a while, because it's too bright for them."

"I can see it, too," Mona said.

"How the hell did you grow wings?" Lance turned from the screen to ask Renault. "It's shocking enough to see you here in daylight."

"Mac, where did those swords come from?" Laronda queried, unable to take her eyes off the television.

"Those swords are a part of me," Mac sighed. "I use them to protect the one who holds the stone. Unless they refuse my help."

"Has that happened?" Ari frowned at Mac.

"Yes. On several occasions. They thought I was of the devil. They lost their lives believing that, rather than understanding that the ones who tortured or sentenced them to death were agents of the Adversary."

"Those times were difficult enough and were made even more difficult by the search for another to hold the stone and attempt to force back the Adversary," Renault explained. "Once the evil gets a firm foothold, it can take centuries to eradicate it."

"You know there was a series of weak vessels during that time, because the strongest were located and killed by the Adversary. He went unchecked for a very long time."

"It's like plugging the big holes in a dike, but the smaller ones still leak enough water to create a flood," Nico said. "I saw it in my dreams," he added. "The Adversary whispers in the ears of many of his servants that they are right to believe as they do, and, by extension, are doing the right thing and the best thing by torturing, mistreating and killing swaths of people."

"And then there are the Adversary's servants who enjoy the pain, death and madness they create," Mac added.

"What about the people who *can* see what we saw?" Mona asked.

"Some will understand what they are seeing. Others will seek answers. Only a few will be called to openly act against the Adversary. Of those few, not all will answer the call. Some will believe that their efforts will be fruitless—or cause their demise or ruin their reputation. They will allow their fears to hold them back," Nico replied.

"Some won't be wrong in that way," Mac said. "This isn't a safe or friendly undertaking, by any means. We've already seen those they've killed, some of whom were resurrected as demons. More will surely die. Those taken from Austin today will most certainly become a part of their army."

"At least we kept some from their clutches," Ari said.

"Half, maybe," Nico nodded at Ari. "Renault's help made things much better."

"Will we get more vampire helpers? For days?" Del asked. "I know some in the Department will be very interested in this."

"And that's exactly why you shouldn't tell them," Nico said. "Unless you find some who can see us through those images of light."

"Maybe it's time we paid a visit to the home office," Laronda turned toward Del.

"I would like to come," Nico volunteered. "I will know which ones are right to join with us."

"Renault, what miracle is this?" Claudio floated into the room.

"I am more surprised than anyone," Renault rose to his feet and dipped his head to Claudio. "Nico says the stone chose me."

"As it had already left its mark on you," Claudio breathed in wonder. "Please, tell me of this day's events, and how this miracle transpired."

"Master Scholar, the Adversary sent his flying demons to attack a festival in Austin. We only managed to save half the intended victims."

"You saved half. Do not think it a failure or only half a victory. Those saved owe you and your comrades their lives. All could have been taken. You prevented that."

"Master Scholar, I have bad news," Alejandro rushed into the room. "Everette's nightclub was attacked and many were killed. The attackers were shouting *death to fags and witches*."

"Is Everette among the victims?" Claudio demanded quickly.

"She has been harmed, but still alive when I received the phone call."

"Where is she?" Ari was on her feet in a blink.

"Can you get us there?" Del turned to Ari.

"I can get us there. Can you get us through the police at the scene?" Ari asked him.

"Yes."

Alejandro rattled off an address not far from Ari's gallery in Deep Ellum. "I know where that is," Ari said. "Anybody here who doesn't want to go?" When there was no reply, Ari transported everyone to a nearby alley, and when Del began to run toward the chaotic scene on the street, the others followed.

CHAPTER EIGHTEEN

*A**ri, Everette is locked in a room in the basement. She can't afford to let the EMTs examine her*, Nico informed her. Del and Laronda had gotten them past the tape and barricades, now they had to find Everette. *I can get us to her*, Nico added.

Then do it, Ari replied.

In seconds, Ari and Nico found themselves in a small room below Everette's nightclub, where Everette was huddled on a bed in a corner, bleeding sluggishly from wounds to her thigh, shoulder and neck.

"We're here to help," Ari held up a hand as Everette moved, preparing to protect herself.

"Honey, why is your hand glowing?" Everette made an attempt at humor.

"She can remove the bullets and repair much of the damage," Nico explained.

"Thank the goddess," Everette let her head rest against the wall behind her.

"Do you want me to hold your hand while she works?" Nico asked.

"I never turn down an offer from a good-looking man," Everette sighed, holding out her left hand for Nico to take.

"Here we go, then," Ari soothed, holding her glowing, shell-imprinted hand outside the neck wound first. Everette gasped when the bullet left her body, slapping into Ari's hand with a small thump.

"Thigh next," Ari breathed as Everette turned her eyes toward the ceiling, refusing to watch. That bullet came out easier than the one in the neck. Everette drew a shaky breath and nodded for Ari to continue.

"Now, shoulder," Ari said. "This one—is lodged in the bone. It may hurt."

"I'll try not to break your hand," Everette told Nico.

"I can protect myself," Nico soothed. "Ari, do what you must."

Ari's entire body began to glow, forcing Everette to close her eyes. The bullet made a bone-scraping noise as Ari pulled it out of Everette's shoulder.

"There, all done," Nico patted Everette's hand. "How do you feel? Is there anything else we can do to help?"

"I feel much better," Everette sighed. "A vamp's body knows when there's something foreign in it, and it can be painful—and terrifying."

"Do you have more clothes?" Ari asked. "These are kinda bloody."

"At home," Everette replied. "This is my emergency shelter, you understand."

"I think we should take her back to the ranch," Nico suggested. "Unless you want to talk to the police. Claudio, Renault and Alejandro are upstairs with Del and the others."

"How many were hit?" Everett asked.

"Most are dead," Nico said. "Only three escaped without injuries. I believe seven were transported to the hospital. There were six gunmen, and they all carried hundreds of rounds for their weapons."

"I couldn't get to any of them," Everette shook her head. "I was in the back, putting an order together for the club, when the shooting started. Bullets were flying everywhere; you couldn't walk through the place without getting hit. I got knocked down, and they all ran out of the place like they'd been jerked on a string. I heard sirens right after that, so I came down here. Paramedics and vampires don't get along when there's been an accident."

"I can get her back to the ranch," Nico told Ari. "If you want to go upstairs and sniff around."

"All right," Ari said. "Let me know if you need anything, and I'll be right there."

"Thank you for your help," Everette told Ari as Nico helped the vampire to her feet. "I wasn't sure what to do."

"We'll figure this out," Ari said. "Go on, Nico."

Nico transported Everette away, leaving Ari in the small room. Squaring her shoulders and taking a deep breath, Ari unlocked the door and walked out, heading for the stairs and the bloody nightclub above.

How is Everette? Renault asked the moment Ari arrived.

She's well enough—we got the bullets out, Ari explained. *Nico took her to the ranch to get some rest.*

"Thank you for helping," Claudio came to stand beside Renault. "Alejandro is assisting with the investigation."

"Do we have a body count, yet?" Ari asked.

"A preliminary estimate is forty-seven, but that number will likely rise," Claudio said. "Everette's place is quite popular, you understand."

"Everette draws people to her," Ari agreed. "I think she's always been that way."

"I agree with that assessment," Renault nodded. "It's why she was turned."

"Del is attempting to get copies of security recordings," Claudio said. "I hope to see them, too. Renault, Alejandro and I are very adept at recalling images."

"I'm wondering whether these gunmen were sent by the Adversary, or if they saw the call to arms on those websites and acted on their own," Ari said.

"Either way, they serve the Adversary," Renault observed. "They will be easy for him to find, if they are not already pledged to his service directly."

"You mean they're easy for him to find, and not so easy for us to locate?" Ari asked.

"Yes. The Adversary is adept at sniffing out those who are amenable to his purpose."

"All who were still living have been transported," Alejandro joined them. "All others are beyond help."

"Do you think Everette should close her business for now? It could be dangerous for her to reopen in this climate," Ari said.

"It will take some time to clean and remodel, once the investigation is concluded," Claudio explained. "I hope she can reopen after that, with no threat to the safety of her guests or herself."

"I hope it will be safe. I'm really worried, now," Ari shivered.

"As are we," Renault conceded. "But we are not free if we are afraid."

Ari lifted her eyes to Renault's. "You're right," she sighed. "It's just a horrible, ironic life we live, huh?"

"As it has always been," Alejandro nodded wisely. "Pointing fingers always create targets, do they not?"

"Yeah. I think I'll check on Lance and Mona."

"We will accompany you," Claudio said. Ari stepped carefully around the perimeter of yellow tape which circled bodies and a crime scene from a nightmare, heading for Lance and Mona, who spoke to a detective near the door.

"Do you need anything?" Nico asked Everette as he showed her to the steps leading into the basement.

"I'll be fine," Everette said.

"It's all right to be worried," Nico soothed. "We're worried, too, because they've widened their hit list from witches only, and fast, too. I'm concerned about who their target will be next time."

"Did this have anything to do with those attacks in Austin earlier?"

"Yes. I can answer questions downstairs if you'd like to lie down."

"Thank you. I do have plenty of questions," Everette confirmed. "Will it upset you if I have some of Claudio's bagged blood?"

"No. I think you need it," Nico replied. "Go on down, I'll be right behind you."

Minutes later, Everette sat on a bed in the basement, sipping from a bag of blood with her back to the wall. "I really want those murderers to suffer. Those people they killed—many of them are personal friends," she said.

"I'm sorry you were targeted," Nico told her. "They targeted my parents—and me, too. My parents died. I only survived because I decided to visit Ari at her gallery across the street, rather than going in to work early."

"You're that one," Everette breathed, studying Nico in the dim light. "Your parents owned that restaurant."

"Everybody else thinks I'm dead. I have to stay hidden to fight the Adversary. They think Ari's dead, too, and she'll stay hidden for the same reason."

"This sounds like a big conspiracy theory," Everette said.

"I know. Except people are dying, and we're the only ones who can stop it."

"Most people don't care about that, as long as it happens to somebody else," Everette pointed out.

"It's sad, but you're right."

"What are you doing to stop it?"

"Well, today we were only half a failure. We managed to save half of those targeted by the demons in Austin. Whatever the final count is, double that and you'll know the number of intended victims. Mac, Ari, Renault and I were there. We saved as many as we could."

"Four of you saved a hundred and fifty-two? That's how many are missing, and if you saved as many as were taken," Everette blew out a breath. "I saw those things on television when I woke—that's what stopped me from getting to the club on time and kept me from being in the middle of the firefight. I stayed to watch the whole thing on the news. The inventory should have been done already, and I would normally have been on the floor when those assholes came in. I wish I could help you in some way, to get back at the ones who are causing all this. I can only help at night, though." Everette's tone betrayed how helpless and depressed she felt.

"I'll say this, then," Nico said. "Get some rest so those wounds will heal completely. We'll see what tomorrow may bring. Good-night, Everette. Pleasant dreams."

"Masks. You can't see well enough past them to get any reliable images," Claudio shook his head when Del ran the images again. "With the little we can see through those clear masks, in addition to their body images, I've determined that all the assailants are male."

"That's what our experts are saying after they've cleaned and magnified the images," Del agreed. "We're going through recordings outside the club—all six rode off on motorcycles."

"You don't think they're blaming the LGBTQ community for what happened in Austin, do you?"

"People do weird shit," Mona drawled. "A therapist might call it displacement. I mean, we saw clear images of demons flying away with their helpless victims in Austin. Why shouldn't they blame the guests in this nightclub for that?"

"All it takes is a rumor nowadays," Ari said. "It's astounding how easy it is to manipulate some people with only a single, non-verifiable allegation. Lies and rumors like these are so loud and raucous, the truth can't make itself heard."

"I'll check in with our group who watches those sites," Del said.

"As will I," Claudio agreed. "We are attempting to track these sources, you understand, but that is difficult."

"If you find anything, will you let me know? Perhaps we can combine efforts to hunt the sources down. This may lead us to a connection of some kind to the ones we wish to find most."

"Of course, but I must warn you; if we have resources in the appropriate areas, you may hear of it afterward. Rest assured, we will obtain information if at all possible, before taking action."

"Well, I appreciate your honesty," Del grimaced. "My Department may not be happy that someone else cut in, but I understand that hesitation could cost us a lot."

"We need to get a better handle on who the next target could be," Lance observed. "If we'd had any idea that this was about to happen," he made a helpless gesture.

"We may have a few suggestions," Claudio turned toward Lance. "The problem, of course, is how to provide information or protection without the Adversary becoming aware and selecting a different target instead."

"You will find that the Adversary is more slippery than an eel, as elusive as a unicorn and able to wear more disguises than a chameleon," Mac said. "And, like the legendary hydra, will only grow more heads the longer he is attacked. The only good news in all this is that it could take two weeks or more for the abductees in Austin to become demon. I doubt the Adversary will send that portion of his army out until its numbers are acceptable. That doesn't mean he won't send the odd ones out now and then, but it will be far more covert than the debacle in Austin."

"How will he build up the number of demons, without an attack on a grand scale like the one in Austin?" Del asked.

"Kidnappings—by the same type that shot up the nightclub. With human involvement, guns, zip ties and duct tape can be convenient and persuasive."

"How the hell can we combat those tactics?" Lance demanded.

"We need more of us," Mac's shoulders drooped. "In the past, we stayed small and mobile, but that's when horses were the fastest mode of transportation. Here and now, it's like emptying an ocean with a single bucket—while it's raining. Back then, the Adversary couldn't create demons where he was; the stone and its previous owners prevented it. Once it left Spain behind, he was also free to leave. My guess is his ultimate goal is to destroy the stone and the one who holds it. Once here, his power appears to be unlimited to do just that."

"You haven't talked about the stone before," Laronda said.

"It's better to keep it hidden," Mac replied.

"What does it look like?"

"Like this." Renault held out his hand bearing the imprint.

"It chose Renault, just as it chose Ari and Nico. They are sworn to fight the Adversary," Mac explained. "It's building an army of its own, but it's taking longer and choosing more carefully than the Adversary has to."

"It's a shell?" Mona studied Renault's palm.

"It's carved of hard jet. You can call it petrified wood, for lack of a better term."

"There are two types of jet," Claudio said, as if lecturing a class. "Soft jet is created by carbon compression and fresh water. Hard jet is created by carbon compression and saltwater. There is a theory among the scholars that this particular jet stone is from a tree that never grew upon this world."

"Is that true?" Del asked.

"I cannot say," Mac neatly avoided answering the question.

"It is nearing dawn, Master Scholar," Alejandro reminded Claudio. "We have been at this most of the night."

"I can take you back," Ari offered.

"Take all of us back," Del pulled the thumb drive containing security camera recordings from the computer in Lance's office. "We can work on this in a more comfortable setting there."

"Nico," Hunter exclaimed after finding Nico hunched over a coffee mug in Janie's kitchen the following morning.

"Hey, Hunter. Is Erly around?"

"He went out with Val earlier, and let me sleep in a little," Hunter admitted. "They should be back for breakfast."

"Barn finished?"

"Yep. Did a good job, too." Hunter pulled out a barstool next to Nico's. "Why do you want to know?"

"Because we have other stuff to get to," Nico said.

"Hunter, would you like juice or milk?" Mary Kate asked.

"I'll get my juice," Hunter dropped off his seat and walked toward the fridge. "Need any help with breakfast?"

"I'm good," Mary Kate smiled at him.

"Want anything while I'm up?" Hunter asked Nico.

"I'd take some juice."

"Good morning, Nico," Ari shuffled in, hair damp from a shower, house slippers on her feet and wearing jeans and a T-shirt. She stopped to put an arm around Nico's shoulders to give him a hug.

"Thanks, Ari," Nico gave her a smile as she walked around the island to pour coffee for herself.

"We have something to do today, don't we?" she asked him as she lifted the coffeepot and filled a mug.

"Yeah. I don't think it'll be easy to watch, either."

"You're talking about the hearings at the state house, aren't you?"

"Yeah. We need to find a seat in the gallery. Renault will have to remember it for Claudio, since he can't come."

"They'll probably record it," Ari said.

"Well, anything could happen, I guess."

"You think something may happen, don't you?"

"I'm worried, yes."

"Then we definitely need to be there. Del and Laronda, too."

"I want Erly and Hunter to come with us," Nico said. "I doubt there'll be anyone allowed in the gallery, so you and I have to get everybody in. Nobody will see us," he added.

"You've worked this out, haven't you?"

"Yeah."

"Have you told Mac?"

"Told me what?" Mac walked in much as Ari had, after getting too little sleep. Dressed in jeans and a T-shirt, Mac had chosen to walk barefoot into the kitchen.

"Take a seat—I'll get your coffee," Ari told him after taking a good look at the lines on Mac's face.

She's worried about you, Nico sent to Mac.

I don't deserve it, Mac replied.

My mother would say Mira lo que trajo el gato, Nico informed him.

Look what the cat brought?

Well, I've seen you look better. It was Mama's version of look what the cat dragged in.

Mac, rather than becoming angry, barked a laugh. It was an infectious laugh, filled with genuine humor.

"Here you are," Ari set a mug of coffee in front of Mac.

"Thanks, Ari." He shocked the hell out of her by lifting her free hand to his lips and kissing it.

"Huh?" was all she could muster after moments of silence passed.

"Nico says I look like something the cat dragged in. I figure that cat would have to be you," Mac grinned at her.

"I figure she could drag you back to her lair and feast on your flesh," Nico teased.

"Uh, I'm not sure I should acknowledge that one," Ari said. "Besides, I don't have a lair—that sounds too arch villain-ey. Plus, I figure he'd be tough to chew."

"I would be," Mac confirmed. "Sit down and drink your coffee before it gets cold."

"Yeah. Need coffee. Make brain work gooder."

"I see what you did there," Hunter leaned around Nico to grin at Ari.

"Don't worry; you'll be old one day," Ari wrinkled her nose at him.

"Yeah, but you'll always be older."

"Can't argue with that," Ari lifted her coffee mug and drank.

"Who's older?" Erly walked in the back door with Val.

"I'm older than anybody in this house," Mac raised a hand. "And, as Hunter pointed out, I will always be older than everybody in the house."

"You may need to explain that sometime," Erly said. "Did you leave any coffee for me?"

"There's plenty of coffee," Ari said. "Come have a seat and I'll get you a cup."

"I won't say no to that," Erly grinned and took a seat next to Hunter.

"So. You were an engineer?" Mac asked Erly.

"Word gets around, I guess," Erly thanked Ari as she set his coffee on the island. "I can fix just about anything, from your roof to your vacuum cleaner."

"How did you end up so far in the back of beyond, then?" Laronda asked as she and Del joined the others in the kitchen.

"Fell out of love with the human race," Erly toyed with his coffee cup. "After Katrina, the insurance company only paid half what my house was worth, and I spent most of my money trying to make them give me what I paid 'em for. Found the place outside Swindall for what little I had left, fixed it up and retired from humanity."

"Do you still own the property in New Orleans—sorry—Nawlins?" Nico asked.

"I do, but that's all it is—an empty lot," Erly shrugged. "Still pay the taxes on it, too."

"The Rangers have investigated it," Del said. "You're right; it's only a bare lot, with a patch of grass front and back. They hit a dead end, looking for you there."

"Are they still blaming Hunt and me for that mess? Like he'd kill his own kin, or I'd kill friends," Erly growled low in his throat, as if his Jaguar was just as upset as the human.

"You're listed as persons of interest, mostly to keep the public at bay," Del replied. "Word was sent through our Department that you were away from home at the time and had nothing to do with it."

"Is that coffee I smell?" Everette swept into the kitchen, with Renault right behind her. "Oh my goodness, the sun is out, too."

"Welcome to daylight," Nico turned to smile at Everette. "Pull up a chair and we'll get you some coffee. How do you take it?"

"Sweet and dark, honey, sweet and dark."

"Reverend Benny and I will be there, although no others will see us," Belhar informed Darnell. "My suggestion is to allow the others to ask questions—as we will direct them to do so."

"You're planning to redirect any accusations?"

"Obviously. You will vote as you desire, and it will become their desire, too."

"Are you saying that I'm actually in charge of the legislature, now?"

"In a manner of speaking," Belhar confirmed. "It's only a matter of time before the judicial branch falls under our sway."

"What about the executive branch?"

"You are so shortsighted, my friend," Belhar revealed pointed teeth as he smiled. "Come now, it's time to make your appearance at the capitol."

"I need to check in with my wife."

"You don't need her," Belhar removed the cell phone from Darnell's hand and tucked it in his shirt pocket. "Your family is but a distraction, you understand. Reverend, it's time to go."

Killebrew, standing nearby, dipped his head to Belhar. Darnell Cheatham didn't fully comprehend what was happening—not yet, anyway. Killebrew understood completely, and he welcomed it.

Everette had chosen a demure, cream silk blouse and black slacks, and left her wig behind so as not to call attention to herself while attending the hearings with Nico and the others. Ari complimented her on her natural hair, which was dark brown with a natural wave. Cut stylishly, her hair swept back from her face, exposing delicate, gold earrings.

We must remain silent, Renault cautioned Everette as she followed him into the empty gallery above the hearings.

I can do that, Everette responded, although being able to communicate silently with several in the group still excited her so much, she couldn't keep the bubbly effervescence from her mental reply.

No matter what you hear, Renault cautioned.

Of course. Everette schooled her enthusiasm this time.

They can't see us, Nico told Everette. *I'm still working on a sound shield.*

You're very talented, Everette smiled. *I haven't seen daylight in twenty years.*

Ari did that for you, I didn't, Nico said. *Just—let me know if you see anything that shouldn't be during the hearing.*

Of course. I'm sorry—I still find this exciting.

Then remember last night, and why you find yourself in this position today. The topic will come up unless I am very mistaken.

Oh. That doesn't sound good.

It isn't. You'll see. They're coming in, now.

Senator Cheatham walked in and took his seat at the curved desk above the witness table, then adjusted his microphone so he wouldn't have to lean in or work to make his voice heard.

His fellow senators filed in and took their seats too, some attempting to make their seat more comfortable; others talking in whispers with a neighbor. Two seats down, his main adversary in the Texas State Senate, Esther Johnson, set a yellow pad on the desk in front of her and clicked a ball-point pen, ready to take notes.

He wanted to remind her (as he often did) that the questioning would be recorded, but there she was, preparing to take handwritten notes.

Of the thirty-one senators in the Texas legislature, only nineteen had made an appearance for today's questioning. Darnell's mouth stretched into a judgmental grimace—all of them should be here. He'd have a word with the Governor later about that.

Squashing yet another desire to taunt Esther in some way, he forced himself to turn away from her as he waited for the first witness to appear—Captain Verlen Belwether from Dallas PD's Central Division.

The Captain finally walked in, flanked by his state representative and an attorney representing the police department.

I hope you have good questions planned, Darnell told Belhar.

Never fear; I know what I'm doing, Belhar replied. *I've done this sort of thing before.*

"You're not on trial here, Captain Belwether," Esther said, before

Darnell could say otherwise. "This is merely a fact-finding mission, you understand. We expect honest answers to some of the troubling questions we have regarding unusual events in the past month."

"Of course," Belwether leaned forward to speak into the microphone. Darnell smiled; he always enjoyed making witnesses uncomfortable, no matter how petty or insignificant it was.

"Captain Belwether," a fellow senator on Darnell's right spoke next. "Is it true that you've known about these—zombie attacks—from the beginning?"

"At the beginning, it was a bombing," Belwether said. "There were no zombies connected with that, not that we know of. Those creatures you're calling zombies—I have no idea what they are or how they came about. Can you explain that, Senator? I sure can't."

"Would you describe these creatures as supernatural?" Another senator asked.

"They're not normal," Belwether shook his head. "I don't know what they are."

"So, supernatural, then," the Senator confirmed.

"I didn't say," Belwether began.

"Do you believe that these supernatural creatures may have been created by supernatural power—negative energy, perhaps?" Someone else queried.

"I have no idea whether there's anything supernatural involved," Belwether was clearly off-balance already.

"But it would have to be—supernatural, that is. These creatures are supernatural by your own admission. Could any normal human achieve this? I think not," the Senator answered his own question.

"If I could just," Belwether attempted to interject his thoughts.

"What about the murders of that witch coven outside Swindall?" The fourth Senator spoke up. "Aren't they supernatural? Could they not have made these creatures to begin with? We've seen that they can turn humans into wolves. If this is true, then perhaps their killing is justified."

"Yes, that could certainly explain things," a female Senator replied. "My question to you, Captain Belwether, is this; are witches attempting to take over our country? Who else could have created these—zombie-like creatures, who can infect others by mere contact? If they can make zombies and werewolves, could they not also create those flying demons we saw only a few blocks from here? Tell me about the cruise ship that was taken in the Gulf. Where are those people now, Captain? Are they perhaps—zombies? Werewolves—or demons, perhaps? Were witches aboard that ship, casting terrible spells?"

"It has come to my attention that at least two members of the murdered witch coven were homosexuals," someone else hissed at Belwether. "Are they aligning with the witches in this? Could this be the reason the nightclub was attacked last night in your district—was someone brave enough to take down some of the enemy for us?"

"That has nothing to do," Belwether sputtered.

"It has everything to do with this, if they are our enemies," the female senator mocked Belwether's attempt to set the record straight.

"You say that this started with a bombing?" the first senator spoke again. "Weren't the owners of that restaurant Hispanic? Don't tell me for a minute that they aren't involved in this plot—they've wanted to invade this country for a long time, haven't they?"

"That's not what we're dealing with," Captain Belwether shouted.

Darnell cast a swift glance in Esther's direction. She hadn't spoken since the beginning, when she assured the Captain he wasn't on trial.

Except that's exactly what was happening—this *was* a trial and Belhar was hitting every hot button topic he could, making far less than logical leaps to do it.

Esther's mouth was set in a grim line as she scribbled on her notepad. He wondered what she was writing. *I'll ask someone to steal it later*, Darnell promised himself before turning back to the circus that should have been a routine questioning.

Ari's hand gripped Mac's wrist so hard it would leave a bruise. *I see it*, he told her. Throughout the questioning, the giant, black-and-brown serpent, invisible to those below the gallery, wound its way through the senators, touching this one or that, and in turn, the one touched would speak and make wild accusations.

Mac wasn't surprised by the accusations, either. All of them, at one time or another, had made their presence known, with the Adversary's blessing.

No doubt, too, the serpent had once been human, but now willingly served the Adversary.

We can't fight it until we know where his human body is, and it isn't with the serpent, Mac told Ari.

Everette looks like she's seen a ghost, Ari said.

Then it's a good thing Renault and Nico are sitting beside her, Mac replied. *Nico may not have any blood left in his hand after this.*

I don't like where this is going, Ari said. *If this continues, there'll be legislation produced by the end of the day to round up all witches, gays and Hispanics, and it'll set off a hunt for werewolves, too.*

Like they don't have a head start on it already? Mac's sending was gruff and unsurprised. *Those subversive websites will send out a call to eliminate them the minute they see any part of this—and they will see it.*

I know.

I can't see the Adversary, but he's close, Nico informed them. *I only need to protect Belwether's mind a little longer—they'll dismiss him soon.*

Thank goodness; I was feeling ill, Renault confessed.

I am ill, Everette countered.

"Thank you, Captain Belwether," someone spoke below. Mac wasn't interested in who dismissed the Captain; only that they'd done so.

The damage was done; now it would only mount higher with each additional witness until the entire legislature was inflamed, and then the inflammation would spread throughout the state.

Followed by the country.

The Adversary loved bloodshed, and he'd never had such a free rein before.

Mac was beginning to feel ill, himself.

CHAPTER NINETEEN

"Technically, we still own the property," Denton Franks waved the insurance check in front of his wife.

"But the Jordans are the ones who covered dead cattle and fixed the hole; they should be compensated for the work they did," she argued. "At least deduct it from the sale price."

"The money for the cattle is being withheld," Denton snapped. "They're saying we knew they were sick, and we neglected the animals. I'm stuck here with a cast on my leg and my father is dead. I'm putting all of this in the bank."

"Then give them the furnishings in the house, rather than making them pay for all of it."

"Not a chance. I just got my truck fixed after that mountain lion wrecked it. You notice it never tried to jump Val Jordan. I'm betting it's a pet, and I'm betting that the cat Dad killed all those years ago was a pet, too. That's why they were pissed off about it."

"All this animosity—for decades—and this is what you have to show for it?" Maurine's hands went to her hips. "Honestly, your father should have let that go rather than allowing it to fester. Besides, he kept the money, just like you're about to do."

Maurine walked out of the room with a bounce in her step,

knowing that Denton couldn't follow her until he reached his crutches, and by that time she'd be out of the house and in her car, driving to her cousin's place in Fort Worth. It was time to leave Denton behind; the kids never came home nowadays because they couldn't stand their grandfather or their father.

She'd call her kids and an attorney once she reached her cousin's house, and that would be that; she'd stayed with Denton far too long as it was. Maybe she'd call Val Jordan, too, and let him know about the insurance check. After all, half of it—and half the property—legally belonged to her.

"I understand what you're saying, Maurine," Val spoke into the phone as he exchanged a glance with Janie. "But once he knows you're filing for divorce, he could refuse to honor the contract and void the sale. Joint ownership requires both owners to agree to the sale."

Val went quiet as Maurine spoke again, then told her; "I understand that it could be foreclosed on if he refuses to sell, and that will hurt you financially. Rather than getting money to split out of the property, neither of you will get anything. It's in his best interest to go forward with the sale."

Val listened for a few moments before speaking again. "No, Burke doesn't handle divorces, but someone in his firm does. Call and ask for Heather Kirkpatrick, all right? Tell her I sent you. All right, Maurine, you take care, now."

Val ended the call, then shook his head at his mother. "Denton Franks will do his best to turn all of this into the worst mess imaginable, just like his father did."

"Seems to be their specialty," Janie sighed. "Do you think Ari and the others will be back for lunch?"

"Let's have sandwiches. Easy enough to fix if they do," Val suggested. "I hope they're having a better morning that we are."

"Can we have something stronger than lemonade with those sandwiches?" Ari and Nico appeared with the rest of their group.

"I don't think their morning was better than ours," Janie quipped.

"Mona and I will help," Renault offered. "I think I can make a sandwich—I've seen it done before."

"I'll help—my stomach is growling for the first time in decades," Everette declared. "And, after that debacle in Austin, with the snake and the other, totally unsatisfactory shit posing as legitimate political undertakings, I certainly need something to get that bad taste out of my mouth."

"Snake?" Janie stopped halfway to the fridge.

"The Adversary's pet has made himself known," Nico told her. "Don't worry, he didn't know we were there and he won't be able to pass the boundary surrounding this property."

"Maybe you should fill us in while we eat," Val said. "Our only problem is that Maurine Franks is filing for divorce. Denton may put the property sale in jeopardy, just to get back at her—and us."

"Sounds like his father's son, all right," Ari grumbled.

"Mitchell is extra crispy," Val opined. "Maybe Denton feels left out. What? Too soon?" He winked at Ari.

Ari lifted a hand to stifle a snicker.

"How fast will all this move, now?" Ari asked. She and Mac sat on a thick limb of Janie's enormous oak tree in a side yard, its shade keeping them cool enough on a sweltering afternoon. Ari's shoes had been left behind outside the back door; she swung her feet as they idly lounged seven feet above the ground.

"You saw how fast it moved today," Mac said. "Did you also notice that the snake didn't visit all the Senators? He touched those who are inclined to his way of thinking already."

"We can draw a line between those who spoke and the Adversary?"

"Yes. But he also may choose to leave some in reserve, so there's no way to point fingers at all of his allies just yet."

"Of course not," Ari hunched her shoulders and bowed her head. Strands of platinum-dyed hair lifted in the breeze. Mac reached out to brush them behind an ear. Ari tried to hide the shiver that coursed through her body. Mac saw it and wisely chose not to comment.

"The Adversary never makes things easy," he remarked instead. "And here, he's been liberated from everything that contains him on this world. He's not pulling any punches, Arianne. He'll try to kill us and everyone associated with us."

"So what do we do? Hide and let him have his way?"

"No. We fight for every life we can save. Those today? They want what he has to offer. We should keep our eyes on all of them, in case they all feel that way."

"Nico and Hunter are checking their voting records, and the bills they've introduced," Ari was back to swinging her legs.

"Good idea. It could help us weed out the undesirables."

"Undesirable to us or to them?"

"Either. Both. If we find allies, they're worth protecting, don't you think?"

"Yeah. I worry that there's not enough of us."

"We always lose people, Ari," he soothed. "But death is more honorable than joining the Adversary."

"Honorable? Yes. Less painful? Probably not. I saw the claws on those demons."

"The souls flee the bodies—it is their final gift in situations like this. These zombies and demons have no souls. Hunger for human flesh and obedience to the Adversary is the sum of their lives."

"You say we have maybe two weeks before the next batch of demons rise?"

"Around that much, I believe. I worry that the Adversary may send out his current horde to feed, however, if he's planted all the new ones."

"A deadly crop." Ari shuddered.

"Yes. These things—they used to follow a very familiar pattern. That pattern is being broken every day, here in this country. Those who take up the Adversary's cause may attack individuals or families. We may be frustrated and of a mind to help, but I warn you, the Adversary has laid traps in the past, using those tactics. We must plan our moves carefully from now on. Look, Del and Laronda are coming this way. Will you take us down?"

"I don't understand why you can't transport yourself," Ari's eyes locked with his.

"The curse," Mac sighed. "The everlasting, fucking curse. Were it not in effect, I could do many things."

"Maybe you should tell me about that, sometime."

"And maybe I shouldn't. Come on, let's go hear what they have to say."

Ari transported him out of the tree, to meet with Del and Laronda.

"Come inside—there are more videos on those websites," Del said, "calling for all their lackwit minions to fight against the current plague of witches, gays, people of color, werewolves, uppity women politicians, or those who don't obey their husbands."

"You're joking," Ari's eyes widened.

"Nope. They took what the legislature denounced earlier, added to it and we now have a massive hit list. I'm not sure the FBI or Homeland Security have enough people to deal with this, should the shootings begin."

"What about the Rangers?" Mac asked.

"Their funding is under the control of the very people we listened to this morning," Del rumbled. "They're on alert anyway but so far, there are no specific threats."

"There will be," Mac shook his head. "We just don't know where, or how many will be affected. Look for the Adversary to ramp up his game, too, and blame the results on the very targets you just mentioned. Later, there will be torture and burning added to the mix; suspicion will run rampant, neighbors will accuse their neighbors; there's no stopping it. Pain, death, fear, hate, greed—those things feed the Adversary."

"But the law," Laronda began.

"I think you'll begin to see that the law works only as long as there are those willing to enforce or obey it," Mac said. "Even their religious laws tell them not to kill, but they find ways around that every time."

"This madness will spread, much like the disease which creates zombies," Nico walked out the back door to join the conversation. "Come inside and see; already there are those touting the cause—and a few who are calling it what it is—unfounded hate-mongering."

"We have decisions to make," Mac nodded deferentially to Nico.

"We should wait until Claudio wakes. Until then, we can gather names of those who have fallen and those who stand against. Some of those we must help."

"Will recordings of the hearings be released to the public?" Ari asked.

"They're supposed to be available," Del replied.

"The ones who saw our outlines atop the building in Austin—will they also see the serpent in the recordings?"

"I," Nico hesitated. "I don't know," he admitted.

"I'll arrange to get copies," Del turned and strode toward the back door.

"Let's take a look at the damage," Mac cupped Ari's elbow with a hand. "It won't be pretty, I warn you."

"There's the snake." Ari sat heavily on the sofa in the game room as Del played the recording of the hearings they'd attended in Austin.

"There's something else," Laronda announced after looking at her cell phone. "Somebody recorded the attack on Everette's club. It's now all over, including the mainstream news."

"Where were they?" Everette demanded, half-rising from her chair. She sat again after Renault's hand dropped on her shoulder.

"Across the street, apparently," Laronda watched the video on her phone. "All six shooters wore motorcycle helmets and black leathers, so we won't get much to identify them. All the tags on their bikes were covered, so there's nothing to go by on that front."

"I want my hands on the person who made the recording," Everette hissed. "He'll tell me who his friends are."

"What message came with the recording?" Renault asked quietly.

"That this is only the beginning," Laronda sighed and turned off her phone. "Everette, you may have a hard time finding anyone willing to put your club back together after this."

"This is so messed up," Everette mumbled.

"What the—is that a giant snake?" Janie walked in with Val.

"Are you kidding me? Is that thing seriously going from one Senator to another, and they don't even see it?" Val demanded.

"Ah. The answer to your question," Mac nodded at Nico. "Some will certainly see the snake."

"They honestly couldn't see the damn thing?" Val frowned at Mac.

"No. Had no idea it was winding its way around that table, touching this one or that. We should be thankful it didn't bite anyone—Nico believes that the bite will automatically claim the victim as the Adversary's property."

"It's not like they weren't for sale before," Janie snorted. "With a few exceptions, of course."

"I think we need to talk to her," Ari pointed at the Chair of the Committee.

"That's Esther Johnson," Val said. "She's our state senator. Mom and I have voted for her the last three elections."

"Why do you want to talk to her?" Janie asked.

"Del, can you reverse the recording? I think I saw something that will tell you why," Ari replied.

"Sure." Del hit the back button on the television remote.

"Stop there," Ari said. Del let the recording play again. "See. The snake passes her, and she pulls her notepad out of the way."

"That's nothing to base a meeting on," Mac began.

"Mac, it may be an unconscious thing on her part, but she deliberately pulled the notepad toward her," Nico looked up at Mac, who stood beside his chair. "I think we do need to talk to her and take a copy of this recording with us."

"You think being that close put her under the Adversary's influence, so she wouldn't physically see the snake?" Mac asked.

"Yeah, but there's one way to find out for sure. Do you know her at all? Will she agree to a meeting if you call?" Nico turned toward Val.

"We donate to her campaign," Janie said. "I think she'll make time for us."

"I'll go make the call," Val headed for the door and the stairs beyond. "I'll let you know if we can get a meeting."

"I want her notepad. She was scribbling on it the whole damn time, and I want to know what she wrote," Darnell told Niall Pratt, Esther Johnson's personal assistant. He pushed an envelope across his desk toward Niall. "I also want to know if she does anything out of the ordinary or sees anyone not on her schedule."

Niall didn't fail to notice that the envelope was quite thick. "I can take photographs of the notes and send them to you. That way she'll never suspect. And, I can send a text or email if she goes off the reservation," Niall responded before reaching for the cash Darnell offered.

"Good enough. Make sure the notes are clear enough to read," Darnell growled as Niall lifted the envelope and stuffed it into the breast pocket of his suit coat. "Send me texts about the rest—on a burner phone."

"No problem," Niall agreed. "You should have the notes by tonight."

"Good. Now get out of here and make sure nobody sees you."

"I will."

Darnell watched as Niall opened the door carefully and peered about before stepping through and shutting it behind him.

"One more thing off my to-do list," Darnell mumbled as he pulled the bottle of bourbon from a bottom desk drawer. Already, many of his colleagues were testing the waters in their districts, looking for constituents who backed their new agendas.

Agendas which fit perfectly with Darnell's views—and those of the Reverend and Belhar.

"Belhar," Darnell spoke to empty air as he poured bourbon in a glass.

"I am here, Senator," Belhar appeared before Darnell's desk.

"Want a drink?" Darnell asked. "Things are going very well. I'm celebrating. Would you like to join me?"

"No, thank you," Belhar waved away the offer. "I do have news, though. Our newest troops may be ready sooner than anticipated."

"Any suggestions for our next target?"

"Many, so we must ponder this with care, you understand. Also, there is the business of taking over the state government, leaving you in charge."

"What about the current governor?"

"While he might be amenable to our plans, he is not you, you understand. You are the best candidate for that job, and you know it."

"Can we get him to step down?"

"That will leave his Lieutenant Governor in charge. No, that will not be the plan."

"What is the plan?"

"Ah, you know how accidents, unfortunate though they may be, often happen?"

"Well, then," Darnell leaned back in his chair with a creak of leather. "I never really liked either of them anyway. Any chance of including that bitch Esther Johnson in the accident?"

"We can certainly put that on the table," Belhar replied.

Lifting his glass of expensive bourbon, Darnell tossed back the shot and grinned at Belhar.

Big John sat in his repair shop office, a corner carved out of the massive, six-bay garage that not only serviced legitimate customers, but even more that weren't legitimate.

His office was a ten-by-ten square with a half wall on two sides topped by dirty glass. The whole space was cramped and cluttered with files, boxes, parts to be shipped and a ledger filled with false records. The whole thing smelled of grease and oil, but Big John was so used to the smell he no longer noticed.

"Paperwork, boss," Big John's right hand man dropped a manila envelope on the desk.

Roger Little never used his proper name; everybody called him Shank. The source of the nickname was a two-year stint in jail, but Big John never brought that up. It wasn't paperwork in the envelope, either, but payment for illegal sales of parts and entire vehicles.

"You see the video on the news from the hearings at the state house?" Shank made conversation. Big John hoped he'd go away—the envelope would be better off in his floor safe instead of lying atop his desk.

"What video?"

"Looks like the legislators are getting on board with those witch killings, plus the attack on that queer bar. They got a bunch of people on their list, and it could be open season," Shank cracked his knuckles. "I don't know whether them werewolves are real, but if they are, I sure would like to bag one of 'em."

"Don't let anybody see you with a weapon, or you'll be right back in gen pop," Big John snapped, disliking the turn of Shank's conversation.

"I ain't that stupid," Shank denied.

Except that you are, Big John frowned. "Don't you have work to do?"

"Yeah. I'll get right on it, boss. I'm tellin' ya, though, we oughta go out hunting witches and werewolves," Shank pointed a finger at Big John as he walked out of the office.

"Not bloody likely," Big John muttered as he lifted the envelope off the desk and rolled his chair aside to get to the floor safe. "A werewolf will hear and smell you coming from a mile away. You harm one of them, you won't be ready for the hurt leveled in your direction."

Nevertheless, the moment the envelope was safely locked away, Big John turned on the small television sitting on one of his file cabinets. "May as well see what the hell he's going on about."

After flipping through several twenty-four-hour news programs, he found what he sought, then gasped at what he saw. "What the fuck, man? Where the hell did that snake come from?"

A knot of terror made itself at home at the base of his spine. He *knew* where that snake came from.

In fact, he knew a lot more about it than he wanted to know. "Don't pay it any mind—you'll be sharing a cell with Shank if you come forward," he reminded himself grimly. "Keep it to yourself, Big John. Keep it all to yourself."

※

"We need your help, Billy Ray. Your cousin, Bobby Ray's gone; it's time you joined us and took your revenge," Killebrew hissed into his phone.

"I just took another job," Billy Ray informed the Reverend. "I sent you a copy of the attack on that bar, like you asked. This new job is an emergency situation that pays a lot. Let me finish that up and I'll head your way."

"When?" Killebrew demanded.

"Right after I find some help to get the job done. Tell me where you are and I'll let you know when I'm on the way."

"Look," Killebrew hissed, "Come to that service station that's in between Malarkie and Boran. Call me from there and I'll give you directions to the place. The pay is the best you'll ever get, so don't take too long, got it? Bring that video camera with you. You're gonna need it."

"Maybe I can be there tomorrow," Billy Ray said. "If the money's as good as you say it is."

"Bobby Ray was happy enough," Killebrew snapped. "Get your ass in gear and get that job done. I'll be expecting your call tomorrow."

※

"I can get the job done tonight," Billy Ray told his latest employer.

"Good. The sooner, the better. No sense in dragging this out. There's extra money in it, too, if it's completely destroyed."

"I think I can make that happen. I just need to pick up a few things, first."

"Whatever it takes," his employer laughed.

~

"We have a meeting with Senator Johnson set up on Thursday afternoon," Val told Mac. "It's the soonest she could fit us into her schedule, after moving other appointments around, you understand. The meeting is at her office in Austin; she has other appointments scheduled right after we see her."

"We'll take what we can get; Nico is really worried, as is Ari. We also need to know if she's sensitive to the serpent's and the Adversary's presence. If so, then she definitely needs protection."

"What does it mean if she's sensitive?" Val was curious.

"She may feel the need to protect herself, but she can't point to anybody and say for sure that they're the Adversary—or his pet serpent. She can't see them for what they are; she'll just feel uneasy. If they notice, she's a big target."

"Then let's hope she can see the snake in the recording. If not, how the hell will we convince her she's in danger?"

"Let's hope she sees what we saw, then."

~

"Claudio and Alejandro are on a conference call," Renault came to find Mac, who sat on a barstool in Val's bar downstairs, having a glass of Scotch. "That means I will be watching the perimeter tonight. Would you like to come with me?"

"Yeah," Mac emptied his glass before sliding off the barstool. "The raven needs some exercise, and since we can still communicate while I'm shifted, I'll ride along on your shoulder if I'm not flying."

"Good. Ari just informed me that she is feeling pain between her shoulders—a sign that something is not right. It never hurts to have another set of eyes when one is searching for the unknown. She also says that she will arrive quickly if we need help."

"I'm surprised she didn't offer to come along."

"She, Nico and Hunter are still searching through voting records for the current state government. They are making lists of who may or may not be among the Adversary's chosen, or those amenable to his machinations."

"The Adversary always seeks to control the seats of power," Mac said. "Once those are under his sway, the persecutions and executions begin. I'll shift to the raven outside, and we'll guard the perimeter together."

"The door's unlocked and the alarm is off. I've done my part, now it's time to do yours," Billy Ray glared at the two he'd hired to finish the job. "You've been paid; get going."

"We'll have it done before ya know it," the taller one spat tobacco to the side before grinning at Billy Ray. The shorter, younger one, standing slightly apart from his partner, was either bored or vacant—Billy Ray couldn't decide which.

Turning his eyes back to the taller man, Billy Ray refused to gaze too long at his tobacco-stained teeth. "Don't forget to shut your lights off driving in," he snapped. "Don't need the neighbors callin' the cops, now do we?"

"Nope." The tall one spat again to emphasize his answer.

Billy Ray watched both climb into the old pickup they'd driven to the meeting; if they had any sense, they'd buy a new vehicle. Except after tonight, they might not need one.

Billy Ray snorted a laugh before climbing into his car—he'd rebuilt it himself. Even its last owner wouldn't recognize it, now. All it needed was a new paint job and he could sell the old '57 Ford Fairlane as a classic.

"You okay back there?" In the dim interior light of the car, he cast a quick look at his pet rattlesnake, Edgar, who lay curled in his fish tank-turned-reptile habitat.

Billy Ray had packed light; a bottle of whiskey, a pistol, video camera, the cannister of powdered uranium he'd bought off a sketchy dealer online, Edgar, and an old duffle filled with jeans and T-shirts. The only thing his employer asked him to carry away was in the trunk of the car. "I got all we need, Edgar," Billy Ray declared as he started the car and put it in gear to drive away.

Wind is from the south tonight, Mac alighted on Renault's shoulder and fluffed his feathers. *Brisk, too.*

Yet the heat still clings to the land, Renault agreed. *I miss the sea on nights like this.*

I don't miss the Costa de la Muerte, Mac said. *The pull of the gate is strong.*

How did you arrive here—you were forced to come in raven shape, no?

Tanker, Mac explained. *I became a mascot of sorts. I followed the stone's pull, only to find that the one the stone chose had given it away. That has never happened before.*

Perhaps she knew something we do not.

I think she did. Nico is young, extremely powerful and resilient. Arianne is the strongest defender a Custodian has ever selected. When you and Everette came to bear the shell imprint, it gave me hope against terrible odds. Perhaps all these things will create difficulties for the Adversary in the long term.

I believe others will bear the imprint, too, Renault said. *This is how we will know our allies. Unfortunately, this very imprint that Everette and I bear is exactly why Alejandro and Claudio are having a conference with other scholars. They wish to know everything about how this occurred—along with the miracle of our walking in daylight.*

I'm worried about that, actually. Do you believe they will turn on you—or demand that Ari or Nico do the same for them?

I do not know. I hope they see the wisdom in holding back; if they are chosen, then they will also bear the imprint. If not, this is not the time to have a falling out, one against the other.

Why didn't they want to speak with you, Renault? This worries me.

As it troubles me. Wait—did you catch that scent?

My scenting ability, man and bird, is far less than yours will ever be. I didn't smell anything.

It smells like, Renault began to run swiftly westward, toward the fence separating the Franks property from the Jordan Ranch.

Trouble, Mac shouted mentally at Ari and the others; the moment Renault vaulted the fence, Mac was tossed from the vampire's shoulder. Flapping furiously, Mac saved himself from a tumbling fall. Once the raven was high enough in the air, he could see the problem for himself.

Two men, he shouted. *Gas cans. Hurry.*

Renault, get back, Ari shouted into his mind. Renault's heels dug into the soil as he struggled to stop after traveling at such a high rate of speed.

Fly, Renault, Nico's calmer voice sounded in his brain.

Without thinking, Renault's leathery wings sprouted from his shoulders, breaking through the fabric of his shirt and unfurling their lengths to lift him high into the air. Nico's and Ari's warning came barely in time; the Franks' house exploded in a giant fireball below him, with two arsonists still inside.

CHAPTER TWENTY

"We couldn't locate Sheriff McCullough," Deputy Warner told Val. All around them, emergency vehicles were parked, their lights flashing, while firefighters doused the still-burning wreckage of the house. "You're sure your man saw two guys with gas cans entering the back door?"

"That's what he saw. Unless they'd already poured gas on everything in the house, it shouldn't have exploded so fast," Val explained.

"You think the gas was turned on? If those two turned it on first, I reckon they were too stupid to live anyhow," Deputy Warner shook his head. "Any idea who'd do this?"

"Denton Franks is probably the first person you want to talk to," Val said dryly. "His wife just filed for divorce, and he's not known to be magnanimous in adverse situations."

"Trying to get insurance money?" Deputy Warner scribbled on his notepad.

"Trying to cheat his wife out of any income they might get from the property. I had a contract to buy the place as is; he decided to void the sale and drag it through the divorce. Maurine, his wife, says it will go back to the bank during that time; Denton can't meet the mortgage payments."

"You know his wife?"

"Yes. She called me about the voided contract yesterday."

"I'll talk with her and Denton," the Deputy tapped his notepad. "Could be a while before that mess is cool enough to find the bodies."

"They're not going anywhere until you do," Val quipped. "What a mess."

"You might think twice about buying the place if it goes back on the market," Deputy Warner said. "After the earthquake and the cattle all sick and dying, then the lightning strike killing the old man, I'm beginning to think the whole thing is cursed."

"Just a string of unfortunate events, Deputy Warner," Renault arrived at Val's side. "That's all this is, combined with anger and resentment on the part of the owner. Question Denton Franks first; I doubt he will be able to withhold the truth for long. Then, write all this in your report."

"I will," the Deputy agreed amiably to Renault's smoothly-placed compulsion. "That's all I need," he flipped his notepad closed. "Thank you for your help."

～

"Where is Denton?" Janie asked as she poured coffee for Val, Mac and Renault.

"Apartment in Abilene, not far from the doctor's office," Val replied. "Maurine said she found it and rented it for three months, while his leg heals. She was smart to get away from him when she did."

"He'll ruin her anyway," Janie sniffed.

"True enough," Val agreed. "Thanks for making coffee for us, Mom."

"I hope we're not interrupting," Claudio floated in, Alejandro close behind. "The ah, Scholars have all taken an interest in recent events and ah, wish to meet you in person."

"Claudio, we can't change all of you, willy-nilly," Mac turned in his seat to study Claudio's face. Vampires were notorious for schooling their expressions so as not to give away their feelings. Mac could see through them anyway, as could Nico and Ari. "Only the deserving will receive the imprint. We can't change that."

"I told them that," Claudio dropped his gaze to the floor. "I am Seventh, you understand, and the one least in standing within the Seven. I must abide by their wishes."

"Or they'll cut our funding, is that correct?" Renault's voice was hard.

"Yes—a part of it, certainly."

"Following this route will lead them to the Adversary's path," Nico arrived with Ari, Hunter and Erly. "Once they are upon that path," Nico advised, "they cannot return. Patience is the key to remaining true to your principles."

"Wise words," Claudio dipped his head to Nico. "I will have patience. I cannot speak for others, however. Only myself."

"I stand with Claudio," Alejandro pledged. "I will have patience, too."

"Marked or not, we have to stand together," Val sighed. "I've seen bad things in my life, but this is out of control. I worry that things will never be normal again."

"Depends on your idea of normal," Erly said. "I've seen a new normal way too many times. Usually it ain't a good normal, either."

"Then I hope we can find a normal we can all live with," Janie said. "There's more coffee, or I have sodas and juice in the fridge."

"Police in Abilene just arrested Denton Franks," Del arrived with news. "Seems he pulled cash money out of his account earlier and can't say where the thirty grand went."

"That's a big chunk of his insurance settlement," Val said.

"The feds were already looking into the transaction when they got word from Deputy Warner about the blowup at the ranch. This is a no-brainer; we'll see if he names the ones he hired. They're booking him into the Abilene jail, but he'll be moved back to this county, most likely."

"What about the two who died?" Ari asked.

"Pulled the bodies out fifteen minutes ago. Should be on their way to the ME by now. Laronda is talking with somebody at the Department; they're passing information back and forth. May not get anything else worthwhile until tomorrow morning."

"Then I'm going to bed," Ari announced. "Wake me if you need me."

~

Mac forgot he was in raven form until he yawned and accidentally poked Ari's lion in the shoulder with his beak.

How had he ended up surrounded by her protective body at the foot of Nico's bed? He only recalled clutching the headboard with his talons when Nico switched off the light.

Are you up or going back to sleep? Ari's irritated telepathy rattled his sleep-fogged brain.

Which one would you prefer? he asked.

Coffee is what I'd prefer.

Then let's go get some.

I'll meet you in the kitchen. Ari gracefully slid off the bed, barely ruffling any of Mac's feathers and taking her warmth with her. He watched as she pawed the bedroom door open and disappeared down the hall. It made him wish he could open doors while he was raven— things would be so much simpler if that were true.

Flapping off the bed, he headed for the bathroom and the clothes he'd left there the night before.

~

"Have a seat," Val invited Ari to take a barstool at the kitchen island. "Cops in Erly and Hunter's old neighborhood arrested the guy Denton hired to burn his ranch house down." Lifting the remote to the kitchen television, he turned off the mute so Ari could hear the details. They had to sit through a barrage of commercials, first, but eventually the news returned.

"The man hired to burn down a ranch house was arrested during a routine traffic stop," a field reporter spoke to her audience.

"Billy Ray Gentry was stopped for failing to signal a lane change, and for driving erratically," a state trooper described the arrest. "During the stop, it was determined that the car he drove was stolen several years earlier. The suspect had a bottle of whiskey in the car with him, along with a pet rattlesnake, some powdered uranium, a pistol that may have been used in a crime, a rug made from the head and skin of a mountain lion, and twenty-five thousand dollars in cash."

"I'll fucking kill him," Ari was on her feet in a flash, the moment she heard about the mountain lion skin and head.

"Is it true the snake's name is Edgar?" the journalist asked, chuckling.

"That's what I hear," the trooper grinned. "Hell of a traffic stop, don't you think?"

"Can the snake be released on his own recognizance? He wasn't involved in the crime," the journalist pointed out.

"We'll see what we can do," the trooper replied with a grin.

"Ari, I didn't know about your dad," Val shut off the television and turned toward her. "They didn't say anything about that in the earlier broadcast."

"What happened?" Mac walked into the kitchen, straightening the collar on his pullover shirt after a lengthy shower.

"They arrested the guy Denton paid to burn down the house," Val said. "He took James Leone's remains from the house before he turned on the gas in the house and left the rest to his patsies, who not only accomplished the goal for him, but ended up not getting the benefit of their portion of the proceeds because they're toast."

"What happens to the remains?" Mac asked, his hands dropping onto Ari's shoulders and beginning a slow massage to calm her.

"Stuck in evidence," Val shrugged. "They draw a clear line between this guy and his presence in the house."

"You think they'll charge him with murder, if he's the one who turned on the gas?"

"I think that's something they'll consider. He certainly planned all this, unless I'm very wrong."

"Sheriff McCullough still hasn't shown up; Deputy Warner has requested that Franks and Billy Ray Gentry be brought back here for charges. They're scheduled for the move this afternoon," Del joined the kitchen conversation.

"Del, can I see you for a minute?" Laronda came in behind Del.

"Sure thing, Lara." Del followed her out of the kitchen.

"Somethin's up," Erly walked in.

"Any idea what?" Val asked.

"I heard McCullough, but that's about it before Laronda came running in here like a ghost was chasing her."

"That's the County Sheriff. We may find out where he's been all this time," Val slid off his barstool. "I'm making a fresh pot of coffee. Any takers?"

Every hand in the room went up.

We'll get him back, don't worry, Mac reassured Ari after removing his hands from her shoulders.

"Thanks," he told Val as two fresh cups of coffee were set in front of him and Ari. Mac turned slightly as Del and Laronda returned to the kitchen.

"Sheriff McCullough's son, Jeremy, was one of the arsonists who died last night," Del said. "Apparently, Jeremy went on a crime spree before buying the gas—he used his father's credit card to buy the fuel, after he shot his father and mother and left them dead on the floor at the house."

"Damn, that's harsh," Erly grimaced.

"They've also found images on the video camera that was found in Billy Ray's car. Seems he recorded the original killing spree where Hunter's aunt was murdered, and the recording of Everette's business getting shot up. That means he had a hand in both. Right now, he's clammed up tighter than a seal on a submarine. Won't talk until he gets his lawyer visit."

"That's a solid lead to the Adversary," Mac stood slowly and leveled a troubled gaze on Del. "He probably doesn't know who the Adversary is, but he's connected, somehow."

"He has the names of the others engaged in those murders," Laronda pointed out. "We'll be looking into that for certain."

"Only if you can reach him before the Adversary does," Ari's voice was a low growl. "This won't get past the Adversary; you can bet on it."

"He'll be killed or rescued, depending on how much he matters to the enemy," Mac said. "The people at the jail should prepare themselves for attack."

"You think we ought to be there?" Del studied Mac's expression, searching for an answer.

"On the one hand, we kill a few of the Adversary's minions and keep the culprit alive. As long as the culprit lives, those around him will be in danger," Nico advised.

"Nico?" Mac turned toward him, worry betrayed in that single word.

"On the other hand, if the culprit dies before the Adversary sends his minions," Nico opened his hands like a book, its pages connected by a single spine.

"You're suggesting we kill the bastard?" Del breathed.

"No. I suggest that we make it appear as if the bastard is dead—at the hands of his most recent employer, Denton Franks."

Del whistled at Nico's suggestion; Mac blinked several times as if attempting to reconcile this version of Nico with the one he'd first met. The one who was a care-free young man, happy to see him and feed him tamales behind his family restaurant.

The stone does things to people, Mac reminded himself and squared his shoulders. He felt responsible, when he knew he had nothing to do with the stone's choices. He was merely cursed with guarding their safety.

"It'll be a race to see who gets to him first," Ari pointed out. "Sit down, Nico. I'll fix you an omelet."

"We can let the Adversary have him," Val offered. "He's not that bright. Not sure how much good he'll be to the opposition. Get two skillets out, Ari. I'll help you cook."

"We need his information," Nico reminded Val. "Even a single lead will be invaluable to us. We find enough links in the chain, eventually we find the hook at the end."

"Nobody's ever found the real hook," Mac reminded Nico grimly. "We only find the human incarnation. We destroy that and the evil is forced underground again."

"Except this time isn't all the other times," Nico countered. "This time, the win or loss could be forever."

"We may be able to help with the information part," Del began. "We have information on his background coming in, and backup sent from our Department. Let's hope they get there before the other side does."

"I'll let them know they may have competition," Laronda said dryly and left the kitchen.

"I'll bring you an omelet," Ari called out to her.

"Thanks," Laronda's reply floated back.

"Billy Ray's been arrested," Killebrew said. "Somebody's bringing your breakfast in from the kitchen."

"On what charge?" Darnell leaned forward to set both elbows on his makeshift desk at the Lodge.

"Arson and possible murder," Killebrew sniffed. "I told him to let those jobs go and get his ass here, but he wouldn't listen."

"Fuck," Darnell cursed. "We have to take care of this and soon, before he talks."

"Hasn't talked yet," Killebrew attempted to settle Darnell's rising temper.

"He knows my name," Darnell hissed. Killebrew didn't like the light in Darnell's eyes, but didn't say anything.

"We can pull him out," he began.

"We're past that. We have to shut him up, and the sooner the better. Belhar," Darnell pounded a fist on the desk.

"How would you like to proceed?" Belhar appeared, smiling as if he'd anticipated Darnell's summons.

"Get rid of the leak," Darnell said. "However you like. The sooner the better."

"Of course." Belhar gave the Senator a wicked grin before disappearing.

"Where's Edgar?" Billy Ray shouted as he was shut up in his cell.

"Don't you worry about your little snake," the guard teased as he walked away.

"Hey, I get a phone call," Billy Ray yelled.

"Shut up, Billy Ray," came from next door.

"What the hell? Franks, is that you, you stupid bastard?" Billy Ray focused on a new target. "You just told the whole jail you know me."

"You just told 'em you know me. Chill, asshole. They already know everything," Denton snapped back. "Now shut your face. I'm trying to sleep in here."

"Like I care if you can't sleep. Live with it, fucker."

"Hey, knock it off," a new voice yelled.

"Shut up," Denton and Billy Ray chorused as the walls to their cells caved inward with an ear-splitting boom. The concrete enclosures collapsed like a castle of sand built too tall to sustain its bulk. What crawled inside the gaping hole caused Denton to faint and Billy Ray to shriek in terror.

"Images go blurry here," Del said as he moved the computer mouse to show the attack. "Franks and Gentry are now missing. No idea whether they survived the assault, but the entire jail had to be evacuated—it's too unstable to house prisoners, now."

"At least they only had five in there at the time," Mona pointed out. She, Lance, Del and Laronda were the first to see the images Del received from the Department. Nico, Ari, Everette, Renault and Mac were having a separate meeting regarding the attack on the county jail.

Lance wanted to be in both meetings, but he didn't say it. He understood that Nico was not only concerned about the disappearances of Gentry and Franks, but also about the impending visit from the remaining Septum Scholarium.

As for Claudio, Lance understood the scholarly vampire was also concerned, but didn't voice his worries aloud. No vampire would, but Lance had become attached to the three who'd come to help. Protecting them if they needed it was now a self-appointed task.

Don't worry, we'll keep them safe, Nico's words flowed into his mind, making Lance jump.

How? Lance directed his thoughts to Nico.

When your worry is that deep, I can pick it up, Nico explained.

What about Gentry and Franks?

They are beyond our control. Living or dead, we cannot use them for information now. Del's background checks will reveal much. Prepare yourself—remember we have a meeting with Senator Johnson in two hours.

Do you know what hit the jail?

We have suspicions.

Will you describe those suspicions?

Enough time has passed since the first demons rose from the island for them to slough away their first molting. I imagine these are the larger, more clever versions sent to collect a liability.

How many times will they molt?

They will grow larger and continue to molt until the Adversary stops them or they are killed.

You're not making me feel better about any of this, kid, Lance said.

There was never a time to make anyone feel good about any of it. We are living in deadly serious times, Detective.

What's our next move, then?

We offer to protect Senator Johnson. Muster your hope that she can be convinced.

You think the state government will be split down the middle, don't you? Lance guessed.

At this point, there is no longer a middle balance. I imagine it will split seventy-thirty at best, and ninety-ten at worst.

With the high numbers going to the Adversary?

Yes, Detective. Exactly that.

"What the fuck are we supposed to do with a cripple?" Darnell stared at Denton Franks, who had a cast on one leg and a hand on Billy Ray's shoulder to prop himself up. "Killebrew, tell me whether he's anything more than demon food."

"He can help me record video," Billy Ray asserted. "Even with a bum leg."

"Then you're in charge of him. We have work for both of you coming up. Either one of you fail me, and you'll both be demon food."

"Aren't you that Sen," Denton began before Billy Ray elbowed him in the stomach, effectively cutting off Denton's speech.

"You will address him as Master," Killebrew snapped at Denton. "Nothing else. Got it?"

"Yeah," Denton wheezed as he attempted to straighten up. "Yes, sir, Master, sir."

"Get outta my office. Rev, get them the best equipment money can buy. We have some primetime TV to record."

"Already on it," Killebrew promised as he herded Billy Ray and Denton out the door.

Jeff Walker shoveled cow and chicken guts over the mounds that the

Most Reverend Benny Killebrew called *the garden*. He said the ones planted there needed to eat to develop properly.

Jeff had already seen more than he wanted of those developments. This was his penance for sticking his nose where it didn't belong, and then trying to milk a little fame out of it.

He couldn't help but wonder whether those people he'd guided into the wildlife refuge had survived, or if they'd been planted in one of Benny Killebrew's gardens, to eventually sprout out of the ground, hungry for whatever they could find to feed them.

As far as he could tell, there was nothing capable of withstanding these creatures, unless somebody wised up and sent the Air Force in with bombers.

"Won't be long, now," a fellow gardener drove along the perimeter of the garden on a small tractor, hauling a trailer filled with more guts and offal. "Boss says there's a special mission waiting for this batch."

Jeff looked up into the unforgiving Texas sun and shaded his eyes. The dust disturbed by the tractor's passing hung in the motionless air, like a deadly virus waiting to be inhaled.

"I don't suppose you know what that mission is?"

"Does it matter, maggot?"

"No, I guess not. Empty the trailer—I got work to do."

"Got kids, maggot?" After dumping his grisly load, the driver ground the tractor's gears as he prepared to drive away. Jeff cringed and clenched his teeth at the offensive noise. The tractor rumbled away, leaving him standing speechless in the dust of its wake.

"Hell, no," Jeff yelled, after returning to his senses.

"Good for you, maggot."

"Val, it's good to see you and Janie," Senator Esther Johnson welcomed them into her office. "Did you bring someone with you?" She politely dealt with the small crowd that had come with Val and Janie.

"They have an interesting story to share with you," Janie began. "I'd appreciate it if you'd hear them out. This is Agents Del Reeves and

Laronda Abrams from a special division of the FBI," she introduced them first. "And this is Ari Leone and Nico Garcia."

"Those names sound familiar," Esther Johnson scrutinized both faces.

"They should sound familiar. They're both listed as missing," Lance stepped forward and offered her his badge. "Lance Elliott and Mona Sparks, from Dallas PD," he introduced himself and his cousin. "We're related to Val and Janie," he added. "These two," he tipped his head toward Erly and Hunter, "are Hunter Pace and Erly Graham. The last two in the back—that's Everette Ellison, owner of Everette's Night Grooves in Dallas, and Renault Retat, a friend."

The Senator looked from Hunter to Erly to Ari to Nico. "Get in my office now. We'll shut the door and ask not to be disturbed."

Esther Johnson watched the recording of the hearings she'd attended earlier in the week. Every time, she blinked and shook her head at the image of the giant serpent, going from one colleague to another.

It was a copy of the official recording provided by the crew working for the state government; she'd requested it after watching the version Del had brought with him for her perusal.

Both copies were the same, and all her visitors visibly relaxed once they were assured she could see the serpent in the recordings.

"This is connected to the zombies?" She blinked at Del.

"Yes, ma'am. And to the abductions in Austin, the mess in the wildlife refuge on the gulf, and the murders in Swindall and at Everette's club. And, just recently, the attack on your county jail, where two inmates went missing. We have a recording of that, too, but the images are blocked out. Nico can probably describe what it was that knocked the wall in to extract the missing detainees."

"They will blame all this on those they target—witches or wiccans, minorities, LGBTQ, asylum seekers, the lot," Laronda explained.

"You're saying that some of my colleagues on the panel may be involved in all this?" Esther's forehead was creased in a deep frown as she watched the recording again.

"Unfortunately, yes. We can't say for sure who is affected, but some of them are or will be."

"Your life is in danger, if we're reading the signs correctly," Lance told her.

"Well, I can't just go into hiding, nor would I want to. If there is evil among us, it must be met head on."

"We agree—up to a point," Val said. "We're offering protection—and information will be provided as we deal with this enemy. You're someone who many people trust to give them the truth. That will make you a big target, if you choose to take on that role."

"What kind of protection?"

"Two day guards—two night guards, who can be rotated on and off with a second squad, but you'll be given round-the-clock protection."

"Who might these guards be?"

"They'll be provided by my Department," Del said. "They're only waiting to hear from me before they begin their protection duties."

"What about the Governor?" Esther demanded.

"We haven't heard a word from him, and two of ours sat and watched the recording with him," Del admitted. "Our two saw the serpent. He didn't."

"This isn't good," Esther breathed, shaking her head and trying to convince herself that this was fact and not fiction. "Before that hearing, I'd have thrown you out of my office for lying. Now," she closed her eyes and breathed a ragged sigh. "What has the world come to?" She opened her eyes and blinked at Val.

"We wonder the same thing," Val agreed. "Del, tell those guards to bring her to the ranch if she needs extra protection. It's the least we can do."

"Senator Johnson, you will receive an unexpected invitation soon," Nico interrupted, his voice flat. "No matter how enticing, the answer should be a polite no."

"I have an invitation to join the Governor and Lieutenant Governor at a ribbon-cutting ceremony," Esther fingered a memo on her desk.

"Call and decline," Nico said.

"If you need advice, here are our numbers," Del handed Esther a card. "Unless we're in the middle of a battle, we'll do what we can for you."

"You really saved people in Austin? Why isn't anyone talking about that?"

"There's another video," Laronda pulled a thumb drive from her pocket and handed it to Senator Johnson. "It's from a rooftop camera. I warn you; the images are graphic and frankly, most people only see a bright light. I think you may be able to see past that."

Lance helped her load the thumb drive onto her computer and begin the video. Esther's eyes opened wide in disbelief as she gasped, "That's—oh, my Lord."

⁓

"Get it in gear, Phyllis. This is going to push our cause across the country," Benny Killebrew snapped at his wife.

"This is too hot," Phyllis mumbled as she pulled the black, hooded robe on.

"Make sure your face is covered—we don't want anybody recognized. Tonight, you're a witch, and we're gonna record you and the others raising my new batch of soldiers."

"You mean monsters." Phyllis' words were muffled by the heavy robe she struggled to fit over her head.

"Shut up, or you'll be one of the offerings instead of the witches. Come on—we got three cameras at three angles. This is gonna make everybody sit up and take notice. Then, they're gonna go out and do our work for us. There won't be a practicing witch or wiccan left in this country after this goes public."

Phyllis wanted to argue with him, but he'd meant what he said about making her an offering. He'd saved several women from the raid on Austin just for this. She shuddered, thinking of the monsters bursting from the ground and devouring the naked, innocent souls

Benny's new deacons had been ordered to tie to stakes in his garden—as the rising demons' first meal.

The video would then be sent to all those websites that he'd pulled to his cause. He hoped to attract the attention of the President and Congress—*to bring them into the fold*, as he often said. And, as usual, donations would pour in to further *the cause*.

Phyllis finally had the oppressive robe situated around her so she could see through the hood's opening. "That's good, Phyllis," Benny nodded as he studied her. "Pull the hood a little farther over your face. Remember the chant I taught you? Make sure you're doing it in unison with the others, and when my soldiers begin to emerge, hold your candle high. You're celebrating, remember?"

"I'll remember."

~

"Just hit record and leave the camera alone," Billy Ray told Denton. "Don't touch it—don't do anything unless I tell you to, okay?"

Denton Franks had a makeshift crutch to prop himself up, but the tip of the whittled branch kept sinking into the ground. "I got it," he growled, jerking his crutch out of the soil for the umpteenth time.

Denton still didn't understand what all the mounds in the field were, and the stench of rotted meat reminded him of his dead cattle.

"If what comes out of the ground scares you, whatever you do, don't bump the camera. Just close your eyes—you're not on the menu tonight."

"What's that s'posed to mean?" Denton snapped at Billy Ray.

"Just don't worry about it. Stand here and pretend you're doing something, all right? If you want to live, that is."

"My leg hurts," Denton whined.

"Well, I'll see if anybody has any pain pills after this is over—if you do your job."

"I'll fucking do my job," Denton hissed through clenched teeth. "When does this rodeo start?"

"Soon. Look, the witches are coming."

"Huh?" Denton almost fell, he swiveled so quickly to see what Billy Ray meant.

"Don't worry; I already got another camera set up to get this part."

Denton watched in horrified fascination as a line of people, dressed head-to-foot in dark robes and carrying tall, pillar candles, approached in the deepening twilight. Following in their footsteps were more black robes, leading shackled, naked women on chains.

Tasting bile in his throat, he watched as the dark robes circled the field and stood at attention while the chained women, most of them weeping, were tied to heavy poles buried randomly in the field.

Then, the chanting began, almost making him forget to hit the record button.

CHAPTER TWENTY-ONE

"*L*aronda and I can stay with Senator Johnson until her new guards get here," Ari volunteered.

"You're the ah," Esther Johnson blinked at Ari.

"Yes. It's nothing to be afraid of—it'll be me, just in another form."

"Senator, the stone wouldn't have marked Ari if she weren't worthy," Nico assured her. "Let her guard you until the others arrive."

"The plane was delayed out of Atlanta—the remnants of the tropical storm caused the delay," Del explained. "They're scheduled to take off any time, now, so it'll be roughly four hours for them to fly in and get to you here."

"I'll stay here with Laronda until Ari gets the others home," Val offered. "I can catch a flight back to Dallas."

"Let me stay instead," Mac rumbled. "I'll stick with Ari and Laronda until the others are here."

"Yes—that works," Nico agreed.

"I hope they don't mind working with me—I have plenty of rescheduled appointments tomorrow," Esther said. "I had to ask my assistant to make apologies, and I really do need to have those meetings."

"Understood, Senator," Val nodded. "We appreciate your time and attention to these matters and accommodating us for this meeting."

"Val, thank you for bringing this to my attention. I would have been completely in the dark if you hadn't come forward."

"We'll be working on strategy with you in the coming days," Del assured her. "This requires careful planning, as you've probably guessed already."

"Yes. Especially if this enemy manages to bring more people to his side in some way."

"He will; we're only waiting to see how he does it," Nico said.

"I'll be back in a few," Ari said. "Are the rest of you ready to go?"

"We are," Del said.

Ari transported the others, leaving Senator Johnson blinking at the empty space in her office.

"I wouldn't have called you, except this is urgent," Niall Pratt, Esther Johnson's assistant breathed into the burner phone he'd bought. "I tried to get in there, but she told me she didn't want to be disturbed. All I could see past the blinds on her office window was bright light." Niall listened intently to the response from Senator Cheatham.

"Of course I have what's needed. Your associate asked me to get it —did he not tell you?" Niall listened while Cheatham spoke again. "I agree that he did the right thing and has your best interests at heart. I only need assurances that I'll be protected."

Niall, peeking through the blinds of his own office window, glanced across the hall at Senator Johnson's closed door. "Yes, she's still in there. I'll be ready when your men arrive. Just give me a few minutes, all right?"

Jeff Walker leaned on his shovel, feeling sick to his stomach. The screams were bad enough as women were eaten alive in a few gulps by

horrific monsters, but an entire section of demons had risen and disappeared without gorging themselves.

Already on a mission, the tractor driver from earlier in the day informed him in passing. Maybe an escape attempt would be better for him than staying to watch the same thing over and over; after all, the demons' victims had died in a matter of seconds.

You're afraid of those few seconds if you're caught, he chastised himself, and wondered who the unlucky target of the newborn demons would be.

Niall checked the clip for his recently-purchased Glock 19. Fifteen rounds in the first clip to bring the old biddy down, and another fifteen in the second clip for anybody else in the office with her.

After all, Senator Cheatham had certainly listened carefully once he'd mentioned the bright light coming from Esther's office. Maybe he wouldn't wait for Cheatham's men. Rising from his desk chair, he stuffed the gun in a front pocket and strode toward the door, only to be blown back against the wall when two creatures burst through his door.

From his position on the floor, he watched as six more ugly, demon-like creatures—much larger than the kind that attacked downtown Austin during the biker parade, crashed through Senator Johnson's door and outer wall.

Niall, intent on watching what happened across the hall, shrieked as the first demon creature bit into his leg. He barely had enough sense left to pull his gun out and begin shooting.

Striking demons with fifteen nine-millimeter bullets only served to infuriate the two attacking him.

Cheatham lied was Niall's last thought.

Ari shrieked in pain as she prepared to return to Esther Johnson's office, the skin between her shoulder blades felt as if it were on fire after she landed in the game room with Janie and the others.

Her first thoughts were for Mac and Laronda as she bent over and screamed in pain a second time. Renault leapt to her aid, as did Everette and Val. And, because they were so close when she transported back to Austin, they ended up going back with her.

Two decapitated demons lay at Mac's feet; he kept his swords moving, fighting off another four. Esther Johnson, whom he'd shoved behind him to protect her, threw anything she could reach at the attacking creatures, distracting them so Mac could rain blows with his blades.

Nearby, Laronda had turned to coyote after emptying her gun at the remaining four creatures. One demon foolish enough to attack her was now missing a foot and a hand.

Capitol guards arrived almost the same moment that Ari, Val, Renault and Everette did. Shots rang out immediately; two demons turned to deal with this new threat while Ari blasted the nearest demon with light from her hand.

Val tugged Esther out of the way as guards continued to shoot erratically at anything that moved. The inner glass wall in Esther's office shattered, sending shards flying toward the occupants inside. Val placed himself between the flying glass and his charge.

Shouts rang out and echoed in the building as more guards arrived. Ari screamed in rage as Renault was hit in the arm by a flying bullet while he and Everette fought the largest demon among their attackers.

"No!" Esther shrieked as Mac, moving forward to decapitate the monster Renault and Everette fought, was hit in the chest by two bullets.

Ari's yowl was high-pitched as Mac went down, and her answering blast of light momentarily stunned any human around her who still lived.

"Ari and Nico are with him now. If there's any hope at all," Janie patted Esther's hand.

Ari had the presence of mind to get Mac and the others out of Esther's office before the Capitol guards could cause more damage. Del and Laronda were monitoring the situation from the ranch, and already in contact with their Department to explain what actually happened.

"You have a lovely home," Esther said, her voice betraying how distracted she was. "You and Val were right, and you came at the right time," she added in a whisper.

Janie didn't want to tell Esther that her assistant, Niall Pratt, had been half-eaten by the demons attacking him. The FBI was on the scene, gathering evidence and taking statements from the handful of guards who'd survived the ordeal.

Del had already reported that Esther was in a safe location—one that couldn't be revealed because she was the main target of the attack.

"We wanted to protect you, and we accomplished that," Janie said, keeping her voice calm. "You're the one people will listen to, when you tell them the truth. The time for hiding these demons—for sweeping the information under the rug—is over. The enemy will lie about them. You will speak the truth."

"How quickly will they lie about it?"

"Nico says soon," Janie sighed. "Come to the kitchen—Mona has coffee, tea and sandwiches ready if you want some."

"All right."

Janie didn't fail to notice how badly Esther's hands shook as she helped her rise from the sofa in her sitting room.

Mac wandered through the mists of his ancient home. He stood upon high, green cliffs, watching the sea fling itself against the rocky coast below with a regular, booming intensity. This was where he'd grown up —but the place was empty. Even the house had sunk into the pit of time and no longer stood where his father built it.

A shudder shook him as his thoughts turned to his last meeting with his father—and the fateful choice he'd made. One that left him standing beside his mother while his father disavowed his only child and went off to war.

Had *She* brought him here—to gloat? To shove this part of his life in his face?

To tell him *She'd* warned him all those centuries ago?

"I don't care," he spoke to the winds stirring the mist. "I gave my heart and it will remain given. It was worth my life." He shivered in the cold winds, only then noticing he was naked. Ari was the love he'd always longed for and refused until now. Nico was like his own son. He loved them both unconditionally.

"You were a young fool back then, Cormac." The Morrigan stepped through the mist, looking as she always did when she appeared to him—as if time and the mundane elements had no hold on her.

"I know it well," he bowed his head to her in deep respect.

"Here. I know this embarrasses you." Holding out a hand, *She* clothed him warmly with a thought.

"Thank you," he dipped his head to her again.

"You recall the warning I gave—should you give your heart completely?"

"Yes, Lady." This bow was deeper than the others, as Mac accepted his fate.

"Good. Your curséd life is over. Go back, now, liberated from my curse. You may freely protect the ones you love with all your heart."

Ari cried out as the second bullet slapped into her palm and Mac's sudden, indrawn breath bowed his back, lifting him off the bed.

Nico's arms went around Mac, pushing his body gently onto the bed again. "All is well," he breathed into Mac's ear. "All is well."

"There it is," Everette pulled the slug from Renault's arm and held it out on the tip of a claw.

"You fought bravely," Renault dipped his head to Everette. "And you have some healing skill as well."

"I may have taken first aid when I was in college," Everette dropped the slug into Renault's hand, then retracted her claws. "Damn. Ruined my nails, too." She studied her hands. "Demon juice dissolves nail enamel, looks like."

"I'm sorry about your nails," Renault held a piece of gauze to his wound, which would stop bleeding momentarily, now that the bullet was out and the vampire healing had taken over.

"Don't be. It was worth a thousand nail jobs just to take that piece of shit down."

"They do have that stench about them," Renault agreed.

"Mac's alive," Hunter almost tripped coming down the basement stairs. "Ari fixed him!"

"Thank goodness," Everette breathed. "High five," she held up a hand for Hunter to slap. He did so with a huge grin.

"Janie said to tell you there's food in the kitchen," Hunter said before running back up the stairs.

"I'm hungry," Everette said.

"I could eat," Renault laughed.

~

"Nico, the curse is lifted," Mac said softly. Ari had left Mac's bedroom to get him a glass of water after she'd healed the bullet holes in his chest.

"I was afraid you'd die," Nico confessed. "I heard the curse in a dream days ago. Thank you for remaining true to yourself and ignoring what we believed it meant."

"All those years, I served because I was held to a curse. Some of those I protected I considered friends. Others were only a task that I was set."

"Until now," Nico smiled.

"Until now. It's finally personal to me to see this through, no matter how it ends."

"Mac, look at your hand," Nico's smile became a grin.

"Huh?" Mac held both hands in front of him.

"Palm up, dude."

Mac turned his hands over. There, on his left palm, lay the imprint of the shell. "*Bidh mi air mo dhamnadh*," he whispered.

"Nah—you won't be damned. Are you hungry? Ari says she'll bring soup for you if you want it."

"I'm hungry," Mac let his head fall back on the pillow. "Thank you —and Ari—for not giving up on me."

"That can't be real—can it?" Val frowned at Del's laptop screen.

"It appears to be real," Del released a pent-up breath. "It looks as if some of those monsters rising are the same ones we dealt with last night. You see these eight here?" He pointed to the left side of the screen. "They rise and disappear. The others—they all fed from the hostages. My Department is working on trying to identify those women among the ones taken in Austin."

"You think the Adversary just stuck some of his people in black robes so they wouldn't be recognized, and expects us to believe those are witches or wiccans?"

"That whole thing was staged—come on, three camera angles? Please. You know some will believe this tripe, though, no matter what. Already the conspiracy websites are blowing up with this mess, and threats against anybody claiming that religion are pouring in. The only reality in that video is that demons rose and women died."

"Then it's only a matter of time before the fake trials and—the rest of the madness begin?"

"That's what Claudio says. By the way, the other Scholars are scheduled to arrive tonight. We can change the venue if you don't want them here."

"No. We'll stand with Ari and Nico, no matter what. We're trying to work out how to get Esther and her guards together, so she can do a press conference and try to put the truth in front of the public, rather than this fucked up business."

Del shut his laptop and shook his head. "That horse is out of the barn and far ahead of us. All we can do is try to appeal to anyone who still has any sense left."

"Del," Mona rushed into Val's study without knocking. "The Governor and Lieutenant Governor were just attacked at a ribbon-cutting ceremony. They and half the crowd at the event are dead—more demons attacked in broad daylight."

"Fuck," Del swore and flipped his laptop open again.

"Guess who's next in line to take the Governor's place?" Lance arrived with Senator Johnson right behind him.

"Who's that?" Del asked while he tapped keys on his laptop.

"It's that peckerhead, Darnell Cheatham," Esther sniffed.

"Senator Cheatham, you have to get here right away," Gerri Dean, his Chief of Staff, sounded flustered over the phone. "The Governor and Lieutenant Governor died this morning. I'm afraid you have to come in and take over, then reassure the public."

"Set up a press conference," Darnell stood and lifted his suit coat from the back of his desk chair. "I'll be there in a few minutes."

Darnell smiled at Benny Killebrew and Belhar, who stood on the other side of his desk, listening to the call on speaker.

"Oh, oh," Gerri sounded more flustered than before. "Willow says the President is on another line, asking to speak with you."

"What does he want?" Cheatham asked.

"He ah, said he supports the ah, cause," Gerri didn't sound comfortable. "When we asked him what that was, he said he only wanted to speak with you."

"Give him this number. I'll be waiting for his call," Darnell said, trying to keep the smile out of his voice. "Terrible tragedy—send my condolences to the Governor's and Lieutenant Governor's families."

"I will, and I'll have Willow tell the President how to reach you."

"You do that." Darnell hung up.

"Well, well, looks like we're sittin' in tall cotton," Darnell chuckled. Killebrew nodded; Belhar wore a thoughtful expression as a fire kindled in his eyes.

"I don't trust any of this," Nico said. He, Ari and Mac had found a shaded spot around the pool and settled there to have a private conversation. "Esther said she was invited to the ribbon cutting, too, and after she was attacked, she didn't show up."

"I don't know what they were thinking, both showing up at the same event," Ari shook her head.

"The Adversary was likely doing the thinking in this. I'm suspicious of this man—the one taking the Governor's seat," Mac said.

"Same here," Nico agreed. "It disturbs me that the serpent we saw at the meeting gave him a wide berth, as if deliberately avoiding the man."

"We need Lance, Mona, Del and Laronda to do some digging on this guy. If he's sneezed wrong in the past few days, I want to know about it," Ari growled. "He's setting up a press conference, and that's going to overshadow Esther's announcement. She'll have to reschedule, and that will only place more innocent people in danger. The crazies will start hunting anybody they suspect of being a witch, wiccan, werewolf, gay or anybody else they plain don't like, and people will die."

"If the Adversary has Cheatham in his clutches," Mac sighed.

Ari lifted her head when the back door opened and Janie and Esther emerged. "They want to talk to us," Nico observed.

"I'll have to reschedule my announcement," Esther said as she and Janie joined the conversation. "All the networks will be covering the Governor's death and Cheatham's rise to power. Plus, they'll show the video of the crowd being attacked and half of them being eaten by those—vermin."

"It's on the national news, too," Janie said. "The President has called Governors in the surrounding states to put their National Guard on alert in case this becomes a bigger problem than Texas can handle."

"How are the National Guard going to help with this problem?" Mac asked. "Those Capitol Guards didn't stand a chance last night against what attacked them. Have you noticed that the local news has skirted that issue? Nobody's saying anything about how those demons were killed."

"Not that it's a bad thing," Ari frowned at him. "At least I got us out of there before anybody could ask questions."

"I hope Del and his Department were able to gloss over the Senator's guests," Nico said. "We don't need to be on their radar just yet."

"I didn't tell anyone who I was seeing—I only told Niall to reschedule that appointment, and then later to reschedule all of them for the day. And then Del told me that they found a cell phone near his body. It was crushed, but they're trying to get information from it anyway. There may be a record of him trying to call for help. You have to admit that the guards were very slow to arrive. It makes me wonder whose side they're on."

"Something to look at, certainly," Mac told her. "Frankly, anyone there at the time should be under scrutiny. Ari tells me that only the guards showed up, but isn't it highly unusual that nobody else would be in the building?"

"I think there were probably many there," Esther agreed. "Half the inhabitants probably have a firearm within reach, too. Why wouldn't they come to help?" Her last question was posed to herself mostly, but it was something that Ari, Mac and Nico had already discussed.

"Interference, perhaps—from the one or ones directing the demons?" Nico mused.

"You think they muted the sound—or managed to make the others ignore it?" Ari's forehead furrowed in concentration as she considered Nico's suggestion. "Can we do that?"

"Is it a good idea to do that?" Mac asked.

"We could sneak up on somebody, maybe?" Janie offered.

"We'll need to know where they are to sneak up on them," Nico pointed out.

"True enough," Janie said. "Mac, do you have any suggestions for entertaining a bunch of vampire visitors? I can't offer them cookies and lemonade."

"They're coming tonight—I forgot about that," Ari sighed.

"I hope they don't try to replace Claudio—he's the one who should be here," Nico said. "If our opinion matters to the Scholarium, they should leave unless they're here to help."

"Senator Johnson, your guards are set up at a safe house in Austin, if you're ready to go," Del said. He and Laronda walked toward the patio to inform Esther of her arrangements.

"Will I be safe enough?" she asked, rising from her chair.

"As safe as anybody can be right now," Laronda said. "Ari, we'll have to impose on you to get us there."

"No problem—where are we going?" Ari asked.

Del rattled off an address in an upscale Austin suburb. "It's armored in brick and steel, with bullet-proof windows and safe rooms in the basement. There are eight guards in residence already—four wolves and four vampires."

"Before yesterday, I'd have said you were crazy," Esther said. "Before yesterday, I would never have accepted such guards. Today, I am grateful."

"I'll come with you," Nico stood with Ari. "I can see this house in my mind. Ari and I will make sure you arrive safely."

"Her guards are fine," Ari sat on the opposite end of the sofa Mac occupied. "Nico went to the kitchen to get a soda. Del's Department also brought in three tech people to watch the security monitors. They check out, too."

"You look tired," Mac told her.

"Says the guy who got shot twice and is still recovering."

"Recovering is a lot better than dead," Mac raised arms above his head in a careful stretch.

"I prefer recovering, myself."

"Ari, I owe you big apologies," Mac dropped his arms and turned toward her.

"Mac, don't," Ari felt heat rise in her cheeks.

"Then I'll tell you this. For centuries, I've been the one to make sure the person holding the stone was safe and protected—as much as they'd allow it, anyway. The other day, when I woke and found my raven cuddled beneath your chin, I felt safer and more protected than I ever have. I—am grateful. To you and to Nico."

"We will fight for you, just as you will fight for us," Ari shrugged and turned away. "We feel you're part of our family, now, as strange as that may sound."

"I haven't had family since I was young and that's a long, long time ago. I ah, feel you and Nico are my family, too. My protection in the past was always part of a curse—something I was compelled to do. This—Ari, I've been freed from that curse. This protection is freely given and my sole purpose from now on."

Vampires are here, Nico informed Ari and Mac.

We'll be right down. Wait for us to go with you for introductions, Mac instructed.

I'm in the kitchen.

"Ready?" Mac asked Ari.

"Yeah. Let's go see how things are going to shake out."

Renault positioned himself beside Alejandro as Claudio prepared to welcome the vampire Scholars at the front door.

"Claudio," First Scholar, dressed in a fine, black silk suit with black shirt and tie, acknowledged the Seventh as he entered the house. Five more Scholars followed him, Claudio dipping his head in respect as each one passed. Renault studied each Scholar in turn before Alejandro offered to lead them into the formal living area.

The one who gazed longest at Renault was Second Scholar. Renault had worked with him before, and he'd held the Scholar in high regard but that could change. Renault stopped himself from breathing a sigh as the last of the Scholars passed him and strode into the room designated for their meeting.

Outside, each Scholar's guards had positioned themselves to protect the house while their charges were inside. Depending upon which way the wind might blow, Renault knew that the guards would eventually realize that Val's werewolf ranch hands also watched the house—and its visitors.

We're on our way, Ari informed him. *Val and Janie are with us. Del and the others are still in the kitchen; they'll only come out if asked.*

Thank you. The Scholars are quite curious—their scent betrays it, Renault replied.

Then we'll try to satisfy their curiosity without argument or bloodshed.

In the past, they have always remained strict but reasonable.

Then we'll see if that has changed.

Claudio wished he had the telepathic ability that Renault had been granted. If it were so, he would beg Ari and Renault to watch carefully if First Scholar sought to delve into his experiences using *Insight*, rather than asking questions.

He'd been through *Insight* before—many times—and was never concerned about surviving it. It was the standard way for Scholars to see the truth, rather than getting it any other way.

This time was different. Few creatures walking the Earth, vampires included, were above jealousy. The only thing that stood between him and his potential demise was the lack of the imprint on his palm and the gifts it conferred.

Renault held that honor; he doubted that Ari would allow anyone to perform *Insight* on someone she and Nico had chosen to bear the imprint.

"The Custodian is on his way, with the Raven Knight and the Protector," Renault announced. "They are accompanied by the werewolves who own this ranch."

Claudio watched First carefully as he digested Renault's information. Would he refuse to see Val and Janie? That would be a direct insult to their hospitality.

"They informed you of this—with telepathy?" First asked.

"Yes, Master Scholar," Renault dipped his head.

"This Custodian—you say he is nineteen years of age?" Second queried.

"Nearly twenty," Nico walked into the room followed by the others. "Age has no significance in this conversation."

"As you say," Second dipped his head to Nico.

"Why can we not hear your heartbeats?" Sixth asked, earning a quelling frown from First.

"Ari and I are experimenting with a new idea—that of muting sounds—and images."

Claudio drew in a breath. "This is why so few came to help at the Capitol, isn't it? The enemy has learned new tricks."

"They may be old tricks, Master Scholar," Ari addressed him formally. "Nico and I think they may have been held back by the ah, location in the past."

"Yes," First breathed. "The spells and the power within that area are certainly something to consider."

"Some of them were held in place by the stone," Mac said.

"Which is no longer there," Second observed.

"The war is here, now," Nico said. "It will be won or lost here."

"We are most interested in learning from Claudio—and Renault— the things which have passed here," First said.

"Then you'll have to ask questions," Mac warned. "Neither Ari nor Nico will allow *Insight* on either."

Third growled low at Mac's announcement; Sixth turned swiftly toward Third.

Ari growled back at Third. Claudio held his breath—here was the one who wanted him—and possibly Renault—to suffer.

With a hiss and movement so fast it was a blur, Third and Sixth attacked First.

Almost as quickly, Third and Sixth, after slicing First's chest and throat deeply, fell to the floor with agonizing shrieks after blasts of intense light hit them.

They're dead, Claudio realized, as Third's and Sixth's bodies began to disintegrate. Nico lowered his hand—he'd leveled the killing shafts of light against both vampires.

Ari rushed forward as First crumpled; both attackers had dealt terrible blows.

"We need him, Ari," Nico knelt beside her as she laid her hands on First.

"She needs room," Claudio warned the others when they crept closer.

"Help—me," First whispered. Ari's hands began to glow. "Nico has faith in you," she told him. "Of course we will help."

CHAPTER TWENTY-TWO

"First is resting well," Claudio replied to Ari's question. After she'd healed the deep gashes Third and Sixth delivered, Claudio and the other Scholars ushered him to the basement to fully recover.

"How are the others dealing with the ah, loss?" Ari sat at the kitchen island, turning a coffee cup in her hands, going over and over the images in her mind of Nico killing two vampires with swiftly honed shafts of light.

Claudio sat beside her; Mac, Nico and the others had gone to bed. The questions for Claudio could wait until the following evening when First felt better, according to Claudio and his fellow Scholars.

"I believe they knew something wasn't right," Claudio admitted. "During our discussions, there was much argument, you understand."

"Nico, Mac and I knew you were troubled, but we didn't want to pry into Scholar business."

"First wanted to send two Scholars here," Claudio sighed. "Fourth and Fifth volunteered, as they have the most battle experience. Third and Sixth would not agree and demanded that they be sent. First made the decision for all to come. Therefore," he didn't finish.

"Therefore, you're two Scholars down."

"They did not suffer long; I only captured a glimpse of brief surprise before their deaths. Dying in sunlight is far more brutal and ah, lengthy."

"They didn't think Nico had the ability or the will," Ari said flatly and sipped her coffee before setting the cup down. "They thought he was just a boy they could manipulate. What about Third and Sixth's guards?"

"They weren't aware of the intended betrayal, and from now on will provide extra security for the rest of us. Second made sure of them," Claudio studied his hands for a moment.

"It'll be okay," Ari covered his hands with one of hers. "If you need to talk," she offered.

"I thank you. As a rule, we aren't comfortable doing such, but your offer is much appreciated anyway."

"Just remember we're in this together," she pulled her hand away and smiled at him. "We'll get through this. I'm going to bed. See you later."

"Kraw."

Mac woke himself up from a dream he was having, and discovered that once again, his raven was burrowed in Ari's fur beneath her chin. He'd settled on Nico's headboard to keep watch. Ari had taken her usual place at the foot of Nico's bed. How they ended up like this without either waking was a mystery.

Ari chuffed a breath; he watched her cat's whiskers tremble. He'd wakened her, too.

Hesitating only a moment, he began to groom her whiskers with his beak—one was curled unnaturally, meaning she'd slept on it wrong.

Or he had.

One of her eyes opened lazily, carefully watching his sharp beak.

Habit, he sent. His raven's chuckle sounded like a rough titter.

You're impossible, she replied.

And yet here we are. Want me to groom your ears? You have nice, tempting tufts inside.

You leave my ears alone. Besides, those aren't tufts, they're called ear furnishings and you have no idea how long I've worked to get them the way they are.

Somebody needs coffee. Want some cream to go with your grumpiness?

If you weren't covered in feathers, I'd bite you.

Do we not like feathers in our mouth?

Shut up.

Will you two stop arguing? Nico scolded. "Come on," he said aloud, throwing covers to the side. "Let's go have breakfast and check the lay of the land."

"We've missed you," Ari hugged Mary Kate after finding her in the kitchen baking biscuits.

"Val sent us to Burke's for our days off," Mary Kate smiled when Ari let her go. "He didn't want to take chances with our safety, and we were slugs while Burke's staff took care of us."

"Is that why you look so rested?" Ari walked to the coffee pot to pour a cup for herself.

"That's the reason. They even did our laundry for us. We were positively slothful."

"Good morning, Mary Kate," Mac walked into the kitchen, his hair still damp from the shower. Nico walked in behind Mac, his hair also damp.

"I like that shower gel you're using," Ari told him. "Vanilla is one of my favorites."

"I like it, too. It makes me think of Mama's baking days."

"You poor thing," Mary Kate turned to give Nico a hug.

"Want coffee?" Ari asked.

"Yes," Nico and Mac answered together.

"You're telling me the President is coming to attend the Governor's funeral?" Val poured a glass of Scotch for himself and Del.

"It's not unheard of, although in this case, it worries me," Del replied. "Governors from other states are also coming or sending Lieutenant Governors to show their respects. The flags will fly at half-mast for a month, but Senator Cheatham is scheduled to be sworn in two days after the funeral."

"That's also something that troubles me—and it really troubles Esther. There's something else, too."

"What's that?"

"Four home invasions last night across the state. Everybody in the house shot to death, and this, written in the victims' blood, on the walls." Del handed his phone to Val.

"Death to all witches?" Val's forehead creased with concern as he handed the phone back to Del.

"It's the rally cry on those websites. In three of those houses, kids died, too."

"Does Nico know?"

"He knows. He says this is not unexpected. Those websites have their followers' emotions running high—they actually believe this shit. Four houses in Texas hit in one night is big, but there were also killings in California, Oregon, Illinois, Tennessee, Georgia and New Mexico."

"Damn," Val swore. "So it isn't just this state anymore."

"Nico predicted it would spread quickly. Neighbors will begin scrutinizing neighbors, and if more videos like the last one show up," Del shook his head.

"What's being done to stop it?"

"This is new, so state and local authorities are scrambling to put out a message. I heard there's quite the argument about what, exactly, the message should be."

"What do you mean?"

"There are some factions in the states hit last night that want to send a message for all witches to confess their beliefs, so they can be protected."

"You're joking. Sounds like that will only paint a bigger target on their backs."

"Exactly what Nico said. Once they're identified, well," Del spread his hands.

"Sounds too much like the Inquisition, when they were tortured to confess."

"Nico says that this enemy is behind all that, too. For some reason, the Adversary has a penchant for destroying those accused of witchcraft, those of the wiccan religion, those who may stand in the way of the killing and torturing, and pretty much anybody else they don't agree with."

"Like Everette?"

"Yes."

"Does anybody know why the Adversary targets witches—and the others?"

"Lycanthropes were targets too, in the past, or so Nico says. That means you, my friend."

"Werewolves tend to be so well hidden, it's difficult to find the real thing," Val sighed. "That doesn't mean that a human can't be accused of such."

"As was the case in the past," Mac said. He and Nico walked into Val's office, since the door was open. "Nico tells me you're curious about why witches are targets. I know why, but the reason is buried in the mists of time."

"We have other concerns to deal with, first," Nico said. "After that, if we're still standing, Mac and I will tell you what we know."

"What concerns?" Val asked.

"I have a feeling that things will take a terrible turn, and very soon," Nico sighed. "Some of us must go to the funeral with Senator Johnson. Something tells me that this event will prove most important to the future."

"Does she know we're coming?"

"Not yet. After the vampires wake tonight, we will pay her a visit

—to determine who will stand beside her and who will guard from a distance."

"Some of my wolves will volunteer if you need them," Val said. "As will I."

"This is the church where the Governor's funeral will be held in Austin," Del set a printed set of plans on the dining room table so those around him could see. "The Lieutenant Governor's funeral is set in his family's hometown of San Marcos, at a much smaller venue. Nico says we don't have to worry so much about that one."

"Please tell me Esther doesn't have to sit near that jizz-stick Darnell Cheatham," Everette muttered.

"Unfortunately, they're both in the same pew, although on opposite ends," Laronda said.

"That means we have to put guards on both sides of her, I think," Nico nodded. "That's the second pew—is the President sitting in the first pew on that side?"

"Yes," Laronda confirmed. "The center section is reserved for family and close friends, right side for colleagues and fellow politicians, left side for other important people. Press will be set up on the rear balcony; they expect an overflow crowd outside the venue, so big tents with large screens will be set up there for a direct feed to the public."

"It'll be televised, too, for those watching at home," Del said. "With a few seconds delay, of course."

"Is that the big church where they refused to take in hurricane victims?" Hunter asked.

"One and the same," Del told him. "They're providing the live feed for the attendees left outside the church. Local television stations will be sending the delayed feed to everybody else."

"Secret Service will be stationed throughout the cathedral," Laronda pointed out strategic spots, "as well as near the President and his entourage in the front pew. All of them will be armed, so don't forget about that."

"We won't be the first ones to attack," Val said.

"You can't say that with certainty," Nico warned.

"Who should be with Esther?" Laronda asked Nico.

"Val and Janie. That would be logical because they're her friends, plus one or two other guards. Renault would be a good choice."

"I'm good with that," Val agreed.

"As am I," Renault nodded at Val.

"We have to get Esther's approval, but I think she'll agree," Janie said.

"I'd like to pair at least one vampire with one of Val's wolves, to watch the crowd outside. I'll consider other pairings for the crowd, too," Nico said. "Del, do you think you could get two pairs inside the cathedral?"

"Let me look into it. Lists are being carefully scrutinized, you understand. I might be able to get one pair in on the left side."

"We'll take whatever we can get," Mac said.

"We're going to the Governor's funeral, so let's get you caught up on video one-oh-one," Billy Ray told Denton. "We'll be upstairs on the rear balcony, officially working for the next Governor of the Republic of Texas."

"My cast is itching," Denton complained. "Do we have to do this now?"

"You saw what happened to those women when the feeding began," Billy Ray snapped at Denton. "Unless you want to be tied to a pole next time, then you'd better listen up. Besides, Governor Cheatham will let us carry pistols—concealed of course. We may be able to sneak in a rifle with our equipment, too. Wouldn't want the reporters to freak. Once he's sworn in, we'll open carry, no matter what."

"Open carry is already the law," Denton huffed.

"Yeah, but not in a place like this, and certainly not when the President will be there."

"The President's coming?" Denton sounded much more interested than before.

"Oh, yeah. Last I heard, he's gonna get behind the whole killing witches thing. Ain't that somethin'?" Billy Ray slapped Denton's shoulder, causing him to wobble where he stood.

"What about the Secret Service?" Denton asked, once he'd righted himself.

"Oh, they'll be packing for sure, so don't do anything stupid."

"I want to meet him—the President. I voted for him. My stupid ex didn't. Shows you how wrong she was."

"Just be glad you got rid of her."

"She probably thinks I'm dead."

"Not a bad thing, either, considering the charges and all."

"Yeah."

"The Rev says there are special plans for the funeral, so keep your eyes open and be sure to keep up on recording it. I'm gonna show you how to pan the camera."

"Pan?"

"Moving from one side to the other, to follow the action. You need to take it nice and slow, so you don't make your audience dizzy or confused," Billy Ray explained. "The camera will be on a tripod like before, so you don't have to worry about a handheld pan. You're way too shaky to pull that off."

"Look who knows so much," Denton sneered.

"Two years of video production in college," Billy Ray said proudly. "I learned a few things before they kicked me out."

"Bad grades?"

"Hell no."

"Why, then?"

"None of your business. Start panning or plan your wardrobe for an invite to demon dinner."

~

"You'll be sitting in the second pew, across from the center section and right behind the President," Gerri, Darnell's Chief of Staff, gushed over the phone. "Willow and I will be at the back of the left section, but if you need anything," she offered.

"Send a message to my wife. She needs to be there, dressed appropriately."

"I will. Oh, this is so exciting. I never thought I'd be the Governor's Chief of Staff."

"Let me know what she says," Darnell cut her off and ended the call.

"Perhaps you should tell her that the Chief of Staff position is already taken," Benny Killebrew said, examining his fingernails. "Phyllis needs to give me a manicure," he mumbled. "As for your Chief of Staff, if you don't want to tell her she's fired, we can arrange another accident."

"Accident sounds fine, but let her finish her assignments, first."

"Sure thing, Governor. I think I already have a good idea on how to make it happen."

"Good. By the way, have you seen Belhar lately?"

"Last night. He said not to worry—he's gonna make this look really good and your legislation will definitely slide right through the House and Senate. He has a special assignment for you but didn't tell me what it was."

"I hope it furthers our cause. Only four places got hit in the state last night. Those numbers are way too low. We need to ramp this up and fast."

"But the other states were a real bright spot," Killebrew insisted.

"Yeah, but we need more from this state. I want all the people behind us in this."

"I think the next few days will take care of all your concerns, Governor."

"Good. Things are looking up, eh?"

"In a manner of speaking, yes."

～

Claudio woke first and sat up, only to realize the sun hadn't set outside. His body clock told him so, which puzzled him greatly. He'd never wakened before the sun set.

Ever.

"Claudio?" First's voice came to him from a cot against the far wall.

"First, are you well?"

"I feel quite fine. Has the sun set? My brain and my body must be confused with the time change."

"London time is quite different from Texas, Master Scholar," Claudio replied as agreeably as he could.

"I should travel more. I haven't been away from my city for more than a century."

"You are welcome to visit any time. The new world is not so bad—when it isn't being stalked by the Adversary."

"Then we will hold hope that the Adversary will fail in his attempt to destroy it, along with everything else."

"Yes. If he takes this country, he will have unlimited weaponry and troops to do his bidding against all the others. It will not end well."

"I know this. It is why I decided to come and bring the others. You saw for yourself that the Adversary invaded our ranks. I am fortunate to be alive today."

"It will be most difficult to trust from now on."

"Master Scholar, why does my hand glow?" Alejandro's question interrupted the conversation.

Claudio drew in a breath as a light kindled in his own palm—and that of First Scholar, too. In seconds, the entire basement glowed from the lights in many palms.

"Mom?" Val walked into his mother's sitting room. The television was on, but she wasn't watching it. Instead, her arms were crossed, her hands tucked tightly against her ribs. "Is something wrong?" he asked right away.

"Val, I," she began.

"Show me," he said gently.

Unfolding her arms, she held her left palm out for Val to see.

Val held out his left hand. Both bore matching scallop shell imprints. "What does this mean?" Janie breathed.

"It means we're among those the Custodian trusts."

What if I'm a little afraid?

"Did you want me to hear that?" Val asked, taking his mother's hand in his own and squeezing it carefully.

"I wasn't sure it would work."

"Mom, I think we're all afraid—some of us more than a little. We have to stand up for what's right, or division and chaos will take this country down."

"I'm not so young anymore," she revealed her biggest worry.

"That doesn't mean you can't make your presence known," Val smiled. "I love you, Mom. More than anything. Come on, dinner's ready."

~

"Well, you said we'd need a ton of tamales," Ari nodded at Nico when seventeen vampires followed their noses into the kitchen.

"Erly, let's take 'em to the big table," Hunter bumped his friend's shoulder with his own. "Follow me," he invited Claudio and the others. "We'll bring the food to you. You're gonna love this."

"I think I can make tamales in my sleep, now," Mary Kate laughed. "Come on, let's get the food on the table."

~

Lance, sitting on his favorite sofa in the game room, studied the imprint in his palm. Mona, Laronda and Del all had one just like it. One minute, his hand was normal. The next, it bore the imprint. He hadn't felt it; it merely was.

He'd discovered that Janie, Val, Erly, Hunter and two of Val's wolves, Henry and Kev, also had an imprint, in addition to seventeen vampires, who'd devoured tamales for dinner as if they were the best thing ever.

Maybe tamales are *the best*, he thought.

"Tamales were outstanding," Mona agreed. She sat on the opposite end of the sofa he occupied, waiting for Nico and Ari to take them to Austin to visit Esther Johnson.

"If we survive all this, do you think we can ever go back to Dallas PD—with what we are and what we know, now?" Lance asked her.

"Probably not. We haven't talked to Belwether in days and he hasn't called us; I doubt it will be a painful break if we don't go back."

"You'll have a place within the Department if you want it," Laronda said. She and Del walked into the game room to join them. Laronda's hearing had caught the conversation long before she reached the doorway.

"Something to consider—thank you," Lance grinned.

"Yeah—normal stuff just feels so—mundane, if you know what I mean," Mona said.

"Ready?" Mac arrived not far behind Laronda and Del.

"Yep," Lance heaved himself off the sofa.

"Ari and Nico are downstairs, waiting," Mac said. "Shall we?"

∾

"Coffee is quite delightful," Claudio sipped with obvious enjoyment. Esther had offered her guests coffee, cookies and small slices of cake upon their arrival.

"I haven't been able to taste anything in so long," Second Scholar sighed after finishing a chocolate chip cookie.

Ari, Nico and Mac, all having coffee, watched the vampire Scholars with barely hidden smiles.

"You're here to discuss the funeral, aren't you?" Esther turned her gaze toward Del.

"Yes. We want to provide protection. Nico suggests that Val and Janie be with you, in addition to one other guard, at the very least."

"I can take up to four guests," Esther replied.

"Then Erly or Hunter would be good choices," Nico said.

"Hunter may be the better choice," Mac coughed.

"Yeah. Sticking a black man smack in the middle of a bunch of white folks makes him stand out like a peacock in a hen house," Erly agreed. "We don't need anybody paying closer attention than they ought to, especially in that crowd."

Laronda dipped her head in a slight nod of agreement with Erly.

"We can put you somewhere in the middle section, though," Del said. "If needed, you can get through a crowd fast, I think."

"Sure can, even if I have to claw my way over wooden pews."

"Well, these pews are padded, but we get the idea," Laronda smiled.

"Haven't you ever wanted to claw the stuffing out of seat cushions?" Erly teased. "If you haven't, you may have to turn in your shifter card."

"I may or may not have allegedly chewed a few in my younger days, but there's no real evidence left behind."

"Statute of limitations has set in," Val opined.

"What is the statute of limitations on cushion destruction? Asking for a friend," Ari said, holding up a hand to fend off accusations.

"I'd say two years—it's fairly standard," Esther laughed.

"We'll have others from the Department outside, watching the overflow crowd," Del broke in, bringing the conversation back to the subject at hand. "More than half won't need to carry a weapon, because they are the weapon."

"Just be careful—you know what those conspiracy websites will make of that if it comes down to it," Lance cautioned.

"Yes, but if the choice is hold back or save lives," Nico countered.

"Saving lives is what we're there for—along with hunting the Adversary," Ari said. "Maybe we ought to start hunting down those websites, too."

"We have people on that," Del said. "But if one gets shut down, there's nothing to stop it from popping up elsewhere."

"Then the people behind those websites may have to be stopped," Mona suggested. "I can help with that, if you want."

"Turn in your notice to Dallas PD, and we'll put you on the payroll permanently," Del told her.

"I'll let you know after this is over."

"Fair enough. Now, let's get down to business—on what our plan is when and if something goes wrong, and then speculate what that something could be."

"It could be anything from an attack of demons to an attack of fake witches," Mac huffed.

"Or a regiment of conspiracy nuts descending on the place with enough rifles and ammunition to kill everybody several times over," Laronda pointed out.

"I'm worried it'll be something we didn't consider," Ari sighed. "Something that will take us all by surprise and paralyze us just long enough to do major harm."

"You mean like the minister and the choir turning into monsters?"

Nico turned toward Hunter, who'd made the suggestion. "Something like that, yeah," he agreed. "Something or somebody we're not looking at too closely, who can transform the whole thing into a killing ground."

"Perhaps we should study the list of attendees—from the minister on down," Esther said. "And consider what damage they can do if they suddenly go nuts."

"Nobody inside should be armed except Secret Service, not with the President there," Del began ticking items off his list. "That leaves physical ability and enhanced physical ability."

"Humans, shifters and vampires," Claudio agreed. "It is a terrible thought that any of the latter could have joined the Adversary, but it's possible, I suppose."

"That's terrifying and against their own self-interest, but that doesn't mean it doesn't or won't happen—we see it all the time," Renault surmised.

"True enough," Esther agreed. "You have no idea how many

politicians I've seen get in bed with the enemy just to put themselves ahead, somehow."

"That sort of thing happens everywhere," Mac said. "And throughout time, too. It's nothing new and there's not much you can do about it."

"Will you be recovered well enough to fight if it's required?" Esther asked Mac.

"Yes. I already feel fit and should be at a hundred percent by Monday."

"I never thought I'd see anyone fighting with a sword outside the movies," Esther told him. "I'm not sure they know what they're doing."

"I'm pretty sure most of them *don't* know what they're doing," he chuckled. "They've never been in a real sword battle for their lives; I'd bet on it. Originally, I fought with a two-handed long sword, but I learned how to fight with two slightly shorter, double-edged blades. I make do with either, but the double-edge lops off heads easier—from a personal standpoint, of course, because just stabbing this enemy won't make him dead. It will only make him angry."

"Like the zombies," Lance nodded.

"Because the zombies are the first stage of demons," Nico agreed. "If they're given safe ground and a food source, they'll become demons. And later, they can pupate again, to become larger, more dangerous demons. What we've seen so far are the ones that Mac can kill with his blades. Bigger, stronger ones?" Nico shrugged.

You're having nightmares again? Mac silently asked Nico.

They don't disturb me like they did before if you and Ari are close by. It's like your strength combines with mine to provide a separation, so I see and hear but they don't threaten me like before.

Good to know, Mac said.

"Does anyone need a fresh drink or cup of coffee?" Esther asked.

"I'll take more coffee," Ari said. Several others asked for the same.

"Let's get down to business and lay out this plan of ours, so we'll know what to do and where to go," Del said as two of Esther's guards went to the kitchen for refills.

"Let's look at the layout of the church again, and pinpoint our positions," Lance suggested. "Then map escape routes and anything else we may need."

"That sounds good to me," Erly said. "I need to count how many people and pews are in the way if Esther's guards need help."

"I wish to know where we can direct the crowd if they're attacked," Claudio said. "First says we should be on the perimeter and ready to do battle if necessary."

"Fourth and Fifth will develop a plan to drive the crowd to safety, but we need a safe place for them."

"There's a storm shelter in the basement of the church, but that's not safe if the building is already compromised," Del replied.

"The nearest building where they can take refuge is a quarter mile away," Laronda pointed out. "It's a bank building, so it might not be the best choice."

"There's a parking lot here," Ari pointed out an area west of the church. "It could serve as a gathering place, if something like that is needed."

"If the crowd panics, it will be pandemonium," Fourth Scholar spoke. "I believe if that happens, the best option will be to fight the attackers and hope the majority of the crowd can get themselves far enough away to save their own lives."

"That's terrifying. Will there be a police presence for the overflow?"

"Yes, and that could prove dangerous to any of ours outside," Del pointed out. "We may have to work around the police firing at demons if they attack the crowd."

"This could turn into a right mess," Erly observed.

"You're right," Esther nodded. "It could become a bloodbath, actually."

CHAPTER TWENTY-THREE

"Two days," Ari hunched her shoulders. She'd slept badly after returning from Esther's safe house the night before. Mac, buried in her fur, had croaked sleepily twice as she twitched in restless, nightmarish dreams.

"We don't know for sure that anything will happen," Janie patted her hand. Both women sat at the kitchen island drinking coffee while Mary Kate put a breakfast casserole together.

"Nico, Mac and I have a bad feeling about it."

"Then let's hope it's not too bad. Burke is on his way; he'll be here for breakfast. He says he has a question for you and Nico."

"Probably about what to do with my gallery, and Nico's parents' will," Ari sighed. "I can't keep the gallery; I know that, now. As for Nico's stuff—I don't know what he wants to do with all that."

"I want to keep the property—for now," Nico said as he and Mac shuffled into the kitchen. "Maybe someday, I'll know what to do with it. For now, I have other problems to deal with."

"You okay?" Mac asked Ari, his hands gripping her shoulders and massaging tense muscles.

"Yeah, just stressed," she told him. *That feels wonderful,* she informed him privately.

I wish we had time for more, he replied. *I'd do your entire back.*

I know about men and back rubs, she snipped.

Good. You know how I feel, then, he teased.

Horny?

I hate that word. I am—justifiably aroused.

Justifiably?

Just watching your muscles ripple in the morning when you slip off the bed, he began. *Your ear furnishings turn me on in ways I cannot describe. Your whiskers are any raven's dream. The way your tail curls lazily at the end when you're pleased, or twitches when you're angry is like ambrosia for my soul*, he added.

You're horny—just admit it.

That takes the art of lovemaking and turns it into crassness.

But what about those times when the need is so overwhelming that the faster you get to it, the better off you are? Ari asked.

Ah—the rush of mutual, undeniable desire. Oftentimes the unplanned act adds to the pleasure, no?

You're trying to stir me up, aren't you?

Is it working?

Mac dropped his hands and ended the conversation when Burke entered the kitchen. He'd been so engrossed in his mental discussion with Ari that he failed to hear the doorbell.

"Arianne," Burke held an open palm in front of her. "Can you explain this?"

"If you wouldn't mind staying here while we go to the funeral," Val told his uncle. "I mean, you're the one who'll have to take care of all this if the worst happens."

Burke turned toward Nico and Mac; Nico nodded his agreement with Val's words. "We need you standing behind us for now," he said aloud. "When the time comes, you'll step into the open with the rest of us."

"I'll make sure that Mary Kate and Francine have a safe place to go on their days off, and guards if they want to shop or go out. The same goes for anyone else," Burke offered.

"You may get some takers," Val said. "Lance and Mona want to check on their houses and pick up clothes. Besides, nobody with that imprint on their hands has had a day off in a while."

"Your staff is welcome here—for the same reason," Janie told Burke. "Can't be too careful right now."

"Perhaps we should meet your staff," Nico said, causing Burke momentary concern. "Renault can come with us," he added. Burke breathed a relieved sigh. Compulsion could be placed so secrets would remain secrets—if it were necessary.

"Renault wants to try Chinese food," Mac grinned. "Maybe all the vamps will want to come along."

"What about you and Janie?" Burke asked Val.

"We're moving cattle to the south pasture. Erly and Hunter really want to help, so I'll stay here," Val replied.

"If Ari goes, I will, too," Janie said. "She can get me back home fast if it's necessary."

"You think Ari wants Chinese food?" Nico turned to Mac.

"Does she like Chinese?"

"She loves the steak and broccoli from Sang's in Deep Ellum."

"They make steak and broccoli?"

"Yeah. It's sliced thin and stir-fried in Sang's special sauce with the broccoli and vegetables. It's so good," Nico replied. "Everything they make is amazing, but the steak and broccoli is Ari's and my favorite."

"I've been to Sang's," Burke grinned. "I'm up for eating out tonight."

"I think we need to visit Deep Ellum, then," Mac told Burke.

"I feel like we've been let out of prison," Ari told Mac. She and most of the crew from the ranch were now lying on lounges around Burke's pool, having a light lunch and drinks.

Burke lived in the Dallas suburb of Highland Park, where his three-story, native rock mansion was surrounded by high walls, lush, green lawns, carefully trimmed trees and shrubs, and flower beds displaying a predominance of burnt orange and white—the colors of the Texas Longhorns football team.

The pool was Olympic-size and the surrounding area was built for entertaining, with many carefully placed shady spots. Padded, comfortable furniture was tastefully scattered about a custom-designed, flagstone patio.

"Burke's wolf likes to swim, so the pool had to be big," Janie explained. "And he usually throws an Independence Day party and barbeque, where people can swim, eat and drink all afternoon—unless it falls on a full moon, of course. Then, he tends to host another party—for OU-Texas weekend."

"OU-Texas?" Mac asked.

"It's when two entire states kinda go rabid," Ari explained. "Some of us prefer to hunker down and hide."

"Ari goes to Palo Duro Canyon around that time every year, so she has an excuse to close her gallery," Nico grinned at her.

"Did you just rat me out?" She leaned around her chair to pretend-glare at Nico.

"Who wants to know?" Nico teased.

"I find the information useful," Janie said. "It's good to know where your friends will be in case they need you, or you need them."

"Gotta admit, it makes sense," Mac agreed, giving Ari a sardonic smile.

"We're back," Mona and Lance, accompanied by Del and Laronda, walked out of the house to join them. They'd stopped in the kitchen to grab drinks and a snack, first.

"Get everything you need?" Janie asked.

"Yeah. Place smells musty since it's been shut up all this time," Mona replied.

"Mine, too. Forgot I had towels in the washer," Lance admitted.

"Bet those were nice and mildewy," Ari said.

"They were—and frozen into a donut shape at the bottom. I just pulled 'em out and chucked 'em in a garbage bag."

"I hope those weren't your good towels," Janie admonished.

"They weren't. I don't think I have any good towels."

"Lancelot Avery Elliott," Janie, sounding scandalized, shook her head. "I'll get you some new towels for your birthday."

"Thanks, Aunt Janie," Lance grinned.

Darnell considered calling Belhar, but he was already perturbed enough to yell at him and yelling at a good servant wasn't the best idea. Belhar had been avoiding him for days, or so it seemed, and Darnell was pissed about it.

After all, Benny Killebrew had seen Belhar several times in the interim, and had passed messages along to Darnell. Belhar should be speaking directly to him, Darnell snorted, causing Phyllis, Benny's wife, to jump as she set a mug of fresh coffee on his desk.

"Sorry," Phyllis apologized. "Benny's out on an errand, and we're nearly out of coffee and a few other things," Phyllis said timidly, her hands betraying her nervousness in Darnell's presence.

"You're telling me we need groceries?"

"Yes, sir, Governor, sir."

"Here," Darnell pulled a wad of cash from a pocket, along with keys to his SUV. "Go get coffee and whatever else we need. I'll tell Benny I sent you out if he asks."

"All right," Phyllis' voice trembled. Turning away, she headed for the door.

"Get some toasted and salted pecans if you can find any," Darnell called after her.

"I will."

"Maybe I'll have a few words with Benny when he gets back, letting the pantry get low like that," Darnell grumped before unlocking his cell phone and placing a call to his current—and soon-to-be-gone—Chief of Staff, Gerri Dean.

He still didn't have an answer from his wife on whether she'd be at the funeral and dammit, he wanted an answer. Gerri had already called several times, but his wife had put off answering every time.

Maybe I ought to bring her out here and let her see how things really are, he mused.

"No," he said aloud. "She'd bring the kids. That won't do."

Phyllis gripped the steering wheel so hard her hands began to sweat. Benny kept her driver's license in a desk drawer; it was the only thing other than Cheatham's cash and keys she'd carried out of the lodge. She had two hours, perhaps, to disappear and abandon the SUV before somebody started looking for her.

Cheatham's pocket money had turned out to be nearly three hundred dollars. She'd never had that much cash in her life; Benny always controlled the money and the checkbook.

She needed shelter—a hiding place. Where could she go?

"Go to the grocery store and leave the car. Maybe they'll think I was kidnapped," she mumbled as if to reassure herself. "There's a bus station not far from the store," she added. "I can walk there and buy a ticket for the first bus going anywhere."

With that plan in mind, Phyllis set her course for Virgil's Supermarket in Fredericksburg.

"I've reserved Sang's private room—it'll hold all of us. Barely," Burke dropped onto the chaise next to Janie's and reached out to pat her hand.

"Ari can get us there—we just need a good place to appear and disappear," Janie leaned her head back and closed her eyes. "I forgot how restful it is, here," she told him.

"I keep inviting you to visit," Burke's voice was gruff. All his life, he'd been envious of his older brother—who'd gotten the ranch and the best woman he'd ever met. He'd built everything he had from the ground up, and now owned one of the most prestigious law firms in Dallas.

Plus, he'd built this home with Janie in mind. He'd added all the things she loved but couldn't have at the ranch, for the times his brother and sister-in-law came to visit. When Brett died, however, Janie closed herself off and focused solely on Val and the ranch. Lately, though, she'd come out of her shell—when Ari and the others needed her.

"I know," Janie responded to Burke's previous statement, breaking into his thoughts. "I haven't thanked you for taking such good care of Mary Kate and Francine."

"They're family," Burke said.

"Yes, they are. Keeping them safe is a priority."

Burke jerked slightly when Mac's voice sounded in his head, with the following words: *You can now say things in private this way, you know.*

Burke, momentarily stunned, took a moment to take a deep breath before letting it out. *Janie?* he sent, as an exploratory attempt.

Burke? Janie's mental response revealed her surprise.

Janie, I ah, Burke floundered.

I know you love me, Janie told him. *I love you, too. I think we just had to wait until the right time to say that.*

Thank the First Wolf, Burke whispered into her mind. *What are we going to do about it?*

I was hoping Val would find someone for himself, she said. *But after this mess is over, maybe we can talk about it? Just the two of us? We're not too old to ah, you know.*

I know. And I like that idea. A lot.

Please don't sound too desperate, Phyllis chastised herself as she spoke with the attendant. The bus station wasn't a station—it was pick up and drop off only. At a service station.

"You can buy a ticket online, but the next bus to Austin won't be here until tomorrow," the service station attendant told her.

"I really need to get there sooner," Phyllis said, attempting to slow the rapid beating of her heart and the trembling of her hands.

"There's somebody local who drives for one of those—you know, pick up and drop off services—like a taxi, except they drive their own cars."

"I only have cash." Phyllis was so frightened by now she nearly burst into tears. Cheatham's SUV was in the grocery store parking lot several blocks away, and she'd dropped the keys in a trash barrel between there and what should have been a bus station but wasn't.

"He may be willing to drive you, but it's nearly eighty miles. I figure that could cost close to a hundred."

"I'd pay him a hundred, if he's willing to take me now," Phyllis warbled. Her throat felt as if it were closing; she gulped shallow breaths as her panic increased.

"Let me call him," the cashier offered and lifted the receiver of the phone at her elbow.

∾

"Sang's is five blocks from my gallery," Ari explained to the group gathered in Burke's spacious foyer. "I still have the alarm codes and an extra key hidden inside; we can land inside and leave from there, too."

Claudio beamed at her; he was the only vampire who'd allowed his excitement to show regarding their outing. The others had dampened their eagerness to go out for a meal; some of them had never had the experience, they were so old.

"Maybe this is a good reason to hold onto the gallery," Burke smiled at her. "Don't worry about the rent—I've already covered it for the next six months. Maybe by then, we'll have everything sorted out."

Ari's cheeks pinkened as she digested the information. "Thank you," she breathed.

"I have a confession to make to you, Ari," Claudio dipped his head to her. "I had an agent contact the buyer for your last painting. I offered him a generous increase to sell it to me. It now hangs in my home—in Tulsa."

"You didn't," Ari's eyes were wide with astonishment.

"I did. The moment I saw it, I knew I had to have it. The light falling upon the rock formation is astounding. You captured it perfectly."

"They call that the Lighthouse," Ari explained. "It's a hoodoo."

"I did some research on the subject," Claudio smiled. "It was informative."

"I still can't believe you bought it," Ari told him. "Okay, are we ready to go?"

"I'm ready," Mac said. "My stomach has been growling for half an hour."

"All right—we'll hurry, since you're about to cave in and all."

"Where's Phyllis?" Benny Killebrew stalked into Darnell's office, interrupting a phone call.

"Just tell her to meet me in the sanctuary at nine-thirty," Darnell shouted into the phone before ending the call. "What the hell, Rev?" Darnell snapped at Killebrew. "Can't you see I'm busy?"

"Where's Phyllis?" Killebrew repeated his question.

"We ran out of coffee and some other stuff. I sent her to the grocery store."

"When?"

"I don't know." Darnell checked his Rolex. "Three—four hours ago, maybe."

"She should be back by now. How the hell was she getting to the store, anyway?"

"I gave her keys to my car and some cash to buy what we needed. You ought to keep a closer eye on the pantry, Rev. I won't tolerate not having coffee when I want it."

Killebrew looked as if he were ready to explode. "That bitch has run off—I guarantee it, and you let her go."

"Chill out, Rev. She doesn't know to jump until you tell her to.

Besides, I can call my service for the SUV—they can tell me where it is at any moment."

"Then you ought to call," Killebrew hissed so forcefully spittle flew from his mouth. "I'm telling you she never made it to the grocery store."

"Fine." Darnell lifted his cell and scrolled through his contacts before tapping one and putting the phone on speaker.

"Hello, Mr. Cheatham, how can I help you today?" The call was answered by an actual person.

"I need to know where my SUV is," Darnell said.

"Hold on and I check on that. Ah, it's at Virgil's Supermarket in Fredericksburg, Texas. Has the vehicle been stolen? I can report it to the police."

"No, no, I loaned it to someone and that's where they should be. Thanks for the info." Darnell ended the call.

"Didn't make it to the store, huh? I told you she's too afraid to do anything that upsets you."

"Maybe she's been abducted, then," Killebrew said. "Or murdered for the cash you gave her."

"Call the store. Have them page her," Darnell was more than done with the conversation. "I have other calls to make, so do it elsewhere."

"Thank you," Phyllis handed her driver a hundred dollars in twenties. He'd dropped her off at the bus station in Austin, as she'd asked.

"No problem," Jack, her driver, said as he stuffed the cash in his pocket. "I think I'll grab something to eat before I go back home."

"Enjoy your meal," Phyllis said and shut the door. Feeling like her legs were made of rubber, Phyllis forced herself upright and walked into the bus station. Glancing around, she located the ticket counter and the agent standing behind it.

"I'd like to buy a ticket to Dallas, please," she told the young man.

"What date and time?"

"Next bus out."

"I have one seat left on the bus leaving in ten minutes," he told her after tapping on a computer.

"How much?"

"It's economy—twenty-nine dollars plus tax."

"I'll take it."

"That was excellent," Mac sighed. Everyone else sitting at the private room table appeared more than satisfied with their meals, too.

"Told ya," Nico prodded Mac with an elbow.

"I'm glad they let us order extra steak," Ari said.

Yeah, Nico responded. *Full moon coming up, huh?*

Exactly, Ari replied. *I'm glad it's two days after the funeral, too. Could become a real mess if that wasn't the case.*

"Please, allow me to pay for the meal," First Scholar argued gently with Burke, who was reaching for his wallet. "I insist, and I have cash."

"All right, but I'll get the check next time," Burke told him.

"This was such a pleasure," Second Scholar said. "It is only fair that we conclude the experience with something else we've never done —tipped for an excellent meal and service."

"Claudio, I have an announcement to make," First said after laying several hundred-dollar bills on the small tray holding the check.

"What is that, First Scholar?" Claudio asked.

"I am promoting Fourth, Fifth and Seventh. Fourth is now Third, Fifth is Fourth, and you are now Fifth Scholar."

"I am twice honored," Claudio dipped his head to First. "I would also like to congratulate my brother Scholars on their promotions as well."

"Way to go, Claudio," Everette raised her glass of wine to the newly-appointed Fifth Scholar.

"Well deserved," Alejandro followed Everette's example.

"As it should be," Renault said and lifted his glass to Claudio, and then to the new Third and Fourth Scholars. "Well deserved all around."

"To our friends," Mac lifted his glass. "May all your endeavors succeed."

~

"The keys are missing and there's no sign of Phyllis," Benny Killebrew snapped. He and Billy Ray walked around Cheatham's SUV, searching for any sign of a struggle.

"Locked up, like she left it to go inside and never made it," Billy Ray muttered. Phyllis had parked mid-row on the east side of the parking lot.

A nearby pole lamp flickered erratically in the night air, ramping up the Reverend's anger. Had the bitch run off, or was she abducted? Either way, he didn't want her talking—she knew too much.

"Is there a bus station here?" Billy Ray asked.

"How the hell should I know? Phyllis liked to shop here for groceries. I never came with her—that's woman's work."

"I'll go inside and ask." Billy Ray loped toward the supermarket entrance. He was back in less than five minutes while Killebrew continued to fume.

"No bus station here, just pick up and drop off. Can't buy a ticket there—has to be done online."

"I guess that rules out the bus, then. Dammit, what happened?"

"I don't know, but even if she did escape, you think she'd talk to anybody? Phyllis is a scaredy cat. Besides, she knows that somebody will come after her if she even hints at talking to the police."

"You'd know about that, wouldn't you?" Killebrew hissed.

"Yeah. I know about that. I heard they're still trying to get the jail fixed."

"And still wondering if you're dead or alive. You and that parasite, Denton Franks."

"Look—how hard will it be to ask Belhar to send one of his servants after Phyllis if she shows up somewhere?"

"Not hard, I suppose."

"Then let's use Cheatham's extra keys and drive this thing back to the ranch."

"We better buy coffee, first, or he'll be pissed."

"Sounds like a fine idea."

~

"Burke? I haven't seen you in forever." A man walked up as Burke and the others prepared to leave Sang's. "I got your message the other day; I just haven't had time to get back with you."

"Hey, Marlon," Burke readily shook the man's hand. "I was just checking on that property next to my nephew's ranch. Has it gone back to the bank, yet?"

"Just about. Sorry the deal fell through the first time. Franks turned out to be just as squirrely as you said he was. Last I heard, he was missing and presumed dead—him and that idiot he hired to burn down the house."

"Well, we'll be interested if it goes up for auction."

"Already have feelers out," Marlon Keating grinned at Burke. "Let me know if you need anything else, all right?"

"Will do," Burke said. "Good to see you, Marlon."

"You, too."

Ari and Nico, shielded by Mac and Renault, walked out of the restaurant behind Burke and Janie, while the others followed.

We'll do some research on Marlon, Del announced as he and Mona walked out together.

Marlon Keating—he's in real estate, Burke replied. *I have a number and an address if you want it.*

I do, Del replied. *Can't be too careful, you know.*

~

"Don't tell me there's a snag with the property this late in the game," Darnell didn't bother saying hello when he answered Marlon Keating's call.

"Nope. You're squeaky clean," Marlon replied. "But I may have information about a cover-up."

"Cover-up?"

"Well, I've had my eye on some property in Deep Ellum—have a client who's interested, you know. It's that property where the Mexican food place was blown up—remember that one?"

"Yeah. Everybody died."

"Including the son. I've been looking into all this, you know, trying to find out who's dealing with it. Turns out, an old friend, Burke Jordan, has been handling all the legal stuff on that property and the art gallery across the street. Well, I saw Burke and a bunch of other people tonight at one of my favorite restaurants in the area. Guess what? One of the people with him looked to be in his late teens or early twenties. Had dyed hair, but he's the right age and everything to be that kid everybody thinks is dead. Now, once you sit in the Governor's seat, would you mind doing a bit of research on that? Somebody's hiding something, I think."

"I can look into it, for sure," Darnell replied. "You did me a big favor with this place, so it's only fair."

"Thanks. My client really wants that property—to build a nicer restaurant, you understand."

"Sure thing. I'll get back to you. Is Wednesday soon enough?"

"Oh, yeah."

Darnell ended the call and looked up as Killebrew walked in with Billy Ray. "We found your SUV," Benny said. "Phyllis is probably dead in a ditch somewhere, and the cash you gave her is in somebody else's pocket. We bought coffee, though, and I'll send somebody else out tomorrow morning to get the rest. Don't worry," Killebrew held up a hand before Darnell could protest. "Belhar will find her if she turns up."

"Where is Belhar?" Darnell demanded. "I thought I'd see him by now."

"Don't worry, he's putting everything together, so it all goes without a hitch," Killebrew soothed. "You'll see him when everything is in place."

Phyllis began to panic after stepping off the bus at the station in Dallas. Where could she stay? Adrenalin had run its course and she felt beyond weary.

"You all right?" The woman who'd sat on the opposite side of the aisle approached her as she stood at the center of the concrete loading area, quietly panicking.

"I ah," Phyllis' voice trembled.

"You need a place to stay? Are those bruises on your arm and neck the reason you're here?"

"I uh," Phyllis swallowed with difficulty.

"There's a women's shelter not far from here. Come with me; I'll put you in a cab."

"But," Phyllis whispered.

"If it's not for you, you can leave tomorrow. Tonight, I think you need a warm bath and a bed."

"Th-thank you," Phyllis stuttered.

"Come on. Let's find that cab."

"Security will be tight in the church parking lot, but there'll be some who park nearby to stay away from the common herd," Shank tapped the paper map of the church in Austin.

"The ones with drivers to come pick them up?" Big John asked.

"I figure some drivers will be waiting in coffee shops, restaurants or something. That funeral will go on for at least two hours. You see the list of speakers?" Shank added another paper on top of the map. "That ought to give us plenty of time to scope out what's available. We have orders for all kinds of stuff, boss."

"Yeah. We do," Big John idly traced the list of speakers with a forefinger. "And, if we can't pick it up there, we'll get information and tag numbers to track it down later."

"Just what I was thinking. If you can get on the roof and let me know when the cars drop off," Shank grinned.

"I can do that," Big John agreed. "I'll go in just before dawn and set up. I'll let you know where the cars exit, so you and the team can keep an eye on 'em."

"Wanna drive to Austin together?" Shank sounded hopeful.

"Nah, I got other business. Just bring the team around eight. I'll call you."

"Okay, boss." Shank tried to hide his disappointment.

"Look, go down the night before and stay in a hotel," Big John opened his desk drawer and pulled out an envelope of cash. "Just don't get too drunk and get to the church on time."

"You got it," Shank grinned. Big John didn't miss the bounce in Shank's step as he walked out of the office, either.

CHAPTER TWENTY-FOUR

"You look so pretty," Ari told Janie. Janie had dressed in a calf-length black dress that flattered her figure. Seventy wasn't old for a werewolf, since their lives were roughly twice that of the average human.

"It was in the closet," Janie shrugged modestly. "Never thought I'd wear it to a state funeral, though."

"Don't let that stop you from wearing it again—you look great in it." The clothes Ari wore to her mother's funeral still hung in her closet at home and she refused to ever wear them again because too many painful memories saturated the fabric.

"We have to live through the day, then, so I can wear it another time."

"Yeah." Ari's thoughts turned dark for a moment. Nico had been uncharacteristically quiet when he awoke earlier, and Ari felt as if the air around them pressed and pressured far more than it should.

"There's danger in the air, isn't there?" Janie said, breaking into Ari's thoughts. "Val says sixteen households were attacked across the country last night. Whole families were murdered—just like before, only this time, more than half the houses were set on fire afterward."

"Because they want to burn witches," Ari shuddered. The

information nauseated her. "We have to find that bastard," she whispered.

"I agree. Anybody could be next. The country is about to kill itself and very little is being done to stop it. They were showing videos on the news this morning."

"I can't watch anymore. It's disturbing and I feel helpless," Ari admitted. "The Adversary must be jumping for joy that so many are willing to take up his banner after looking at actual murders and false narratives on a website or two."

"It's like everything is fractured, and nothing fits together anymore," Janie sighed. "What a mess."

"We're ready," Val walked into Janie's bedroom, where she and Ari were talking.

"Coming," Ari told him. "You ready for this?" She searched his face.

"Yeah." Val wore a grim, determined expression. "Come on—let's get this over with."

~

At this point in time, I'm usually stepping back and letting the Custodian and his protectors handle the job, Mac took one last glance at his reflection in the mirror. He, Hunter and Nico had spent the day before finding suits that fit to attend the funeral.

It was fun to spend the day going out with Ari and the others to shop. He almost forgot the Adversary for a brief time while they laughed, teased, had lunch and picked out clothes. Today, the Adversary was very much on his mind, along with the fact that he was prepared to do battle—not for himself but for those he loved.

"A long way from what it's been in the past," he told himself and strode out of his bathroom to join the others.

"You clean up nice," Ari teased him. He grinned at her. The raven in him inspected the bits of black crystal beading on her jacket collar; they glinted in the morning light. Maybe he'd ask her to buy more clothes with sparkles—he liked it.

"We're meeting Esther at her place and driving from there," Val said. "They have two limos to carry those of us going inside the church and several black SUVs from Del's Department to carry the rest of us to the overflow pavilions. Ari?" he nodded to her, as an indication he was ready for transport.

"Here we go," Ari said, and pulled all of them with her to Senator Johnson's safe house in Austin.

Big John's eagle perched in a shaded space below the church's roof. Around his neck hung a pouch which held his cell phone and a lightweight pair of boxers. With the enhanced sight of his alternate form, he carefully watched early arrivals and the security setup surrounding the parking lot.

The rest of his clothing was roughly a mile away, stuffed in the notch of a tree. Shank and the others were parked in businesses outside the church property, searching for select vehicles. He'd relayed information to Shank after briefly becoming human on the church's roof, then turned to his eagle form and found a niche to hide.

With a high-profile funeral like this, the elite would be attending in droves, which made the job of finding the vehicles he wanted as simple as choosing food at a buffet.

He'd done this before—at football games, concerts and anywhere the public gathered in large numbers.

It was part of the reason he'd been in Austin before, and was snatched by those—things.

Lucky to be alive, he thought as a Maybach Cabriolet entered the parking lot.

"Got the Maybach's license plate," Shank's low voice sounded through the push-to-talk app on his phone. *"We must be livin' right, boss. May be able to pick that one up today."*

That's what Big John thought, too, since vehicles like the Maybach usually stayed in an alarmed garage or storage facility. Shank didn't expect a reply—he knew Big John didn't want to alert anyone to his presence by speaking aloud at this point—a crowd had already gathered and he needed to maintain silence.

And, if Big John were in human shape, he'd have a Bluetooth device in his ear to keep the other side of the conversation quiet. There was so much that nobody knew about him, and Big John liked to keep it that way.

"Vintage Rolls," Shank crowed. *"They're comin' out of the garages today, just like you said they would."*

"Have you ever worked in a bar before?" Assistant manager Richard Wayne asked the walk-in applicant.

Phyllis shook her head at the man interviewing her. "But the ad asked for a cook. I'm a good cook."

"Do you have a problem working in an establishment like this?" Richard waved an arm at the mostly-refurbished bar area of the nightclub.

"I don't."

"Does it bother you that this bar was attacked—and people died here?"

"It bothers me that innocent people were killed for no reason."

"Good answer," he offered her a tight smile. "It bothers me, too, and it really bothers the owner. She'd be doing this interview if she weren't out of town for a few days. Look, the bar won't be open for another two weeks, but frankly, we could use somebody to cook and clean while the rest of us are getting things back together. How about cooking lunch and dinner for the crew until then, and we'll see if you'll fit in."

"Like a trial run?"

"Yes. You can take a look at the menus today. Let me know if there's anything on it that you don't know how to make. We have dinner shows on Saturdays now and then, and we'll need special menus for those days."

Phyllis took the menus he handed her and skimmed them quickly.

"I think I can make all this, and a lot of other things besides," she told him.

"All right. Come in tomorrow morning at eight; I'll send someone out to shop for supplies with you, since you're telling me the bus will drop you off here. You and Kenny can use the bar's van. Get everything you need to put lunch and dinner together for at least three or four days."

"Thank you," Phyllis sounded breathless. "I appreciate your faith in me."

"We'll see you in the morning," Richard said. "Welcome aboard."

"What is that?" Janie breathed as the limo turned into the massive church parking lot. While the air had felt heavy all day, once they traveled onto the property, a sense of absolute dread gripped all of them.

Ari's warning tingle between shoulder blades had become a full-blown burning. She shuddered; Mac gripped her hand tightly, easing some of the tension.

"That's the Adversary's doing," Nico hunched his shoulders. "Just —do what you can to push it away from you."

Ari, Nico sent to her, *remember what we talked about last night. It's important.*

I will.

"It feels evil," Senator Johnson's mouth tightened as her dread mounted; she felt more than uncomfortable and she didn't have the imprint on her palm.

"At least Del wangled more seats inside for us," Ari sighed. "Nico, do you think the vamps and werewolves outside will be able to handle —whatever is coming?"

"I don't know," Nico appeared troubled. "This—they're not holding back, Ari."

"Maybe we should take Esther away from here," Janie breathed. "I don't think any of us are safe, but she's the most vulnerable."

"We can't let the Adversary know that we feel any of this—it will show our hand and convince him to be more subtle in the future," Mac told her. "We have enough people around her to provide protection—as well as we can, anyway."

"Janie, stop worrying," Esther patted her hand. "We'll either get through this or we won't."

"Look at those huge tents on the grounds," Val breathed while staring out the limo's window. "They're expecting a huge crowd. That's not good."

I don't like this at all, Ari informed Mac and Nico as she leaned forward to look out Mac's window.

We can't do anything about the crowd now, Nico sounded unhappy. *We can only do our best. We can't save everybody, remember? We can only stand against the Adversary's minions and give as many people as we can a fighting chance.*

"We're here," their driver announced through an intercom. He'd driven them to a side door of the church, beneath a portico. All the VIPs would be dropped off there while their limos and vehicles were parked in a roped off portion of the lot.

Val helped Esther from the car; Mac gave Janie his hand. Behind them, the second limo in their motorcade dropped off Erly, Hunter, Mona, Lance, Del, Laronda and Everette.

"Let's get inside—I feel like we have eyes on us," Mona shivered.

"Come on, then," Lance took her arm and pulled her into the church.

The vans following the limos had already broken away to drop Claudio and the other Scholars and guards off, including Kevin, Henry and several other werewolf ranch hands who'd volunteered.

They were assigned to watch the crowd and report any activity connected to the Adversary. The Scholars dispersed amid a growing human crowd, their guards following discreetly. Werewolves patrolled in twos around the perimeter, as if they were searching for a premium spot to view the funeral on the many large screens set up beneath tents.

"I never felt anything like this in my life," Henry observed as he and Kevin walked beneath a corner of the outermost tent. "Can't smell anything different, but there's something there, for sure."

"Yeah," Kevin's voice was close to a growl. "Like I want to rip into whatever it is, and it just isn't visible enough to attack."

"You think they're hiding in plain sight?"

"Hiding, no question. It's like they found a way to become invisible."

"I'm calling Val." Henry pulled his phone from a pants pocket.

"President's motorcade coming in," Kevin hissed as Henry held the phone to his ear.

"It's Henry. Give me a minute," Val stepped to the side of a hallway leading to the church's sanctuary.

The others stopped, too, allowing attendees who'd come in behind them to go ahead.

"Yeah?" Ari heard Val say softly into his phone. He listened for a few seconds before saying, "Okay, I'll let them know." He ended the call and blinked at Ari and Nico.

Henry says he thinks the enemy is here—he just can't see them or smell them.

I feel that way, too, Ari replied. *Like they're all around, trying to suffocate us.*

We've been working on concealing ourselves from sight, Nico turned to Ari. *Do you suppose they've perfected it?*

If that's the case, we could all be dead and just don't know it yet, Mac said. *What they haven't been able to do so far is keep us from feeling their presence. Listen up, everybody. Keep your eyes and ears open. We could be surrounded already, and not know it.*

Let's go, Nico said. *The President is coming, and they'll want to clear this hallway for his use.*

Darnell was invited to ride to the church with the President. Not only that, but the Rev and Belhar had also been asked to join President Horne and both Senators who'd come with him.

He was enjoying a drink in the back of the limo with the President and one of the Senators when they arrived at the church.

"Give my men a few minutes to clear the hallways," President Bertram Horne lifted his glass of whiskey to Darnell. "Can't be too careful, eh?" He emptied his glass before turning to Belhar and Benny Killebrew. "We'll be dismantling the Department that worries you so much," he told them.

"What Department is that? Did I miss something?" Darnell demanded.

"Nothing of importance," Belhar waved a hand, dismissing Cheatham's concern. "Just clearing the way—you know—for bigger and better things."

"To bigger and better," the President refilled his glass and lifted it. Darnell, still concerned and more than curious, schooled his expression and clinked his glass against the President's.

Nothing about this feels right, Mona reported. She and Lance were seated in the back row of the center section, on the end. Across the aisle, in the left section, Del and Laronda sat.

Halfway down the center section, Everette and Erly were seated, and two rows in front of them and on the opposite side, were Mac and Ari.

Esther, Val, Janie, Renault, Nico and Hunter sat in the second pew on the right side. So far, Senator Cheatham, who'd be sworn in as the next Governor, hadn't arrived with his entourage, and the President's front pew was also empty.

Around them, people spoke in whispers, but the gathered voices became a loud rumble that washed through the crowd. Ari caught low voices expressing their doubts regarding the Senator, and others voicing their support for Cheatham as Governor.

The bier at the center front already bore the Governor's casket—an elaborate, polished black box with gold and silver trim. His widow was seated front and center, with other family members around her.

Never stick me in one of those things, Ari indicated the expensive casket. *Just have me cremated or leave me in Palo Duro Canyon to feed the birds and animals.*

Ari, stop being morbid. It makes me uncomfortable, Mac chided. *Today, especially.*

The President is coming in, with Cheatham behind him, Val announced.

Does anyone else feel that vibration? Renault asked.

The floor is humming, Erly said. *It ain't the church choir, either.*

Something is happening outside, Claudio reported, before he shouted *No!* into everyone's mind. *Demons are rising*, he cried. *They are everywhere.*

"Turn!" Henry yelled as he ripped off his shirt and ran through the nearest tent with Kevin right behind him. "Get the kids out of here," he added before he became wolf and human speech was beyond him.

Kevin, following Henry's example, came out of his shirt quickly and became wolf, shedding the trousers he'd worn and leaving them on the grass as he dodged a screaming, fleeing crowd.

Before him, a winged demon erupted from the manicured lawn, long, talon-like fingers grasping for any human within reach. Kevin howled as a woman was snatched from her husband's arms and gobbled down while her blood dripped and smeared across the demon's grotesque features.

Without thinking, Kevin launched himself at the monster, tearing into its throat as it struggled to claw through his fur. In this instance, however, Kevin had the element of surprise on his side, as he gripped the thin neck in his jaws and clamped them shut.

Ari nearly tumbled into Mac as the humming vibration in the church's floor turned into something resembling an earthquake. Already, attendees were pushing and shoving to escape their pews and head for the doors.

Look at the President, Nico sounded alarmed.

There, standing beside the right, front pew, the President and his entourage were in the center of an unnatural calm. At that moment, both wide, double-sided doors into the sanctuary blew open, revealing four, ten-foot tall, winged demons, all of which had to duck beneath the opening to enter.

All the fleeing, screaming guests turned quickly and ran toward the back doors located on both sides of the pulpit and choir. Those doors also burst open, and demons flew in, snatching easy prey to devour before the real killing began.

Pews overturned as people crashed into one another, attempting to escape the carnage and commotion. Blood flowed down the aisles; Ari watched it as she and Mac knelt between pews to avoid attack.

We need a door opened, or they'll all die, Ari sent a desperate message as she and Mac flattened themselves to the floor to keep from being hit by two large demons.

We're closest to the outside doors, Lance said. *Right now, we're under an overturned pew, but we can crawl to an open space.*

So can we, Del reported.

Do it, Nico said. *But stay hidden while you're doing it, or they'll be on you immediately. They're trying to draw us out*, he warned. *Don't reveal yourselves until I command it.*

On it, Laronda called back as she and Del crawled between pews until they were positioned behind the carved, wood cubicle at the back that held sound and lighting boards. There, they waited for Lance and Mona to join them.

Hurry, Nico urged. *We're all on the floor, and things could get interesting fast.*

What are we waiting for? Everette begged. *There are dead people piled up all around us.*

For the human Adversary to show himself, Nico replied calmly.

Thank goodness, Del acknowledged Lance and Mona's arrival. All four cringed as a human head dropped next to them, splattering warm blood everywhere. *Ignore that,* Del snapped. *We have work to do.*

Raising shell-marked hands in unison, they fired at the bottom of a set of exit doors, filling that portion of the sanctuary with blinding light while blowing the doors down and frying two demons in the process.

If they thought the demons were in a frenzy before, they now ramped up their attacks three-fold. *People are running toward the doorway we cleared,* Del gave a desperate report. *But the demons have increased their attacks. Not many are getting out that way. We'll try to open the other exit.*

Claudio and Alejandro fought in tandem with Fourth Scholar and his two guards. Forming a small circle, they stepped as one through the crowd outside, fighting off encroaching demons while humans ran screaming around them.

Somewhere in the crowd, First Scholar and his guards worked to carry children away from the carnage. Second Scholar had set up a safe space off the church grounds at the designated concrete parking lot, hoping it would prove difficult for demons to emerge through a harder surface.

There, First Scholar and his guards delivered armloads of wailing children, and sometimes their only remaining parent with them.

Claudio knew, without anyone telling him, that all the police sent to the venue for protection were already dead; there'd been few gunshots after the demons erupted. Their initial focus on law enforcement had given some humans enough time to escape rampaging demons, but too many others had fallen or were trampled in the maddened rush to flee from the monsters.

Bodies lay everywhere, staining meticulously trimmed grass with their blood. Too many times, Claudio was forced to stand astride a human body or parts of one, in order to move with his fighting circle and continue the battle.

Big John watched the carnage taking place below and felt ill. He recognized the creatures attacking the humans—all too easily.

He could have reported the location of their lair. He could have done it anonymously, and he hadn't. He'd only thought of keeping his skin—and his freedom—intact.

Across the way, children were being carried to the parking lot of another building. He watched as three demons began flying after a man carrying three children toward that safe place.

Wait—*that wasn't a man, was it? Going that fast?*

No. Vampires *did not* survive in daylight, but no human was capable of what he was seeing. Then, surprising him even more, a large dog raced from the side, leaping and crashing into a diving demon just before it reached the vampire.

Except—it was no dog that tore into the unsuspecting creature—that was a *werewolf.*

The vamps and shifters had chosen to fight this enemy, yet here he was, cowering in a safe place beneath the roof.

Below, like a flood, humans suddenly ran out of the church as if the devil himself were after them—as could be the case, in Big John's opinion. Sure enough, a legion of flying demons left the church right behind them.

Odds are not in your favor, Big John, he chastised himself before the eagle dropped off his perch and launched himself toward the enemy below.

Darnell, standing near Belhar and the President, gaped at the slaughter about him. Even more shocking, the President laughed as a woman was sheared in half right in front of him by a swiftly passing demon. The top half of the body rolled toward the President, stopping about two feet from his expensive, Italian shoes.

This—this was what Belhar had prepared in secret for him, on what should have been *his* day?

"Stop this," Darnell grabbed Belhar's arm and shouted in his ear, before screaming in pain and pulling his hand back, his palm burned and smoking.

You think you're in charge? Belhar's mouth pulled into a malevolent grin, displaying his many, pointed teeth. *You haven't been in charge since I found you in the Cave of Zugarramurdi in Spain, you know that?*

Is it time? The President turned toward Darnell, a wicked light in his eyes.

We'll let him see the big surprise before we make him one of the et Inpaenitens *and the lowest of my servants,* Belhar replied.

Reverend, keep an eye on him—make sure he doesn't get away before the ritual, the President said, turning back to the show outside Belhar's shield.

It will be my pleasure. Benny Killebrew became the serpent and wrapped himself around Senator Darnell Cheatham, who was so shocked he couldn't move to prevent it.

Henry ran, but the demon would overtake him quickly. He understood that and dodged beneath a tent, while the demon plowed through the sturdy canvas overhead like a hot knife through butter. The shrill scream of a bird of prey sounded behind him the moment a clawed hand scraped Henry's ribs, throwing Henry off balance and rolling him across the blood-slickened grass and into a pile of broken folding chairs.

The bird screeched again before Henry could get on his feet; he pulled himself up in time to witness an eagle harrying the angry demon. If the eagle didn't leave, the demon would have him.

Henry leapt toward the demon, savaging his neck to force the demon away from the bird who'd saved him. While the demon flailed, hitting Henry several times with a clawed fist, the eagle returned and clamped his talons on the creature's wrist, flapping furiously to keep the hand away from the werewolf.

A running vampire rushed by, and, reaching out with an extended claw, decapitated the demon, barely ruffling Henry's whiskers while he did it.

Henry let go of the bottom half of the demon's neck and turned toward the eagle, who, now on the ground, turned a questioning eye in his direction. Nearby, another demon attempted to tackle Kevin. Without a word, Henry and the eagle rushed to his aid.

Ari, I'm not sure this is a good idea, Mac warned as her mountain lion clawed its way beneath pews toward the pulpit and the casket before it. Mac, completely irritated, crawled along behind her.

The Governor's widow is still here, Ari's telepathic message was a growl in Mac's mind. *If she's still alive, I intend to help her. But I have to get to her, first.*

Nico? Mac sent, irritating Ari.

Telling on me? she snapped at him.

He needs to know, Mac shot back.

Ari, let Erly and Everette handle this, Nico ordered.

Erly and Everette aren't nearly there. I am, Ari insisted.

We're on our way, Everette responded to Nico's request.

I'm here, and, Ari stopped speaking while Mac shouted *No!*

CHAPTER TWENTY-FIVE

*L*ily Anderson, amid the chaos and death around her, had crawled to her husband's casket and knelt beside it. With one hand touching the polished surface, she understood that she, too, was going to die.

Where were these creatures from—hell itself? She had no other explanation. As for the accusations that witches had done this, well, in her mind, witches and wiccans had existed for a very long time, and were this kind of thing possible, it surely would have happened before now.

No, this was new. Another enemy had stepped onto the world stage, just as her sister told her—the sister who served as the Mother Superior in a local convent.

"Hannah, I think you're right," Lily whispered her sister's given name as the coffin burst open and a hungry demon crawled out of it, forcing Lily to scream and scramble backward.

~

"Ari, no," Mac shouted into the din as the demon burst from the Governor's coffin and scrambled to dislodge itself from the confined space. Its goal was clear enough; attack the Governor's widow. Ari's mountain lion leapt toward the coffin, hitting the lid with her front feet and bringing the heavy top down on the demon's head.

Then, using that as leverage for her back legs, which landed squarely behind her front paws, she leapt again, touching down beside Lily Anderson. Then, turning, spitting and fuming, she guarded the woman as the demon once again attempted to extricate itself from too small a space.

Mac's raven flew swiftly toward Ari's location without thinking, while Erly and Everette shouted in his mind that they were on the way. Overhead, demons circled, like a massive kettle of vultures flying over a carcass.

～

Renault, Nico shouted at the vampire as he left Nico's protective shield to help Ari and the others.

I am sworn, Renault replied, before his wings jutted through the suit he wore. With a leap, he landed next to the coffin, decapitating the demon before the creature could reach Ari and the Governor's widow.

Above them, demons screeched and flapped, while the sound of it echoed through the church like thousands of bats in a cave.

Get away from the pulpit, Nico shouted, as Del, Mona, Lance and Laronda rushed toward Ari and the others.

～

Henry growled as he took a step back. Kevin and the remaining werewolves did the same as demons stalked toward the only survivors remaining near the property—the children and parents rescued by the vampires. All the other humans were either dead or still running, while the sounds of sirens could be heard in the distance.

This new round of first responders wouldn't survive any better than the last two; Henry understood that well enough. All that stood between the children and these murderers, were four werewolves and nine vampires. They'd started with seven and sixteen, respectively. Except for those around him facing this final threat, all the others were lost.

But the eagle survived.

Somewhere behind him, the bird perched on the roll bar of a small pickup, warily watching the demons advance as the children and a few parents huddled around the vehicle. Henry knew the eagle was a shifter and wondered briefly why it had chosen to join their fight.

Even if he flew away, the winged demons would be on him in an instant.

Hold steady, Claudio's voice entered his mind. *Nico has asked us to wait a few more seconds before we release our light.*

Everette, Erly shouted as his jaguar attempted to pull Lily Anderson away from the pulpit. Ari growled and hissed at the demons circling above. Lily had fainted after seeing a demon crawl from her husband's coffin.

I have her, Everette scooped up the woman and raced toward Nico, leaving Erly behind with Ari.

Mac's raven stood upon the pulpit and squawked, although his voice was drowned out by the shrieks of hundreds of demons.

The humming is back, Laronda said as her coyote leapt upon the dais where Ari stood. Not far behind her, Del, Lance and Mona ran, until shots rang out and Del dropped to the floor.

Laronda's coyote ran back to Del, while more bullets peppered the floor—someone high above the floor in the back was shooting.

Ari, no, Nico shouted again as she turned from mountain lion to human in the space of a blink, standing naked at the altar as she lifted a hand at the gunman.

There, in the balcony where the news crews had set up, stood two men. One was still manning his camera while the other fired a semi-automatic rifle.

Denton Franks, you die, Ari hissed at the shooter and raised her hand.

Ari! Nico screamed as Denton fell from the balcony, already dead, victim of a light so bright and focused nothing human could withstand it.

Get away from the pulpit, Nico shouted. *Somebody get Del—he's still alive.*

Demons scattered above them, seemingly terrified as the humming became a roar so loud it resembled an avalanche.

Ari! Mac, no longer in raven form, dragged her and Erly away, just as the floor beneath them rose up and then burst open like an erupting volcano.

Now, Nico screamed at anyone who could hear him, as a twenty-foot-tall demon, covered in fire and scorched earth, crawled out.

Shafts of light from every direction hit the enormous demon, only to bounce away, ineffective. Standing and lifting massive arms, the giant demon punched fists through the church's roof, sending beams, roofing materials and debris skyward.

Inside the sanctuary, flying demons surged through the new opening like a swarm of angry hornets, leaving the enormous demon alone to fight this stage of the battle. Roaring loudly enough to shake the entire building, the abomination stepped forward to attack the Adversary's enemy.

You see, that wasn't so difficult, Belhar smiled at President Bertram Horne. *They always make mistakes and reveal themselves. The light betrays them. Now, they die. Do you wish to stay and watch, or shall we leave this place?*

I could use a drink, the President replied.

Very well. Reverend, bring our newest slave. He'll be transformed soon enough.

Ari cursed herself as she tossed blast after blast against this giant—the Adversary must have been nursing this one since the beginning, to create a demon so large and so impervious to their weapons.

Nico was right to hold back—he must have suspected something like this could happen. Blinking through tears of frustration, she continued to hurl blasts at the demon's head, but all she could accomplish was momentarily blinding him.

Back up, Nico ordered. *Toward the door. Val, Janie, Hunter, get Del, Esther and the Governor's widow out of the building. The rest of you, guard them. Make sure they leave safely.*

Nico, I'll stay and hold him off, Mac said. *Ari, go with them.*

This is my fault, she replied. *I'll stay with you. Nico, go. Save yourself and the others.*

The others will go; I still have something to do, Nico said.

Ari's head turned swiftly toward Nico, only to watch him disappear.

Hold on, we're coming, Lance shouted as Claudio fired light at the swarm of demons that had fled through the church roof. He and his companions had already taken the first set down, but the defenders were weary against this new threat.

Nevertheless, Claudio lifted his shell-marked hand and fired his light, weakened as it was, at demon after demon, blinding them, then decapitating them with the claws on his other hand.

Help couldn't come soon enough; in fact, they might not arrive in time to save any of them. Claudio wept as First Scholar, true to the last, rushed to defend Henry, who fought beside him.

As if they knew who he was, a score of demons attacked First Scholar at once as he shoved the werewolf behind him. Focused beams of light hit the pile of clawing demons, blasting them apart.

Lance and the others had arrived; only two demons broke away at the last, surely knowing that their mission was accomplished.

First Scholar lay on the hard concrete, his head separated from his body. He'd sacrificed his life to save another. All around him, the battle continued with their reinforcements firing lethal blasts at the remaining demons.

Claudio dropped to his knees beside First Scholar's body, his body shaking with grief as he wept.

~

Mac's blades were in his hands as he and Ari backed away from the massive demon.

Ari, Mac sent, *I really didn't want it to come to this.*

Ari, who'd become mountain lion again, growled low in her throat. *I'm sorry, Mac. I didn't know my foolishness would kill both of us.*

That's not what I'm talking about, Mac dismissed her apology. The demon stepped forward, towering above them and casting them in deep shadow as he blocked the sunlight pouring through the broken roof.

Nico knew what he was doing, Ari. He knew you'd save the deserving. He knows something about me that nobody else has known —for a very long time. A part of me that I refused—that I didn't want. Nico knew, Ari. That secret has been blocked from every Guardian— until now. I'm the one who needs to apologize, and after today, if you no longer want anything to do with me, I'll understand.

What the hell are you talking about? Mac, we have to survive first, and the way things are looking, that's not gonna happen.

The demon stomped a foot, bringing more of the roof down around them. *He won't even have to hit us to kill us*, Ari shouted at Mac. *He'll just bring the whole place down and try to crush us that way.*

"Demon," Mac yelled, lifting his blades. "Attack us and die."

~

"No need to rush," Belhar snapped at the Secret Service agents surrounding the President. "Not all of you will be leaving with us, you know."

"The Senators certainly won't be leaving with us," President Horne turned a nasty grin on both men, who'd remained fearful and silent during the massacre in the sanctuary. "You'll be our sheep at the slaughter—to convince all the others to align with our agenda," Horne's grin widened.

"Wait."

Horne, Belhar and all the others turned swiftly, to find a young man standing in the hallway before them. Belhar blinked, but he couldn't bring the face into focus.

It didn't matter; every Secret Service agent had their weapon drawn and trained on the newcomer's chest. "Who the hell are you?" Horne demanded.

"Nobody important," Nico replied. "But I do have a request. Anybody who doesn't want to follow the President, raise your hands. Be honest, please; your life depends on it."

Both Senators, three agents and Darnell Cheatham, now handcuffed and held by Benny Killebrew, attempted to raise his.

"Thanks," Nico said. "Now, Mr. President, and I use that title sarcastically, I'll trade you this," he held up a small, black object, "for all the people who raised their hands."

"What the hell do I need that for?"

Belhar, who'd hidden himself behind too many spells to count to remain invisible, stepped forward and whispered in Horne's ear.

"That's the stone, you fool—I can feel the power pulsing off it. I'll trade anything to get it, including your sorry ass. Tell him we have a deal."

The demon, still towering over them, hesitated. *What the hell is going on?* Ari frowned at the monster, before turning the frown on Mac.

With blades still high in the air, Mac repeated his challenge, only this time, he called the demon a coward.

Ari's eyes widened in terror as the demon roared again, shaking more of the building down before leaping toward Mac.

Shrieking, Ari relocated to the doorway, ready to ghost away if she couldn't save—*what had Mac become?*

What the hell is that? Horne shouted as the building shook amid a second roar; one far louder than the first. A roar so loud it temporarily deafened all of them.

Nothing to worry about—probably your master's overly large demon, Nico informed the President as the roar continued without abating. *Do you want this or not?* He held the stone between a thumb and forefinger.

Take it, Belhar breathed into Horne's mind.

Give it to me, Horne held out a hand.

Catch, Nico grinned, tossing the stone toward the ceiling.

Grab it before it disappears, Belhar's desperate command betrayed his fear as the roaring in the chapel continued and the entire building began to shake.

Killebrew responded to Belhar's order. The man became the serpent; the serpent leapt toward the stone, which seemed to linger high in the air while several people vanished around him.

No, Belhar yelled as Benny opened his fanged mouth to capture the small carving, and inadvertently swallowed it whole.

Ari, curled in a ball of fur near the outer doors of the sanctuary, was terrified her ears would bleed if Mac didn't shut his mouth soon.

There he stood, toe to toe, size for size with the Adversary's massive demon, screaming in its face while it held arms up, warding off the ear-splitting, mind-bending noise.

Covered in lumps and bumps across bronzed skin, Mac had huge, pointed ears pierced with many gold rings, wild black hair, a fearful visage and two ornate, jeweled blades that fit his current size. Armor covered his chest; the skin of an unknown animal covered his loins. In all of Ari's life, she never imagined anything like this.

Ari jerked as Mac's roar abruptly ended. Turning in her direction, he gave her a grin that would frighten anyone else. Ari found it comforting in a strange and dreadful way. Mac turned back to the demon, who remained stunned by Mac's vocal assault. Without hesitation, Mac decapitated the creature quickly with a mighty sweep of each blade.

Arianne, Nico's calm voice called out. *Do you remember what you did when Franks' sick cattle threatened Val's ranch?*

I do, Ari's reply was shaky as she watched the demon fall, almost in slow motion.

Do the same for this church, please. Oh, and don't forget to take Mac with you when you leave. I'll get the others. We have healing to do and deaths to mourn.

~

Nico, it was hard not doing what you told me, Ari sighed. She'd found him in Janie's kitchen the following morning.

Nico, huddled over a mug of fresh coffee, lifted his eyes to watch as Ari filled a cup for herself. *I asked you to listen to the shell. I knew it would tell you to hold back from hitting that demon with everything you have. The Adversary was watching; I could feel it, although I could only see the President, Senator Cheatham and a few others inside that shield. The Adversary was there and he didn't need to see— most of what you and Mac can do.*

"Ari, it's not about listening to me," he said aloud as she took the barstool next to his. "It's about following your heart and doing what you know is right. How is Del this morning?"

"Better. Laronda and Mona are fussing over him. Now, tell me what Mac is," she said. "He's back to himself—at least the human-looking self, anyway, and he's worried that I won't accept him for what he is."

"I was afraid of that," Nico sighed. "Ari, he rejected his father's heritage when he was young, choosing his mother's race and form instead—that of a shapeshifting raven. The other half, well, that's Fomorian."

"Huh? The mythical giants of Ireland?"

"That's one description, sure," Nico nodded. "Except he's not mythical. Does that scare you? Do you not want to be around him anymore? I forced him to reveal this part of himself, Ari, because we need that heritage."

"I don't think of him as any different than the rest of us, except that he's a lot bigger," Ari shrugged. "I feel bad that he feels bad."

"Do you still love him?"

"I thought I'd killed him with apparent foolishness," tears obscured Ari's vision. "Of course I love him, but he can't feel the same—he was always upset and angry when I'd go off-script. At least Denton Franks is dead," she lifted a shaking hand and brushed moisture off her cheeks.

"Denton Franks *is* dead," Mac agreed as he, Val and someone Ari didn't recognize, walked into the kitchen. "They pulled his body out of that pit of rubble this morning," he poured three cups of coffee. "That means Denton's widow can now sell the property to Val without any legal obstacles."

"We're gonna need that property," Val sighed, taking a chair for himself. "We have new recruits, looks like, and we need a place for them to stay. Everybody, this is Big John, new recruit, eagle shapeshifter and expert car thief. Janie, Lily and Esther are with Erly, Hunter and Renault at the barn, getting information from that idiot, Darnell Cheatham. Nico, I hope you know what you're doing with that one," Val shook his head.

"If Nico hadn't pulled him away with the others, he'd be the newest member of the *et Inpaenitens*." Weariness was expressed in Claudio's voice as he floated into the kitchen. "We sacrificed First and Fourth to that bastard's ambition," he added.

"Then once we have as many answers from him as we need, I'll hand him to you for vampire justice," Nico told Claudio.

"I will give him to the Council, and they will deliver justice,"

Claudio nodded as he accepted coffee with cream and honey from Mac.

"That is more than acceptable to me," Val agreed.

"Me, too," Ari said.

"At least his soul will be his own when he dies," Nico murmured. "We have the location of his compound, by the way. They are currently growing more demons to replace what was lost in Austin."

"I can take care of that," Ari began.

"In a few days," Nico held up a hand. "Right now, the Adversary and his new human puppet, President Horne, believe they have the stone. They merely have to wait a few days for it to ah, pass into their hands. When that moment arrives, we will destroy what Cheatham and the Adversary built, informing the Adversary twice over that he does not have the real stone."

"You gave him one of our carvings?" Ari breathed. "Outstanding."

A corner of Nico's mouth lifted in half a smile. Mac walked around the island to pull out the chair next to Ari's and sit down. He smiled shyly at her. She bumped her shoulder against his.

"By the way," Mac put an arm around her, "I love you, too."

EPILOGUE

"*D*amn, I wanted to ride with the President, and I didn't even get to shoot anybody," Billy Ray complained aloud as he set two video cameras on Senator Cheatham's desk at the Lodge. Denton had gone crazy, shooting at people instead of paying attention to his camera. He'd died for that lapse of judgment.

This ain't Cheatham's desk anymore, Billy Ray reminded himself.

"You're right—it's not that fool's desk any longer."

Billy Ray almost fell, he was so startled by the voice and unexpected appearance.

Sitting in Darnell Cheatham's desk chair was someone new. He didn't look like Belhar, but he held a hint of the same—Billy Ray didn't know what to call it—not quite a smell and not quite a feel.

This one spoke with a notable accent, too, which he couldn't place. "Call me Master Pierre," he said. "I am Belhar's agent. I see things have become lax here. Beginning now, that will change. Everything will be done according to my wishes, and by my schedule. Understood?"

～

383

While a nearby television screen blasted the news of the tragedy in Texas, along with the revelation of the President's miraculous survival, Directors Smith and Jones, vampire and werewolf, tapped their codes into a computer linked to a secure, private server.

On the screen, a single question appeared.

Do you wish to proceed with operation Blackout?

Smith tapped the enter key.

"Our operation is officially underground," Jones sighed as the entire system shut down. "All our agents will destroy their records and disappear. The President has gone rogue and eliminated the Department, as was feared would happen when it was created. Shall we meet again at the designated location?" he turned toward Smith.

"Assuredly," the vampire replied. "You know what I have to accomplish first, however."

"I do. Good luck, my friend."

"And to you as well."

~

"House cleaning?" The President lifted an eyebrow at Belhar's statement as Belhar and Reverend Killebrew stood before the Resolute desk in the oval office.

"Yes—those who refuse to support your cause, sir. They must be released from their duties, and others will be brought in. It will be accomplished expediently, once we present ourselves to Congress. Then, we seed the courts with our judges and the trials will begin."

"I like the sound of that," President Horne smiled. "Yes. Let's do this," he grinned and slapped a knee.

"First, the Reverend and I must attend to some business," Belhar said. "It requires perhaps a day or two for the ah, passage of a necessary item," he glanced briefly at Killebrew, who'd been fool enough to swallow the stone. "Along with the arrival of more of my underlings," Belhar continued. "Some, you may find willing to serve in newly-vacated positions."

"You've done well for me so far," Bertram nodded. "I trust your judgment."

"Yes," Belhar smiled. "Exactly what I hoped for."

"Burke, I didn't expect to see you again so soon," Marlon Keating moved his newspaper so Burke could sit across from him at his favorite coffee shop in Austin. "Who's this with you?" he turned toward the man who'd walked in behind Burke.

"This is Renault," Burke introduced his companion, who pulled a chair from a nearby table and sat adjacent to Marlon. "I ah, heard that you were interested in handling the property left behind after the restaurant bombing in Deep Ellum—that you already have someone interested in buying it. Word also has it that you believe you saw a survivor of the family who owned the property not long ago," Burke continued.

"Who told you that?" Marlon frowned. "I don't ever disclose my clients or my business, you understand."

"We have this information on good authority," Burke offered a forced smile. "Who's interested in the property?"

"I'm not telling you anything," Marlon began to rise from his chair.

"Sit," Renault said pleasantly. Marlon found himself obediently sitting in the chair.

"Now," Renault said, "Tell us everything you know about that interested party. Don't leave anything out. Afterward, you'll forget all about us—the prospective buyer—and that property."

The End

This story will continue in *Exile, Ancient*, Book 2 of the Lion and Raven series